Strictly BUSINESS

STEPHANIE ALVES

Editing: Wonder and Wander Editing Co.
Cover designer: Coralie.renards

ISBN: 978-1-917180-14-6

This book contains detailed sexual content, graphic
language and some other heavy topics.
You can see the full list of content warnings on my website
here: stephaniealvesauthor.com

Happy Reading!

Also by Stephanie Alves

Standalone

Love Me or Hate Me
Holly's Jolly Christmas

Campus Games Series

Never Have I Ever (Book #1)
Spin The Bottle (Book #2)
Would You Rather (Book #3)
Truth Or Dare (Book #4)
The Final Game (Book 4.5)

 # Playlist

🔁 ⏮ ⏸ ⏭ 🔀

▶ **Skin**
Rihanna

▶ **Lights on**
H.E.R

▶ **TiO**
Zayn

▶ **House of Balloons**
The Weeknd

▶ **All To You**
Sabrina Claudio

▶ **Addicted**
Jon Vinyl

▶ **Yeah I Said It**
Rihanna

▶ **Sweat**
Zayn

▶ **Shameless**
Camila Cabello

▶ **Earned It**
The Weeknd

▶ **Butterflies**
Isabella LaRosa

▶ **Worship**
Ari Abdul

▶ **Prisoner**
The Weeknd ft Lana Del Rey

Author's Note

Alright, let's cut to the chase. *Strictly Business* is a book that will have you blushing and kicking your feet at every interaction these two characters have. But let's be honest. You're not here for sweet glances and shy smiles. You're here for the filth. And trust me, I *delivered*.

Inside these pages you'll find:

- So much praise
- Breeding kink
- Overstimulation
- Hand necklaces—because diamond necklaces are overrated
- Spanking
- Bondage
- Sub/Dom relationship
- Voyeurism and exhibitionism
- Face sitting (as she should)
- Delayed gratification – aka suffering, but hot
- Spitting
- And of course, good ol' fashioned anal

If you're still here, congrats—you're my kind of reader. Now, grab a drink (hydration is key), maybe a fan (you'll need it), and prepare for one hell of a ride.

For those who prefer hand necklaces over diamond necklaces.

CHAPTER ONE

Amara

I wonder if heartbreak can actually kill you.

Can love break you so completely that your heart just… stops? No warning, no second chances. Just pain, pure and unrelenting, until your body decides it's had enough.

I spent the entire weekend in bed, staring at my ceiling, waiting for the Grim Reaper to show up and finish me off. Spoiler alert: he didn't.

Instead, I woke up this morning with a headache, an empty ache in my chest, and the crushing realization that heartbreak doesn't kill you. It just makes you wish it could.

The elevator doors slide shut, and I catch my reflection in the mirrored walls. Puffy eyes, blotchy cheeks, and hair that's barely hanging onto the idea of a bun.

I look like a mess and feel like a mess. But at least I made it here. Out of bed, down the subway steps, and into my office building. Progress, right? Never mind that I'm still replaying Friday night on a loop in my head, like a broken record.

Four words. That's all it took to rip my world apart. Four stupid, gut-wrenching words from the man I thought I'd spend forever with.

I cheated on you.

The memory hits like a sucker punch, and I press my fingers to my temple, willing the ache in my chest to leave.

If heartbreak doesn't kill you, it sure as hell comes close.

I should have seen it coming. The late nights at the office. The sudden work trips that didn't quite add up. The fact that we hadn't slept together in… Let's just say I've lost track of how many days it's been since my orgasms started relying entirely on my own imagination.

The red flags were all there, waving frantically in my face.

But nope. I missed every single one.

Instead, I let myself get cozy in our little routine. So cozy that now I'm heartbroken, living in a rundown apartment forty minutes from work, with only Pumpkin, my overly clingy kitten, to keep me company.

My lip wobbles, and tears blur my vision, but I force them back. I will *not* cry at work.

The ding of the doors opening snaps me out of my spiraling thoughts, and I blink hard, squaring my shoulders as Jade comes into view, her hands on her hips and a frown on her face.

Her eyes sweep over me. "You're late."

I plaster on a smile, trying to act like I'm not one wrong word away from falling apart. "I overslept." My voice sounds hollow, even to me.

Her perfectly arched brow shoots up. "Amara Winslow? Oversleeping?" Her voice goes up an octave, drawing the attention of a guy passing us with his coffee. Great. Just what I needed. An audience.

I shrug, juggling two coffees and my laptop as I collapse into my desk chair, which probably costs more than the rent on my new shoebox of an apartment. The pink overload of my desk stings my eyes.

Normally, the bright sticky notes, pink pens, and pink and white keyboard, would make me smile. Today, they're just mocking me with their brightness.

Jade perches on the edge of my desk, crossing her legs. Her red lips purse as she studies me. "You look terrible."

I let out a short, humorless laugh, dropping my bag onto the floor. "Thanks."

Her eyes narrow, lips pressing into a thin line. "Your hair looks like it hasn't seen shampoo in days, you have horrendous dark circles under your eyes, your lipstick's all over the place, and—" She stops mid-rant, her gaze snapping to my face. Her expression shifts, her eyes widening, fire blazing in them. "You've been crying. What did he do?"

I swear, Jade's like a bloodhound when it comes to sniffing out a meltdown.

She's never liked Liam. Not from the moment he drunkenly flirted with her at the office Christmas party two years ago. He'd been a little too tipsy, made a scene, and hit on every woman in the room, including her. I'd brushed it off at the time, told her he was just drunk, but looking back… he was just being a jerk.

I never liked when Liam drank. It was like a switch flipped, and suddenly, I didn't recognize him. Maybe it was the real him all along, and I was too blinded by love to see it.

My eyes drift to the framed picture on my desk—me, Pumpkin, with her ridiculously cute pink bell, squirming to try and get away from Liam, who's standing beside us, flashing that smile of his.

This picture used to make me smile. Now it just makes me want to throw my coffee at the wall.

3

Was he already sleeping with her when this was taken? How long had he been lying to me? How did I not see it?

My throat tightens. I haven't told anyone what happened. No one knows, not even my grandma, who's been blowing up my phone all weekend.

But Jade's waiting. Patient. Expectant.

And finally, it spills out.

"We broke up," I whisper, the words tasting like ash in my mouth.

Sophie, from the desk next to mine, gasps so loudly I'm pretty sure the whole office heard her. "*What*? You broke up?"

The room goes still, freezing around me as they wait for me to speak.

"Yes," I say, the word heavy in my chest. I wipe a tear away, but it's no use. It falls anyway.

"Oh, honey, no." Sophie lifts out of her chair, her arms wrapping around me in an instant. "Don't you dare cry over that bastard. He doesn't deserve a single one of your tears."

But I can't help it. I lost everything. My home, my happiness, the future I thought I was building. He made me believe I was the only one. That I was special. And I trusted him. Completely. Now, here I am, alone, feeling like a complete idiot.

Jade's still quiet, and it's starting to freak me out. Her face is too calm, too still.

"I can key his car," she adds, her voice serious, no trace of a joke. "I have a disguise, no one would ever know it was me."

I blink at her, unsure if she's being serious or if she's just trying to make me laugh.

"Why do you have a disguise?" Sophie asks, looking confused. "What would you even need it for?"

4

Jade shrugs, her lips tipping up into a smirk. "For things I can't discuss, seeing as your boyfriend's a lawyer."

Sophie rolls her eyes. "You don't even know if Liam did anything. Amara could've been the one to break up with Liam."

"I hope so," Jade replies, letting out a low whistle. "We both know she could do so much better than him."

"That, we can definitely agree on," Sophie adds, a laugh escaping her lips.

I brush off their teasing and turn my monitor on, desperate for anything to distract me. "Can we please not talk about it?" I mutter, picking up one of the sticky notes hanging from my screen and fiddling with it. "I barely slept all weekend, and I still need to get through all these applications for tonight."

I scroll through hundreds of them, each one from a woman vying for a spot beside Nicholas Blackwood—the city's most eligible billionaire, or as I like to call him, *my boss*.

I can't help myself. I glance at each photo, comparing them to me. Tall, blonde, thin… The kind of woman I'll never be. A sharp ache hits my chest, and I can't stop the thought that pops into my head.

Is this the type of woman Liam cheated on me with?

I push the thought away, refusing to let it linger, and focus on the screen. I swipe past polished headshot after polished headshot, wondering which one might actually catch Nicholas's attention.

"She's beautiful," Sophie points out, tapping the screen on a blonde with bright blue eyes who recently graced the cover of *New York's Finest*. She practically glows, the kind of beauty that's made for the Blackwood arm-candy role.

I follow her gaze, and then I spot it. The rock on the woman's finger. Huge, sparkling, and definitely a dealbreaker.

"And engaged," I say, quickly clicking her profile off the list.

It's not the first time I've had to toss a taken woman's name. I guess loyalty isn't a priority when Nicholas Blackwood's in the picture.

"You think Nicholas would care?" Jade asks, raising a brow.

A nasty twist of doubt churns in my stomach. Jade's right. Nicholas probably wouldn't care. Hell, he probably doesn't even bother learning their names.

"Even if he doesn't care," I say, dragging her application into the trash, "he wouldn't want the scandal that would come with it."

A tap on my desk makes me glance up.

"Hey, ladies." Ethan, a business mogul known for owning the most exclusive nightclubs in the state, and Nicholas's childhood friend, flashes us a grin that could melt the panties off a room full of women. "Busy at work?"

"Unlike some people," Jade shoots back, crossing her arms.

Ethan blows her a kiss. "Love it when you flirt with me, babe."

"I'd rather set my hair on fire," she replies dryly, and I swear I can hear the eye roll in her voice.

Ethan chuckles, turning his attention to me. "Is Nicholas in yet?"

"Not yet," I reply.

He nods, gesturing behind him with his thumb. "I'll wait for him."

With that, he turns and heads toward Nicholas's office—the only one in the building with a door. Guess the boss needs his privacy.

Jade and Sophie crowd around my desk, eyes glued to the screen as we go through the endless parade of applicants.

"Ooh, what about her?" Jade adds, pointing a manicured finger at a brunette who's so stunning, it's like she was plucked straight out of a magazine. "She's a dancer. Think he'd appreciate the flexibility?" she teases.

A flush creeps on my skin as I swipe the application away, dragging it to the trash. I don't let myself think too much about what happens after these dates. It's not part of my job description. My focus is finding someone who looks good next to him. What happens next?

Not my business.

Though, if I'm being honest, I've thought about it. A lot. Sometimes when I'm alone and in the mood for self-inflicted torture, I scroll through gossip blogs. Him with a new girl every other night, each one more stunning than the last.

"He likes blondes," I say, moving to the next candidate. It's a fact I've picked up from observing the very few women he actually gives the time of day.

"He does?" Jade raises an eyebrow, flicking her dark hair over her shoulder. "Damn. Should I dye my hair?"

Sophie snorts. "Please. Like you have a shot with him."

Jade gasps, clutching her chest dramatically. "Rude."

Sophie shrugs. "Just being honest. None of us could snag him, even in our wildest dreams. Well, not *my* wildest dreams, since I have a loving boyfriend who I adore more than anyone."

My face drops at the reminder of the 'loving boyfriend' I thought I had.

Sophie swallows hard, an apologetic look crossing her face when she sees mine drop. "Sorry. I didn't mean to—"

I wave her off. "It's fine. Just—Let's move on."

At least Jade's single. She'd rather die than be in a relationship—her words, not mine—so I don't have to worry about being reminded of my failed one.

Jade lets out a dreamy sigh, her legs crossed and her pleated skirt inching up. "I wonder what he's hiding under those suits."

My face goes red, and I immediately focus on my screen. "I'm officially out of this conversation."

"Oh, come on!" Jade prods, leaning closer. "You're single now. You can finally admit you have a crush on him."

I press my lips together, narrowing my eyes at the screen. "I do not have a crush on him. Nicholas Blackwood is my boss. I get his coffee, I do his dirty work, and that's it."

At least, that's what I keep telling myself.

But Jade's slender finger taps lightly on my shoulder. "What does Nicholas look like without a shirt?"

I choke on air. "How should I know?" I reply, my brain immediately trying to block out the image. But, of course, it doesn't work. It lingers despite my best efforts.

"You're his assistant." Her smirk stretches wider. "Doesn't that mean you bring him a change of clothes when he spills coffee on himself?"

"That only happened once," I defend, meeting her gaze, which is practically glowing with amusement. "And I didn't stick around to watch."

Jade clicks her tongue, shaking her head like I'm a lost cause. "What a missed opportunity. I would've whipped out my phone and filmed a little movie," she quips, her blue eyes sparkling with mischief as she clearly plays out the scenario in her head.

And, despite myself, I start to imagine it too.

My mind drifts to Nicholas in his office, unbuttoning his crisp, white shirt slowly. Each button popping open, revealing a teasing glimpse of his toned chest. I can practically hear the fabric tearing as he rips the shirt off in frustration, his muscles glistening in the dim light from the spilled coffee... before he—

"Oh look. I made Amara blush," Jade interrupts, pulling me back to reality. Warmth spreads across my face, and I quickly try to hide it, but it's no use. Jade laughs, poking my cheek with a mischievous grin. "Babe, you're as red as a tomato."

I swat her hand away, embarrassed and irritated by the image that slipped into my mind. "I have pale skin," I mumble, turning my attention back to the screen. "I can't exactly help it."

Jade's laughter bubbles up from behind me. "It's adorable how shy you get when we talk about Nicholas."

Sophie shoots Jade a warning look. "Stop teasing her."

Jade just waves her off with a grin. "Oh, come on. It's too easy."

"I'm not shy," I mutter, trying to sound convincing, but the warmth in my face betrays me. "I just don't like thinking of him like that when I work with him," I say, trying to push the image of Nicholas out of my mind.

Jade leans in closer, crossing her arms over her chest. "You might not want to, but you definitely *like* thinking about it. I know *I* do," she adds, smirking.

I open my mouth to protest, but before I can, a voice cuts through the tension.

"Good morning, ladies."

Sophie straightens up, and Jade tilts her head, her eyes narrowing as she looks over at our boss, Nicholas Blackwood, who's walking past my desk.

9

"Hi, Mr. Blackwood," Sophie greets him, slipping into a professional tone.

"Good morning, sir," Jade adds, trying, and failing, to hide the mischievous glint in her eyes.

Nicholas gives them a brief nod, his eyes scanning them before landing on me. "Amara." My name rolls off his tongue like melted butter... Smooth, rich, and way too tempting. My stomach does a little flip as I meet his gaze, and my heart beats just a little faster than it should.

"Can I see you in my office?" he asks.

"Of course," I reply, swallowing hard, suddenly hyper-aware of how much of a mess I must look. My hair's probably frizzing out of control, and I'm pretty sure I have coffee stains on my sweater.

With a sharp nod, Nicholas turns and strides toward his office, his tailored gray suit hugging his broad shoulders in a way that's completely unfair to my concentration. The door swings shut behind him as soon as he enters.

"Phew," Jade sighs, dramatically pressing the back of her hand to her forehead. "Anyone got a change of panties?"

Sophie rolls her eyes, clearly over Jade's antics. "He's our boss, Jade."

"So?" Jade shrugs nonchalantly, a teasing smirk spreading across her face as she glances at me. "You say that like you've never watched a rom-com." She pauses, eyes glinting with mischief. "*Can I see you in my office*? Is it just me, or is that code for sex?"

I shoot her a glare. "It's code for work," I say, turning off my screen and standing up.

Jade lets out a dramatic scoff, nudging my shoulder. "Yeah, I bet he works you *really* hard."

Warmth floods my face, and I grab Nicholas's coffee, trying to ignore the way her words make my mind wander. I head to his office, knocking twice before hearing a low, "Come in."

I push open the door, and Nicholas's gaze lifts as I step inside. My eyes fly to Ethan, who's lounging in one of the chairs with that laid-back grin of his. He smiles at me, tipping two fingers in a casual salute.

I place Nicholas's coffee on the dark, polished wood of his desk, which looks like it came straight out of a high-end catalog, so clean and perfectly curated, it makes my desk look like a disaster zone by comparison. The bookshelves lining the walls are filled with decorative pieces, none of which are books.

"Thank you," he murmurs, taking the coffee with a slight nod. He sips it, his eyes briefly meeting mine before he shifts his focus back to the screen in front of him.

"You're welcome," I reply. I can't help but notice how the waistband of my pleated skirt feels tighter than usual, and I adjust it slightly, trying to make it more comfortable. I blame the emotional eating I did over the weekend.

"If this is about tonight, I'm so sorry for the delay, but I can assure you I'm almost done."

He pulls his gaze from the screen, his thick brows furrowing as he focuses on me. "Tonight?"

I can't help but take a second to appreciate the sheer perfection of this man. His strong jawline and dark hair give off a Henry Cavill vibe, effortlessly handsome in a way that makes you do a double take. His muscles are straining against the fabric of his shirt, and I can't shake Jade's comment about wanting to see what's underneath.

I clear my throat, trying to push those thoughts out of my head. "Yeah, the… the date you asked me to set up."

His brows relax. "Oh. Right." He shakes his head, lips pressed into a tight line. "Sorry, I completely forgot." He turns back to his computer screen. "You can send me her details once you've chosen."

I blink. Normally, he has me narrow the list down to a handful of candidates, from which he picks his favorite. "You want me to choose?"

His eyes meet mine, and he gives a subtle nod. "I trust you."

I swallow at his words. "Okay. I'll take care of it."

He nods, eyes already back on the screen. "Actually, I called you in here to let you know this week's going to be a little hectic," he begins, fingers tapping rapidly on the keyboard. "I've got a few things I need your help with for the board meeting, so I'm going to be working you hard this week." He pauses, gaze locking onto mine with a focus which makes my heart do an involuntary flip. "I hope that's okay."

Jade's teasing words echo in my mind, and a flush spreads across my face. "Yep," I say, my voice cracking a little. "Not a problem."

Nicholas narrows his eyes, studying me. "Are you okay?"

Crap. I nod quickly, forcing a smile. "Perfectly fine. I should get back to my desk."

He leans back slightly, watching me with an intense, calculating look. Heat rises in my face as I turn and quickly slip out of the door, my heart pounding in my chest.

Once the door clicks shut behind me, I take a deep breath and square my shoulders, walking back to my desk where Jade and Sophie are deep in conversation. The moment they see me, their eyes lock on mine.

"So… what did the boss want?"

I narrow my eyes at them, the memory of my flushed face and their relentless teasing still fresh in my mind. "I hate you guys."

CHAPTER TWO
Nicholas

R ed eyes.

Red fucking eyes.

The door clicks closed behind Amara as she leaves, but the image of her face lingers.

I'm used to seeing Amara's warm, green gaze, flecked with gold that catches the light. Used to looking away from those eyes before they make me think too much. But today, they're dull, rimmed with red. Her lips look swollen, her whole expression shadowed by sadness.

She's been crying.

I don't make a habit of involving myself in my assistant's life. Or anyone else's here, for that matter. But the thought lingers, an unwelcome itch at the back of my mind. What happened to make her look like that?

My mind drifts to her boyfriend. Or maybe ex-boyfriend. The memory of him showing up at the office Christmas party two years ago comes into mind. He'd turned what should have been a good time into a public embarrassment for her. She'd been mortified, her face bright red as she apologized to everyone in sight, practically dragging him out of the building. I don't even know if they're still together.

A throat clears, and I'm startled to remember I'm not alone. Ethan's still sprawled in the chair across from my desk, one leg crossed casually over the other, his smirk firmly in place.

"Forgot I was here, didn't you?" he asks, the amusement in his voice grating.

"No," I lie, dragging my gaze back to the papers on my desk.

"Sure you didn't." He leans forward, elbows on his knees, and grins. "What's got you so distracted, Nicholas? Don't tell me it's work. You're not that boring."

"What do you want? I'm busy."

"It shows," he replies, his voice dripping with sarcasm as he leans back and laces his fingers behind his head. "I heard you got a date tonight?"

I finally glance up, pinning him with a look. "Apparently. I forgot about that."

"Forgot?" He chuckles. "Who forgets about a date? She must be real special."

"You're one to talk," I retort, raising my brow. "When's the last time you went on an actual date?"

"Touché." He chuckles. "So, you bringing her to the club?"

I shake my head, letting out a scoff. "Not going to happen."

"Why not? You've been MIA lately. Don't tell me you've gone soft."

"None of your concern," I reply dryly. "Just know I won't be back."

"Are you sure about that?" he asks, arching a brow. "There's a new room and—"

"Not going to happen," I interrupt. "Just drop it."

He leans back again, crossing his arms this time, but the smirk doesn't budge. "You're really going to deprive me of the joy of seeing your broody face in my club? It's tragic, honestly."

"You'll live," I deadpan.

"*Fine*," he sighs with exaggerated defeat, dragging the word out. "But when you're bored out of your mind tonight, just remember my offer still stands. New room, Nicholas. You'll love it."

I give him a pointed look. "Don't hold your breath."

The intercom dings, and Amara's name flashes on the screen. I press the button, clearing my throat. "Everything alright?"

Maybe she wants to leave early, though in the two years she's been my assistant, she hasn't taken a single unscheduled day off. It's one of the things I respect about her. She's dependable, punctual, and professional. I can't stand tardiness or flakiness, and Amara has never once let me down.

"Mr. Blackwood, Alexander is on the phone. He wants to speak with you, sir."

My jaw tightens at the mention of my brother's name. Across from me, Ethan groans, tipping his head back dramatically.

"Put him through," I reply.

"Seriously?" Ethan asks, his face twisting. "You're actually answering his calls? If it were me, I'd tell your cute little assistant to block him."

My pulse ticks at the *cute assistant* remark, but I push it down. "That's different. You're not his brother."

"Thank fuck for that," Ethan mutters with a low whistle.

A second later, my phone rings. I answer, barely opening my mouth before Alexander's voice cuts through.

"Forwarding my calls to your assistant, Nicholas? Do you even realize how that looks? Delegating me to—"

"To my very competent assistant?" I cut him off, letting a trace of boredom seep into my tone. "If you'd prefer to wait on hold, or better yet, schedule an appointment, I'm sure Amara would be happy to add you to the list."

Ethan leans back in his chair with a smirk as I juggle Alexander's rant on the phone. He crosses his arms, clearly enjoying the show. "This is better than Netflix," he mutters, just loud enough for me to hear.

I ignore him, my focus on Alexander's grating tone.

"Don't play games with me, Nicholas," Alexander snaps, his irritation crackling through the line. "We both know why I'm calling."

Of course we do. This isn't a brotherly check-in; this is about the CEO position. The position he's been gunning for since our father passed. The position I now hold, much to his never-ending frustration.

"Dad wanted a leader to take over the company, not some... figurehead," Alexander continues, his voice dripping with disdain. "He needs someone with experience. And I have that."

"Experience throwing tantrums? Absolutely," I reply, my tone as cold as the glass of scotch I'm already considering for later. My fingers tap against the desk, wanting this conversation to be over.

Alexander's voice pitches higher, his frustration boiling over. "You've never even wanted this role. You know this was meant for me."

"Yet, here I am," I say, my voice clipped. "And here you are, calling to whine about it. If Dad thought it fit to put me in charge, perhaps it's because he recognized something you still can't grasp. Leadership isn't about clocking hours or racking up years. It's about vision, restraint, maturity—"

"Don't lecture me," Alexander snarls, cutting me off. "I've earned this."

"Then act like it." Silence stretches between us. "Do your job, Alexander, and leave me to do mine."

I can almost hear him grinding his teeth through the phone. He hates being called out, hates it even more when he knows I'm right.

"Fine," he bites out, his words like venom. "Enjoy your petty victory while it lasts."

The line goes dead, and I set the phone down with more force than necessary, the sharp click echoing in the room, his words clinging to me.

You've never wanted this.

The irony is, I didn't. Alexander was the one who obsessed over it since we were kids, groomed by my father to take over, which only made sense, seeing as he's the oldest. But as the years went on, and Alexander became interested in... other endeavors, dad turned to me. Our father made his choice, and I'm determined to honor it, no matter how little support I get from Alexander.

"Wow," Ethan scoffs from across the room, with a slow clap. "That was... heated. You two always this friendly, or is this a special occasion?"

I glare at him, but it only makes his grin widen. Ethan thrives on chaos, especially if he's not the one in the middle of it.

"Don't you have somewhere to be?" I grit out, my focus locked on the screen in front of me. The endless to-do list stares back, a reminder that I don't have time for Ethan's nonsense today.

"Not really," he replies, casually crossing his arms and sinking further into the chair. "But I'm happy to stick around for whatever you need. Moral support, commentary… think of it as a favor."

"How generous of you," I say dryly, swiveling my chair away from him toward the window and lift onto my feet.

"Kinda jealous of your office," Ethan murmurs. "Ever have kinky sex in front of the windows?"

I glance at him over my shoulder, one brow arched. "Do you ever think of anything else?"

He shrugs, his lips quirking into a grin. "Not really. My mind's a fun place."

"I'll bet," I mutter, turning back to the view. The city stretches out before me, the Blackwood Hotel prominently visible in the skyline—a towering reminder of my father's legacy. It's my responsibility now, my name on the line. I should be focused on proving I deserve this.

But instead, my thoughts drift to her red-rimmed eyes.

Goddamnit. What the hell is wrong with me?

I run a hand through my hair, the tension knotting in my shoulders as I move to the bar. Grabbing a glass, I drop in two ice cubes and pour a finger of scotch.

"Jesus." Ethan scoffs from behind me, his tone dripping with amusement. "Your brother must've really screwed you up if you're day drinking."

Brother. Right.

"You know what would help you blow off some steam?" he continues, his grin audible even before I turn around. I don't need to hear the rest. I already know where this is going.

My jaw tightens as I face him. "Get me a fucking invite."

Ethan's grin spreads wider. He stands, pulling a keycard from his jacket pocket and holding it out to me. "Already got one right here."

19

CHAPTER THREE
Amara

"Y ou see? Even Mark Darcy broke Bridget's heart," I mutter dramatically, wiping my nose on the sleeve of my sweater. Pumpkin stretches lazily on my lap, her eyes fluttering shut. She doesn't care about my emotional breakdown. Of course she doesn't. She's a cat. Her priorities begin and end with food, naps, and plotting my demise when I forget to give her a treat.

"There's no hope for me if they can't make it work," I sniff, sinking further into my couch of despair. Pumpkin purrs in reply, or maybe she's just mocking me. It's hard to tell.

But then a knock at the door jolts me out of my pity spiral, and my heart leaps into my throat. I glance at the thin, useless curtains covering the window. The faint glow of the streetlights filters through, confirming that, yep, it's late. And dark. And definitely not the time for unannounced visitors.

My first thought? *Serial killer*. My second? *Do I have time to grab a weapon*?

I don't have time to do anything but stay frozen in place, staring at the door in panic.

When the knocking doesn't stop, I groan and drag myself off the squeaky couch-bed hybrid. The cold floorboards send a shiver up my spine, but I shuffle toward the door, wondering if I'm about to be murdered with pizza crumbs on my clothes.

I reach for the door handle, mentally cursing the builder who decided a peephole wasn't needed. Seriously, who designed this?

But when I finally twist the handle and crack the door open, it's not a random stranger or a serial killer. It's Jade and Sophie. Standing in my hallway.

Sophie crosses her arms over her chest, scanning the interior of my apartment, and the hallway, like someone would a crime scene—with mild horror.

Jade, on the other hand, breezes past me, scrunching her nose and arching an eyebrow. "You don't even have space to breathe in here." Her arms fling out wide, only to crash into my fridge and the wall.

"What the hell are you doing here?" I ask, rubbing my eyes with the back of my hand. I just wanted to watch a cheesy movie, drown in ice cream, and cry into Pumpkin's fuzzy paws until I passed out.

Sophie kicks the door shut with her foot and Jade spins around, her brows raising as she assesses my pink, strawberry print pajamas, a smirk curling up her lips. "Nice pajamas," she teases.

I cross my arms over my chest, giving her a look. "They're comfortable," I shoot back, shaking my head when the realization of them both being in my apartment—which I didn't tell anyone about—hits me.

"How did you guys find me?" I ask them, glancing between them. Jade's heels click on the floors as she walks over to the coffee table, picking up the empty carton of Ice cream toppled on its side.

Sophie—whose eyes are still darting around the small, cramped space, from the mismatched furniture to the dishes piled up in the sink, to the laundry half-folded on the tiny pull-out couch—folds her arms, standing by the door like she's afraid to get too close. "We went to your place, looking for you. Liam told us you moved out?" Her head tilts slightly. "He tracked your phone and told us where you were."

I blink, my pulse quickening. I don't know how I feel about my ex still having access to my location.

"I told you guys we broke up," I say with a shrug.

Jade places her hand on her hip, glaring at me. "Yes, but you never told us you were the one who moved out." Her voice drops a notch. "And to this place, no less," she adds, shaking her head. "You could've come to us, Amara. I would've let you crash at my place without a second thought."

I get it. I know they're frustrated, and honestly, I'm frustrated too. I should've told them. But…

I cross my arms tighter around myself. "I didn't want to tell anyone," I admit, glancing down at the worn rug beneath my feet. "I just… I felt embarrassed. And I couldn't stay there another second," I confess. "Not when—" I pause, swallowing hard as the memory rushes back. "Not when he slept with someone else on our bed while I was at work."

The silence that follows is thick. I can feel Jade's anger building as she inhales sharply. Her eyes widen in disbelief. "He did *what*?" she asks, her voice cracking with fury. Her fists clench at her sides. "I'm going back there right now and kicking his ass."

"Jade, stop," I say, stepping in front of her before she can do something crazy. We both know there's no stopping her once she's set on something.

Jade's eyes narrow as she glares at me. "I'm not letting him get away with this. We need to do something about it."

Sophie clears her throat, unwrapping her arms and placing a hand on Jade's shoulder. "I don't think getting arrested for assault is going to help Amara."

"I look good in orange," Jade adds with a grin, flicking her straight brown hair behind her shoulder. "Now, are you going to help me, or am I going to have to take him down myself?"

I sigh, rubbing my temples. "Jade, you need to calm down. He's not worth it." Jade's fierce. She'd die for her friends, no questions asked. But Sophie and I both know we have to keep her in check because, let's be real, she'd also *kill* for us without a second thought.

"Amara's right," Sophie adds. "That asshole doesn't deserve a single tear or a single drop of sweat, from you or anyone else."

"He *cheated* on you." Jade frowns. "I might be allergic to the idea of relationships, but cheating? That's a hard no in my book."

Sophie chuckles, tilting her head at Jade. "Who would've known?"

Jade smirks, clearly relaxing a bit more with each passing second. "I'm a woman of many talents," she says with a shrug.

"Back to your cheating ex," Sophie interjects. "Why the hell did he get to stay in the apartment anyway? Why were you the one who left?"

I press my lips together, the question hitting me like a punch in the gut. Because I couldn't stand to look at our room anymore. I couldn't bear to think about all the times we'd been together, wondering if she had been in our bed those days. I couldn't stay there, not with him, not with the memories haunting me. So, I packed up, grabbed Pumpkin, and left.

I press my palms to my face, fighting back the emotions. "I really don't want to talk about this," I murmur, sinking onto the pull-out couch, which creaks under my weight.

"Good." Jade plops down beside me. "Because we're not talking." I lift my head, giving her a confused frown. "We're getting drunk."

I blink. "Excuse me?"

She tilts her head. "Staying in isn't doing you any favors, babe. You need to get your ass in a sexy dress, the shorter, the better, and come out with Sophie and me and get shit-faced drunk."

Sophie lets out a breath, running a hand through her blonde hair. "We all have work tomorrow, Jade. Maybe getting drunk isn't the best idea, considering it's a Monday."

Jade shoots Sophie a glare, tilting her head in challenge. It makes me laugh, because no one can say no to Jade. Not even Sophie, apparently, as she lets out a sigh. "Okay, maybe a few drinks won't hurt."

Jade grins and lets out a whoop. "See? Even Virgin Sophie is on board. Come on, Amara. Say yes."

"Excuse me." Sophie frowns. "Do I need to remind you I'm in a relationship? I get constant sex."

Jade scoffs, raising an eyebrow. "I'm sure," she drawls. "Missionary position and all."

"I like that position," Sophie replies, her voice quiet, brows knitted together.

Jade tilts her head, pressing her lips into a smirk. "Sure you do, hun," she says, before turning back to me with a glint in her eye. "So, what do you say?"

I laugh, shaking my head. "You guys are ridiculous."

Jade's grin widens as she nudges my shoulder with hers. "You love us anyway."

And I do. I thought keeping everything to myself was the best option, but I should've known that telling them would make me feel better. Just having them here, bickering and joking, is already helping me forget what happened with Liam... *almost*.

"It's your choice, Amara," Jade adds, her smile settling. "If you want to sit in this dusty, crusty, musty apartment and cry at cheesy rom-coms," she gestures toward the TV, where Bridget Jones is still playing in the background, "just say the word and I'll run—well, not run, because... *ew*, I don't run—I will strut downstairs, head to the nearest grocery store and pick up every single flavor of ice cream I can find."

God, that sounds depressing. All I'd need is *All by Myself* playing in the background, and I'd be starring in my own rom-com. Except it wouldn't actually be funny. Or romantic.

I chew on my bottom lip, glancing between the girls, who are both waiting for my answer. I love them for being the kind of friends who would sit with me while I cried into a pint of ice cream without hesitation. But that's not what I want.

"Okay," I say, taking a deep breath. "I'll go."

"Fuck yes!" Jade claps, jumping up with a grin. "That's my girl."

Sophie pulls out her phone, shifting as she starts typing. "How long are we staying out?" she asks. "I need to let Sebastian know when we'll be home."

Jade rolls her eyes dramatically. "You want to invite him and handcuff him to your wrist all night too?" She shakes her head, laughing. "Just tell him you'll be home late. Don't worry, I'll bring you back unharmed and untouched," she teases.

Her eyes meet mine, glinting with mischief. "Now, let's find the hottest, skankiest dress you own." I don't even have a chance to protest as she pulls me toward the pile of crumpled clothes in the corner.

I groan, letting out a long exhale. What the hell did I just agree to?

CHAPTER FOUR
Nicholas

My palms are damp, sticking uncomfortably to the polished wood of my desk. I grip the edge tighter, like it might somehow anchor me… or at least stop my hands from shaking.

Focus. Get it together.

I've done this a thousand times before. I've made presentations, pitched deals, closed contracts. There's no reason for me to be nervous. Not now. Not with this.

The air is thick with the scent of fresh leather and expensive cologne. Across from me, Robert Jensen, the CEO of Jenkins International, taps his pen against the polished mahogany table. His eyes flick from me to the other three men sitting around the table. David Owens, head of acquisitions; Claire Rivers, the CFO who could probably crush me with a single glance; and Simon Reynolds, the consultant who thinks he knows everything. He's the youngest in the room by a solid twenty years, the only one even remotely close to my age.

But he blends right in with the rest of them—tailored suit, smug expression—all of them holding my future in their hands.

No fucking pressure.

"Mr. Blackwood," Robert begins, tapping his pen against my desk. "We've been looking over the Blackwood brand and its success in the U.S. and we're confident expanding internationally is the next logical step."

I nod, my gaze flicking to the pen he keeps tapping on the table.

I wish he'd cut that the fuck out.

I've heard this pitch a hundred times. Europe, Asia, South America—hell, we've been talking about it for months. This is what my father wanted for as long as I can remember. A global brand. He had the vision, the drive, the passion to take this empire global. But he passed before he could accomplish it. And now it's my responsibility. To honor him. To finish his unfinished business.

It's everything I've worked for. And yet, despite all that, it feels like the weight of the world is pressing down on my chest, making it harder to breathe.

Robert clears his throat, leaning forward as the pen tap-tap-taps against the table, then stops. "But there's something holding us back."

I sit up straighter, instinctively gripping the edge of the table. The smell of fresh coffee lingers in the air, but it does nothing to calm the storm brewing inside me. Holding them back? What the hell is he talking about?

"And that's your image," Robert continues, the goddamn pen tapping again like he's trying to drive me insane.

My image?

I've given everything to this company. Every waking moment, every late night, every holiday. I've sacrificed it all to keep the Blackwood name intact. To make sure my father's legacy doesn't get trampled by some shiny new competitor. I've fought for this. I've bled for this.

"I'm sorry?" I ask, my voice strained, unsure if I'm even hearing them right. "What about my image?"

For a brief moment, my mind flashes to my brother. Though we don't exactly look alike, his name's been dragged through the mud more than once. And if this has anything to do with him...

My jaw tightens, the muscles in my neck stiffening.

Robert clears his throat. "The thing is... Blackwood Hotels is synonymous with luxury, exclusivity, and... family values." He looks around the room for a moment, the tension thick in the air. "We've done our research, and there's been a bit of a discrepancy in your personal life. The tabloids have had a field day with your... romantic history."

A cold chill runs down my spine. I can feel my heart rate spike, my pulse thudding in my ears. Are you fucking kidding me?

Since my dad passed, the world has been watching me and the Blackwood family, waiting for us to fail. We were in freefall, struggling to keep the company afloat after months of ignoring the financials. My brother, stumbling through life, drowning in alcohol, unable to cope with my being CEO. And I... I failed. I watched the company slip through my fingers.

So, I did what I knew best. I made headlines. I staged some club outings, let myself be seen with women, whatever it took to get people talking again, to bring the attention back. It worked, for a while. Bookings picked up. Investors were interested again. But now... now it's all coming back to bite me in the ass.

David shifts in his seat, clearing his throat. "Look, Nicholas, we know a man like you is entitled to live how he chooses," he continues, his voice measured but serious. "But for Blackwood Hotels to succeed internationally, we need you to represent something more… something stable. A family man. Someone we can rely on."

Family. The word sounds foreign to me. I've been running on fumes for so long, entirely focused on saving this company, doing whatever it takes to keep it afloat, that the thought of stability—of settling down—slipped too far into the background, out of my reach. They want someone committed, someone married or engaged. And I'm nowhere near that.

"With all due respect," I say, my voice tight with frustration, "I think I've shown my capabilities to run this business."

Robert's gaze softens for just a moment before he leans back in his chair, his fingers steepled in front of his face. "You have," he adds, but there's a hesitation there I can't ignore. "But most of the attention surrounding Blackwood Hotels has come from your personal life. Your romantic escapades. That's the narrative the media's picked up on. And while it may have worked to generate buzz, it's also been a distraction."

Fuck. He's right.

I've let my personal life spill out into the public eye, thinking it would help the business. It worked, for a time. But now, it's only serving to undermine me.

Before I can respond, Claire speaks up, clearing her throat. "We all agree you've kept the Blackwood name relevant. But what we need is someone who can take it from gossip columns to the Forbes list."

The rest of the board nod, their faces neutral, calculating.

"And if you can't do that…" Robert lets the sentence hang, his words heavy with implication.

My pulse quickens. Sweat clings to my palms. This is it— the deal I've been working for, my chance to fulfill my father's legacy—and I'm on the edge of losing it.

Just as it all threatens to crush me, a soft knock echoes through the door. My head snaps up, my heart stuttering in my chest. The door swings open, and Amara steps in. Her wide eyes flick to the members of the board, and a faint flush spreads across her face.

"I'm so sorry. I forgot the meeting was today, and—"

"That's okay, Amara," I say, my shoulders loosening just a little. I push myself up from the chair, moving toward her. Her confused gaze meets mine, her green eyes clouded with uncertainty. A small smile tugs at the corners of my lips as I step closer. Without thinking, I take her hand.

The room falls dead silent.

Amara gasps, her eyes flicking down to our joined hands. I can feel the weight of their stares, the pressure building in the air, and something inside me snaps.

I turn to face them, my grip on Amara's hand tightening. A wide smile spreads across my face, and the words tumble out before I can stop them.

"Have you met my fiancée?"

CHAPTER FIVE

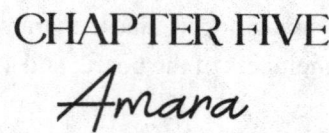

I'm still drunk.

There's no other possible explanation for why Nicholas Blackwood, my boss and notorious *too-good-looking-for-his-own-good* CEO, is holding my hand like it's no big deal and calling me his *fiancée*.

I feel the blood rush to my cheeks, and I briefly wonder if I'm about to pass out. This is just a very, *very* vivid dream while I'm inebriated... right? But when my head starts to pound from my questionable decision to take those tequila shots last night, I know for sure this isn't a dream.

"I don't understand," the man at the center of the group speaks up, his brow furrowed in confusion as he glances from me to Nicholas. The others—dressed in suits that probably cost more than my rent—echo his disbelief with silent stares.

I can't say I blame them. I'm just as lost.

I glance at Nicholas, whose fingers are still casually wrapped around mine. The man's grip isn't letting go anytime soon, and when his eyes meet mine, I swear, time stops. He looks at me like I'm the only one in the room, and it's honestly kind of terrifying.

But also *extremely* hot.

One of the other guys clears his throat. "My apologies, Mr. Blackwood, but we were under the impression you weren't seeing anyone."

Nicholas doesn't even flinch under their questions. Instead, he tightens his hold on my hand. I glance up at him, and his gaze catches mine, with a silent request to follow his lead.

"Fortunately, your assumptions are wrong," he replies in the polished tone that somehow manages to make everything sound so plausible.

His eyes linger on mine, way too intense, and I have to remind myself that we're surrounded by people. I try not to notice the heat blooming in my chest or the way his gaze seems to burn into me, memorizing every single detail.

I have no idea what kind of alternate universe I've stumbled into, but it sure as hell doesn't feel like the one I left last night.

He finally looks away, his gaze drifting back to the board. For a split second, his fingers loosen in mine, and I brace myself for him to pull away, to backpedal on whatever wild story he was just spinning. But then, with zero warning, he laces our fingers together like it's the most natural thing in the world.

"We're engaged," he announces, his voice dripping with confidence. No doubt. No hesitation. Just a hundred questions swirling in my head.

I blink up at him, my jaw practically scraping the floor. Seriously? He's sticking with this?

"Engaged?" the older guy at the head of the table repeats, his brows furrowing as he taps his pen against his chin. "I'm sorry, Mr. Blackwood, but when exactly did this... relationship begin?" His tone is polite, but the skepticism is thick enough to cut with a knife.

I swear, my skin goes clammy. Lying isn't exactly my strong suit. Pretending? Even worse. And right now, I'm standing here like an idiot with no freaking idea what's going on.

"Recently," Nicholas replies, his voice as steady as ever, his finger gently trailing over the back of my hand. And, of course, the goosebumps are back. *Great.* "Very recently."

Like, thirty seconds ago, to be exact.

I bite down on my cheek, fighting the urge to blurt something—anything—that would make this less painfully awkward. But all I can do is stand here, praying I don't look like I'm about to melt into a puddle right on the spot. Their gaze travels over me, assessing, judging, looking for cracks in the story, weighing whether I'm worthy enough to stand by a man like him.

But I already know the answer.

I'm not.

There are a lot of things about myself I like—qualities someone might even come to love someday. But I'm not delusional enough to think Nicholas would ever be one of those people. He's too polished, too confident... too far out of my league.

I don't belong in his world, and definitely not in this room, surrounded by businesspeople in suits that probably cost more than my entire yearly paycheck.

As much as I try not to admit it, Nicholas is a walking, talking Greek god. With a body that should come with a warning label and a face straight off a runway. Every inch of him screams power and control, from the sharp lines of his jaw to the way his suit fits him like it was made just for him.

And I'm just the assistant. The girl with hair that's always a bit too frizzy, thanks to drugstore shampoo. The one who never quite fits in. The girl with a bunch of shirts shoved in the back of her closet, collecting dust because they're way too small, waiting for some miracle to make them fit again. We're galaxies apart, and I'm pretty sure everyone here can sense it.

"We've kept our relationship quiet to avoid the press," Nicholas continues. I can't help but admire how effortlessly he handles this, like he's been doing it his entire life. "But I can promise you, while the tabloids paint a very different picture of me, I am a family man to my core."

I glance up at him, unable to hide my surprise. I swear, if he ever decided to trade his suit for a movie script, Hollywood would be knocking down his door.

"Isn't she your assistant?" one of the board members asks, breaking my trance.

My stomach drops. Shit. Am I about to get fired? Is this some twisted test? Will HR hear about this and boot me out the door?

I try to pull my hand away from his, but Nicholas's grip tightens, his fingers weaving through mine with a possessiveness that sends a shiver down my spine. He doesn't flinch. Doesn't waver. Doesn't even blink.

"She is, yes," he affirms with a sharp nod. He's so sure of himself, so utterly confident, in a way I'm not sure I'll ever be.

"Well," the gentleman in the center clears his throat, his pen stopping mid tap. He leans back in his chair, an almost amused glint in his eye. "That changes things." Nicholas's hand tightens around mine at those words. "We'd love to move forward now that we know you're… pursuing something more stable."

Nicholas nods once. "I appreciate that. And I would love to continue this discussion another day, but right now my fiancée needs me." The word strikes like a chill, crawling up my spine.

I freeze for just a second, caught off guard by how casually he drops it.

Nicholas doesn't seem fazed. Without missing a beat, he stands and walks to the door, turning the handle. "It was nice to meet with you today."

One by one, they stand and file out, each of their gazes lingering for a fraction of a second longer than necessary as they pass me, I hold my breath, forcing a smile that feels more like a grimace, trying to channel even a sliver of Nicholas's confidence.

"Congratulations," the man in the center says, his gaze flicking toward me.

"Thank you," Nicholas responds with a short nod.

The man's eyes stay on me a moment longer than necessary, my heart pounding under his scrutiny. Finally, he gives a brief nod and turns, the door clicking shut behind him.

Nicholas stays by the door, his hand on the handle, and for a brief moment, his gaze shifts downward as his fingers slowly slip from mine.

"*Fiancée?*"

It's the only word I can force past my lips, the only thing my brain can latch onto right now. I can't make sense of what's happening. What he just said. What this all means.

Nicholas lets out a slow breath, his gaze locking with mine as he turns toward me. "I can explain."

I cross my arms, trying to keep some semblance of control, even as the tequila still clings to my system. Dressing up, getting drunk, it all seemed like a great idea at two a.m. But now? Not so much, especially with this bombshell he just dropped. "Please do."

Nicholas steps away from the door, his jaw tensing, and I catch the flicker of discomfort in his eyes. It's subtle, but it's there. He's not as calm as he's pretending to be.

"Before my dad passed," he starts, voice rough, almost like the words hurt to say, "he had plans to take Blackwood Hotels international. He wanted Blackwood to be a global empire. It was everything to him. But then…" He exhales sharply, shaking his head. "He died before he had the chance to. And when I took over as CEO, I did everything I could to keep his dream alive, to make sure his vision of Blackwood in every major city around the world became a reality."

I blink, and shake my head, clearing out the last traces of the party fog. "I'm sorry, but I don't understand," I reply. "What does *any* of that have to do with me?"

His jaw clenches, the muscle ticking visibly as his gaze locks onto mine. "I'm sorry," he grunts, his voice low. "I should never have dragged you into this. The board… they told me they wanted someone who came across as a 'family man.' And, let's face it, I clearly wasn't what they wanted, not with my—" he pauses, his lips pressing together as he swallows, "my dating life all over the tabloids. The deal was about to fall through because of it. And then you… you walked in, and I—" He stops, running a hand through his hair in frustration as his eyes soften. "I'm sorry, Amara."

God, he has got to stop saying my name like that. It does things to me I don't even want to think about. His Adam's apple bobs as he swallows, his posture stiff. He's clearly just as uncomfortable as I am.

And yet, I ask the last thing I ever expected.

"How exactly would this plan of yours work?"

His eyes widen just a little, like I've shocked him as much as I've shocked myself. I can't believe I just asked that. I can't believe I'm even thinking about this.

Nicholas takes a slow breath, straightening his tie and smoothing a stray strand of hair away from his forehead. He's in control again, and I can see it in the way he shifts into pitch mode.

"It wouldn't be for long. The board's already on board, and we've got the resources to make this happen. All I need is to convince them I'm serious about this. About… you."

Color rushes to my face, and when his gaze narrows slightly, I know he sees it. Great. Just what I need—my emotions all over my face.

The idea of pretending to be Nicholas Blackwood's wife, or fiancée, or whatever this charade is, fills me with dread. The paparazzi would have a field day. The tabloids would have my face plastered all over them, dissecting my every move. I don't think I could handle it, especially if he takes the company global. It won't just be New York, but the whole world watching us, judging, expecting me to be something I'm definitely not.

I shake my head, stepping back until I bump into the edge of his desk. The cold wood presses against me as I struggle to catch my breath. "I'm sorry. I just can't."

I lift my eyes to meet his, and for a second, I catch the faintest flicker in Nicholas's gaze… Disappointment, maybe? It's gone so quickly I wonder if I imagined it. He nods, his voice softer now. "Of course. I understand. I didn't think this through. I'm sure your boyfriend wouldn't be okay with it."

The mention of Liam churns my stomach. "No, it's not that. We, uh… We actually broke up."

His eyebrows lift, just a tiny bit, the surprise flashing across his face. "I'm sorry."

"It's okay," I mutter, trying to brush it off with a shrug. "We just… grew apart," I lie.

It's bad enough being cheated on by your boyfriend of five years, let alone having to bring it up with your boss.

Nicholas nods, his hand lifting thoughtfully as he hums under his breath. "If a boyfriend isn't the issue, may I ask what is?"

His gaze locks onto mine, dark and intense, and I can't help it, he pulls me in, despite every part of me telling me not to. I *don't* want to be attracted to him. But it's hard not to, not with the way he looks at me. Every woman seems to fall for his charm, and I'm apparently no different.

"It's frowned upon for bosses and assistants to… date," I say, my voice shaking slightly, betraying me when I see him take a step closer. His gaze never leaves mine, and I hate how my pulse quickens in response.

He smirks as he steps even closer, his presence overwhelming. "True, but not unorthodox."

I shake my head, trying to focus. "I just… What will people think when they hear we're… engaged?" The word feels alien on my tongue, like I'm saying something that doesn't belong to me. Once upon a time—hell, even five days ago—I thought I'd be getting engaged to Liam. And now here I am, being asked to pretend to be my boss's fiancée.

Nicholas's smirk deepens, and my grip tightens on the desk behind me. "They'll think you came into my office for more than coffee runs."

A rush of color floods my face as his words crash over me. I shake my head, unsure whether I heard him right, wondering if he really just implied that we...

"I don't..." I pause, gathering my thoughts. "I don't understand how this would work. No one will believe this."

He stops in his tracks, his brows furrowing, eyes locked onto mine. "What do you mean by that?"

What do I mean? How can he not see it? Surely, he must understand why some people would find this impossible to believe.

I exhale, my neck hot and tense. "I don't look like the girls you're usually seen with, Mr. Blackwood," I say, my voice quieter than I intend, unwilling to meet his gaze. Afraid of what I might see in his eyes.

The silence stretches, and I brace myself for him to agree, maybe even apologize, and suggest this plan be scrapped. But then his voice breaks the silence, low, rumbling, and somehow darker than before, sending a shiver down my spine.

"Is that what the problem is?" His eyes lock onto mine, dark and piercing. "You don't think I'm attracted to you?"

The air thickens, pressing down on me from all sides. I try to stand my ground, but my heart is racing out of my chest. "Are you?" I ask before I can stop myself, immediately regretting the words as they slip past my lips.

It must be the alcohol still lingering in my system making me see things. There's no other explanation for the way Nicholas's eyes slow their scan of my face, taking in every detail, every inch of me, until they finally land on my lips. He takes a step closer, and my breath catches in my throat. My lips part instinctively, like they've been waiting for this moment, and then—

"Mr. Blackwood."

The interruption is sudden. Two quick knocks at the door, and Nicholas steps back, once, twice, eyes flicking over me from head to toe before turning to face the door.

"Yes?"

The door swings open, and Sophie appears, her eyes widening when she sees me. Her gaze flicks back and forth between us, before landing on him.

"I'm sorry to interrupt, sir. Amara's line was ringing off the hook, and I hadn't seen her for a while, so I picked up the phone."

Nicholas doesn't immediately respond, his eyes flicking to me, as if just now realizing that I'm still here, still caught in the middle of whatever this is.

"Alexander wants to speak to you, sir," Sophie adds, her voice now laced with a touch of concern.

Nicholas closes his eyes, a vein popping in his neck as he exhales sharply. "Thank you, Sophie." He turns toward her, his posture stiff. "I'll take it from here."

Sophie nods and glances at me, her eyes filled with questions, but I just clear my throat and make my way to the door.

"I should…" I murmur, struggling to finish the sentence as I step away from his desk. Nicholas gives me a brief nod before I close the door behind me, his words still clinging to the air.

I know Sophie must have a million questions—as do I—and she doesn't even wait until the door closes before tugging me by my elbow.

"What the hell were you doing in there for so long?" she asks, lowering her voice as we walk toward our desk.

I let out a heavy breath, shaking my head. "You wouldn't believe me if I told you."

CHAPTER SIX
Nicholas

New York is beautiful. Especially at night. The lights scattered across the city, the skyscrapers towering over the streets below. But as I stand by the window, staring out at the skyline, Alexander's voice echoes in my head, drowning out everything else.

He didn't even give me a chance to avoid him today. The second he found out I'd met with the board to discuss expansion of the hotel, my phone lit up with his name, over and over again, until I gave in.

His words linger, sharp and unyielding, carving their way into my mind. The doubt, the jealousy, they stick, like a shadow I can't shake, no matter how hard I try.

I've heard it all before, but for some reason, it hit differently this time. It's because for the first time since stepping into this job, I'm starting to think he's right... I'm questioning if I actually have what it takes.

If this deal goes south, it's on me. My father's empire—his legacy—is going down with it. I wanted to prove to myself I could do this. That I could fill my father's shoes, but with every step I take, it feels like I'm digging myself deeper into a hole I can't get out of.

I close my eyes, drag in a shaky breath, and try to let it out slowly.

The soft knock on my door pulls me from the downward spiral of my thoughts. The creak of the door follows, and I don't need to turn to know who it is.

Amara steps inside, heels clicking against the polished wood floor, a stack of papers balanced in her hands. Her expression is calm, professional as always, but I notice the subtle tells. How her lips press together just a fraction too tightly, how she avoids looking at me. The hesitation in her steps tells me everything. She's still thinking about earlier.

So am I.

"I'm just… leaving the papers you asked for, sir." She places the papers on my desk with meticulous care, her gaze fixed on them, before she turns around and walks toward the exit.

Before she reaches the door, I say her name.

"Amara."

She freezes mid-step, her shoulders stiff, and when she finally turns, her eyes flick downward, refusing to meet mine.

"We were interrupted before," I say, gesturing to the chair in front of my desk.

She doesn't move right away, her hesitation hanging in the air. I can practically see her weighing her options, deciding whether to stick around or make a run for it.

I lean forward slightly, resting my forearms on the desk. "We need to finish our conversation."

She hesitates, her gaze flicking toward the chair, then back to the floor. She lowers herself onto the chair, slowly, but I catch the tension in her face. The way her brow furrows, the slight clench of her jaw… She's nervous. And it unsettles me more than I care to admit.

I shouldn't care. Her nerves shouldn't bother me. But as I watch her sit, a strange tightness coils in my chest, impossible to ignore.

I move from behind my desk and settle on the edge of it, close enough to make my presence known but leaving her the space she clearly needs. She doesn't look at me. Her eyes flick toward the stack of papers on my desk, then down to her lap, where her hands fidget restlessly.

I study her for a long moment, remembering our conversation earlier, the hesitation in her voice.

She thinks I'm not attracted to her.

I almost laugh at the absurdity of it.

Attraction? That's the least of the issues here.

It's a problem, just how much I'm attracted to her. A problem I've tried my best to avoid. The last thing I want to do is complicate things in the workspace. Dating an assistant is a cliché, one I've worked hard to avoid. And yet…

I shove the thought aside. Focus. There's too much riding on this conversation to let myself get distracted.

Her fingers twist together in her lap, and she finally breaks the silence. "I don't know what you want me to say," she murmurs. She shakes her head, her shoulders tight. "What am I supposed to say here?"

She's still avoiding my eyes, but I see the way her chest rises and falls with each shallow breath, like she's struggling to find the right words.

"You can say anything you want," I tell her, leaning in just a little, wanting her to know she has control. Her eyes flick to mine—*finally*—and the uncertainty swimming in them hits me square in the chest. "You won't lose your job for speaking your mind, Amara," I add, holding her gaze when she tries to look away. "Say yes, say no, tell me to go fuck myself if you don't want to do this. Whatever it is, it's your call."

The words linger between us, and slowly, a faint smile tugs at the corner of her lips. It's small, cautious, but it's there. She's listening. She's thinking about it. But there's still hesitation in her eyes. I can see it, feel it.

"But if your concerns are about what we discussed earlier…" I pause. Then, before I can stop myself, I lift a hand and gently cup her chin. Her skin is warm, soft, and the contact sends a shock through me I'm not prepared for. My thumb brushes over her cheek, slow and careful. She doesn't pull away.

"My attraction to you isn't an issue."

Her eyes flicker to mine, searching, hesitant. I see every question she's too afraid to ask reflected in the green of her gaze.

"No?" she murmurs, testing, her voice as soft as the touch of her breath.

I hold her gaze, unflinching. "No."

She exhales slowly, struggling to wrap her head around everything, and the last thing I want to do is add to it.

"I didn't mean to make you uncomfortable." I lower my hand.

"No," she whispers, shaking her head. "You didn't."

"I know this is a lot. Take your time. Think about it. There's no rush," I lie.

We're absolutely in a rush. The board won't wait forever, and eventually they'll want some proof that we are truly engaged. But I won't push her.

I straighten my tie, more for something to do with my hands than anything else, and take a step back, giving her room. "If it's compensation you're worried about, don't be. That's not a problem."

Her head snaps up at that, her brows furrowing slightly. "You'd *pay* me?"

"Of course," I reply, without hesitation. "It's only fair. You're doing me a favor."

I pull open the drawer and reach for my checkbook, scribbling a number that's more than generous. When I slide it across the desk to her, she doesn't reach for it. Instead, she stares at it for a beat, then back at me.

"Amara," I say quietly, leaning just slightly toward her. "This is your call. No pressure. No expectations. If you want to walk away, I won't stop you."

Her eyes dart between me and the check, her brows pulling together before she finally reaches for it, her fingers brushing the edge of the paper.

When she flips it over and sees the number I've written, her breath catches.

"Are you—this is insane, Nic—Mr. Blackwood." Her voice cracks, and the way she almost says my name, soft and unguarded, stirs something inside me. She's always been the epitome of composure. I've never heard her voice waver like that. Never seen her so thrown off balance.

She pushes the check back toward me. "I can't accept this," she whispers, shaking her head.

Before she can pull away completely, I reach out, covering her hand with mine. "Don't do anything rash, Amara. Not yet. Take the time to think it through," I continue. "You don't have to decide right now. When you've made your choice, I'll accept it. Whatever it is."

I mean it. Every word. I need her to know that I'm not trying to back her into a corner, not trying to force her into something she doesn't want.

But… God, I need her.

Her gaze lingers on where our hands still meet. For a heartbeat, neither of us moves, neither of us dares to speak.

Then, without a word, she pulls her hand away, her fingers slipping from beneath mine, the check clutched tightly in her hand. She clears her throat, a small, quiet sound, and nods. "I'll think about it."

I don't breathe until the door clicks shut behind her and I'm finally alone.

No matter what happens next, I'll respect her choice.

Even if it shatters everything I've built.

CHAPTER SEVEN

Amara

"Come on," I grunt, when the key jams in the lock as I try to open the door to my apartment.

I grunt, twisting it harder, but it doesn't budge. I curse in frustration that this has become my new routine every time I come home. Shifting my weight, I lean my shoulder into the door, turning the key again with a forceful click. A little shove, and the door finally gives, swinging open with a creak. I stumble into the apartment, breathing a sigh of relief as I kick the door shut behind me.

Pumpkin is already by my feet when I enter my apartment, weaving between my legs with a soft meow.

"Missed you too," I murmur, managing a tired smile as I drop my bag on the floor and take a long, deep breath. I used to love coming home. It used to be my quiet refuge. Undressing, slipping into pajamas, and sinking into the couch while watching a movie. But now? Now, I dread it. This place feels suffocating, the ceiling too low, the space too cramped. My stuff is crammed into every corner of this tiny studio, making it look more like a storage unit than a home.

The thought of Liam coming home after a long day of work, stepping through the door of our apartment, makes my fists clench. I toss my keys into a chipped bowl by the door and let out a frustrated sigh.

Screw him.

Screw him for moving on without a second thought when all I ever did was love him. Screw him for leaving me with nothing but this cramped apartment and a heart that feels like it's been run through a blender. The worst part is how unaffected he seemed when he broke my heart. Calm. Unbothered. Like none of this—like *I* never mattered to him.

I shake the memory off and kick off my shoes, crossing the cramped space to the kitchen. The fridge groans when I open it, and I half expect the light not to come on, but it flickers to life, revealing a single egg and a nearly empty carton of milk.

"Great," I mutter to myself. "Guess it's breakfast for dinner, again."

I crack the egg into a bowl, watching the yolk break and pool, and a tightness forms in my chest. Cooking for one is depressing. The kitchen feels empty, quiet, just me and the hum of the fridge.

Pumpkin circles my feet again, meowing insistently, her tail brushing against my ankle. I glance down at her, a tired smile tugging at my lips. "Maybe I should get you a friend," I say, whisking the egg in the bowl. "A couple more cats, and I'd be a full-blown, crazy cat lady."

She purrs as if in agreement, and I shake my head, trying to push the thought away. At least cats don't break your heart. They don't pull the rug out from under you just because something better came along.

My phone buzzes from the makeshift coffee table—an old wooden crate I found on the curb—and I glance over, reluctantly stepping away from the sizzling pan, and pick it up.

A pang of guilt hits me when I see Grandma's name flashing on the screen. I close my eyes, squeezing the phone in my hand. I haven't spoken to her in days, and I can already picture the concern in her voice. But I can't bring myself to tell her about Liam. She always warned me he'd break my heart one day, and now here I am, her words echoing in my head, too late to matter.

I pick up the phone, trying to make my voice sound normal. "Hey, Nanna."

"Oh, darling," she sighs. "I was starting to worry. Is everything okay?"

"Yeah," I lie, but the word feels weird in my mouth. I glance around the apartment—peeling wallpaper, clothes in heaps—and feel a sinking pit in my stomach. "Just been... busy."

"You haven't answered your sister either," she continues, the guilt twisting tighter in my stomach. "She was ready to jump on a bus and come up here to find you."

"No," I say quickly. "No, don't let her do that." I wince at the thought of Annie seeing me like this. "You need her there with you, Nanna. You don't need to worry about me."

"Darling, I'm fine." The words come out too easy, too practiced. I know she's not fine, she hasn't been for a long time.

I can hear the effort in her voice when she says, "You worry too much, sweetheart." Like she's trying to convince herself as much as me. "I want to hear what you've been up to. You must've been super busy to not answer my calls. What did you design this week?"

I let out a sigh and sink into the pull-out couch, the springs protesting with a loud creak. I've been lying to her for years now, ever since I graduated college. I had big plans—design and architecture. I'd always loved the idea of interior decorating, of creating spaces that felt lived in, real... like home.

But reality hit hard after graduation. No experience meant no designer job. So, I took the assistant position at Blackwood & CO. It was supposed to be temporary, just a stop until I could get my foot in the door, gain some experience, and finally move into design like I'd always dreamed. But somehow, here I am years later, still an assistant. Comfortable, sure, but stuck in a job that wasn't part of the plan.

"A few things," I say, forcing the words out, wanting her to believe I'm okay, that I'm living the life she always dreamed for me.

"I'm so proud of you," she sighs, her voice thick with pride and hope. It makes my chest tighten. "You should visit soon, darling. I miss you so much."

I swallow hard, trying to push down the lump in my throat. "I'll try, Nanna. I promise."

We say our goodbyes, and I hang up, the silence settling over me. Pumpkin jumps onto the couch beside me, curling up on my lap, and I run my fingers through her soft fur, closing my eyes for a moment. The silence in the apartment is louder than ever.

I'm jolted back by the smell of something burning, my stomach dropping as I remember the egg on the stove. "Oh, shit." I rush over, coughing as smoke fills the cramped apartment, fanning the air with one hand while yanking the pan off the burner with the other. Of course, the smoke alarm doesn't work—not that anything else in this apartment does.

I scrape the charred mess into the trash, too exhausted to even think about ordering takeout. Looks like sleep's on the menu tonight.

Opting for an early night instead of sinking into my misery, I pull off my sweater and start unbuttoning my blouse. When I catch a glimpse of myself in the small mirror leaning against the wall, I immediately look away, my stomach twisting. Looking at my body is something I haven't been able to do in a long time, knowing I'll only be able to focus on the stretch marks, rolls and flabby skin. Everything Liam wasn't attracted to.

Trust me when I say, attraction to you isn't an issue.

A warmth spreads up my body at the memory of his voice— rich, low, as Nicholas lifted my chin and looked me straight in the eyes. The moment flickers in my mind, making my body heat up.

I shake the thought away, and slip into my pajamas, pulling the ribbon out of my hair. I crawl into bed, pulling the duvet up to my chin, but my mind won't quiet. My gaze drifts to the corner of the room, where I catch sight of the check he wrote me.

The money would be life-changing, so absurd that I haven't even allowed myself to believe it's real. But faking an engagement with New York's most eligible bachelor? That's insane… right?

And yet, the thought creeps in, insistent, nagging at me. *What do you have to lose?*

I hesitate, my finger hovering over my phone. I scroll to his contact, my pulse quickening. Our conversations have always been brief, professional… nothing like today, where everything's shifted.

I chew on the thought for a moment longer, and before I can convince myself to back out, my fingers move, typing without thinking.

Me:

When do you need my answer by?

His reply comes almost immediately, as if he's been waiting for me to reach out.

Nicholas:

> You can take as long as you need.

> But I'd appreciate an answer by the end of the week.

Three days. Just three days to decide if I want to fake an engagement with my boss and completely change my life.

Me:

> What will you do if I decline?

This time, there's a pause. The typing bubbles appear, disappear, and reappear. When the message finally arrives, it feels like an eternity has passed.

Nicholas:

> I don't know.

That three-word answer sits heavy in my chest. Nicholas has always had a plan for everything. He's always been the type of guy who controls every detail of his life. I've never seen him flustered, never seen him without an answer. And now, with this decision hanging in the air, I can't shake the guilt curling in my stomach. This deal means everything to him. To his business.

Me:

Exactly how long would this
engagement last?

The dots appear again, his response almost immediate.

Nicholas:

Is that a yes?

My heart stutters. I set my phone down and close my eyes, his question pressing against my chest, suffocating me with a choice that could make or break my life.

Saying yes would change everything.

And I don't know if I'm ready for that.

CHAPTER EIGHT

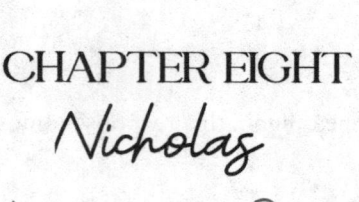

Nicholas

I don't get distracted.

Ever.

Not once in my life have I let anything pull me off course. My entire world is built on control, on knowing every move before it's made. And yet, here I am, with last night's text playing on a loop in my mind, taunting me.

Was that her way of saying yes?

Everything I've worked for—the future I've spent years planning—is dangling from the hands of my assistant and I can't do a single thing about it except wait.

Lifting my arm, I glance at my watch. *Ten a.m.* Usually, by now, my coffee is sitting on my desk, and she's briefed me on my schedule for the day with her usual crisp efficiency. But not today. Today, there's no coffee.

No update.

No Amara.

It's not like her—at all.

My stomach twists uncomfortably, the thought creeping in that I may have pushed her too far. Did I overstep? Did my offer make her uncomfortable? My jaw tightens at the possibility of her leaving the company over this.

Losing her would be a disaster. Not just because of the deal on the line, but because replacing her would be a monumental pain in the ass. She's a damn good assistant. Hell, she's the best I've ever had.

And that's the only reason—*the only reason*—why I press the intercom button and call her in.

"Amara, can I see you in my office, please?"

Releasing the button, I adjust my tie, leaning back in my chair as I wait. The silence stretches longer than usual. Then, finally, there's a soft knock at the door.

"Come in."

The door creaks open, and there she is, hovering in the doorway, looking hesitant. "You wanted to see me?"

Her voice is soft, and though she's clearly trying to mask it, the pink tint on her skin betrays her nerves.

"You didn't answer my text last night," I tell her, ushering her to come inside.

She takes a tentative step, and closes the door behind her, standing a few feet away, twisting her fingers positioned in front of her stomach.

My lips twitch despite myself, and I lift my hand to rub my mouth, attempting to cover my amusement. Two years she's worked for me. And yet after all this time, she still gets flustered around me as if it's the first time we've met.

"I was tired," she murmurs, her lips pressing into a thin line. "I fell asleep."

Bullshit.

I can read her emotions pretty clearly—unfortunately for her—and I can see the lie swimming in her eyes as clear as day. She got scared. Didn't know how to respond. And while that hesitation means there's still a chance she'll say yes… there's also a risk she'll say no.

And that would be a really big problem for me.

But I meant every word of what I told her. Her decision changes nothing about her position here.

"You still have time to think about it," I tell her, pushing myself up from my chair. Walking around my desk, I sit on the edge, crossing my arms as I watch her carefully. The uncertainty in her eyes is driving me crazy, making it impossible to focus.

Her green eyes lift to meet mine, and for a moment, I'm caught off guard. *God, that green.* I've never had a favorite color, but hers? It could convert a man. Bright, fresh, and tinged with gold. They're so vivid, so expressive, that I could lose myself in them if I'm not careful.

"And you'll really pay me that amount?" she asks.

I nod. "Every cent," I tell her, hope rising when she widens her eyes. "I'll promote you, too," I add, throwing out the offer as a way to sweeten the deal.

Her lips part, surprise flickering in her eyes. "What?" She shakes her head, clearly thrown off. "I don't—"

"If I remember correctly," I cut her off, "when you applied for this job, you mentioned wanting to become a decorator. Correct?"

She hesitates, her fingers twisting even harder before she nods. "Yes, but—"

"I can make that happen."

For a moment, she just stares at me, like she's waiting for the catch. But there isn't one. Truthfully, I've kept her close because she's exceptional at her job. But if she agrees to this, I'll ensure she gets her dream job, even if it means she's no longer by my side.

"You'll really promote me?" she repeats, as though testing the words. "I'll be a designer?"

I nod again. "Yes. As soon as the deal is finalized, I'll handle the transfer myself. You'll work as a decorator at our New York City hotel, and we'll go our separate ways."

Amara glances away, her expression shifting as her thoughts race through her head. Looking down, she fidgets with her hands again and my muscles coil, my heart pounding as I wait for her answer.

"You only date blondes."

My brows furrow. "What?"

She shakes her head, her eyes flicking to mine. "The girls you date… they're all blondes. Thin. Tall. Models. Everyone knows you have a type, Nicholas. And it's clearly not me."

She looks down at herself, and the muscles in my neck tighten at the sight of her self-doubt.

I take a step closer, my eyes locking onto hers with an intensity that has her holding her breath. "Amara," I say, my teeth grinding. "You pick them."

She blinks, confusion flickering in her eyes. "What?"

"You pick my dates," I clarify. "Every single one. The choice has always been yours."

She opens her mouth, but no words come out. I take another step closer, my presence towering over hers. "And you're wrong," I add, each syllable cutting through the air. "They're not my type."

She swallows, the sound loud between us. "No?"

I shake my head, a slight smirk tugging at my lips, my hands clenched at my sides before I do something I'll regret. "Not even close."

Her lips part, just slightly, and my eyes instantly drop to them. *Shit*. I take a step back, the air between us thick and hot and so fucking dangerous. Her eyes flicker, and for a brief moment, I wonder if I've pushed her too far. But then, she surprises me.

"Yes."

I hold my breath, the silence between us stretching. "Yes?" I repeat, needing to hear it again.

She nods, her chin tilted just enough to meet my gaze. "Yes. I'll do it. I'll be your..."

"Fiancée," I finish for her, my lips curving into a smirk.

The pink in her skin darkens, but she nods again. "Right. Fiancée."

"You're sure?" I ask, leaning in just slightly, unable to resist. "Completely sure?"

"It's a lot of money," she admits, lifting her chin with an almost defiant edge, meeting my stare.

A smirk pulls at my lips. At least she's not pretending to have some noble reason. She owns her decision. I like that.

"And you're prepared for everything that comes with it?" I press, watching her brow furrow. "People will be all over you. They'll scrutinize your every move. Dig into your past. Make assumptions." My gaze drifts down to the fluffy cardigan wrapped around her shoulders, her white blouse, the buttons straining slightly across her chest, and the pleated skirt she loves to wear, hugging her figure a little more than usual. "Some of them will say you slept your way to the top."

Her eyes widen—*so damn green*—and I watch as my words hit her. "I hadn't really thought of that," she admits, shaking her head, the reality of it sinking in.

"You should. You'll get the money, the job, the promotion, but there will be consequences. I'll protect you, Amara," I assure her. "I'll bury the rumors, pay to keep your life out of the press... but even my name has limits."

She hesitates, her hands twisting together. "How long will this last?" she asks.

I rub my chin, thinking it through. "If everything goes as planned? About three months."

Three months. Less than that, really.

It might seem like a long time, but I know it'll pass in the blink of an eye. And when it's over, we'll both have exactly what we want.

She nods slowly, her lips pressing into a thin line. "Okay. I'll do it."

The tension in my body eases, but I keep my expression neutral.

"Great," I say, rounding my desk. "I'll have my lawyer draw up the contract."

She turns to leave, her heels clicking against the hardwood floor, her fiery ginger hair catching the light as it spills over her dark blue sweater.

"Amara," I call, stopping her in the doorway.

She glances back over her shoulder, waiting, her eyes locked onto mine.

I can't let her leave without saying something, because if it wasn't for her, I'd be screwed. My entire future, everything I've worked for, would be up in smoke. "Thank you."

She doesn't speak, just gives a small nod before slipping out the door.

And just like that, she's gone. The faint trace of her perfume fills the space, leaving an odd emptiness behind.

The deal is as good as sealed, my future within reach.

Now is not the time to lose my head over any woman.

Especially not my assistant.

CHAPTER NINE

Amara

What the hell did I do?

This was a mistake. A massive, irreversible, life-altering mistake.

I sink into my chair, staring blankly at my computer screen, trying to convince myself I haven't just torpedoed my entire life. But then my inbox pings, and there it is.

Contract Details – Blackwood Proposal.

My stomach flips, nerves twisting tighter as I hover over the email.

Do not open it.

Just delete it and pretend this never happened.

But, of course, I can't. With a resigned sigh, I click.

The email opens, with the contract attached. Swallowing down my nerves, I double-click, and the document fills the screen. My eyes dart over the text, the legal jargon practically leaping off the page. I try to focus, but all my brain seems to catch are fragments.

Business arrangement... three-month timeline... promotion... no outside romantic entanglements...

And then I see it.

The promotion. The salary bump. Everything he promised me and more.

Interior Design Lead for the new Blackwood properties.

It's all there, staring back at me in crisp, black-and-white, a dream I've spent years chasing.

This should feel like a victory. I should be excited, proud, like I've finally made it. But instead, there's this dull ache in my chest, this sinking feeling that whispers I'm trading a part of myself for something I should've earned on my own.

Am I really ready for this?

My fingers hover over the keyboard. I could back out. Walk into his office, tell him this isn't for me, that I'll find another way. I could go back to being the invisible girl who blends into the background.

But then I think of my tiny apartment. The cracked tiles in the kitchen I can't afford to replace. The rent that swallows my paycheck whole every month.

I don't have a choice.

Before I can second-guess myself, I hit print, grab the contract, and make my way to his office. My heels click against the hardwood floors, my pulse pounding louder with every step.

When I reach his door, I stop, my hand hovering over the handle.

This is it. The moment everything changes. Once I walk in there, there's no going back.

I knock twice, my knuckles brushing against the cool wood.

"Come in."

His voice is calm, controlled, like always.

I push the door open, and find him adjusting his cufflinks, his jacket draped over the back of his chair, and his tie slightly loosened.

Even off-guard, he's intimidatingly perfect.

"Amara." His dark eyes meet mine. "I take it you've read the contract?"

"I did," I say, stepping inside and letting the door click shut behind me.

"And?" His brow arches, waiting for me to continue.

I set the contract on the edge of his desk. "It's... a lot."

His lips twitch into a faint smirk, the kind that makes my stomach flip despite my better judgment. "It's a legal document. It's supposed to be."

"Right." My fingers fidget with the hem of my sweater, but I force myself to breathe.

"Was there a problem?" he asks, his voice smooth but firm. "You're free to change anything you don't agree with."

I swallow hard, my fingers twitching at my sides, unsure what to do with them. "There's a clause about no outside... romantic relationships."

His smirk vanishes, replaced by a look I can't quite read. He straightens, crossing his arms over his chest as his dark eyes bore into mine. "That's correct. I thought it would be best to maintain appearances."

I nod, my throat suddenly dry. "Right. Appearances."

He tilts his head, like he's dissecting my every word. "I don't think it would send the right message if you—or I—were seen with someone else during this arrangement."

"Of course. That... makes sense."

But my brain isn't cooperating, because now it's stuck on Nicholas Blackwood—powerful, controlled, untouchable— being abstinent for three whole months. And an even more dangerous thought follows. There's nothing in the contract about us being... involved.

My stomach twists as I gulp, trying to focus. I'm sure it's an oversight, something I could mention to him right now, and he'd correct it with a few strokes of a pen.

But I don't.

"And this... deal will end on August 31st?" I ask, squeezing my hands into fists as his gaze lingers on me.

"That's correct," he confirms with a nod, his fingers brushing his chin. "That'll be more than enough time to secure the deal with the board."

I nod, swallowing the lump in my throat. For him, this is all so clear-cut. So simple. For me... it feels like stepping into an active volcano.

He straightens, adjusts his tie, and steps closer. "It's normal to feel hesitant," he continues, his voice softening just enough to make my stomach flip. "We don't know each other that well."

A surprised laugh escapes me. "I know everything about you," I counter. "I've been your assistant for over two years. I know your coffee order, your schedule, the way you organize your desk, your preferred brand of pen..." I trail off, because if I keep going, I'll expose just how much I've noticed about him. How much I've paid attention.

A low sound rumbles from his chest, something between a scoff and a snarl, and the hairs on the back of my neck rise. "You might know those things about me," he says, stepping even closer, his dark gaze practically pinning me in place. "But I can promise you, Amara... you don't really know me."

My breath catches, his words pressing against my ribs. I don't know if he's daring me to dig deeper or warning me not to.

His eyes flick down to my lips—so quick I might've imagined it—before snapping back to mine, as intense as ever. "There's a charity gala on Saturday," his voice cuts through the silence. "The board will be there. It's crucial I make a strong impression. It'll be the perfect opportunity to show them I'm serious about this deal."

I nod as I clear my throat, looking up at his tall figure. "And you want me to find you a date?" I ask automatically, already used to his routine.

His eyes flash with something I can't quite read as his lips curve into a slow smile. "No. *You're* my date."

I blink, thrown completely off guard. "Excuse me?"

"We'll be announcing our engagement at this gala," he clarifies, his words sending a shiver down my spine. "You'll be my date to every event from now on."

I open my mouth to respond, but no words come out. His gaze lingers on mine for a moment longer before he steps back, the faintest smirk still playing on his lips.

Reaching into his coat pocket, he pulls out a sleek black card, holding it between his pointer and middle finger. "Buy yourself a dress. On me. Money's no issue."

It's every girl's dream to hear those words from someone who could make it happen without batting an eye. And yet, while my fingers itch to snatch the card, my pride screams louder. I'm already taking more from him than I ever thought I would.

"Mr. Blackwood, I—"

"Nicholas," he cuts me off.

I blink. "Excuse me?"

"You're my *fiancée*, Amara." His voice dips lower, the word curling around me like smoke. "I think you can start calling me by my first name."

He says it with such ease, like it's already a fact. It sends a shiver down my spine, one I have no business feeling.

I could correct him, remind him that this isn't real, but the way he says *fiancée* has my mouth going dry, and suddenly, I'm not so sure I want to.

"Nicholas," I say carefully, the name foreign on my tongue. His eyes darken, just for a second, and I swear I catch the flicker of a smile before it's gone. I lick my lips, suddenly too aware of the intensity of his gaze, and continue, "While the offer is very generous, I don't think I can—"

"I'm a billionaire, Amara." His brow arches, and the corner of his mouth twitches, daring me to argue. "One dress won't make a dent in my accounts." He steps closer, holding the card out to me again. "Take it. Buy a dress, buy ten if you have to. Shoes, bag, whatever you need. It's on me."

I reach for it, my fingers brushing his as I take the card and slide it into my pocket.

"Any more… hesitations?"

I shake my head, and his lips tip upward in approval.

Turning back to his desk, he grabs the contract and a pen—a Montblanc, of course—and slides them across the desk toward me as I stare down at the contract.

This is it. Once my name is there, there's no undoing it.

Flicking my hair over my shoulder, I step forward and take the pen, removing the cap.

You're doing this for the promotion. For the money. For your future, I tell myself.

The scratch of the pen as I sign sounds louder than it should, and when I finish, I cap the pen and set it down carefully, stepping back as if distance will make this less real.

Nicholas watches me, his sharp gaze pinning me in place. He nods, tipping his chin. "That'll be all."

Dismissed. Just like that. As if I didn't just sign my life away to him for the next three months.

I turn and walk out of his office, closing the door behind me. I lift my head and catch a few pairs of eyes flicking toward me. I know the moment the news of our engagement gets out, the whispers will start. People will tally up how many times I've been in Nicholas's office, the long hours spent with the door closed, and I'll be the center of every office rumor.

I square my shoulders, forcing myself to walk toward my desk without looking back. I made this choice for me—for my career, for my future. And I won't let the whispers, or the sideways glances make me second guess it.

When I finally sit at my desk, I take a slow breath, trying to push the tension out of my body.

Bianca pops her head over the divider between our desks, her brow furrowing. "Everything okay?" Her voice is soft but probing. She knows me too well. "You were in there for a while."

I hesitate for just a second, searching for the right words. "Yeah, just some things to sign." It's not a lie. Not exactly.

Bianca doesn't press, but I catch the flicker of curiosity in her eyes as she gives me a thoughtful look but doesn't say anything else.

I turn my attention back to my screen, my fingers hovering over the keyboard. I try to focus on the emails in front of me, but the knot in my stomach refuses to loosen.

STEPHANIE ALVES

This is it. The decision is made. I'm committed to this deal.

But even with that certainty, I can't shake the feeling that everything's about to change.

CHAPTER TEN

Amara

"**H**oly shit." Jade's eyebrows shoot up.

I watch her closely, pressing my lips together as she processes the news.

A second later, her eyes widen even more. "Holy shit," she repeats, making me breathe out a laugh.

"You've been saying that all day. I thought you'd have moved past the shock by now."

Jade shakes her head, her hands thrown up. "You honestly can't expect me to move on so quickly from this. This is huge!"

I knew this would be a shock—hell, it shocked the hell out of me, too—but I didn't expect her to lose it like this. I guess I didn't expect to break her either.

She shakes her head, flopping down onto my bed. "You can't expect me to not react." She rubs her forehead as if trying to clear her thoughts. "The other day you were telling me about your breakup with Liam, and now you're... engaged to our boss?"

"It's not real," I remind her, with a shrug. "Just a little white lie until we both get what we want."

There's no clause in the contract that says I can't tell someone, but I know if news got out about this, it would be detrimental, for both Nicholas and me. I've been avoiding my grandma and sister, knowing they'll have a million questions when they catch wind of all this, starting with why the hell I didn't tell them about Nicholas, and what happened with Liam. But I needed to tell someone, and telling Jade feels like the safest choice.

Plus, she caught me in a store earlier today using Nicholas's black credit card, so I had no choice but to tell her.

I'm not an actress, I never claimed to be one, so when she asked, I froze, panicked, and blurted it all out.

A scoff escapes her. "It's more than a little white lie. Are you sure there's nothing going on between you two?" Jade asks, her voice laced with suspicion, as she waves her hand in the air. "I mean, are you making up this whole… business deal to cover it up? Because if there is, I wouldn't judge you, you know that."

"I know you wouldn't," I say with a smile. "And that's one of the reasons I love you. But no, it's not real." I shake my head. "I just happened to walk in when he was meeting with the board. He would have picked anyone for the job. I'm just a pawn in his game, helping him win. Nothing more."

And that's the truth.

I might imagine lingering glances, even the occasional warm touch, but when it comes down to it, this is just a coincidence. If Jade had been the one in the room that day, she would have gotten the job. They'd be engaged right now, and they'd be a much better match.

I push the thought aside as Jade scoffs, clearly not buying it.

"I'd say you're playing your pieces too." She grins, holding up the black card Nicholas gave me. Before I can stop her, she's waving it in front of me, and I quickly snatch it back, narrowing my eyes at her.

I know Nicholas made it clear that my purchases won't make a dent in his wealth, but I'm sure Jade would be more than happy to burn a hole in his pockets.

"He told me to buy a dress," I explain, slipping the card back into my clutch. "I didn't want to embarrass him by showing up to the gala wearing one of my old, raggedy dresses. That's the only reason I took him up on the offer."

Jade laughs, shaking her head as she eyes me. "Embarrassment is the last thing he'll feel." Her gaze scans me from head to toe. "You already know you're stunning, but tonight…" She whistles, her eyes gleaming.

I tilt my head, amused. "Did you just whistle at me?"

"Hell yes." She grins. "You look hot."

"You're just being nice," I say, dismissing her compliment with a wave.

She shakes her head, a knowing smile tugging at her lips. "Trust me," she insists. "When Nicholas sees you in that dress, I don't think he's going to remember that you're his assistant, or that this is just a business deal. Because honey…" She raises an eyebrow. "He might be your boss, but he's also just a man."

Warmth floods my face at her words, and I shoot her a playful glare. "You're delusional."

She hums, leaning back on my bed and crossing her legs. "I'm right," she corrects.

I glance at the mirror, my eyes roaming over my reflection as I nervously tug at the fabric. The dress clings to places I'd rather not draw attention to. Finding something in such a short amount of time is difficult enough, but for a bigger body like mine? It feels impossible. The embarrassment of walking into store after store, feeling like I didn't belong, hits me all over again. And sure, maybe I didn't belong there, but this dress…

I smooth my hands over the soft silk material of the floor-length black dress Jade picked out. The huge slit running up the side shows off my thick thighs—one of my biggest insecurities.

I swallow the lump in my throat at the sight of the dress clinging to my body, wanting to tear my eyes away, and luckily, my phone rings and I grab it, seeing Nicholas's name flashing on the screen.

"It's him."

"Answer it," Jade urges, her voice teasing. "You can't keep your *fiancé* on hold."

I roll my eyes, shuddering at the word, especially when Nicholas says it with such intensity it makes me forget my own name. I definitely don't need Jade reminding me of it.

Taking a deep breath, I accept the call and bring the phone to my ear. "Mr. Blackwood?"

"Amara," Nicholas's voice comes through, deep and thick. "What did I tell you about calling me that?"

"Sorry, Nicholas." Saying his name shouldn't make me blush, but the heat still creeps up my skin anyway.

"Much better," he says, his low voice making my pulse race. "My driver informed me he's outside your apartment. Are you almost done?"

I glance at the clock, eyes widening as I realize how little time I have left. I look over at Jade, who's completely distracted, bopping Pumpkin on the nose.

"Yes, I'll be right down."

"I'll be waiting."

I hang up the phone and grab my clutch, stuffing my phone and lip gloss inside. "Nicholas's driver is downstairs," I tell Jade, panic rising in my chest.

"Calm down. Everything's going to go great." She flashes me a reassuring smile. "You look amazing."

For once, my appearance is the least of my concerns. I shake my head, the anxiety clawing at me. "What if I embarrass him, or slip up about the engagement or—"

"Okay." Jade stands, walking over to me and placing her hands on my shoulders in an attempt to calm me. "Breathe, woman. You're giving *me* a panic attack."

I inhale deeply, my shoulders relaxing as I blow out slowly.

"Everything will be fine," Jade assures me. "You're going to do great, and the board will love you so much, they'll offer Nicholas the deal on the spot." Her grin makes me breathe out a laugh, the knot in my stomach starting to unravel.

"Awfully confident in my skills, aren't you?"

"I'm confident in *my* skills," she corrects, flopping back down onto the bed with a shrug. "And you look hot as hell because of me," she adds, pointing at herself. I arch a brow, and she lets out an exaggerated sigh. "Okay, fine. You might have a little something to do with your hotness." She narrows her eyes. "But I take full credit for the dress."

I shake my head, laughing. "Credit's all yours."

Leaning down, I kiss my cat on the head, then take one last look at myself in the mirror, adjusting my dress. The smooth fabric slides over my body, and I flip one side of my hair over my shoulder before waving Jade goodbye. She blows me a kiss in return.

As much as I love that Sophie has a loving boyfriend, I'm thankful for Jade on nights like these, to help me build the confidence I need when I'm doubting myself.

I press the elevator button, the metal doors creaking closed. My stomach twists with familiar anxiety as it lurches downward. I hold my breath, praying I don't end up stuck in this rickety thing.

After what feels like an eternity, the doors finally open, and I breathe a sigh of relief. Stepping out, I'm greeted by the sight of a sleek black Mustang parked outside. The tinted windows, which stick out like a sore thumb in this part of town, make it clear that this must be Nicholas's driver.

The window rolls down, revealing an older man with salt-and-pepper hair, wearing a sharp black suit.

"Amara?" the driver asks.

I nod, already feeling like I've stepped into some bizarre dream. Or maybe it's a reality show. This doesn't feel real, and I'm just waiting for it to be ripped out from under me.

The driver opens the door, and I slide inside, a little unnerved by how classy everything is. This isn't my world, and every second spent in it only makes that more obvious.

A few moments later, the driver slides into the front seat, and the car starts moving. I watch the city pass by, the lights reflecting in the windows as we drive to the gala.

Eventually, the car slows to a stop, and I glance out the window, seeing the gala entrance ahead. I suck in a breath, reaching for the door handle, only for it to be opened before I have the chance. I look up to see Nicholas standing there, dressed in a sleek tuxedo, his hand extended toward me.

"Thank you," I murmur, my voice a little shaky as I place my hand in his. He gives me a gentle tug, helping me out of the car. The moment my feet hit the ground, my nerves kick into high gear.

Especially when Nicholas's gaze slides over me, his eyes scanning me slowly from head to toe. The silence stretches between us, and I notice the subtle clench of his jaw as his eyes linger on me for what feels like an eternity, until they finally meet mine again.

He doesn't speak at first, just holds my gaze. "Glad you could make it," he finally says.

I nod, my heart pounding in my chest, wondering what the hell he's thinking. Does he like the dress? Does he not?

The silence stretches again before he adds, "I got you something."

My eyebrows raise, surprised, but before I can ask what it is, he reaches into his jacket pocket and pulls out a rectangle box. My breath catches as he opens it, revealing a beautiful silver necklace that sparkles, the diamonds catching the light.

"Wow," I breathe out, completely stunned. "It's beautiful."

"Only fitting," he says smoothly, "that my fiancée would wear the best."

I absentmindedly reach up, tracing my bare décolletage, suddenly remembering I forgot to buy jewelry—which a billionaire's fiancée definitely wouldn't forget. A rush of warmth spreads across my face as I glance down at the luxurious piece nestled in the velvet box, realizing he expects me to wear it.

The thought of putting that necklace on makes my palms sweat, and I shake my head quickly. "It's stunning, really, but I can't wear that," I tell him. "It's way too expensive."

Nicholas raises a brow. "You're my fiancée, Amara," he murmurs, pulling the necklace out of the box. "It's my job to spoil you."

I press my lips together, unsure how to argue with that. Before I can try, he steps closer, his sharp cologne filling the space between us.

"Turn around."

I hesitate for half a second before doing what he asks, turning to face the night sky. The cool breeze brushes against my skin, but it's nothing compared to the shiver I feel when Nicholas's hands graze my neck. His touch is light but firm, and I'm hyper-aware of every little movement as he gathers my hair and gently drapes it over one shoulder.

My heart pounds as he places the necklace against my skin. The cold metal makes me shiver, or maybe it's the way his fingertips skim my neck as he fastens the clasp. I hold my breath, staring out at the city lights, trying to ignore how intimate this all feels.

"Look at me."

I let out a slow exhale and turn around to face him. His eyes immediately find mine, lingering for a moment before they drop to the necklace resting against my collarbone.

"Beautiful." A small smile tugs at his lips.

For a minute I let myself think he's talking about me, but I know he means the necklace. I lift my hand, tracing the small diamonds decorating my neck.

He keeps his eyes on me for a while before his hand reaches out. "Shall we?"

I glance at his hand, before sliding mine into his as we walk toward the entrance.

This might not be my world—might not even be real—but for the next three months, I think I could get used to this.

CHAPTER ELEVEN
Nicholas

I thought this would be easy.

It might have been a rash decision, in a moment of panic, but I've done nothing but think of what this arrangement would be like for us. I managed to convince myself that this would be like any other business deal.

But it turns out, I was wrong.

So fucking wrong.

Asking Amara to be my fiancée is a problem I didn't see coming.

I steal a glance at her as she walks beside me, her long black silk dress catching the low light, the smooth fabric clinging to every inch of her body. My jaw tightens involuntarily.

Fuck, she looks beautiful tonight.

For two years, I've seen Amara in sweaters and skirts that hid her figure. And although I tried not to, I always thought she was beautiful, in a quiet, understated, girl-next-door kind of way.

But this?

I've never seen her like this.

She looks like she's stepped straight out of one of my wet dreams, the silk of her dress catching every movement, her soft waves cascading over one shoulder, framing her face. And that dress… *God, that dress*. It's enough to drive any man to distraction.

I force my gaze forward, clamping down on the unwelcome thoughts spiraling in my mind. I have work to do tonight, people I need to impress. I can't afford to let her distract me.

Focus.

The clinking of glasses, the low hum of polished conversations, the faint notes of a string quartet playing in the corner are all familiar. Comfortable, even.

I've done this before. I've walked into rooms like this, with a date on my arm to maintain appearances. It's never affected me. It's always been a necessary part of the game.

So why the hell is having Amara's soft hand in mine muddling my head?

When her hand tightens in mine, I glance down, catching the flicker of unease in her eyes as she scans the room.

"Are you okay?"

She nods, her throat moving with a gulp as she meets my gaze. "Just feeling a little... out of place," she admits, her eyes darting around the room again.

I stop, gently cupping her face with my hand and lifting her chin to make sure she focuses on me. "Amara, we're here to announce our engagement. People will be asking questions, talking about the wedding, taking pictures..."

Her eyes widen, the realization settling in, and I can't help but stroke her cheek, her lashes fluttering at the touch.

"Are you sure you can handle it?"

She's quiet for a few seconds, my breath hitching as I wonder if she wants to back out, but she nods. "I'm sure. I can handle it."

I glance down at her, arching a brow. "I think now's as good a time as any to announce our engagement."

Her eyes widen, the tension returning immediately. "Wait. You want to do that now?"

I give her a reassuring look. "We can't avoid it forever. The sooner we do it, the sooner it's done."

She takes a deep breath, the uncertainty still lingering in her eyes. I can't blame her. It's strange for both of us, but we're in this together.

I scan the room briefly, catching the event coordinator's attention with a quick nod. The music dips, and the room quiets, everyone's attention shifting toward us.

"Ladies and gentlemen," I begin. "If I could have your attention for a moment."

The room settles, conversations fading as eyes turn in our direction. Amara shifts beside me, her hand tightening around mine. I glance down at her, offering a reassuring smile. She gives me a small, nervous one in return, her eyes flicking around the room before focusing on me.

"I'd like to take this opportunity to share something important," I continue. "I'm proud to announce that Amara and I are engaged."

I can hear Amara's breath catch beside me, so I squeeze her hand gently, trying to calm her.

"We're excited to begin this next chapter," I add, making sure my gaze stays on her, offering her the assurance she needs. "And we wanted to share the news with all of you."

The room goes quiet for a moment, the silence almost heavy. I can feel people waiting for more, and a hint of doubt crosses my mind, wondering if people can see through us, and know this is nothing but a ruse.

Then someone calls out from the back. "Congratulations!"

A ripple of applause follows, and the room shifts again. People start chatting, drinks are raised, and the music returns softly to the background. The tension in the air—and my shoulders—begins to lift.

The room starts to pick up again, people talking and laughing, and I lean in closer to her. "You okay?"

She looks up at me, offering a small smile. "I think so," she replies. "That wasn't as bad as I thought it would be."

I nod, relieved. "I guess it's official now."

"Yeah." Her lips twitch into a slight smile. "I'm engaged."

"Partly," I add with a playful grin, reminding her—and myself—that it's all just for show.

She lets out a quiet laugh, shaking her head. "Right."

"Blackwood."

I look up, spotting Robert Crestwell raising his hand in greeting. He finishes his conversation and makes his way toward us with his wife.

"Robert Crestwell is on the board," I whisper, lowering my voice as I pull my hand from her face and place it lightly at the small of her back. "You might remember him. He's the one with the incessant pen tapping."

Amara lets out a soft chuckle, the tension leaving her shoulders as a small smile tugs at her lips. She looks up at me, her eyes softening. "Yeah. I remember."

I squeeze her waist lightly. "Good. He was a little skeptical when I announced the news, which means we need to convince him we're in love and engaged. So, if he asks any questions, just let me handle it."

She nods as we head toward him.

"Crestwell," I greet, offering my hand. "Good to see you."

He gives me a firm shake, his eyes drifting to Amara, and a smile spreads across his face. "I see you've finally brought out your fiancée tonight. Glad to see you finally announced the engagement."

His wife, Eleanor, steps forward, her eyes flicking between us. "That was quite a show, Nicholas," she adds, her smile widening when her eyes land on Amara. "And you, my dear, are quite a sight."

Amara offers a polite smile and nods. "Thank you. It's a pleasure to meet you both."

Robert laughs lightly. "It's about time. Blackwood's been keeping this one under wraps, hasn't he?"

I lift my shoulder in a shrug. "Some things are better left private."

Eleanor lets out a chuckle, her gaze sliding to Amara. "So, are the wedding plans already underway, or are you keeping those a secret too?"

Amara glances up at me, and I catch the flicker of panic in her eyes.

"We're still enjoying the engagement period before we officially start wedding planning," I reply, giving her a reassuring look, noticing her shoulders relaxing a little.

Eleanor hums thoughtfully, her gaze narrowing. "Well, don't wait too long," she tells us. "Venues book up quickly. You'll want to get on that soon."

"We'll keep that in mind," I reply, giving her a smile.

Robert lets out a chuckle, tapping me on my back, leaning in slightly. "Between you and me... the board is fully prepared to offer you the deal." My body relaxes at his words. "This is exactly the image we want to present to the world, Nicholas. It's nice to see you so... in love."

My spine tenses, my body freezing at his words as I pull back and offer him a smile, knowing this is all fake. Every bit of it. I force myself to swallow, nodding as he pats me on the back and heads toward the drink table.

This is what I wanted. The ruse is working, and the deal is as good as mine. I just need to keep this up.

Twisting my head, I turn, looking for Amara, finding her in the corner, talking to a group of women. Her smile is tense, and I reach up, tracing the amused smirk on my lips as I watch her.

How she can look like *that* tonight and still act like the shy girl who gets flustered talking to me, I'll never know.

"Tell me this is a joke." I turn around and see Ethan, nursing a glass of bourbon, his eyes wide. "*Engaged*, Nicholas? What the fuck?"

Shit. I forgot about this loudmouth, curious bastard. I let out a sigh, feeling a headache already creeping in. "It's... complicated."

"It always is with you," Ethan quips. "So why don't you uncomplicate it for me? Because I've been standing here trying to figure out how Nicholas-fucking-Blackwood, a man who works 20-hour days, and has no interest in a relationship whatsoever, somehow managed to *propose*. To his assistant no less."

Jesus, I'm never going to live this down. I let out a sigh, meeting his eyes.

"It's fake," I grit out.

He pauses, reeling back in shock. "What?" He shakes his head. "What do you mean it's fake?"

"It's not real," I clarify, narrowing my eyes when he tilts his head, confused. "I needed her help convincing the board I was in a serious relationship. And she just so happened to walk in the door."

His jaw drops. "You're fucking with me. Tell me you're fucking with me."

I don't reply immediately, my jaw tightening, and Ethan takes my silence as an opportunity to continue.

"Wait a second." He pauses, leaning in. "Is this why you bailed on the club last week?

The question hits a nerve, and I stand straighter. I had every intention of attending his club, needing to relieve some stress, needing to let go of everything and just feel. But I couldn't.

"She has nothing to do with it," I tell him. "I just didn't feel like going."

He snorts. "Bullshit. You were more than willing to accept an invitation, so why didn't you go? Couples are welcome at the club, you know. First session's on me."

"Not going to happen."

"Why? Is she not into it or something?"

The image hits me before I can stop it. Amara in the club, her hand in mine, her cheeks flushed as I lead her inside. The thought sends a rush of heat through my body, and I have to clench my fists to steady myself. My assistant has no idea who I am and what I like to do when she packs her bag and leaves the office. Or *liked* to do, I should say.

"She doesn't know about it," I admit, wanting him to shut the fuck up already. Thinking about Amara that way is not fucking good. The world might think she's my fiancée, but she's still my assistant. My very off-limits assistant.

Ethan hums, a smirk curling on his lips. "Interesting. And what do you think she'd say if she did?"

I grind my teeth, attempting to force the image of her out of my mind. Amara isn't the type of woman who belongs in a place like that. She's… soft. Sweet. Innocent in a way that makes me feel like the biggest bastard on the planet for even thinking about her this way.

"Drop it, Ethan," I warn him.

"Relax." He nudges my shoulder. The bastard's enjoying this way too much. "I've gotta admit though, it's kind of fun seeing you like this. All wound up over a woman. Never thought I'd see the day."

"Were you not listening when I told you it's not real?" I snap, my patience wearing thin. "Nothing's going on between us."

He chuckles, low and dark and fucking annoying. "So, you're telling me you're not interested?"

Christ, I feel a headache coming on. "That's exactly what I'm saying," I lie through my fucking teeth.

His eyes flick to Amara, and he whistles, a slow, cocky grin spreading across his face. "You're out of your mind," he mutters, eyes raking over her. "She's cute as fuck in her usual black skirt, but tonight…" He groans, his voice deepening, making my blood boil.

"Ethan," I warn.

"What?" His grin widens. "Nothing's going on between you two, right?"

I don't reply, and he takes that as a challenge.

Without missing a beat, he crosses the space toward her, and I watch, teeth clenched, as he speaks to her. She smiles up at him and he takes her hand in his, kissing her knuckles.

I clench my fists, my knuckles cracking, and my teeth grind together. Why the hell does the thought of him touching her—of him flirting with her—infuriate me so much?

He looks back at me, still grinning, and winks.

I lose it.

I storm across the room, my hand grabbing the front of his jacket and yank him away from her. Before he can even react, I land a punch right into his arm.

"What the hell man?"

"Stare at my fiancée like that again, and I'll deck you. Friendship be damned."

Ethan laughs, rubbing his arm. "I thought you said you weren't interested?"

I grit my teeth, my patience snapping. "Shut the fuck up."

Before I can stop myself, I cross the room, my gaze locked on her fiery orange hair, gleaming under the lights. My heart thuds in my chest when she turns around, her eyes meeting mine.

"Ladies," I say, cutting through their conversation as I approach Amara and gently take her arm. "If you'll excuse us." I pull her away, the tension in her body easing as I lead her further from the group. "Fun conversations?" I ask with a smirk, raising an eyebrow.

She lets out a soft laugh, her shoulders relaxing. "They all had a million questions about the wedding, and I had no idea what to say," she admits, shaking her head slightly. "Did you know flowers need to be booked twelve weeks before the wedding?" she asks, her voice incredulous. "That's three months away."

I chuckle, amused. "I didn't know that, actually," I reply. "Good thing we won't be getting married."

"Yeah," she chuckles, letting out a relieved sigh. "I see why brides go crazy now. There's so much planning."

I don't know squat about wedding planning. I've never been close to it and don't plan on being any time soon—which is exactly why I needed her in the first place. But I nod, playing along, tugging her arm lightly to make her look up at me.

"If you want to leave, just let me know. We don't have to stay here all night."

She tenses, shaking her head quickly. "No, I'm fine. Besides, you need to impress the board."

"Trust me," I say, leaning a little closer, inhaling the warm vanilla scent that clings to her. "They're impressed."

Her green eyes meet mine, wide and uncertain. For a split second, I think she might say something more, but instead, her gaze flickers to my mouth. My throat tightens. Her plump pink lips part just enough to draw my attention, and in that moment, I forget how to breathe.

Christ. She looks beautiful.

The sharp clinking of champagne glasses breaks the moment, dragging my attention back to the crowd. I glance up and freeze. A group—hell, nearly everyone in the room—is staring at us, glasses raised, and grins plastered on their faces.

"To the happy couple!" Robert's voice rings out, his glass lifted high. "C'mon, give us a kiss, Blackwood."

The cheer rises around us, and my shoulders stiffen. I glance at Amara, who's just as frozen as I am, the faintest crease forming between her brows.

"Kiss! Kiss!" someone calls out, and the room erupts, the chant spreading like wildfire.

I swallow a groan, jaw tightening as I look at Amara again. She glances up at me, her expression flickering with nerves, and I know there's no way out of this.

I've had no issue kissing any of my previous dates in the past, and if I decline this kiss with her right now, it'll look suspicious as hell, and every eye in here is on us.

I lean down, my hand sliding to her waist. "Relax," I murmur against her ear, low enough that no one else can hear.

I lift her chin with my thumb and her breath hitches. Her eyes flutter as they meet mine before they close, and I take that as permission, erasing the distance between us to brush my lips against hers.

I think there's applause and some cheering, but I couldn't care less, because all I can focus on is the way she tastes. Sweet and warm, and faintly of champagne and despite my better judgement, I tip her head back, deepening the kiss.

She gasps into my mouth, her fingers clutching at my shirt like she's holding on for dear life. And *fuck*, I don't remember the last time a simple kiss felt like this. Like the ground beneath me was no longer solid, like the world had narrowed down to nothing but her.

My grip on her waist tightens instinctively, my fingers digging into the soft fabric of her dress. I don't want to pull away. Hell, I don't think I could even if I tried. All I want is to keep kissing her—forever, if she'd let me.

But just as quickly as it started, it's over.

Amara pulls back abruptly, her chest rising and falling with a sharp inhale, her lips glistening and just slightly swollen. For a split second, her wide eyes meet mine, and something unspoken passes between us.

The cheering from the crowd finally registers in the background, loud and relentless, but she doesn't look away. Neither do I.

I've kissed plenty of women before. It was always... fine. Routine. Practical. Forgettable. Clinical, even. But this? There was absolutely nothing clinical about what just happened.

My tongue darts out, grazing my lips as if to confirm it wasn't a hallucination. Nope. Still there. They still taste like champagne and something entirely Amara. My skin burns, like her plump, swollen lips have imprinted themselves on me.

A slap on my shoulder jolts me out of my thoughts. I whip my head around to find Ethan grinning at me. "Hell of a kiss, Nic."

I roll my eyes, shrugging him off. "Don't you have better things to do?" I mutter.

He chuckles, and I barely register him moving away because I'm already looking back at Amara. She blinks up at me, her lips parted like she's still catching her breath. For half a second, her walls are down, and I catch a glimpse of... something. Then she recovers, her signature professional smile snapping into place like armor.

"That was... a good call," she says, letting out a light laugh that doesn't quite match the way her fingers fidget at her sides. "I'm sure they bought it."

A good call?

They bought it?

I force myself to nod, but my chest tightens as I watch her spin on her heel and head toward the drink table, a little too quickly, like she's trying to outrun what just happened.

My eyes stay locked on her as she walks away, her hips swaying in a way I can't help but notice. Her hair, loose and slightly mussed from my hand, bounces with every step. My fingers curl at my side, itching to reach for her again, even as my brain screams at me to get it under control.

She's treating this like nothing more than business. A job. A role to play for the sake of the contract. And she'd be smart to keep it that way. We both would.

That's what we agreed on.

But no matter how hard I try, I can't stop replaying that kiss. The way she tasted. The soft gasp she let out. The way her lips molded to mine like she'd been made for this. For me.

The night isn't over yet, but as I glance back at her, pretending to focus on the champagne flutes at the table, one thing is painfully clear.

This deal just got a whole lot messier.

The car ride back to Amara's place is suffocatingly quiet. Amara stares out the window, her fingers fidgeting with her clutch. Since the kiss between us, she's been trying her absolute hardest to keep her distance, mingling with the women at the gala instead of standing by my side.

Whereas I, like an idiot, spent the entire night trying—and failing—not to look at her.

I couldn't tell you a single detail about the conversations I had tonight, but I could tell you exactly how many times her eyes found mine. *Zero*. I can count the times she laughed, the tilt of her head when she smiled, even the way her lips wrapped around the rim of her champagne flute. I memorized it all. God knows why.

I couldn't keep my eyes off her, and yet, she's doing everything possible not to glance my way.

Christ, this ride is taking forever.

I glance at my watch, each passing minute making the unease in my chest grow. My jaw tightens when I notice the streets outside the window, their dim lighting and cracked sidewalks unfamiliar and frankly, sketchy as hell.

When the car slows to a stop, Amara reaches for the door handle without a second thought.

"Amara," I call out, halting her. I don't know why I do. Maybe because I'm replaying that kiss in my mind, maybe because she still hasn't looked at me, maybe because the idea of her getting out of this car in this neighborhood terrifies me… or maybe because… I just don't want her to go yet.

She freezes, her hand hovering over the handle before she turns her head, her green eyes finally meeting mine.

"I'll walk you up," I offer, trying to convince myself this is purely a practical decision.

She blinks, clearly startled, before shaking her head. "That's really not necessary. I'm fine."

Fine.

Sure.

Except every bone in my body is screaming that she's not. Not here, not in this neighborhood, and not after that kiss that we still need to talk about.

"That wasn't a question." I open my door, stepping out into the cool night air. By the time I round the car and open hers, she's staring up at me like I've lost my damn mind.

"Nicholas—"

"I'm walking you up," I interrupt, extending a hand to her.

Her lips press into a thin line, but she takes it anyway, her soft palm fitting into mine as she steps onto the sidewalk.

The walk to the building is quiet, the only sounds coming from the clinking of her keys and the occasional hum of a passing car. When we reach the cracked blue door, she pulls it open with a creak that echoes down the dimly lit hallway.

"This is where you live?" The words slip out before I can stop them, my eyes scanning the peeling paint, the flickering overhead light, and the unmistakable smell of damp.

Her shoulders straighten as she presses the elevator button. "It's a little old, but it's fine," she mutters.

Fine. There's that word again.

The elevator arrives with a groan, the doors jerking open. Inside, it's as dingy as the rest of the building, but Amara steps in without hesitation. I follow, the doors closing us into a silence so thick and heavy, it's unbearable.

"We can talk about it," I say, cutting through the silence. "About what happened back at the gala."

I understand why she'd be so worked up about it. She's my assistant. A great one. A professional one who never once stepped out of line. And yet—

"That wasn't in the contract," she says suddenly, making me glance down at her.

"No, it wasn't," I admit, rubbing my chin, the short hairs rubbing against my fingers. "But you're supposed to be my fiancée, Amara. There's no world where I wouldn't kiss you looking like *that*," I tell her, my eyes scanning her from head to toe, drinking her in, memorizing her before she steps foot in her apartment, and I have to close my eyes to picture her again.

Her eyes snap to mine, wide and unblinking, her chest rising and falling with each heavy breath she takes.

"It would've been suspicious not to," I add.

"Suspicious," she echoes, her brows knitting together.

I nod. "Of course. I've kissed plenty of dates before. This is just another part of the act."

A muscle in my jaw tightens, and for a moment, I think I've pushed too far. "Do you... want to amend the contract?" I ask her, my mind and body and every other part of me rebels at the idea of never being able to kiss her. But the last thing I want to do is make her uncomfortable in any kind of way. "To add a no-kissing rule?"

Amara stares at me, her lips parting slightly as if she's about to say something, but then she stops, pressing them into a thin line.

The elevator hums quietly around us as the dull light glows over her. Her cheeks are still flushed from earlier—whether from the gala or the kiss, I don't know—but it's a sight I can't seem to look away from.

Finally, she exhales and shakes her head. "No."

Her answer sends a jolt of relief racing through me. My lips twitch into a small, involuntary smile, but I quickly disguise it by rubbing a hand over my mouth.

Get it together, Nicholas.

But all I can think about right now is when the next time I'll be able to kiss her will be.

The elevator dings, its doors sliding open to reveal another dimly lit hallway. I follow her as she walks to her door, her keys jingling as she unlocks it and nudges it open with her hip.

Her fingers clutch her purse, her knuckles whitening as she avoids my gaze. "I made it home safe. Thank you for walking me up, but you can go now."

My eyes narrow, my gaze flickering to the peeling paint on the hallway walls, the flickering light overhead, the faint sound of someone shouting in the distance.

"Mind if I come in?"

She stiffens, her gaze darting behind her to the door. "Um… my space is pretty small, so…"

I shrug. "I don't mind."

Her lips part like she's about to protest, but instead, she lets out a soft sigh, turning to push open the door, stepping inside, and I follow, my stomach tightening the moment I see where she's been coming home to at night.

My jaw clenches as my gaze sweeps over the space. The walls are a dingy off-white, the wallpaper peeling in more places than not. The furniture is mismatched and worn, looking as if she found it in the trash.

Amara drops her purse onto the arm of a sagging couch, moving toward a kitchenette that's nothing more than a counter and a mini fridge. She keeps her back to me, her shoulders stiff.

"Do you want anything to drink?" she asks, her voice clipped, as though she's trying to rush me out.

I don't answer. My eyes are still taking in the space, the cracked tiles in the kitchen, the water stain on the ceiling, the faint sound of someone's television bleeding through the walls.

How the hell can one of my employees—my assistant, whom I pay a pretty healthy wage to—live somewhere like this?

The fridge door squeaks as she opens it, and the sound yanks me out of my thoughts. "Nicholas?" She glances over her shoulder, her voice cutting through my thoughts.

STEPHANIE ALVES

The thought of her coming home to this every night makes something twist in my gut. Because this isn't just small—it's suffocating. Because she deserves better.

I should say none of that. I should walk out, get in the car, and let her go. But I can't.

Before I can stop myself, the words tumble out of my mouth. "Move in with me."

CHAPTER TWELVE

Amara

I must be dreaming, because Nicholas—my boss—did not just say what I think he just said.

"Excuse me?"

"Move in with me, he repeats, his voice firm. I blink, wondering if this is a joke, or if I'm hallucinating, my brain refusing to believe it. But Nicholas's face remains still.

I shake my head, laughing nervously. "This is crazy."

"You living here is crazy," he counters, his gaze scanning my tiny apartment, his brows furrowing. "This place isn't safe for you to stay in, Amara. Especially not after tonight."

"What does tonight have to do with anything?"

"Our engagement announcement," he says, as if it's obvious. "Tonight, we made it official that we're engaged. That you're mine." Those simple words—that shouldn't mean much—cause the air to get stuck in my lungs. "After today, you'll be as much a public figure as I am, which means everyone's eyes will be on you. Always."

My body stiffens at the thought, his words sinking in.

"If people find out you live here," he continues, his voice quieter now, as if the words themselves pain him. "That the wife of a billionaire lives here…"

"Fiancée," I correct quickly. "It won't get as far as marriage," I remind him, shaking my head. "No one will care, Nicholas."

"You're wrong." His voice deepens, his frustration evident as he takes a step closer, the only thing between us being the couch. "I care, Amara," he says, his eyes meeting mine, dark and intense. "And I can't, in good conscience, let you stay here."

"Nicholas, this is absurd." I shake my head. "I've already taken so much from you. A payout, a promotion…" My hand brushes the silky fabric of the dress he bought me. "This dress."

"It's all yours, Amara." His voice softens. "All of it. The dress, the promotion, the empty guest room in my penthouse. Take it," he urges. "It's yours for the taking."

"I can't," I murmur, shaking my head. It feels like one too many favors, one too many handouts, and I refuse to take advantage of him.

"I'm not taking no for an answer." His jaw tightens. "I'm not leaving you here."

"You don't need to do that, Nicholas. None of this was part of the contract."

A moment of silence passes between us as Nicholas makes his way past the couch, approaching me. The air feels thicker, the apartment feels smaller as he towers over me. "No," he agrees, his body so close I can smell his cologne. "But you work for me, and that makes you my responsibility. You're my assistant. *My fiancée*," he adds, and there's an emphasis on the word that makes my heart flutter unexpectedly. "And I take care of what's mine."

His words send an unexpected shiver down my spine, and I suck in a sharp breath, trying to ignore the butterflies stirring in my stomach, wondering—hoping—that his words mean more, even though I know better.

But despite my better judgement, I glance at his lips, remembering the way they felt against mine earlier. The heat of his kiss, his control as he slid his tongue against mine, taking what he wanted...

I snap myself out of it, shaking my head. "I can't just move. I already paid the lease for a year."

He shrugs. "I'll take care of that."

"My things are all here," I tell him. "My cat—"

"I love cats," he cuts me off.

I blink. "You can't be serious."

He rubs the back of his neck, his usual smirk widening. "Okay, so I've never actually had a cat, but how bad could it be?"

"Pumpkin doesn't like men," I warn, still not sure if I'm seriously entertaining this. "She hated my ex." Liam couldn't stand her, and the feeling was mutual. Pumpkin would claw at his face any chance she got. Maybe she knew he was a piece of shit before I did.

"Good thing I'm not him."

Yeah. Really good thing.

"You're my fiancée, Amara," he says again. He doesn't say the word *fake*. Not once. Maybe it's because we both know the deal, and he doesn't mean anything else by it, but hearing it does something to me I can't explain. "You're living with me, and that's the end of that."

I glance around my apartment. Small. Cramped. So dreary and depressing it feels like it might cave in on itself any moment. I think about his penthouse, the clean, pristine sheets he must have on the bed—*god, a real bed*—and let out a sigh, my shoulders sagging.

"Okay."

Nicholas smiles, just the slightest lift of his lips, and nods. "Get your things," he orders. "I'll wait."

"Now?" I ask, my eyes widening.

He nods. "I'm not letting you sleep here. The thought of you staying in this place..." His jaw tightens, like he's physically restraining himself. "Get the essentials, and I can send someone back for the rest."

I nod, taking a step toward the cracked leather armchair piled with clothes. I grab a bag and start stuffing it with whatever I can—my toothbrush, a few shirts, some toiletries.

Pumpkin's claws dig into my leg, and I glance down to see her hissing at Nicholas, backing away like he's the devil incarnate.

"This is Pumpkin?" he guesses, raising an eyebrow at my cat, who's now glaring at him.

"Yeah, sorry," I chuckle, shaking my head. "I warned you. She doesn't like men. My ex used to kick her out of the bed because she liked to sleep in the bed with me, and... well, let's just say Pumpkin holds a grudge."

"I think I'm siding with Pumpkin," he replies with a smirk that makes my legs feel like jelly. Or maybe it's the champagne.

"Got everything?" he asks, gesturing to the two bulging trash bags I'm holding.

"Yeah, I think..." I glance around one more time, my eyes landing on a pile of old shirts in the corner. The ones I haven't worn in years. The ones I've kept as a stupid reminder of my college days. I hesitate, then leave them behind. I don't need them anymore. I haven't been that size since Liam and I first got together. He used to tell me to hold onto them, to use them as 'motivation'.

I suck in a breath at the painful reminder. How did I not see the signs sooner?

When Pumpkin hisses again, my thoughts are pulled away, seeing Nicholas take a step back from her.

"I think it's best if I take the bags, and you take the cat," Nicholas offers, grabbing the heavy bags from my hands before I can even protest.

I chuckle in agreement as he heads out of the apartment.

An hour later, we pull up to what I can only assume is Nicholas's place as the car stops in front of an impressive, towering building.

The door opens and Nicholas is standing in front of me, reaching out his hand. My lips curl into a smile and I stretch out my hand, but the moment my hand touches his, Pumpkin claws at his palm.

"Christ." Nicholas lets out a chuckle, yanking his hand back. "I think I spoke too soon on the loving cats statement."

I chuckle softly as I step out of the car. "Regret asking me to move in yet?" I tease, watching him out of the corner of my eye.

His gaze doesn't waver from mine, and a smirk creeps across his lips. "Not even a little."

Before I can reply, Nicholas grabs the bags from the trunk and heads toward the entrance.

I glance around, my eyes widening at the sight. Even the neighborhood is a world apart from mine. The streets are clean, the buildings tall and modern, glowing in the city lights like something out of a movie.

When we step inside, it's like stepping into another dimension. The space is huge, and everything is so sleek and elegant it almost makes me dizzy. The marble floors shine beneath us, and the air smells fresh, free of the musty odor my apartment had.

I can't help but stare in awe, glancing toward the huge spiral staircase in the center of the entrance, four elevators lined up beside it.

I don't even realize I'm stood in the middle of the building, just staring, until I see Nicholas approaching from the concierge. "Ready to go up?" he asks.

I nod as I follow him to the elevator. He taps his keycard, and the elevator hums to life, the doors sliding shut.

The ride up is short, and before I know it, the elevator doors open. Nicholas gestures for me to step out, and I do, my breath hitching when I catch sight of his penthouse.

"This is where you live?" I ask him, unable to keep the wonder out of my voice.

I turn to face him, and my breath catches as he shrugs off his suit jacket, revealing a crisp white shirt that hugs his body in a way that makes my heart skip a beat.

Why is he so ridiculously attractive? And why can't I look away?

I glance down at Pumpkin, who's still curled up in my arms. Her wide eyes are locked on Nicholas, and without thinking, I cover her eyes with my hand.

"You're too young for that," I whisper when she paws at my hands, meowing in protest.

"Where *we* live," Nicholas corrects, his eyes flicking to mine.

"At least for the next three months," I remind him.

He nods in agreement. "And when this is done between us," he continues, "I'll make sure to find you somewhere decent to live. Somewhere that doesn't look like a crime scene."

I sigh. "Nicholas, that is—"

"Very necessary," he interrupts, voice tight.

Our eyes lock for a second, and I swallow down my words, knowing there's no use in arguing with him.

He gestures toward the hallway. "Why don't I show you to your room?" he asks. "You must be tired."

I nod, still caught in this weird dream-state, half-expecting someone to pinch me and snap me out of it.

Nicholas leads me down the hall and opens a door to a room so massive, I nearly choke on my own spit. It's ten times bigger than my entire apartment.

"This is the guest bedroom?" I ask, blinking in disbelief.

He nods. "The other is down the hall, which I turned into an office." Pulling something out of his pocket, he holds it out to me. "This is your key card. It's how you'll get in and out of here."

I reach out and take it, feeling the smooth material of the card between my fingers. *God*, even the key card feels expensive.

"I already talked to the concierge and let them know you'll be staying here," he tells me. "And don't be surprised if you see a cleaner in the morning. She usually comes when I'm at work, but you might still catch her."

I nod, my mind still trying to catch up with everything that's happening.

He presses his lips into a thin line. "If you need anything, my bedroom is right down the hall."

I nod again, unable to do anything but nod like an idiot.

"Goodnight, Amara." His voice is thick and gruff, causing a chill to creep up my spine.

"Goodnight, Nicholas."

He nods, dipping his chin before he turns around and walks toward his bedroom, the door closing a few seconds later.

I stand there for a long moment, staring at the king-sized bed. The crisp white sheets and the plush pillows calling my name.

"Welcome to your new home, Pumpkin," I whisper.

Pumpkin jumps from my arms, strutting toward the bed and purrs as she stretches out, curling into the middle of the mattress, making herself comfortable without a second thought.

At least someone's adjusting to the luxury faster than I am.

CHAPTER THIRTEEN
Amara

I wake up to Pumpkin licking my face.

Liam used to hate it, but it never really bothered me. I like to think it's her way of giving me little kisses.

What does catch me off guard though, is the light spilling in through the sheer, white curtains.

I blink a few times, my brain slowly booting up, trying to recall where the hell I am and if I've somehow entered an alternate universe, until it finally hits me.

This isn't my apartment, or an alternate universe.

I'm in a New York Penthouse.

My boss's penthouse.

Wiping the sleep from my eyes, I sit up and glance around the room, trying not to gape like I did when I first walked in last night. But it's impossible. The hardwood floors gleam, polished to perfection, the vanity across from the bed looks like it was ripped straight out of an old Hollywood set, and the bed...

God, this bed.

Stretching out on the mattress, I sink into it deeper, wondering if it's made of actual clouds.

I could write a poem about this bed.

It probably wouldn't be good, considering I've never written a poem in my life, but I'd still try.

Rolling onto my stomach, I grab my phone off the nightstand, only to see a series of missed calls lighting up the screen.

Crap.

I completely forgot that the news of our engagement would be plastered everywhere by now.

I swipe through the notifications, my stomach sinking with each one.

A few more texts from my sister, along with a string of missed calls from my grandma.

But then, my eyes catch on something else. I linger on his name, the sight sending a weird, unsettling feeling through me.

Liam:

> You're engaged? What
> the fuck?

My heart clenches. I haven't heard from him since he broke my heart. And now, after seeing me with someone else, he wants to contact me?

I stare at the message for a moment, wondering what on earth his message even means. But there's no point in replying.

I can't deal with him now. Or ever again, really.

What would I even say to him anyway?

I ignore his message, swiping away until I see a chain of texts from Sophie.

Sophie:

> Are you kidding me?

> How did this happen?

> Why don't I know about it?

> What is going on?

I close my eyes, hating that I'm lying to them. The engagement was supposed to be a solution to Nicholas's problem and my chance to finally get what I've always wanted. But it feels like everyone and their dog has something to say about it. Social media, the news—hell, even my hairdresser probably knows by now.

My thumb hovers over the reply button, but I can't bring myself to type anything.

The lie feels too big, too tangled, and I don't know how to get myself out of this.

I swipe all the messages away and set the phone down.

I know I'm avoiding the inevitable conversation. I'll have to talk to them eventually.

But not today.

Today, I'm going to pretend I don't have to deal with any of it.

At least, until I go to work.

I shuffle out of bed, dragging the covers with me, and head straight for the wall of windows hidden behind thin curtains. My eyes widen at the sight in front of me, the entire city sprawled out below me. I've lived in New York for over five years, but I've never seen it like this.

How the hell did this even happen?

Last night, I was on the arm of a billionaire, announcing to the world that we're engaged. And today? My entire world has flipped on its head in less than twenty-four hours, all thanks to my boss. The man who casually told me to move in here like it's the most normal thing in the world. Like he wasn't offering me a place big enough to fit my entire childhood home.

"I need coffee," I mutter, dragging myself away from the stunning view before my brain starts spiraling.

First order of business? Shower. Second? Caffeine.

I shuffle toward the bathroom, my eyes widening when I enter the bathroom. It's insane, like something out of a luxury magazine. Double sinks, a massive mirror, and a shower that looks like it belongs in a five-star spa.

The shower in my apartment had the worst water pressure known to man, not to mention it was crusted with limescale. But this? This is what dreams are made of.

I can't wait to step into this thing.

I strip out of my pajamas, letting them pool on the marble floor, and step inside the glass-walled shower. Reaching out, I twist the sleek gold knob, anticipation building as I imagine the warm water hitting my skin.

Nothing happens.

"Huh?" I twist it the other way, frowning.

Still nothing.

I jiggle the knob, giving it an extra push this time. Not a single drop of water.

"No, no, no…" I mutter, twisting it again with a bit more desperation. I press my palm against the wall for leverage and give the damn thing one final turn.

Still. Nothing.

"Are you kidding me?" I groan, dropping my head against the cool glass door.

All I wanted was a nice, hot shower to clear my head and maybe wash away the insanity of the past twenty-four hours.

"This cannot be happening," I mutter, my forehead still pressed against the glass.

Grabbing a fresh, white towel, I wrap it tightly around myself and head for the door. Maybe there's someone around who can help. Nicholas mentioned he had a maid who came in the mornings. Maybe she'll know how to fix the shower.

With one hand clutching the towel and the other reaching for the door handle, I pull it open and—

Wham.

I slam right into a solid, very male chest.

"What the—"

A deep voice rumbles above me, and I stumble back, my brain struggling to catch up.

And then it happens.

The towel slips.

It takes a beat—one painfully long beat—for my brain to process the situation. But by the time reality sinks in, I'm standing there. Completely. Butt. Fucking. Naked.

In front of none other than my boss.

"Oh my God!" I yelp, frantically grabbing for the towel as it falls in what feels like slow motion.

Nicholas's jaw tightens, his gaze snapping upward to the ceiling as if it's suddenly the most fascinating thing in the world. "Amara," he says, his voice low and gravelly, "what the hell are you doing?"

"I—I didn't think you'd be here!" I stammer, clutching the towel to my chest as if my life depends on it. My heart pounds so hard I can feel it in my throat, my face heating like I've been set on fire.

"Clearly," he mutters, his tone dry.

His eyes flick downward for half a second—just a second—before snapping back to the ceiling.

I scramble to readjust the towel, fumbling so badly I'm surprised I don't drop it again. My fingers have apparently forgotten how to function, and I'm left clutching the towel like it's a shield against my growing humiliation.

This cannot be happening.

"Why are you here?" I blurt out.

His brow lifts, though his gaze remains firmly fixed above my head. "I live here."

"Well, yeah, but—I thought you'd left for work by now." I gesture wildly with one hand before realizing it's better to keep both hands on the towel.

His eyes finally meet mine, dark and unreadable. "Can I ask why you're wandering around… like this."

"I wasn't wandering," I sigh. "The stupid shower isn't working."

"And your solution was to walk out here naked?"

"I didn't know you were home."

"Well, I am." Silence stretches, and his eyes flick down, landing on the towel and then back to my face. "What do you mean the shower isn't working?" he asks.

I lift my shoulder. "I mean it's broken. Or cursed. Or both."

His lips twitch, like he's fighting a smile. "Cursed?"

"It's not my fault," I grumble, tightening the towel around me. "I twisted the handle twice, and nothing came out."

"Must be a problem with the plumbing. That bathroom hasn't been used in years," he replies, dragging a hand through his hair.

"Maybe you should've mentioned that before I got naked," I mutter under my breath.

His lips twitch. "What was that?"

"Nothing," I say quickly.

He crosses his arms, leaning slightly against the doorframe. "You can use mine."

I blink at him. "Yours?"

"Yes, Amara. My shower. Unless you'd prefer to stay like this all morning?"

His gaze flicks to the towel again—a flicker so quick it might as well have been imagined, but the tightening of his jaw says otherwise.

"Oh, no, I couldn't—"

"Don't argue," he cuts me off. "This is your place now, too. I'll get someone to fix the other one. In the meantime, you'll use mine."

I open my mouth to protest, but his tone stops me. Instead, I nod, mortified and flustered.

"I'm sorry," I say quietly. "I didn't know you were here and—"

"Stop," he cuts me off, stepping closer. His hand brushes my arm, warm and firm. The touch lingers, his fingers curling slightly as if deciding whether to let go. Then, with a soft sigh, he does. "Don't apologize." His jaw ticks. "*Please.*"

"Okay," I murmur.

"Come on." He turns and gestures for me to follow, his stride confident as he moves down the hall.

I hesitate, clutching the towel tighter before trailing after him, my thoughts spinning. My boss. His shower. Naked. *This is going to be a long morning*.

My mind is still spinning with the mortifying image of him walking in on me, rolls and all, as Nicholas leads me down the hallway.

He doesn't say anything, the only sound is the soft click of our footsteps on the hardwood floors.

Just before we reach the end of the hall, he stops in front of a door, pushing it open. His room is even more intimidating than mine—dark, sleek, and impossibly neat.

"The bathroom's through there." He tilts his head, nodding toward a door on the far side of the room.

"Thank you." I hover awkwardly, unsure if I'm supposed to say more, but he doesn't move, his eyes lingering on me just long enough to make my pulse quicken.

Gathering what's left of my dignity, I shuffle toward the bathroom. But before I can reach the door, his voice cuts through the silence.

"Amara, I think it's best if you stay at home today."

I turn, startled. "What?"

"Our engagement is everywhere, and people will have questions. The press will be crazier than ever. Stay home. Let me handle what I can. Just until it dies down a little."

I press my lips together, reluctant to argue, and nod.

He gives a single nod in return before adding, "And from now on, you'll be riding with me to work."

I blink at him, trying to process. "What are you talking about? I always take the subway."

"Not anymore," he replies. "Not while you're my fiancée."

I freeze, my brain short-circuiting at the casual way he drops the word. "Nicholas. We're not actually—"

"We are, as far as anyone else is concerned," he interrupts. "You agreed to this arrangement, and that includes letting me take care of you."

"I didn't agree to being chauffeured," I reply, my arms folding across my chest instinctively, even though it nearly dislodges the towel.

His gaze flickers downward briefly, and his lips press into a thin line, as if he's holding back a comment. "You're living in my house, Amara. It's my responsibility to make sure you're safe."

"I don't need a ride, Nicholas. I can manage just fine on my own."

He takes a step closer, the space between us shrinking. "You're not taking the subway. End of discussion. Now, get in the shower."

Without another word, he turns and strides out, leaving me standing there in my towel with a boatload of conflicting feelings.

Heading into his bathroom, I close the door and let the towel pool at my feet, before stepping into the shower. It's as sleek and luxurious as the rest of his space, with dark tiles and gleaming fixtures. The water is hot, cascading down my back, washing away the tension knotting my shoulders.

I close my eyes, letting out a sigh of relief as I smooth my wet hair back.

Maybe living here won't be so bad after all.

That is, if I survive my boss's *very* distracting presence.

CHAPTER FOURTEEN
Nicholas

Work has been my normal for so long that it feels less like a job and more like the natural order of my life. Meetings, deadlines, negotiations—this is where I thrive. The predictability of it. The control.

I need control.

And yet, right now, my focus is nonexistent. My desk is buried under folders and contracts demanding my attention, but I can't stop thinking about Amara. Specifically, about this morning.

I can't get it out of my mind. The sight of her, all smooth skin and fucking untouchable.

She's supposed to be my fiancée, and yet I can't touch her. Can't look at her. It's torture. Living with her is harder than I ever thought it would be, and I only have myself to blame for this idiotic idea.

This arrangement was supposed to be straightforward. A partnership, a mutually beneficial deal. But every time I look at her, every time I catch the faintest whiff of her vanilla perfume or hear her soft voice, I feel my carefully built control slipping.

It's working out in my favor however, considering the meetings I have lined up this week to discuss the merger. I just need to focus and not let my head get distracted.

My phone vibrates on the desk for what feels like the hundredth time today, and I glance down, seeing Alexander's name flash across the screen once again.

Alexander thrives on making my life hell. I have no doubt in my mind that he's calling to stick his nose in my engagement since he knows marriage is the last thing I have ever wanted.

I lean back in my chair, debating whether to answer. I already know why he's calling. The news of my and Amara's engagement spread like wildfire this morning, and… it's good. It's what I wanted. It's what I need for this deal to go through. But with that, comes the thousand and one lies.

Running my tongue over my teeth, I swipe to answer before I can talk myself out of it.

"Wow," Alexander starts, his tone already dripping with condescension. "The prodigal son answers his own phone. I half expected to be redirected to your assistant… or should I say your fiancée? What's her name again?"

"Alexander," I say flatly, cutting him off. "What do you want?"

He snorts. "What do I want? I want to know what the hell you're playing at." He laughs, low and sharp, the sound crawling under my skin. "I'll admit, the engagement was a nice touch. Almost convincing. But come on, Nicholas. You? Engaged? You don't even date."

My jaw tightens. "My personal life is none of your business."

"Wrong. It's everyone's business now, thanks to your little PR stunt. You don't do anything without a reason, so what's the endgame here, Nick? Trying to make the board believe you're suddenly some family man, ready to settle down? Because let me tell you, they're not stupid."

I let out a slow breath, refusing to rise to his bait. "I don't have to explain anything to you, Alexander."

"Oh, but you do," he snaps. "Because when this blows up—and let's face it, we both know it will—I'll be there to pick up the pieces. And don't worry, I'll make sure everyone remembers who really deserves to be in that chair."

"Is that so?" I ask, leaning back in my chair. "Because from where I'm sitting, it looks like you're spending more time obsessing over my life than focusing on your own job. Maybe if you put half as much effort into your work as you do into tearing me down, you wouldn't still be fighting for scraps."

The line goes silent for a moment, tension thick between us.

"Careful, Nicholas. You're not untouchable, no matter how much you think you are."

I chuckle quietly, my tone sharp. "Remember who gave you your current position, Alexander. Without me, you'd still be sitting in middle management. So maybe think twice before biting the hand that fed you."

"You think you've got it all figured out," he snaps, his composure cracking. "But luck runs out. Watch your back, brother. It'd be a shame if your little charade fell apart before you signed that contract."

He hangs up before I can respond, and I set my phone down slowly, the muscles in my neck tense.

Alexander is bitter. Bitter that he'll never sit in my chair, no matter how much shit he throws at me. Bitter that no matter what he says or does, I'll always be one step ahead.

And he knows it. That's why he's trying so hard to rattle me.

But he'll learn soon enough. I don't break. And I sure as hell don't lose.

I glance at the computer screen, at the open contract I should be working on, but my attention snags on a tab I forgot to close—a news article from last night's gala.

I click on the article, and there we are, front and center kissing. Her chin's tipped up toward me, and my hand's resting on her waist like she belongs in my arms.

My eyes drift lower, examining her in the way I'd never allow myself to in person. Her hand catches my attention—or, more specifically, the lack of something on it.

No ring.

It's a detail that shouldn't matter, but it does. Pulling out my phone, I type a quick message.

Me:

Are you busy tomorrow?

Her reply is almost immediate.

Amara:

Well, I have work.

Me:

Take the day off. Your boss won't mind.

Amara:

I'm not complaining about that.

I rub my mouth, a smile creeping on my face.

Amara:

Can I ask what this is about, sir?

Sir. God help me. The woman lives with me, everyone thinks we're engaged, I've seen her in a towel—in nothing—and she continues her professionalism with me when all I can think of is how I caught a quick glimpse of her pink nipples before I shot my head to my ceiling.

Me:

> I need you to go somewhere with me.

Amara:

> I can't exactly say no… seeing as I live with you now.

My brows knit together, and I fire off another message.

Me:

> You can always say no. Living with me doesn't mean I own you, Amara. You might be my fiancée, and I might be your boss, but you're your own person.

There's a pause before her next reply.

Amara:

> I'd love to come.

The corners of my mouth twitch. Tossing the phone onto my desk, I try to redirect my focus to the screen in front of me.

But it's no use. My thoughts keep drifting back to her, to the way she looked this morning, the warmth in her eyes, the way my name sounds on her lips.

This was supposed to be a simple business arrangement.

Instead, it's turning out to be a testament to my self-restraint.

CHAPTER FIFTEEN
Amara

I step into the living room, spotting Nicholas sitting on the couch, scrolling through his phone, one ankle resting on his opposite knee. He looks sharp, as usual, in a suit that hugs him in all the right ways—broad shoulders, slim waist, long legs.

I gulp, my throat suddenly dry. God, he's ridiculously good-looking. It's unfair, really.

Three days I've been living here, and I've never seen him in anything other than a crisp suit. Not that I'd have much opportunity to. I've been in my room as often as possible, still too aware of how out of place I feel in this penthouse, like an uninvited guest crashing a world I don't belong in.

The soft click of my bedroom door closing draws his attention. His head lifts, and his eyes find me immediately, sweeping over my outfit.

I tug at the hem of my blazer, feeling exposed under his gaze. Normally, I stick to my oversized sweaters, long skirts, and sneakers. But this is the first time since the engagement was announced that Nicholas is taking me somewhere—somewhere public. Somewhere where people will be looking at us. At *me*.

So, I've traded my usual clothes for something more polished—a white shirt tucked into some fitted pants, a blazer draped over my shoulders, and pointed-toe heels that click softly on the floor. This outfit feels foreign, stiff... but necessary. I need to look the part, even if I don't feel it.

Nicholas's gaze lingers, his sharp eyes taking me in, and for a second, I feel bare, as though he can see straight through the effort. His brows lift slightly, and my face warms as the memory of him seeing me naked resurfaces.

"New look?" His deep voice sends a shiver down my spine. He sets his phone down, rising to his feet in one fluid motion.

God help me. He's not wearing a tie today. That means his neck—thick, strong, and entirely too distracting—is on display, and it's almost worse than when he's all buttoned up.

I clear my throat, gripping the strap of my bag tighter. "Is this okay?" I ask, my breath hitching at his expression. "For where we're going?"

He takes a slow step closer, his head tilting slightly as his eyes continue their journey across my outfit. "Where are your sweaters?"

His question catches me off guard. "What?"

"Your sweaters," he repeats, like the word offends him. "You wear those oversized things to work all the time." His nostrils flare. "Where are they?"

"I..." I stammer, thrown off by the sudden interrogation. "I thought this would be more appropriate."

His brow arches, a flicker of something sharp crossing his face. "Appropriate?" he repeats.

"For where we're going," I clarify. "I figured people might look at us, photograph us, and I just wanted to look like someone who belongs with you."

Nicholas doesn't say anything at first. He just looks at me. His eyes roam slowly over my outfit again, lingering longer than they should, before finally snapping back to mine.

"I know I don't look like the kind of girl that would be seen with you," I continue, "but I thought at least—"

"Get changed."

My brows shoot up. "Excuse me?"

"You heard me."

I blink, my lips parting as I shake my head in disbelief. "But I thought—"

"You thought wrong," he cuts me off, the muscle in his jaw flexing. "You think this is what I want?" He exhales through his nose. "This isn't what I want. Not even fucking close."

I hesitate, glancing down at my outfit. "You don't think this looks good?"

"What I think," he cuts me off again, stepping even closer, "is that you look uncomfortable as hell in this." He tugs lightly at the sleeve of my blazer, his fingers brushing my arm. "And I don't want you to be uncomfortable or pretend to be someone else. You don't need to prove anything to anyone. Not to me, not to them." His eyes meet mine, dark and intense, stealing my breath right out of my lungs. "Unless you like wearing an outfit that you can't lift your arms in, go back into your room and put on the sweaters you love so much."

I gape at him, my brain short-circuiting. His jaw clenches, the muscle ticking. For a second before he turns on his heel and walks to the bar, pouring himself a glass of water.

"Get dressed, Amara," he says over his shoulder, his voice gruff.

I turn, retreating to my room, seeing Pumpkin curled in a pumpkin-shaped ball on my bed. Nicholas's words echo in my mind as I peel off the blazer and pants, feeling immediate relief. He was right. This outfit is uncomfortable as hell, itchy, stiff, and *so* not me.

I grab my favorite pink sweater from the closet, slipping it on with a sigh of relief. The soft knit hugs me in all the right places, comforting and familiar. I tuck it into my favorite skirt, swap the heels for sneakers, and glance at my reflection.

It's not glamorous. I don't look like the fiancée of a billionaire. I just look… like me.

My shoulders slump as I grab my bag and step out of the room. Nicholas looks up immediately, his gaze sharp and assessing. His lips part slightly, and he drags a hand over his mouth, like he's trying to hide something.

"Much fucking better," he murmurs, his voice rougher than before.

My heart skips.

"You ready to go?" he asks.

I nod, following him out the door, my heart pounding in my chest.

"This is our ride?" I stop in my tracks, staring at the sleek black helicopter parked in front of us. My voice is laced with disbelief as I take in the polished exterior and spinning blades, the sound somehow already making my stomach churn.

Nicholas hardly spares it a glance as he keeps walking, one hand tucked into his pocket, his tailored suit moving as fluidly as he does. "Where we're going is a little far to drive," he says simply, like he does this every day, which, knowing him, he probably does.

"So, we're taking a *helicopter*?"

Nicholas glances over his shoulder, dark sunglasses shielding his eyes. "Unless you'd prefer to sit in a car for four hours?"

Four hours. My brain stumbles over the number. Where on earth is he taking me? I don't ask because I'm still stuck on the fact that we're about to leave the ground in that deathtrap.

Before I can find the words, Nicholas opens the door and steps inside like he's done this a million times.

"Where's the pilot?" I ask, looking around to see if there's anyone else coming that will fly that thing.

He pauses, one hand on the edge of the seat as he looks at me like I've just asked if the sky is blue. "You're looking at him."

I blink. "*You're* flying this?"

Nicholas raises a brow. "Something wrong with that?"

Yes. A lot of things, actually. "Are you even qualified?"

His lips twitch, but not enough to call it a smile. He shrugs, stepping fully inside. "I've been flying since I was sixteen, Amara. You'll be fine."

Fine. *Sure*. Because who doesn't casually pilot helicopters in their spare time?

"Get in."

I hesitate, staring at the open door like it's about to swallow me whole, and climb in, muttering a quiet prayer under my breath.

The interior is even more intimidating than the outside. The seats are sleek black leather, the dashboard packed with an overwhelming number of buttons, switches, and levers.

I climb into the seat, carefully smoothing down my skirt, and fumble with the seatbelt, my nerves making my fingers clumsy.

"Relax, Amara," Nicholas murmurs, his voice soft and low as he reaches for the seatbelt.

"I can do it," I say quickly, fumbling with the buckle. My hands are shaking, and of course, it won't click into place.

"Clearly."

Before I can respond, he leans over me, one hand brushing against my stomach as he pulls the belt into place.

His hand lingers just a second too long, his knuckles grazing my side as he buckles the strap. The space between us feels suffocatingly small, his cologne—clean, sharp, and expensive—filling my lungs.

"There." His voice is low, almost rough, as his eyes flick to mine. "You're secure now."

I don't say anything. I can't. My pulse is hammering so hard I'm sure he can hear it.

Nicholas pulls back, settling into his seat like he didn't just steal all the oxygen from the cabin. "You ready?" he asks, putting on his headset and flicking a series of switches.

No. Not even a little. But I nod anyway, gripping the edge of my seat like it might save me from falling out of the sky.

Nicholas wraps his hands around the dual controls, moving with precision as the helicopter lifts off, the ground dropping away faster than I'm prepared for. My stomach drops as we rise higher, the city shrinking below us. My eyes squeeze shut, my knuckles turning white as I cling to the seat.

"Amara," Nicholas's voice cuts through the noise after a moment, his voice clear through the headset. "Open your eyes."

I shake my head tightly, keeping them squeezed shut.

"Are you—" He pauses, and I hear the sharp exhale of breath through the line. "Amara. Are you afraid of heights?"

"Not… afraid," I manage to say, though my voice betrays me with a shaky tremor.

"Don't lie to me." I risk opening one eye, catching the faintest flicker of irritation in his profile as he glances at me. His jaw is tense, his hands relaxed on the controls as the helicopter levels out. "Are you scared?"

I force myself to nod, heat creeping up my neck. "A little," I admit.

"Why the hell didn't you say anything?"

"I didn't think it mattered."

"It matters." His tone is clipped, but the words feel heavier than they should. "Of course it fucking matters. I wouldn't have brought you up here if I'd known." He curses, shaking his head. "I just thought you were doubtful whether I was qualified or not. I didn't think you had a fear."

I hesitate, my gaze flicking to him. He looks completely at ease, like he was born to do this. "It's fine," I say quietly.

Nicholas's grip tightens slightly. He shoots me a look. "Don't you dare say it's fine. I would never put you in this position if I knew."

I don't respond, my hands still clutching the seat as we fly higher, forcing myself to loosen my grip on the seat.

"I didn't know you flew helicopters," I say, trying to distract myself.

"I told you, Amara. There's a lot you don't know about me," he replies.

I glance at him, his profile stark in the soft cabin light. He's right. I don't know him. Not really. Not beyond the obvious details, like how he takes his coffee—black, no sugar—or how every suit he wears looks like it was made to fit him and only him.

I shift my focus outside, and this time, the view doesn't twist my stomach as much. "It's beautiful up here," I admit.

"It is," he agrees, his voice softer now. I turn to look at him as he leans back just slightly, his grip on the controls steady, like this is the most natural thing in the world for him. "Flying is one of my favorite things."

His shoulders, usually held with the tension of someone always ready for the next move, are looser now, and there's something in his expression I've never seen before.

"Up here, it's quiet," he continues. "No deadlines. No meetings. No bullshit. Just me and the sky." His words catch me off guard. "The color of the sky at night is my favorite sight in the world," he adds. "And the city lights glowing beneath it? Closest thing to magic I've ever seen."

I don't reply, too caught in the way his voice dips as he speaks, like he's letting me in on something private.

"You okay now?" he asks after a few minutes, glancing at me briefly, his brows drawn together in concern.

I nod, realizing that, somehow, I am. "Yeah. I guess it's not so bad up here." I shift in my seat, settling in. "Besides, I trust you."

His eyes flick to mine, and something shifts in his expression. He doesn't respond right away, but when he does, his voice is low and firm. "Good. Because I'd never let anything happen to you, Amara."

Something in his voice makes my stomach flip, and it has nothing to do with the height.

CHAPTER SIXTEEN

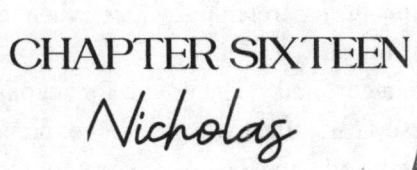

Nicholas

*H*oney.

Fiery orange with flashes of molten gold, like it's been set on fire and tamed just enough to fall in waves. It's lush, rich, and sweet and so fucking distracting, every movement of it pulling my focus. That's the only thing running through my mind as I watch my assistant walk ahead of me, her orange hair swaying with each step, while the flashes of paparazzi cameras blind us as we step through the door into the jeweler.

God, I need to get a hold of whatever the fuck it is brewing inside of me every time my eyes find hers.

I've been fine for two years. Two solid years of keeping my attraction to her in check, only seeing her as my assistant. But now…

My neck feels tight, my heart pounding against my chest as I glance over at her, wide-eyed, staring at the jewels. Her green eyes are bright with wonder, and I can't help but feel a pull in my gut.

My lips twitch, unable to hide my amusement at how genuinely excited she is. I haven't seen anyone this stoked in a long time… Ever, really, since I've always been surrounded by people who all come from the same high-society bubble. I like it. A hell of a lot more than I'm willing to admit.

"Mr. Blackwood." My head snaps from Amara to Mr. Carrington, his grin stretching wider when our eyes meet. "Glad to see you, sir."

I give him a curt nod. "Thank you for accommodating us."

"Of course, Mr. Blackwood. We've prepared a private viewing for you and your fiancée as per your request," he says, making Amara's head snap toward us, her eyes wide.

"You closed this place down for us?" Amara asks, her voice quiet and reserved, making me shiver. Is it possible to be attracted to a voice, because... *fuck me*. Sexiest voice I've ever heard.

"Of course," I reply with a teasing smile, savoring the way she gulps. "You're marrying a billionaire, *honey*."

Her eyes go even wider at the nickname, and I can't say I don't enjoy it. I love how easily I can shock her with just a word. It's like I'm addicted to that reaction, and damn, I want more. Maybe with her lips on mine next time.

She relaxes once she remembers we need to play the part of the happy couple, and she lets out a soft breath, her shoulders dropping slightly in a way that makes me ache for her.

"Would you care for some champagne?" Mr. Carrington asks, sliding over a tray with two flutes.

"Thank you," I say, reaching for a glass, my gaze flicking to Amara. She eyes me cautiously, unsure.

She reaches for a glass herself, murmuring a soft, "thank you," before taking a sip.

I see it in the way she looks around the room, the way she hesitates before moving or speaking. She thinks she doesn't belong here.

It pisses me off that she feels that way. I hate that she thought changing herself would somehow make me happy. It's not that I didn't like the outfit—I liked it more than I probably should've—but when she stepped out of her room in that tight, stiff outfit, with that uncomfortable look on her face, I hated it. She didn't look like Amara. She looked like someone she thought she had to be, and all I wanted was to pull those clothes off her and get her back into those cozy, oversized sweaters that are all her.

My jaw clenches.

I need to get these thoughts out of my head.

I'm her boss.

I'm not supposed to imagine her pale skin, completely bare and exposed. I'm not supposed to fantasize about what she'd feel like in my hands. I'm definitely not supposed to stare at her lips and remember the taste of her kiss.

I clear my throat, forcing myself out of the haze of thoughts when I see Mr. Carrington showing Amara the array of rings he's laid out for her.

Amara glances over her shoulder, her eyes locking with mine, uncertainty swirling in them. "These are for me?"

I nod, stepping closer until my hand lands on the small of her back, covered by a sweater I can't seem to get out of my mind. "I thought you'd like to pick out your ring," I say, catching Mr. Carrington's watchful gaze. He—like everyone else—doesn't know the engagement is fake, so while we need to sell it, I also want Amara to feel at ease. "You can pick whichever one you want," I add, motioning to the display of rings.

She steps forward slowly, her eyes flicking over the diamonds, sapphires, and emeralds. The stones catch the light, each one more breathtaking than the last, but Amara doesn't reach for any. She just stands there, absorbed in thought, her gaze distant.

I watch her, mesmerized by the way the light hits her eyes, the way her fingers brush against the glass, the little movements she makes when she thinks no one's paying attention. I'm not sure how I'm supposed to focus on anything else. She's tying me in knots, and I'm beginning to wonder how much longer I can handle it.

She inhales sharply, shaking her head—like she always does when she's trying to brush something off—and takes a step back. "No, Nicholas, this is—"

"Necessary," I interrupt, just for her ears as I take her left hand in mine, my thumb swiping over her empty ring finger. She looks up at me, those green eyes knocking the air out of my chest. "No one will believe you're my fiancée if you don't have a rock on your finger."

Her lips part slightly, processing what I've said, and she glances at the rings again before meeting my gaze. Something in her expression twists inside me.

"Excuse me, Mr. Carrington," I say, glancing at the jeweler who's watching our interaction. "Could we have a moment alone?"

He hesitates for a beat before placing the display down on the glass table, nodding as he steps back. "Of course. Just call out when you're ready."

I nod, relieved to be left alone with her. I need to figure out what the hell's going on inside this woman's head. When Mr. Carrington leaves, I don't let go of her, instead pulling her closer to me. Her gaze meets mine—wide, vulnerable—and I frown at the tightness in her shoulders. "What's going on, Amara?"

She shakes her head again, avoiding my question.

"I thought every girl's dream was to be surrounded by diamonds," I say, trying to lighten the mood, tilting my head.

She lets out a strained laugh, and I hate it. "It is," she sighs, the smile fading too quickly. "But…" She stops herself, biting her lip.

"But?" I press, needing to know what's going on.

She lifts her head, finally meeting my eyes, and exhales softly before shaking her head. "I've thought about this for a long time," she starts, her voice quieter now, her gaze dropping to the rings. "Getting proposed to. Getting married." She sighs, a deep, heavy breath, and I feel it in my chest. "I thought it would happen sometime soon, and I was so excited for it," she admits. "And now, the first time I put a ring on my finger…" She pauses, her voice wavering. "And it's all fake."

Her eyes close, and I can see the tension in her face, the sadness she's trying to hide. I don't know what to say at first, unsure of how to make it better. So, I don't. I stay silent, just holding her close, hoping that my presence can offer some comfort.

"I always thought I'd have a small wedding," she continues. "Nothing big or over-the-top. Just a few people. Family, friends. A simple, intimate ceremony."

She doesn't look at me when she says it, her fingers tracing the smooth surface of the display of rings, the sadness in her eyes slicing through me like a knife. She's thinking about her ex. That asshole who didn't deserve her, who couldn't give her what she needed, who left her feeling empty.

"I wanted ducks."

I furrow my brow. "Ducks?"

She nods, a small smile tugging at the corner of her lips. "I wanted a small pond with ducks, in the fall breeze with leaves falling, and peonies everywhere." Her shoulders drop. "I know it sounds silly compared to what you're used to," she glances up at me, "but that's what I've always imagined."

I feel a twinge in my chest at her words. I want her to have that. I want her to have whatever she wants.

I pull her a little closer, gently squeezing her hand. "That doesn't sound silly at all," I say, my voice low, trying to offer some comfort. "It sounds beautiful."

She looks up at me then, her eyes glistening just slightly. "Maybe someday," she murmurs, her voice quiet.

"Maybe someday," I echo, my thumb brushing over her knuckles. "I hope I don't overstep," I say, "but from what I remember of your ex, he didn't seem like the kind of guy who'd be willing to give you what you just explained to me."

She laughs, but it's a low, bitter sound, one that cuts straight through me. "No, you're right," she admits with a heavy breath. "He wasn't."

I want to say something else—something to make it better, to fix the look in her eyes—but she continues, and my chest tightens at her next words. "Maybe that's why he cheated."

The words hit me like a punch to the gut, but I can't tell if it's the thought of her ex or the way she says it that gets to me the most.

"Maybe I pushed him too much," she continues. "I shouldn't have talked about wedding plans so much or shown him the folder I made for ours. I should've known better."

I don't think—just act. I step closer, my hand reaching out before I can stop it, my palm gently cupping her face. She looks up at me, startled for a second, but I don't back away. *I can't.*

"Don't," I say, my voice hard, the words coming out more intense than I mean. "Don't you dare lower your standards for some bastard who wasn't willing to give you what you wanted."

She gulps, her skin warm against my hand. I can feel the tremor in her. "You deserve more than that, Amara," I continue. "I have no doubt in my mind that there's a guy out there who'd fall flat on his face just to give you everything you want and more."

Her breath catches. I see the tiniest flicker in her eyes, the softness in her gaze as she stares at me. She doesn't say anything for a moment, but I can tell I've gotten through to her. And god, I want her to know just how much she deserves better than the way she's been treated.

I hold her hand in mine, my thumb brushing against her bare ring finger. I can't stop myself from saying it, even though I'm not sure I should. "For what it's worth, I may never understand your idea of marriage, Amara. But I'm grateful you're my first fake wife."

Her lips twitch. "First, huh?" she teases.

I shrug. "Who knows? There may be other deals I need to close after you and I are done."

Her smile falters just a little, and I hate myself for reminding us this will be over someday. She lets out a hollow laugh that makes my stomach twist. "Yeah."

Needing to do something—anything—to distract myself from the look in her eyes, I glance down at the rings, tugging Amara with me.

"Pick one," I tell her, her hand still in mine as I rub her empty ring finger once again. "Don't worry about anything else but picking your dream ring."

She hesitates, glancing up at me with that look of disbelief. "Any ring?"

I nod. "I'll even let you keep it once this is done."

Her eyes widen. "You can't be serious."

I lift my shoulder. "I won't have a need for an engagement ring once we're done, Amara. You keep it. Wear it, sell it, whatever you want to do."

Her brows furrow slightly as she processes my words. "But what about when you get married in the future?" she asks. "Won't you need it then?"

The question hits me harder than I expected. I never saw myself getting married, and while this isn't real, Amara is the only person I see myself ever giving a ring to.

My jaw tightens at the thought of a future with anyone else. I step closer to her, our bodies now an inch apart. I let her hand go, my fingers trailing up to her chin, and tilt her head back so she meets my gaze. "If I ever do get married in the future, I won't be giving her your ring." Her eyes widen, her breath hitching as she looks up at me. "This one is *yours*, Amara," I say. "Only yours."

She gulps, her eyes locked on mine, the moment stretching on longer than I'm comfortable with. When she finally glances down at the rings, her fingers graze the display, her touch so delicate, and she stops on a simple ring—an oval diamond with a gold band. I tilt my head slightly, studying her expression.

"Is that the one?" I ask her.

She nods, tapping the glass. "I think so."

A smile tugs at my lips, and I clear my throat, standing straight, calling Mr. Carrington back in.

He immediately launches into a detailed explanation about the diamonds and metals used, but honestly, I couldn't care less. My focus is entirely on Amara, on the way she looks at the ring, the way her smile grows as the jeweler takes it out of the display and hands it to her.

She examines it carefully, her pretty lips curling into a smile that could light up a room. Her eyes widen as she falls more and more in love with the ring. God, her smile is something made by the angels, directly for me.

When she hands the ring to me, I take it with steady hands, my heart hammering in my chest. I lift her hand slowly, sliding the ring onto her finger, my eyes never leaving hers. The moment it slides into place, my heart bangs against my chest and I know that something between us has shifted.

This might be a fake engagement, but my attraction to her is anything but fake. I want her. Bad. And I'm already wondering how the hell I'm going to spend the next four hours in the car with her, never mind the next three months.

CHAPTER SEVENTEEN

Amara

Whispers follow me like shadows today, clinging to every step I take through the office. It's my first day back in the office since Nicholas and I announced our engagement, and *nervous* doesn't even begin to cover how I'm feeling.

Two coworkers hover near the glass doors, leaning in close. Their conversation dies the second they see me. They look away quickly, pretending not to notice me as I walk past, but I still hear those damn whispers.

"Do you think it's true?"

"With him? No way. She's not even his type."

My face burns, and I try to keep my head high, doing my best to ignore the stares and murmurs, but the words settle under my skin, prickling with every step.

This is why I told Nicholas I wanted to walk in alone today. It's better this way. No audience, no scene. I don't need the extra attention right now.

It's bad enough that my sister and grandma have been blowing up my phone since the news of our engagement got out. I panicked, told them it wasn't real and hoped to god they would believe it.

But I know at some point, they'll have questions… questions I'm not ready to answer.

I glance at my desk, seeing Jade and Sophie deep in conversation. Jade spots me first, her eyes laser-focused on my hand. Before I even reach my seat, she's out of her chair and grabbing my fingers.

"Holy shit, look at that rock!" Her voice is so loud, I swear half the office hears it. I wince, glancing around to see eyes flicker our way.

"How much did this cost?" Jade's voice is tinged with awe, her wide eyes practically glued to the diamond on my finger. Sophie shoots her a glare which makes Jade shrug. "What? I might buy myself one."

Sophie scoffs. "I don't think you could afford a ring like that even if you worked your entire life."

My heart races at the reminder. "I don't know how much it costs... but it must be a lot since we flew in his helicopter to get there," I tell them.

Both of their eyes widen in shock.

Jade's jaw practically hits the floor. "What?"

Sophie, however, shakes her head, her brows tugged together. "I still don't understand how you were suddenly engaged to Nicholas Blackwood?"

My head snaps toward Jade. "You didn't tell her?" I ask, assuming she would have told Sophie about the fake engagement the first chance she got.

Jade shrugs. "Nope, you told me not to tell anyone."

Sophie's expression flickers with confusion. "Wait. She knows? *Jade* knows and I don't?"

I let out a sigh. "She found out when I was shopping."

Sophie's eyebrows knit together. "Found what out? Someone tell me what the hell is going on."

I chew on my lip for a moment. Screw it. What's one more person? "It's not real," I say quietly. "The engagement... It's just a means to an end until Nicholas can secure a business deal."

Her expression shifts, staring at me, her eyes wide with disbelief. "Wait." She shakes her head. "What?"

I nod, my gaze dropping to my hand, the weight of the ring still unfamiliar. "Nicholas needed to convince the board he was settled down and ready to take on the international merger," I explain. "The fake engagement will be over in three months."

Sophie doesn't respond right away, staring at me for a beat. I can practically see the wheels turning in her head as she processes what I've just told her. She finally looks up from the floor, her eyes meeting Jade's. "And you kept this to yourself the whole time?"

Jade shrugs, a smirk tilting her lips. "I know how to keep secrets." She gives us a knowing look. "You wouldn't believe how many secrets I have."

Sophie narrows her eyes. "That kind of scares me."

Her smirk widens. "It should."

Sophie lets out a small huff of disbelief, reaching for her coffee. "Where were you yesterday?" she asks. "I came over to your place, but you weren't there."

"Yeah, I uh…" I press my lips into a thin line, knowing I'll never hear the end of it. "I kind of moved in with Nicholas."

Both of them freeze, their wide eyes locked on me.

Sophie slowly swallows the coffee down with a loud gulp, placing her mug back on her desk. "*What*?"

Jade shakes her head. "Okay, I had *no* idea about that."

Sophie's brows tug together. "You guys are living together, engaged, and you're telling me nothing's happened between you two?"

I shift in my seat, the pressure of their stares making me squirm. "No," I say, shaking my head quickly. "Nothing. Seriously. It's just business. We're under contract."

Jade raises an eyebrow, leaning back and crossing her arms. Her gaze sharpens as she examines me. "And where in the contract does it say you have to live with him?"

I let out a long breath, my fingers tightening around my mug. "It doesn't," I admit. "But when he saw my apartment, he… told me to move in with him."

Jade lets out a scoff. "I told you to move in with me, and I didn't see you pack a single bag."

"It's not like that," I assure them, my shoulders tense. "He was just worried and—I don't have time for this. I need to work." I turn toward my monitor, clicking open the list of tasks I need to tackle today.

"Uh-huh. Sure. Change the subject all you want, but we both know you're lying to yourself if you think you two will make it three months without fucking." Jade's voice drips with amusement.

I roll my eyes, keeping my focus on the screen. "Trust me, that won't happen."

Her eyes twinkle, and she winks at me. "Whatever you say, babe. We love a good slow burn."

I feel my face heat up, and I quickly glance away. "Don't get your hopes up," I mutter. "Nicholas would never be with someone like me."

Jade laughs. "Please tell me you're kidding." She waits for my response, but when I don't give her one, she scoffs. "Amara, babe. You're hot. Your ex was a piece of shit who made you think you're not desirable, but that's the farthest thing from the truth. Trust me, that kiss between you two at the gala? You don't kiss someone like that if you're not attracted to them."

Trust me when I say, my attraction to you isn't an issue.

The memory of Nicholas's words comes rushing back to me, and the knot in my throat tightens as I wonder if she's right.

Just as I'm about to respond, the elevator doors open, and a delivery guy steps in, holding a bouquet of flowers.

"Amara?" he calls, looking around the room.

I furrow my brows, not sure what's going on. I raise my hand. "That's me."

He makes his way over, handing me the bouquet. My frown deepens as I take it from him. It's beautiful—soft pink and white peonies. My favorites.

I glance up at him, confused. "I'm sorry, I think you've got the wrong person. These can't be for me."

He glances at his phone, then back at me. "Amara Winslow?"

"Yeah… That's me."

He nods, offering a polite smile. "Then they're for you." With that, he turns and heads back into the elevator.

I stare down at the flowers, my heart racing, the knot in my throat refusing to loosen. Jade is practically grinning, looking like she's enjoying every second of this. "Are those from—"

"No." I shake my head. "They… can't be, right?"

Sophie taps me on the shoulder, a little too eagerly. "Uh… babe." I glance up and see the elevator doors open again. Another delivery guy steps in, carrying an even bigger bouquet than the first.

My head spins. "He didn't."

"I think he did," Jade adds with a chuckle. "Oh boy, I love it when I'm right."

"Amara Winslow?" one of the delivery guys calls out, scanning the room.

"That's her," Jade says, pointing directly at me with a grin. "Right here."

Before I can even process what's happening, another delivery guy walks in, then another, and another. They keep coming, one after the other, each with a bouquet in hand. Hundreds of peonies... The flowers just keep piling up, and I can barely catch my breath. By the time the last delivery guy steps in, I'm standing in the middle of a forest of flowers, my arms full of bouquets.

The whole office is watching the spectacle unfold, and I can feel their eyes on me.

"Wait, there's a card in this one." Sophie hands me a small pink card that's tucked into one of the bouquets.

I take the card from her, and read the words, my stomach fluttering like crazy.

You deserve to have everything you've ever wanted.

My breath catches in my throat. I glance up at Jade, who's watching me intently, her lips curled into a mischievous smile.

"Can I be the maid of honor at your wedding?" Jade asks, snapping me out of my thoughts.

I roll my eyes, my heart pounding. "There won't be a wedding," I tell her, trying to keep my voice steady despite the fluttering in my chest.

Jade just laughs, clearly not buying it. "I wouldn't be so sure about that."

CHAPTER EIGHTEEN

Amara

I'm still not used to living here. Every morning, I wake up in shock that this is my life—at least for the next couple of months—especially when I open my curtains and see the most beautiful view of New York City right outside my bedroom window.

Pumpkin, however, adjusted to the luxury the second we moved in. She's still curled up in her bed, and I'm pretty sure she hasn't moved since last night.

I reach for my phone, checking the time. Nicholas is probably long gone by now, so I roll out of bed and stretch, running a hand through my hair, still a tangled mess from sleep. I quickly grab my clothes, throw the covers off, and head for the door, dying to get into his massive shower with its five different water pressures and hot, steamy water that feels like silk on my skin.

"Come on, Pumpkin." She stretches in her bed, then slowly climbs out of her bed, her little feet tapping on the floor as she makes her way over to me. I can't help but smirk at how lazy she's gotten since we moved in.

I open the door, letting her pass, but as I look up, my heart stutters in my chest. There he is, standing right in front of me. *Nicholas*. He's in his perfectly tailored suit, looking like he just stepped out of a magazine. I don't think I've ever seen him in anything else. Never in sweatpants, never in a t-shirt. It's always that sharp, sophisticated look that makes him seem untouchable.

"Do you ever not wear a suit?" The words come out before I have a chance to filter it and my eyes widen as his eyes, dark and intense, travel slowly over my body, lingering on my soft pink pajamas covered in little red hearts. When his gaze finally meets mine, my stomach does a little flip.

His lips twitch, and he raises an eyebrow. "When I shower," he says, before adding, "and when I fuck."

My cheeks burn instantly, my stomach flipping. I quickly glance down at my feet, trying to hide the blush creeping up my neck.

"Morning," he murmurs, with a chuckle, his voice still husky from sleep.

"Morning," I reply, my voice hoarse as I try to clear the fog of sleep. "I thought you'd already left for work."

He raises an eyebrow. "Is it a problem that I haven't?"

"No. Of course not," I say quickly, shaking my head. "I just thought—"

"You don't need to hide when I'm here, Amara." I bite the inside of my cheek, knowing he's caught onto what I've been doing.

He steps closer, the soft click of his shoes on the hardwood floor sharp in the silence. I can feel his presence, like an electric current in the air between us. "I've been leaving for work later and later, waiting for a chance where I'd finally see you in the mornings," he admits, and I feel the air around me thicken. "And yet, I never get the chance... until I see you walk out of your room on the security cameras right after I enter the elevator."

My heart pounds as my brows furrow, unsure what to say. I had no idea he did that, and part of me wants to ask why. Why does Nicholas Blackwood want to see me in the mornings? I swallow harshly, keeping the questions inside.

"I just didn't want to impose."

"You're not imposing. This is as much your apartment as it is mine, Amara. Stop acting like you're not supposed to be here."

My chest tightens slightly at his words. "I wasn't—" I begin, but he cuts me off.

"I'm serious, Amara," he says, his tone softening slightly, but there's no mistaking the intensity in his eyes. "I meant what I said. I want you to have everything you've ever wanted."

My breath catches at the reminder of the card he sent along with the flowers, and my eyes wander around the apartment, noticing the flowers scattered across the living room.

"I appreciate the gesture," I tell him, "but these were unnecessary." Nicholas raises an eyebrow, his smirk playful. "Everyone was looking at me," I continue, my face burning at the thought of the delivery guys and the curious eyes in the office.

His smirk widens as he leans in just a little. "I'm sorry." His low voice makes my skin break out into chills. "Next time, I'll adorn you with flowers in our home."

My heart skips a beat at the words *our home*. "Next time?"

He doesn't reply, smiling instead, amusement flickering in his eyes. "I have a proposition for you."

I raise an eyebrow. "What kind of proposition?"

Nicholas reaches for the glossy magazine laying on top of the kitchen island. "I've been meaning to hire a decorator for my place." My gaze flickers to the furniture layouts scattered across the pages. "But I want you to do it."

My brows knit together, unsure I heard him correctly. "Wait... you want *me* to decorate your apartment?"

"Yes."

I'm silent for a moment, my mind spinning. "But... why me?" I ask, still confused. "You could hire someone else, someone who—"

"I could," he interrupts, offering the magazine to me with a flick of his wrist. "But I want you to do it. You've still got that card I gave you, right?"

"Yeah," I say with a nod. "I do."

"Good." His lips curl slightly. "Use it. Buy whatever you want. I trust you."

My breath catches in my throat as he steps closer, his eyes locking on my hand. I don't move, frozen as his fingers brush mine, testing whether I'll pull away. I don't.

He lifts my hand between us, and his thumb traces the diamond ring on my finger slowly, before he brings it to his lips, pressing a soft kiss to the back of my hand.

"It looks good on you," he murmurs, the words sending a shiver down my spine.

I gulp, my pulse skipping. I'm dizzy from his gaze, the warmth of his touch, and the way his presence fills the room.

Finally, he lets go of my hand, his fingers lingering for just a fraction of a second longer than necessary. "I'll be back later." He steps back, but his eyes don't leave mine. "You have the place to yourself until then. But I don't want you hiding from me again. Got it?"

My chest tightens, my heart pounding in my ears as I meet his gaze. I straighten my shoulders, fighting the flutter in my stomach. "Got it," I whisper,

Without another word, his footsteps echo down the hall as he disappears into the elevator.

I step into his room, the door slightly cracked open, and close it quietly behind me. My eyes take in every inch of his room. The space where he sleeps, where he works, where he… does whatever else.

It's not like any room I've ever seen before. Dark wood furniture, sleek and modern and utterly him. His bed is large— too large for someone who sleeps alone, I tell myself, even as my gaze flickers over the sheets. I quickly look away, biting my lip as my thoughts wander.

How many other women have been in here? Used this bathroom, this bed, stood in this very spot I'm standing in now?

I turn toward the bathroom, pulling myself away from my own spiraling thoughts, and step into the shower. The water turns on, and I close my eyes tilting my head back, letting the water envelop me.

My eyes drift to his products, neatly arranged along the glass shelf—shampoo, conditioner, body wash. They're all high-end. Expensive. But it's the scent that catches my attention. I lean forward, inhaling deeply. It's not just any fragrance. It's his smell, mixed with wood and something spicy. My teeth tug at my bottom lip when my legs start to shake, my core throbbing as I imagine him in the shower, pouring body lotion onto his hand before he dips down and—

I snap out of the fantasy when I realize the shower head is between my legs, hitting my clit with delicious pressure, and I let out a moan, pulling it away.

This is so wrong. He's my boss. I'm in his shower, using the shower head he uses every day, to make myself come. My cheeks heat as I finish showering, trying desperately to ignore the throbbing in my core.

Once I'm done, I step out of the shower, reaching for one of his thick towels. It's soft and fluffy, the fabric clinging to my skin as I wrap it around myself. I hesitate for a moment, looking out into his bedroom. The room smells like him. Cologne, wood, and something familiar. I take a step out of the bathroom, my fingers grazing the dark wood of his desk. There's a stack of papers—some documents I can't make out, some pens, a half-drunk cup of scotch. But it's the bed that pulls me in.

The sheets are soft, white, too perfect. And before I know what I'm doing, my fingers trail over the comforter, and I catch myself wondering if the pillows smell like him. The thought of them, of the way his scent would linger on the fabric, makes my stomach flutter.

I take a seat on his bed, my heart pounding. I imagine him here, in this space. My fingers are still slightly damp from the shower as I slide them over the comforter. I can feel him here, even though he's not.

Before I know it, my head sinks into his pillow, closing my eyes as images of him flood my thoughts. His voice. The way he looks at me. I can't stop it. I picture him standing over me, his hands on my skin, and suddenly, the tension building inside me becomes too much.

My fingers move before I can even think to stop them, slipping under the towel, tracing along my skin. Every thought pulls me deeper, his touch, the look in his eyes. I can't think about anything else as my fingers move closer to the spot aching, begging for attention. The pressure builds, and my body responds to the thoughts swirling in my mind.

God, how long has it been since someone touched me? Liam and I hadn't slept together in a long time—probably since he'd been out fucking someone else—and I only had my own fingers to satiate me. But since moving into Nicholas's penthouse, I haven't dared to touch myself, too aware that I'm in his place, his bed, his room.

But the pressure is too much to ignore, and I let go, imagining him in this bed, his hands on me, his voice in my ear as I lose myself in the fantasy.

A moan spills free from my lips as I circle my clit, feeling how wet I've gotten from a simple fantasy. My towel pulls apart and I widen my legs, keeping my eyes closed, too focused on the pleasure curling up my spine as my fingers move faster, needing the pressure to explode.

You're my fiancée, Amara.

The line between the dream and the real blurs, and I let the moment take over, picturing his dark eyes, his deep voice pushing me further to the edge.

When I shower… and when I fuck.

Oh, god, I'm gonna—

"*Don't stop.*"

The deep voice shocks me, and at first I think it's fantasy Nicholas talking me through the orgasm, but my fingers freeze as I open my eyes. My heart stops when I see my boss standing at the door, his eyes narrowed at the sight of me laying in his bed.

Naked.

Wet.

And playing with my pussy.

CHAPTER NINETEEN
Nicholas

"**D**on't you dare fucking stop, Amara."
My voice is rough, my eyes narrowing at the sight of her fiery orange hair sprawled across my pillows, a white fluffy towel underneath her, and my ring glinting on her finger as she teases her sweet little clit.

Fuck. Me.

I can't breathe, my cock painfully hard beneath my pants, straining against the fabric as it throbs at the sight of her.

I lift my gaze to hers seeing the panic coursing through her eyes as she lifts her hands from between her thick thighs, attempting to grab the towel and shield herself.

Too fucking late.

"Where do you think you're going?" I ask, the towel slipping away from her grasp. I watch, mesmerized, as the flush spreading across her cheeks tells me she was painfully close to coming on my bed.

She gulps, shaking her head as she tries to sit up, attempting to cover herself once again. No chance of that. I've already seen all of her. And fuck, I want to see more. I want to memorize every inch of her, trace every freckle, every stretch mark. I want to devour her like an art piece.

"I—"

I lean forward, my hand landing beside her thighs, my body hovering dangerously close to hers. "You came into my bedroom. You laid yourself out on my bed and started to touch your pussy." I can hear her heartbeat in the air between us, hammering as my words work echo between us. "And now you're going to finish what you started."

Her breath hitches, and her fingers tremble, torn between covering herself and returning to where they were just seconds ago.

Her chest rises as she breathes hard. "I didn't mean— I thought—"

"I know what you thought," I say, the scent of her sweet cunt traveling to my nose, making my mouth water. I fight to keep my eyes locked on hers. "You thought I wouldn't be home. Thought no one would find out how you like to play with your needy pussy in my bed."

Her lips part, her breaths growing heavier.

"Tell me, Amara. Do you do this often?"

She swallows, shaking her head as she attempts to cover herself again. I tilt my head, studying her.

"Was your pretty little clit throbbing, honey? Were you burning with need, unable to take it anymore?"

She nods before biting her lip, a soft moan escaping her throat.

The sound goes straight to my cock. *God*, she's breathtaking. I can't stop myself from leaning in closer, inhaling deeply as her scent surrounds me—sweet, intoxicating, a blend of my body wash and her natural heat. I drink it all in, letting it consume me. I run my eyes down her body, savoring every inch of her soft skin, the curve of her hips, the swell of her breasts. I want to memorize every single detail.

"I'm here now," I say, my voice a rasp, thick with pure fucking hunger. "And I want to watch you."

Her pupils dilate, darkening those mesmerizing green eyes. A shiver runs through her body, goosebumps rising on her flushed skin as she hesitates. I take a step back, pulling out my desk chair and sitting across from her. I haven't felt the touch of anyone except my own hand for far too long so I can only imagine how much she needs to let go.

"Part your legs for me," I command, my voice growing deeper as my cock hardens. "Show me that sweet cunt."

Her breath catches in her throat, as her hands slowly drift back between her thighs. I can't take my eyes off her fingers, the way they hover over her wetness, teasing herself so softly it's almost unbearable.

My cock twitches in my pants as I watch her touch herself, her fingers circling her clit. My eyes lock on her ring, glistening as she moves. Each small stroke is torture, but it's also the most beautiful thing I've ever seen.

Fucking stay in your chair.

This isn't about me. Not right now.

"That's it," I encourage her. "Show me how my fiancée touches herself when she thinks no one is around."

Amara lets out a soft gasp at my words, her fingers trembling as they make contact with her sensitive flesh once more. I watch, transfixed, as her movements grow frantic, faster, harder, her eyes fluttering closed.

"Keep your eyes on me," I rasp, the words coming out rough, hoarse with need. "I want you to look at me while you do this."

She obeys, her gaze locking with mine as her fingers pick up speed. A soft moan escapes her lips, and I feel my cock twitch in response.

"Fuck, that's it," I murmur, my voice rough with desire, keeping my eyes fixed on her wet cunt, glistening with her arousal. "You look so beautiful like this, spread wide open for me, drowning in pleasure."

Her back arches slightly off the bed as she continues to pleasure herself, her free hand gripping the sheets tightly. I can see the tension building in her body, her movements becoming more frantic. Her hips start to roll, chasing the sensation of her own touch.

"Tell me what you're thinking about," I urge, wanting to push her to the edge.

She bites her lower lip, hesitating for just a moment before the words tumble out. "You," she admits, stealing the air from my lungs. She swallows as her eyes meet mine, still somehow shy and reserved, despite her being naked on my bed, touching herself. "I'm thinking about your hands on me," she whimpers, her voice driving me to insanity. "I'm imagining it's you touching me like this."

A groan rumbles in my chest at her admission. My hands clench by my side, resisting the urge to replace her fingers with my own.

Not yet.

No. Fuck that. Not at fucking all.

Nothing can happen between us. She's my assistant. I'm her boss. We've got a contract to fulfill and then she'll be out of my life for good.

This is the furthest it can go. Just once. Just to blow off steam, release the tension building between us. We'll go back to normal once this is done. But first, I want to see her come undone by her own hand.

"Keep going," I encourage, trying to push away the desire building inside me. "Show me exactly how you like to be touched."

Amara's fingers move faster, her breath coming in short pants now. Her back arches off the bed and I can see the tension building in her body as her thighs begin to shake.

"Push a finger inside," I tell her. "Fill up that needy, empty hole for me, honey. Make yourself come."

The way her thick thighs rub together as she shifts, the soft swell of her stomach and hips drives me to the brink of insanity as she widens her legs even more and her fingers trail down, circling her pussy before she slowly slides one inside.

"Fuck," I grunt, wanting—needing—to stroke my cock as I feel a spurt of precum in my pants. Fucking hell. This woman has me almost coming in my pants. I push my hand down on my thick erection growing in my pants as I keep my eyes on her, not wanting to miss a single moment.

Her lips part on a delicious soft moan as she thrusts her finger inside her tight, wet hole, and my tongue swipes across my lips when I finally see how pretty and pink she is.

Christ, I want to touch her. I want to drag myself out of this chair and grip her thighs in my hands, spread her pussy lips with my thumbs and bury my face between her legs until I drown in her.

I can *hear* how wet she is every time she pulls out her glistening finger before she thrusts it back inside her. The sounds she makes as she fucks her finger has me gripping onto the leather chair, my jaw ticking, my body hot as fuck.

"Fuck yes," I grunt, my cock throbbing with the need to feel *something*. "Are you close?"

She nods frantically, her eyes never leaving mine. "Yes," she gasps, pulling her finger out, before thrusting it back inside. Again, and again. "I'm so close. Oh god."

Christ, I want to see it. I want to see her flushed skin and her pretty pussy tightening around her finger as she lets go and comes on my bed. "Then come for me," I tell her, licking my lips, wishing I could taste her. "Let me see you fall apart."

With a cry, Amara's body tenses, her back arching off the bed as she orgasms. Her fingers work frantically against her clit as waves of pleasure crash over her. I watch in awe as she comes, her face flushed, and eyes glazed with ecstasy.

Fuck. Fuck. *Fuck*. My cock grows, throbbing in my pants, twitching with the need to come so fucking bad.

I shake my head, trying to keep my control as Amara's body relaxes back onto the bed, her chest heaving as she catches her breath once her orgasm subsides. I can't take my eyes off her, drinking in every detail of her post-orgasmic glow.

She looks so beautiful, so perfect. My hands twitch, wanting to approach her, wanting to press my lips to her body, to touch her.

I clench my hands into a fist.

I fucking can't.

Lifting myself out of my chair, I hover over her, watching her, ingraining this into my memory. I can smell her, can almost fucking taste her on my tongue, and goddamn I need to do just that before I lose my mind.

Gripping her hand—the same one that's hovering between her legs—I lift it up, bringing her soaked middle finger to my mouth. My jaw ticks as her eyes lock on mine, questioning, wondering what I'm about to do.

The need inside me builds and fucking builds until I can't take it anymore. Closing my mouth over her middle finger, I suck her into my mouth. My cock aches as I let out a groan, my mouth filled with her sweet, heady taste that makes me want to drop to my knees right fucking now.

God damn. This could convert a man. Could make them give their life away and live to serve her.

Amara's soft, pretty moans drive me insane as I swirl my tongue over her finger, sucking her wetness, savoring her taste for as long as I can, because I know… I know that once this moment fades and I leave this room, none of this can happen again.

Pulling her finger out of my mouth, I lick my lips, still tasting her on them and Amara's eyes widen, her breasts heaving as she stares at me.

"Fucking delicious."

I drop her hand, seeing her eyes drift to my cock, which is undoubtedly hard for her, and I let my eyes roam over her again, sweat beading on her forehead, strands of dark orange hair clinging to her face. My jaw clenches, knowing I can never look at her like this again.

I avoid her gaze, turning away and walk out of my room without a word, the door clicking shut behind me. I don't look back as I head for the elevator, pulling out my phone to call my driver.

I need to get the fuck out of here.

CHAPTER TWENTY
Amara

I'm getting uncomfortably used to this bedroom, considering it's the only place I hide whenever Nicholas is home.

Pumpkin scratches at the door, and I sigh, knowing she wants to go to the living room. She's getting too used to hanging around Nicholas, which is weird since she's always hated men. Or maybe it was just Liam.

I sit on the edge of the bed, phone in hand, rereading Jade's text, the pressure in my chest building.

Jade:

> I'm at the club already. You guys need to get your asses out here.

Sophie:

> Henry and I are already in our pajamas having a movie night.

Jade:

> Boooo. Amara, come on. You're my saving grace here.

It would be so easy to go out and try to forget about Nicholas, but it would be no use. The memory of the last few days torments my mind, day and night. It's been almost a week since that day in Nicholas's bedroom, since he watched me, *tasted me*, and then left... like nothing happened.

Since then? Nothing. Not a single call into his office, no rides to work, absolutely nothing. At the office, it's like I'm invisible, just cold, snappy emails that might as well be from a robot. And at home? Even worse. He's hardly ever here, and when he is, he actively avoids me, locking himself away in his office like he's trying to erase me from his life. The thought twists my stomach. Does he regret that night? Does he wish it never happened?

Of course he does. He wouldn't be acting like this if he didn't. And the worst part? I can't stop thinking about it. I can't let it go, no matter how much I try. I can't stop picturing his eyes on me, his deep voice commanding me, his groans as he took my finger in his mouth.

I let out a sigh and type out a reply to Jade's message.

Me:

I'm tired, I think I'll just stay in tonight. Maybe next time.

Jade:

Are you actually tired, or are you fucking your boss?

Sophie:

Jade!

Jade:

What? We're all thinking it.

There's a pause, and then I see Sophie typing.

Sophie:

> I was thinking it. Sorry.

Great. Everyone thinks we're sleeping together, and the minute anything even *remotely* close to that happened, he bolted out of the room like I had a flamethrower aimed at him.

Me:

> None of that is happening. I'm just tired. Pumpkin and I are also having a movie night.

Jade:

> Riiiight. Just remember. Safe sex is great sex.

I throw my phone on the bed with a deep sigh. My stomach rumbles and I'm sick of seeing the same four walls every single day. I need to get out of this room.

I push myself off the bed, heading for the door. As I step into the hallway, I hear the soft clinking of pans. My heart skips a beat. Nicholas is home.

I freeze, my hand gripping the doorknob. For days, I've been avoiding him, pretending like nothing's changed between us, since it's clearly what he wants. But it has. The second we crossed that line, everything shifted.

I take a deep breath, trying to pull myself together. Slowly, I open the door, stepping into the kitchen, and my eyes lock on him the second I do.

He's standing by the stove, wearing a thin gray T-shirt and… sweatpants? I blink, a little stunned. I've never seen him like this. Casual. Relaxed. He's always in a sharp suit, so polished and in control. But now? That confident, authoritative air is gone, replaced by something different. Something that has my pulse speeding up.

I bite my lip, watching him for just a second too long. Then, Pumpkin meows from the doorway, pulling me out of my thoughts. Nicholas glances at the sound, his eyes locking with mine. My breath catches in my throat as he looks me over, his eyes flicking down like he's remembering that day—the one we're actively avoiding talking about.

His lips part, and then my name slips from them. "Amara."

The sound of it makes my whole body tense, reminding me of the moment everything between felt a little too real... before he bolted.

I take a small step forward, trying to steady my breathing.

"Hi," I mumble, my voice quieter than I want it to be. "Sorry. I was hungry, and... I didn't know you cooked."

He doesn't answer right away, but his eyes stay on me, and the silence stretches between us. "I told you, Amara. You don't know me."

I press my lips together. He's right. I don't know him, not really. I thought I did, but now I'm realizing just how wrong I was. I didn't know how dark and intense his eyes could get, how commanding he was, how... dirty his words were.

I shiver at the thought, instinctively pulling my arms around myself. I take another step into the kitchen, lingering near the doorway, unsure of what I'm supposed to do, what I'm supposed to say.

The tension in the air is nearly suffocating, pressing down on me with every breath I take. That day is all I can think about, and I'm doing my best to pretend it never happened. But it did.

No matter how hard I try to ignore it, the memory of him is seared into my mind.

My gaze drifts to him as he grabs his mug, the herbal scent filling the room, and takes a sip. "Are you just going to stand there?"

"I'm thinking."

"Dangerous," he mutters, a slight smirk tugging at the corner of his lips. My brows furrow, hating that he's acting so normal like that day didn't happen, like he didn't leave me naked and alone in his bed.

"You drink tea?" I ask, wanting to move past the awkwardness.

He lifts a shoulder. "At night. Helps me sleep." He flicks his eyes back to the pot, like he can't stand to look at me for any longer. "You're not allergic to anything, are you?"

I shake my head, then take a step closer as he holds up a wooden spoon, offering it to me.

"Here," he says. "Taste this."

I lean in, and close my lips around the spoon, his gaze flickering to mine, lingering for a beat longer than usual.

"It's good," I say, straightening up as I swipe my thumb over my lip to catch any stray sauce. "Could use a bit more salt, though."

His brows furrow. "Really?" He grabs the spoon back, tasting it himself. "I think it's perfect."

I scoff. "And you're an expert all of a sudden?"

His eyes narrow, and I feel the intensity of his gaze all the way through me. "You seem to forget, Amara. I know what tastes good."

The air between us is thick. Too thick. I can't stop replaying that day in my head—the way his mouth closed around my finger, the way he groaned, low and needy.

"Amara." His voice is like a drag of smoke, deep and dangerous, and suddenly, I can't remember my own damn name. His eyes flick down to my lips, my own parting on a gasp, and then—

Everything goes dark.

"What the hell?" I mutter, blinking into the blackness. I can't see a damn thing as I turn my head toward his windows, but the city lights are also out.

Then I hear the click of his phone lighting up, and Nicholas's face glows as he checks it before letting out a sigh. "Power's out," he says, already on the move. "Looks like the whole city's down."

I hear him rummaging around, a drawer opening, the scratch of a match. A tiny flame flickers to life, casting shadows on his face. He lights a candle, then another, and the room fills with warm, flickering light.

"Pasta wasn't cooked yet, so there's no food until the power comes back on," he tells me, lifting his sleeves as he sits at the table.

Great. Because this night wasn't awkward enough.

I sit down on the stool beside him, folding my hands in my lap. Turning my head, I glance at the side of his face, the candlelight dancing across his features. The muscles in his jaw tense, and he turns his head slowly toward me. Our eyes meet, silence stretching between us, and I suck in a breath, unable to stand it anymore.

"Nicholas." His eyes harden. "About that night—"

"Amara," he cuts me off, his voice low, gravelly, and so damn firm it causes a shiver to crawl up my spine.

I know he wants to drop it, avoid the subject altogether. But I'm not doing that anymore. Not after days of silence, of pretending like I haven't been losing my mind over it.

I shake my head, locking eyes with him. "I can't keep pretending it didn't happen."

His jaw tightens, a muscle in his neck twitching like it might snap. "It never should have happened. It was a mistake, Amara. That's all."

A mistake. The word lands like a slap. I should've known it was nothing more than an impulse. But hearing it from him—so cold, so dismissive—it feels like a knife in my chest. I feel the lump in my throat, the anger rising.

I force a tight smile, trying to bury the sting. "Right." My voice breaks a little. "Of course."

I turn, needing to escape the suffocating tension, but before I can get far, his hand catches my wrist, yanking me back to him.

"Amara." His voice drops lower. My pulse quickens, and his fingers tighten around my wrist, pulling me closer to him.

I don't dare look at him. I can't. "Let go of me, Nicholas."

He doesn't let go. His grip tightens, sending a heat through me that I hate myself for feeling. "Amara." He says my name again, like it's some kind of curse. His voice is tight now, strained, like he's holding back. "Fuck. You don't get it. I can't—We can't—"

"I get it, Nicholas," I cut in, the words tumbling out too fast. "You're not attracted to me. You were caught up in the moment, and now you regret it." I swallow the rejection down, tugging my wrist from his grasp. "Now let me go." I yank my arm away from him, my feet carrying me toward my room. It's dark, and cold in there. But I need to get away from him.

"What? What the hell are you talking about?" he calls from behind me, but I keep walking straight ahead.

"Amara," his voice rises, and I squeeze my eyes closed, wanting to bury myself in my bed and erase this whole damn night.

"Amara, come here."

I don't turn around. My steps quicken as I near my bedroom door, my hand reaching for the handle.

"Fuck," he groans, his voice dripping with frustration. "I think about you."

I freeze, my hand just inches from the door, my heart hammering. Nicholas lets out a harsh breath behind me. I want to turn and look at him, but I also want him to keep going.

"I think about you," he repeats. "Every day. Every night." My pulse spikes. "At work. At home. In the shower. In my bed. It doesn't matter when or where; you're in my head. All fucking day."

I gasp quietly, my lips parting at his confession, his footsteps the only sound between us as he moves closer.

"I've thought about that day more than I want to admit," he continues, his voice growing closer with each step. "More than anything else."

My fingers grip the door handle as his breath brushes against my neck.

"I think about it every damn day," he murmurs, his hands finding my hips. Before I can even process, he spins me around and his eyes lock onto mine.

"How the hell could you think I'm not attracted to you?" His voice is low as he presses against me, something hard brushing my stomach.

I stare up at him, letting out a gasp. He curses under his breath, rough and jagged, his eyes closing for a moment as he breathes in sharply.

And then he steps back, his hands dropping from me, frustration painting his features. "Fuck," he mutters, running a hand through his hair. "I shouldn't have done that." He sighs. "I shouldn't have watched you that day. I shouldn't have touched you. You're my assistant, Amara. I'm *paying* you to pretend to be my fiancée, so I can secure this deal. I moved you into my apartment. Made you touch yourself for me." His voice falters as if the words themselves cut him. "I shouldn't have done any of it. I should have turned the fuck away and left you alone."

His eyes are filled with sympathy, guilt swirling in them, but something about the way he looks at me only makes my desire for him grow hotter. He never once said he regretted it, never once said he didn't want it to happen.

"I shouldn't have climbed into your bed and touched myself."

"Fuck," he mutters, closing his eyes, his face tight. "Please. Don't bring that up right now."

I shake my head, stepping closer, my heart hammering in my chest as I close the gap between us. "There's nothing in the contract that says anything about us."

His brows furrow, confusion flashing in his gaze. "What?"

"You said we couldn't have any outside relationships," I remind him, my body burning. "But there's nothing in there about us. Nothing in there saying we can't..." My words trail off, letting him fill in the blanks.

A breath leaves him, his eyes darkening with something that makes my pulse race. "You checked."

It's not a question. It's a statement. Heat floods to my face, tinting my cheeks with red, which I know he can see.

"Why did you look it up?" he asks, his voice rough as he moves toward me, closing the space between us. His gaze burns into mine under the flickering candlelight. "Hmm?"

I suck in a breath, my heart racing from the intensity of his stare. I can't speak. The words lodge in my throat.

"Did you want it to happen?" he presses, his voice hushed but commanding. "Did you want me to find you naked and horny on my bed?" His eyes narrow, like he's daring me to lie.

I can hardly breathe under his intense gaze, my body trembling. "Yes," I whisper, the word slipping out before I can stop it.

"Fuck." His voice is strained as he steps closer. His hand moves to my hip, his fingers brushing the soft fabric of my sweater. The moment his skin touches mine, my whole body shivers.

"We can't," he murmurs, his breath hot against my skin. "This... this isn't right."

I tilt my head slightly, looking up at him, trying to keep my voice steady despite the pounding in my chest. "Why not?"

He doesn't answer right away. His eyes flicker with something close to pain, like he's caught in a battle inside his mind. I take a step closer to him, and his hand grips my hip a little tighter, the heat from his palm searing through the layers of clothes.

"You were hard earlier," I whisper. "I felt it."

His eyes flash, and I swear I see something dark flicker in them, but then he's back to his usual controlled self. "Amara," he warns, his voice low and taut, the kind of sound that sends a shiver up my spine.

"Were you thinking about it?" I press, my throat dry. "Thinking about me?"

He inhales sharply, his jaw clenched. "I told you, I can't *stop* thinking about it. About you lying in my bed, naked… *Fuck*." He grunts under his breath, and I almost wish I hadn't pushed him so far, but I can't stop now. I want to know. I need to know.

I slide my hands up his t-shirt, feeling the soft fabric stretch over the muscles of his chest, and wrap my hands around his neck, keeping my gaze locked on his. "Do you regret it?" I ask. The question slips out before I can stop it, and I brace myself for the answer.

He steps forward, his chest brushing against mine. His hand slides around my back, pulling me in closer, his body heat making everything else fade away. "You're the last thing I could ever regret."

Before I can process his words, his lips are on mine, quick and hungry… *urgent*. I melt into him, my hands still resting on his chest, feeling the rise and fall of his breath through the fabric of his shirt. His hands slide down to my hips, pulling me closer, like he can't get enough, I reply by pressing against him, every inch of me craving him.

"God, how do you taste even sweeter than the last time I kissed you?"

A soft moan slips from my throat as his hands slide down to my waist, pulling me closer. His body is solid against mine, and I feel the heat radiating off him, my skin burning where we touch. His lips trail fire along my jaw, then down to my neck, making every nerve in my body light up.

"You're driving me crazy," he mutters, his voice rough. His fingers tug at the hem of my sweater, brushing the skin of my waist, and I can't stop the shiver that runs through me. "Tell me, Amara. Tell me you want this too."

"I do," I breathe. "I want all of you."

His groan vibrates against my lips, raw and needy, and his hands slide up my back, pushing my sweater higher. I melt into him, every part of me aching for more, for him. It's like he knows exactly how to touch me, to make me lose my mind.

"You're so damn beautiful," he murmurs against my lips, his hands framing my face, glancing down at me with a shake of his head. "These fucking sweaters you wear all the damn time drive me crazy. All I want to do is rip them off and see what's underneath."

My heart stutters at his words. Before I can respond, his lips capture mine, pulling me under until I'm lost in him completely. The cool press of the kitchen island against my back jolts a gasp from my throat. I don't know how we ended up back here, and I don't care. All I can feel is him, his touch, his heat, drowning out everything else. His hands roam under my sweater, mapping every curve of my body. He presses closer, his warmth surrounding me, his fingers brushing the edge of my bra. When his palm cups my side, just under the swell of my breast, my pulse stutters.

Alarms ring in my head. He's feeling my skin, soft and pudgy, covered in stretch marks, and I stiffen, knowing I look nothing like the women he's been with in the past.

"You feel incredible," he murmurs, groaning against my neck before his lips trail to the hollow of my collarbone, pausing as his breath fans over my skin as if he's savoring the moment. "Fuck, I should stop." He groans against my skin, his tongue licking a path. "But I don't want to."

For a moment, his words make me falter. The lingering doubts creep in, uninvited. Whispers reminding me of every imperfection I have, everything I've kept hidden from everyone. Everything my ex didn't like. My hands still against his chest, my breath hitching.

He notices immediately. His hands move to cradle my face, his thumbs stroking softly along my jaw as he leans in close. "Don't," he grits out, as if he can read my mind. His hand slides up to cup my cheek, tilting my face so I'm forced to meet his gaze. "Don't you dare hide from me."

"I just…" I pause, my eyes dropping from his. "What if I'm not what you're expecting? What if…" My words trail off, and I shake my head, not even sure how to explain the knot of fear tightening in my chest.

A flicker of something crosses his face. "You forget," he adds with a smirk, "I've already seen you spread out bare for me." His eyes darken. "And I loved every second of it."

Heat rushes to my face at the memory of Nicholas seeing me so exposed. My body reacts without warning, warmth flooding my skin at the thought of it.

"You don't have to hide from me, Amara. Not now. Not ever." He brushes his lips over mine, before pulling back just enough to whisper, "Let me show you just how much I want you."

The certainty in his voice shatters the last of my doubts, and I can feel the heat building between us. Slowly, he moves, his hands tracing the familiar curves of my body, his lips leaving a trail of fire along my neck and collarbone. In one smooth motion, he pulls my sweater over my head.

His eyes darken, taking in every inch of me, before his hands move to the clasp of my bra. He undoes it effortlessly, the fabric falling away, and my breasts spill free, exposed to him. A breath hitches in my throat as his gaze lands on me, a deep, possessive hunger in his eyes that sends a thrill through me.

"You're incredible," he murmurs against my skin, his hands sliding to my hips, gripping me tighter. "Every inch of you is perfect to me, exactly the way you are. And I'll prove it to you all night if I have to."

My breath catches, my body aching for him. "Then don't stop," I whisper, pulling him closer.

Something dark flashes in his eyes, his lips twitching into a grin as his fingers skim the waistband of my jeans. He leans in, lips brushing my ear, his breath hot against my skin. "Wasn't planning on it."

I can't think, let alone speak. My hands tangle in his hair, pulling him closer, desperate for more. My fingers find the hem of his shirt, lifting it slowly until he wrenches it off, our lips parting for one agonizing second before the fabric is tossed aside. My body arches into his, silently begging for his touch. He answers instantly, his mouth crashing back into mine. The kiss deepens, his tongue sliding skillfully against mine, leaving me breathless.

My hands slide to his bare chest exploring the hard lines of his stomach.

His breath catches, and he flashes me a grin. "Careful, honey," he teases. "I'm trying to take this slow, but if you keep that up, I'm not going to be able to hold back."

"Who said I want you to go slow?" I challenge.

His grin widens, a rumbly laugh escaping him. "You really don't know what you're asking for." His hands tighten on my hips, his thumbs tracing slow, maddening circles against my skin, the cool air hitting me as his hands travel lower, pushing my pants, exposing more of me.

Before I can respond, he lifts me effortlessly, placing me on the kitchen island before kneeling in front of me, and my breath catches at the sight. The only thing separating us is my cotton panties—and the ache between my legs for him.

"You're stunning," he whispers, his eyes locking onto the fabric, dark with admiration and raw want. His grip on my thighs tightens like he can't get enough of me. "Every. Single. Inch."

His lips brush against my stomach, kissing the soft skin as he trails lower, teasing me with what's to come. I know he can see every roll on my belly, every stretch mark, but the way he kisses me, groaning against my skin, has me forgetting all about it, breath hitching in anticipation.

His lips travel lower, and I feel the heat of his breath before he presses the softest kiss right over my panties, making my whole body jolt. My hands find his shoulders, anchoring me to him as I fight to catch my breath.

"You don't have to—" I start, but he cuts me off with a kiss to my inner thigh.

"Believe me when I say," he murmurs, his voice dark and commanding, his hands pushing my legs wider, "I fucking want to."

CHAPTER TWENTY-ONE
Nicholas

I've fucked a lot.

Throughout the years, I've had my fair share of women. I love the chase, love the feel of a tight, pink pussy stretching around my cock, legs wrapped around my waist. And tits. Fuck, I love tits. Small, big, perky, heavy, I didn't care, as long as they were in my hands or my mouth.

But since signing that contract, I haven't even looked at another woman, let alone touched one. And right now? Right now, it's like I've never touched a woman in my life. My cock is straining against my pants, harder than it's ever been.

I've never wanted anyone like I want her. Never in a million years thought this would happen. And yet, here she is. Laid out for me, her legs parted just enough to make my mouth water.

I press my face to the soft skin of her inner thigh, breathing her in. She smells warm, intoxicating, like everything I've ever craved but never had.

My hand slides up her thigh, my thumb grazing the edge of her panties. The heat radiating from her is unbearable, and my cock throbs with the need to sink into her, to make her mine. Slowly, I hook my finger under the cotton and pull it aside.

She's beautiful. Wet, pink, and perfect in every way.

My tongue drags over my bottom lip as I take her in. I need her. Need to taste her, ruin her, claim her in ways that will make her forget anything that isn't me.

A low groan rumbles in my throat as my fingers trace her seam, slick heat coating my skin. She shivers beneath my touch, her body soft, pliant, and so damn eager. I dip lower, circling her clit with slow strokes, my cock throbbing in time with every soft sound spilling from her lips.

"You want me to eat this pretty pussy, honey?" My voice is rough, gravelly, the words dragging from deep in my chest. My fingers tease her, stroking just enough to make her gasp but not enough to give her what she needs.

Her body jerks, her hips tilting up as if begging for more. Her breathing quickens, and her cheeks flush a deep, beautiful red. She nods, frantic, but that's not good enough for me.

"Words, Amara," I coax. I need to hear her say it, to beg for it. "Tell me what you want."

Her lips part, her eyes fluttering shut as a shaky whimper escapes her. "I... want—" Her voice cuts off with a sharp inhale when I press my thumb harder against her clit, drawing slow, torturous circles that have her shaking with anticipation.

"Want what?" I push, my thumb never relenting. "I can't give it to you if you don't tell me."

Another sweet moan spills from her lips, and it takes everything in me not to dive in and devour her. But I wait. I want her uninhibited, stripped of any hesitation, free to feel and say everything she's holding back.

"Your mouth," she finally breathes, her voice shaky, her cheeks burning. "I want your mouth."

I hum against her skin, letting my lips brush the soft curve of her thigh. "You want my mouth... here?"

She shakes her head, her frustration deliciously obvious.

"No?" I murmur, letting my lips trail closer to her glistening heat. I press a kiss against the thickest part of her inner thigh, just shy of where she needs me most. "Then… here?"

Her whimper is pure desperation, her hips bucking, seeking relief. I grin against her skin, the sound of her frustration only fueling me further.

Her thighs clamp around my head, caging me in as she seeks relief from my teasing. The pressure is intoxicating, and a groan rumbles from my chest at the thought of her cutting off my air with those thick, perfect thighs. *What a way to go.*

Gripping her thighs firmly, I wrench them apart. My gaze flicks up to her flushed face, her lips parted, her eyes hazy with need. She's breathtaking. "Tell me what you want," I murmur, my voice dropping to a low whisper as I press a featherlight kiss to her knee. "I'll give it to you, Amara. All of it. You just have to say it."

Her chest heaves, her breath hitching in her throat as her gaze locks with mine. "I want…" she starts. "I want you to touch me."

My cock pulses painfully at her words, her raw honesty hitting harder than any touch could. "Like this?" I ask, dragging my fingers along her soft pussy.

"Yes," she breathes, before she gasps, louder this time. "More. Please, Nicholas."

Hearing my name fall from her lips, needy and desperate, sends a bolt of heat through me. I'm so close to losing control, but I hold on, savoring every second of her unraveling.

"Keep talking, honey," I demand. "Tell me everything you want. I'm not stopping until you do."

Her breathing stutters as my fingers continue their slow, torturous strokes, circling her clit in a rhythm that keeps her teetering just on the edge.

She's trembling, her breath coming in ragged gasps, a broken whimper slipping free. "Nicholas... please."

"Please, what?" I murmur, my lips hovering over her. She shivers as my breath ghosts over her skin. "Be specific. I need to know exactly how you want me to ruin you."

Her face flushes a deep crimson, but her desire burns hotter than her embarrassment. "I want... your mouth," she gasps, her voice breaking as my thumb presses harder against her swollen clit. "I want you to taste me. Please, Nicholas, I want you to lick my pussy."

"That's more like it," I praise. "Such a good girl when you finally use your words."

Hooking my fingers into the hem of her panties, I tug them down slowly, savoring every inch of her revealed to me. Her thighs part instinctively, and the sight of her—bare, glistening, and so beautifully vulnerable—has a groan rumbling deep in my chest.

"So damn pretty when you're dripping for me," I murmur, my voice thick with hunger. I drag my tongue over my bottom lip, dying to taste her. "I bet you taste even better."

A shiver wracks through her, her lips parting on a sharp inhale. She's practically vibrating beneath my hands, and I haven't even started.

A soft, broken whimper escapes her throat as I lean in, and press my tongue flat against her, groaning at the intoxicating taste of her slick heat. Her fingers tangle in my hair, tugging hard as her hips buck against my face. The needy, breathless moan that spills from her lips is music to my ears, and I want more.

"Stay still, baby," I command, my voice vibrating against her skin. "I'm hungry."

My tongue circles her clit, alternating between firm flicks and slow kisses. Her thighs quiver around my head, her soft cries growing louder with every pass of my tongue. Each whimper, every plea, only makes me hungrier, my grip on her thighs tightening as I feast on her.

"You taste so fucking good," I rasp between licks, my cock rock hard. "I could stay down here all night. I'd happily lick this sweet cunt until you forget your own name."

Her thighs shake, her body tightening as she teeters on the edge of release. "Nicholas, I—" Her voice breaks, a desperate sob of pleasure. "Oh god… I'm going to—"

"Come for me," I rasp against her, my words pushing her over the edge. "Let me feel you fall apart."

Her body arches against me, her climax ripping through her as she cries out my name. I hold her steady, my tongue never relenting, working her through every pulse, every shudder. I savor her, drinking in her pleasure like a man starved.

When she finally collapses, breathless and boneless, I pull back just enough to meet her gaze. My face is damp with her orgasm, and I can't help but grin.

"Holy shit," I murmur, brushing a hand over my jaw as I take in her blissed-out expression. "You needed that, didn't you?"

Her flushed cheeks and glazed eyes say everything, but she still manages a breathless, "Yes."

I hum, gripping her thigh. "He didn't take care of you properly, did he?" I ask, reveling in the fact her shitty ex-boyfriend never made her feel like this. "No one's ever made you feel this good," I murmur pressing another soft kiss to her thigh. "No one's ever taken their time to worship this gorgeous body, have they, honey?"

She bites her bottom lip, shaking her head, and fuck if that doesn't send a surge of possessiveness through me. The idea of anyone not cherishing every inch of her infuriates me—but it also ignites something primal inside me.

Her blush deepens as her gaze meets mine. "Not like you."

"Good." I rise to my feet, cupping her face in my hands. "Because we're not done yet."

Her breathing hitches, lips parting in a desperate gasp as tug down my sweatpants, along with my boxers in a single motion. Her eyes widen at the sight, a deep blush creeping across her skin.

I pull back slightly, my eyes scanning her face, breath coming fast. "I don't have any condoms," I admit. "I don't bring girls here."

Her eyes drop to my hard cock, standing at attention for her. "I always used condoms with Liam."

The name brings a sharp sting, the anger bubbling inside me. Hate hearing his fucking name from her lips. I want her to remember no one but me.

I grip her thighs tighter, spreading them wider as I press her back against the cool surface of the kitchen island. "You want me to fuck you bare?" I ask, teasing her slick, soaked cunt with the head of my cock. "You want to feel my cock inside of you with no barriers?" The sight of her like this—flushed, needy, utterly at my mercy—fuels every raw, possessive urge burning through me.

She looks at me, a faint flush spreading across her cheeks. "Yes."

"You're soaked for me, Amara," I groan, running the tip of my cock through her cunt, gathering the evidence of her need for me. "Look at this mess. I want every drop of it." I lean closer, my breath warm against her ear. "You want this? You want me to fill you, stretch you wide around me?"

"Yes," she breathes, her voice breaking on the word, desperate and pleading. "Please."

I want to sink into her, to feel her tight, wet heat pulling me in, but I hold back, my jaw tight as I grip her hips. "I'm not going to make love to you, Amara," I warn, my tone low and edged with hunger. "And I'm not just going to fuck you."

Her breath catches, her wide eyes locking onto mine, anticipation and need warring in her expression.

"I'm going to own you," I murmur, my voice thick with promise. "Every moan. Every whimper. Every inch of this body belongs to me tonight."

A shiver courses through her, and I feel the way her body responds to my words, how her thighs quiver, how her breath hitches, how her need presses against me.

"Do you want that, honey?" I murmur, my cock sliding between her wet, eager pussy, teasing her clit. "To be mine? To let go and let me take care of every single one of your needs?"

She nods, her hips bucking against me.

"Use your words," I demand. "Say it for me."

"I want to be yours," she whispers. "I want you to own me."

"That's my good girl." My praise is rough, my voice thick with approval, and I see how her body responds, arching, craving more. "I'll pleasure you, make you feel so fucking good, but in return you'll do exactly what I say and follow my instructions. Understand?"

She nods eagerly, but I grip her chin, tilting her face so she can't look away.

"Words, Amara."

"Yes, Nicholas," she breathes, her voice shuddering with need. "I understand."

I press forward slowly, letting her feel every inch as I begin to push inside her. Her body resists for a moment, tight and scorching hot, and the sensation of her tight pussy nearly undoes me. Her nails dig into my shoulders, her eyes squeezing shut as she gasps.

"Holy shit. You're so big," she whimpers, breathless. "I—I don't know if—"

"It'll fit. You'll take every inch of me. I'll make sure of it."

Her hips tilt up instinctively, seeking more even as she shudders beneath me. I reward her bravery with a slow thrust, sinking deeper, the stretch pulling a cry of pleasure from her lips. "That's it," I grunt. "This is yours. It's all yours. *Take it*."

Her breathless moans spur me on. Each stroke has her arching into me, her body gripping me tighter, the sound of her wet pussy filling the room.

"Fuck, you feel like heaven already," I groan, brushing her hair back to see her face. "Goddamn, I'm addicted." Her moans grow louder as I grip her face, running my thumb over her swollen bottom lip. "I'm fucking addicted to you."

I needed this—needed her—and *Christ*, this is a mess of complications and mistakes I never make. But I'd do it all again just to have her like this.

"Never had such good... *fuck*." I thrust deeper, her tight heat wrapping around me like a vice. She's so wet, her slick cunt coating my cock.

Her hands clutch my arm as I hold myself inside her, savoring the way her body flutters around me. Then I pull back and slam into her again, her cry echoing in the room.

Her nails dig into my skin, and the urge to completely claim her burns through me. I want her restrained, her hands tied behind her back, waiting for my command. I want her on her knees, looking up at me with those wide, trusting eyes. I want my hand wrapped around her pretty little throat.

But something tells me sweet, innocent Amara isn't ready for that... yet.

"Nicholas," she moans, tipping her head back. "I'm so close."

"That's it," I coax. "Come on my cock. Let me feel you."

My thumb finds her swollen clit, circling it in time with my thrusts. Her moans grow louder, her legs stretching out straight as her orgasm crashes into her. She clenches around me, her release flooding my cock, and I groan, my body losing control.

"Oh fuck," I grunt, thrusting faster as my own orgasm overtakes me. "Take it all, baby. Every fucking drop."

I empty inside her, the sensation so overwhelming I can barely see straight. My thrusts slow as the aftershocks ripple through me, her body still trembling in my arms.

I pull out carefully, watching as my cum spills from her, slick and glistening. The sight sends a surge of possessive satisfaction through me, my breeding kink roaring to life.

"Holy shit," I mutter, running a hand over my face.

Amara's face is flushed, her body spent, but her eyes glaze over with exhaustion and satisfaction as she hops down onto the floor, her hands pressed against my chest.

I'm not done, though. I want more. I want all of her, everything she has to give. My tongue runs over my bottom lip, my body burning with a deep need for her.

"If you can still walk, then we're not fucking finished."

Sliding my hands under her ass, I lift her effortlessly into my arms.

"Oh my God, Nicholas, what are you doing? Put me down!" she squeals, her voice laced with disbelief. "I'm too heavy—you're going to hurt yourself!"

"Heavy?" I laugh, pressing a kiss to her temple. "Honey, I bench more than this before breakfast."

"I'm serious. Put me—"

A sharp, unexpected slap to her ass makes her gasp, and I can't help the satisfaction that rushes through me. "Don't argue," I warn. "We both know you'll lose."

"Where are you taking me?"

"We're not done yet," I say, pushing the bedroom door open. "I want to make you come again."

And again. And again. Making her come has become my favorite new pastime. And I know exactly how I want to do it.

I place her down gently on the ground before lying back on the bed, licking my lips. "Come here."

Hesitantly, she kneels on the bed, crawling toward me, her expression a mix of confusion and desire. I curl my hand around my cock, feeling it harden at the sight of her body—soft curves and round edges. Fuck, she's beautiful.

"Sit on my face, Amara."

Her eyes widen, the shock and arousal flashing across her face. "Excuse me?"

"I want you to ride my face," I rasp, my hands reaching up to grip her thighs, pulling her closer. "I want you to come all over my tongue. Let me taste every inch of you."

She glances down at herself, a mix of hesitation and desire in her eyes. "But I'm... I'm full of your cum."

I lift myself up, grabbing her and pulling her onto me. I widen her legs, positioning her to straddle my face. She gasps, her eyes locked on mine as she hesitates, uncertainty flickering in her gaze.

"Sit, baby," I command, tapping my mouth. "Right here."

She sucks in a breath as she glances down at herself. "My ass is big."

"I'm aware," I reply with a chuckle, squeezing her full ass cheek in my hand, loving every inch of her.

"My thighs are thick, Nicholas. I'll crush you."

I smirk, tightening my grip. "The thicker the thighs, the sweeter the prize."

She blushes, the flush spreading across her skin, and it makes my cock twitch with anticipation as I pull her down further. "Now lower that sweet cunt onto my mouth, Amara. I'm dying for it. I'll gladly die if it means tasting your pussy. Grab onto the headboard and ride my face."

A needy moan escapes her as she finally surrenders, her thighs clamped on either side of my head. She moves against me, the heat and slick pressure grinding into my tongue, and it's pure perfection.

Her hands leave my hair, gripping the headboard above her as she steadies herself, her body now completely in my control. Her pussy is drenched with her arousal and my cum, and I lap at her relentlessly, drinking her in. She anchors herself, the movement of her hips becoming more urgent, every shudder, every breath, telling me she's on the edge.

"Oh god. That feels… Don't stop," she moans, encouraging me to continue.

I grip her hips tighter, pulling her closer, my mouth closing around her as I kiss her clit, sucking gently at first before letting my tongue flick over it, teasing, tasting. I make love to it with my mouth, desperate, starving for the taste of her, every movement driven by the need to make her come.

"Fuck, I love eating your pussy," I murmur against her, my voice rough with hunger.

Her body shivers above me, her breath coming in sharp gasps, and I feel the tension building in her, the way her thighs quiver as she rides my face, unable to hold back. I slide my tongue deeper, the pressure building. "Come for me, Amara. I want to feel you come all over my tongue. Let me taste every drop."

Her cries fill the room, a mix of pleasure and desperation, as she shatters once more, her body convulsing in the sweetest release. "Fuck yes," I groan, savoring the way she clings to me, every muscle in her body shaking as she gives in to me completely.

When she finally collapses against me, breathless and dazed, I press one last lingering kiss to her swollen flesh, my lips brushing gently over her sensitive skin.

Gripping her hips, I lift her from my face, dragging her down my body, her ass grazing against my hard cock, sending a jolt of desire through me. "Don't get comfortable yet. I want to fuck you again."

She swallows, her eyes flicking down to my hard cock and grinds her ass against it, forcing a groan from my throat.

"You want that?" I ask.

She answers without words, lifting her ass slightly. She grips my cock in her fist and positions it just right before slowly lowering herself onto me.

I groan as the heat of her pussy surrounds me, my hands tightening on her hips, guiding her down. I feel the stretch, the way she adjusts to me, and I can't hold back. The sensation of her tight, slick pussy is almost too much to bear.

"Ride me, honey," I grunt, thrusting up into her. "Show me how much you need me."

"Nicholas," she moans as her hips begin to move, slow at first, tentative. I watch her, mesmerized by the way her body reacts, the way she rides me, inch by inch, her eyes locked on mine.

I reach up, my hands gripping her hips, guiding her down harder, faster. Her moans fill the room, and I can't get enough. I want her to feel every inch of me, want her to come again.

"I can feel you tightening around me. You're going to come again, aren't you?"

She nods, her tits bouncing as she rides my cock, her hands pressed against my chest. I'd pay good money to have this sight on a canvas.

"Let go," I urge her. "Let me feel you."

Her body convulses above me, her cunt clenching around me as she shatters, her orgasm rippling through her. I hold her tightly, my own release exploding as I feel her tighten around me.

When she finally collapses onto me, completely spent, I hold her close, my fingers running through her hair.

"You did so good for me," I murmur, pressing a soft kiss to her forehead. "So fucking good. I'm so proud of you, Amara."

She lets out a small laugh, breathless and shaky. "Proud of me? For what?"

"For trusting me," I say as I meet her gaze. "For letting me take care of you."

Her cheeks flush, and she looks away, but I don't let her hide. I tilt her chin up, so she has no choice but to look at me.

"You were amazing, Amara," I praise, seeing her eyes light up. "I want you to know that."

She nods, her lips pressing together, and I let out a breath, closing my eyes as I pull her into me.

This was a line I told myself I'd never cross, but now there's no turning back.

And I don't regret it at all.

CHAPTER TWENTY-TWO

Nicholas

I've never been the type of guy who stays in bed once my alarm rings. It's a waste of time. Lying here, doing nothing while I could be knocking things off my to-do list makes my mind race.

But today? I'm almost willing to make an exception.

Because if this is the view that greets me every morning, maybe I can learn to enjoy staying in bed for a little longer.

A slow, satisfied smirk tugs at my lips as I look down at Amara. She's sprawled across my bed, her dark orange hair spread out on my pillows, completely bare. I can't take my eyes off her. The sheet only just covers her, leaving just enough to drive me crazy, teasing me with the curve of her hips.

I let my fingers trail lightly over her skin, tracing the outline of her jaw, the curve of her cheek. It's soft—so soft—and I can't help but revel in the sensation. I've never had a woman in my bed. Never had a woman stay over. She's the only exception. The first and last.

Last night was incredible... She was incredible, and the urge to do it again hits me like a tidal wave. My body reacts instantly, my cock hardening at the thought.

I try to ignore it, leaning down to press a quick kiss to her lips. They're plump and pink, so inviting, like fresh cherries. As I pull back, I feel her stir beneath me. She hums softly, shifting closer, her body finding mine instinctively.

Just as I'm about to kiss her again, I hear the unmistakable sound of little paws padding across the floor, a soft click of a door opening, followed by the familiar pitter-patter that can only mean Pumpkin's here to ruin my moment. Either that, or she's here to attack me for stealing away her owner.

I glance down at Pumpkin, who's now jumped onto the bed, purring like she owns the damn place. I narrow my eyes at her. "She's not yours anymore," I mutter under my breath.

The little furball blinks at me, before letting out a low meow.

I roll my eyes. "Fine. How about we share her?"

Pumpkin responds with a soft purr, as she curls up on Amara's head, licking her face. Damn cat is kissing my woman. Amara's eyes flutter open and she blinks at me in confusion. Realization hits her a few seconds later, her lips tugging into a smile as the memory of last night floods back.

I can't help but chuckle, leaning down to press a kiss against her lips. "Morning, honey."

"Morning," she rasps, her voice thick with sleep, and *god damn*, it makes everything inside me tighten. I want to stay in this moment, right here with her, but reality is a bitch. I've got an office to get to, phone calls, meetings. But Amara... This woman... She makes everything else seem irrelevant.

I groan, pulling her face up to mine again, my lips crashing into hers. My cock stirs, needy and desperate. She responds with a soft moan, her legs parting instinctively, giving me room. Pumpkin jumps onto the floor, and I grin as I kiss her harder.

I win. She's mine now. Pumpkin: 0, Nicholas: 1.

"Nicholas," she breathes, her hands pushing gently against my chest, breaking the kiss. Her green eyes meet mine, wide and unsure. "What happened last night?"

I arch an eyebrow, a teasing grin curling my lips. "I know I fucked you hard, but didn't realize I'd given you amnesia."

She squints, shaking her head, her expression confused. "No, I remember," she says, her cheeks coating with a delicious shade of pink. "I mean... What does this mean... for *us*?"

Ah. The dreaded talk. I roll off her, releasing a long breath as I try to gather my thoughts.

I wasn't planning on any of this. I just wanted her. *God*, did I want her. And last night, she was right there, telling me she wanted me too. I let go of my control just enough to indulge in what was in front of me without thinking about the consequences.

But now? Now, I'm not sure what to do with all this.

I sit up and look at her, her green eyes wide with uncertainty, waiting for me to put this mess into words.

"The contract ends in two months," I begin, running a hand through my hair. "It wouldn't be smart to... start something. I'm not even sure I want a relationship. Ever. And I don't think you're in the right headspace for something serious, not so soon after..." I stop, my throat tightening at the thought, unwilling to say his name.

She relaxes, her shoulders dropping slightly as if she's been holding her breath. I exhale, relieved that at least we're on the same page.

"We both want each other. That much is obvious. And since the contract says we can't date anyone else, and everyone already thinks we're together..." I shrug. "I say we keep going."

"Keep going?" she repeats, her eyes searching mine for clarity. "For how long?"

"Just until the deal's finalized. After that, we go our separate ways."

I watch as she processes my words. Finally, she nods slowly. "Two months."

A smile tugs at my lips, the tension in the air easing, and I lean in a fraction closer. "Two months enough for you, honey?"

Her shy smile spreads across her lips. "I'm sure I'll get sick of you by then."

A laugh rumbles from deep within me. I reach for her, my thumb brushing over her bottom lip, pulling her closer. "Yeah? We'll see about that."

Amara chuckles, her fingers trace lazy circles against my chest.

I study her for a moment. "What's going on in that pretty head of yours?"

She hesitates, then exhales. "It's nothing."

"Amara."

Her fingers still against my skin. "It's stupid."

"Try me."

She bites her lip, then finally meets my gaze. "It's just… hard not to wonder, you know?"

I don't need to ask what she's talking about. I already know. *Liam.*

My jaw tightens, but I force myself to stay relaxed. "Wonder what?"

"If I wasn't enough." The words are quiet, but they land with the force of a punch.

I shake my head instantly. "Don't do that. Don't give him that much power."

She lets out a humorless laugh. "Easier said than done."

"Then let me make it easier for you." I shift, rolling us so she's beneath me, caging her in with my arms. "Liam cheated because he's a selfish asshole, he's a piece of shit, and that's on him. It's not because you weren't enough."

Her lips part slightly, but she doesn't argue. Doesn't push me away.

I dip my head, letting my lips brush against hers, just enough to tease. "You know how I know?"

"How?" she breathes.

I smirk. "Because I only had you once and I'm already addicted."

I brush my lips against hers, our tongues dancing together, kissing her until the only thing she can think about is me.

"We need to go to work," she murmurs against my lips, when I kiss her again.

"Tell your boss your fiancé fucked you so hard you can't move," I tease with a smirk.

She chuckles, shaking her head. "As much as I'd love to, if we're late, everyone will know why." Her cheeks flush with embarrassment, and a grin spreads across my face, loving that idea.

I dive in, kissing her again. "Don't tempt me, or I really will pin you down and keep you in this bed for hours."

"I'm serious, Nicholas," she chuckles, breaking the kiss. "I'm all sticky from last night, and I still need to shower."

I groan, the thought of her full of my cum making my blood heat, and I move in to kiss her again. But before I can, my phone buzzes on the nightstand.

I let out a frustrated sigh and grab it, seeing Robert's name flash on the screen.

"Good morning, Nicholas," Robert's clipped voice comes through the speaker. "I was wondering if you had time to talk today."

I sit up, stretching a little as I try to shake off the grogginess. Amara stirs next to me, glancing over with tired eyes. "I wasn't expecting you to drop by," I mutter, rubbing my face.

"I wasn't planning on it, but there are a few things we need to go over."

I glance at Amara, who's watching me curiously. "Of course. I'll be there soon."

"Work?" she guesses.

I nod, pressing my lips together. "Robert wants to see me."

Her brows furrow, the concern deepening. "You think he knows?"

I take a slow breath. If Robert found out the engagement wasn't real, it'd be a huge problem. Not just because the deal would undoubtedly fall through, but... My gaze flickers to Amara. This would end between us.

"I don't think so, but who the fuck knows."

I blow out a breath, my mind swirling with the possibilities of what Robert could want. Amara's concerned gaze lingers on me, but I can't focus on that right now—not when I'm more distracted by the soft curve of her lips and the warmth of her body beside me.

I lean in, capturing her lips with mine in a kiss. Her hand slides up my chest, pulling me closer, and for a moment, everything else fades into the background. There's nothing but her.

But—of course—Pumpkin decides this is the perfect moment to jump up onto the bed and cockblock me.

I pull away from her lips with a groan, and Amara chuckles, scratching the cat's head as Pumpkin purrs contentedly against her chest. "Are you hungry, baby?"

I roll my eyes, irritated, as Pumpkin snuggles into Amara, purring softly with her eyes closed. I let out a sigh. I did agree to share Amara, and… she's kind of cute, I guess.

"Come on," Amara says, rolling out of bed. "Let's go get you some food."

As she stands, the sight of her full ass greets me, and I pause for a moment, just watching. The curve of her hips, the way her skin glows in the morning light. I drag a hand down my face. All I want is to stay in bed with this woman, but work—and her damn cat—are ruining that plan.

Amara gently places Pumpkin on the ground before pulling on a silk robe. The cat follows her out of the room, tail flicking.

I lie back against the bed, hands behind my head, watching her every move, my lips curling into a smile.

Then my gaze shifts to the ground, where Pumpkin turns her head back to look at me and lets out a *meow*.

My jaw practically hits the floor as I glare at her, as she follows Amara out the door.

Nicholas: 1, Pumpkin: 1.

CHAPTER TWENTY-THREE
Nicholas

I can feel eyes on me.

It's not unusual. I'm Nicholas Blackwood, after all. But today, it's different.

Whispers ripple through the air, following me the moment I step into the office. My shoulders instinctively straighten as I make my way through the sea of desks, not sparing a glance at anyone.

Amara insisted on coming in ten minutes earlier than me this morning. She's trying to avoid the attention that would surely bring if we walked in together. Personally? I don't give a fuck about the gossip. I'd much rather stroll in with her, hand in hand, and kiss her right here in front of everyone, making it crystal clear who she belongs to.

I scan the floor, my eyes sweeping across the rows of desks until they lock onto her. She's sitting at her desk, laser-focused on her monitor, her long hair pulled back in a sleek ponytail. I spot Jade leaning over, nudging her with her elbow. Amara turns her head, and the instant our eyes meet, her cheeks flush a shade deeper than usual.

A subtle smirk tugs at my lips, and I give her a small nod as I walk past.

"Amara," I greet her, the memory of how I said her name last night making my lips twitch. She blushes even harder, and it's impossible not to enjoy the effect I have on her.

"Mr. Blackwood," she replies, with a cool professionalism that makes me almost scoff. Just this morning she was moaning and gasping my name in the shower, and now I'm just "Mr. Blackwood." Yeah, okay.

I nod at her, the brief eye contact between us enough to send a jolt of heat through my veins. But there's no time to linger. There's work to do.

I turn on my heel and head toward my office, pushing the door open. I sit back in my leather chair, waiting for Robert to arrive. The office is silent except for the faint hum of the city below. My mind, however, is a whirlwind of thoughts... specifically of Amara.

I can't stop thinking about last night. The way she looked, the way she felt. Her soft moans, the way she melted against me, so fucking responsive. I bite the inside of my cheek, feeling the heat flood my body at the memory.

Unable to take it any longer, I grab my phone and type out a message.

Me:

> Mr. Blackwood? Baby, you were screaming my name so loud this morning the walls nearly caved in.

I smile to myself, leaning back further in my chair when I see her typing.

Amara:

> Nicholas. We're at work.

Me:

> And I can still smell
> you on my fingers.

Amara:

> Nicholas… You know I blush
> like crazy. People will be able
> to tell something's going on.

I chuckle. I can practically see her now, biting her lip, trying to keep cool.

Me:

> I know, baby. And I love it. I can't
> wait to see that blush tonight.
> Maybe I'll make it match your ass.

I lean forward, my cock stirring at the thought of her beneath me again.

Her reply comes quickly.

Amara:

> Nicholas!

I smile darkly, knowing I've got her on the edge, making her squirm.

Me:

> I just want to hold you.

> And kiss you all over.

> And then eat you out.

I can almost feel her shiver, her thigh quivering around my head as I lick her sweet cunt.

Amara:

> Oh god…

Me:

> Fuck. I can practically hear you moan already. My cock is so hard.

Amara:

> Nicholas. I'm begging you.

I press my lips together, biting back a groan.

Me:

> Don't worry, baby. You'll be begging me for something else tonight.

My phone buzzes again, but before I can respond, the sound of a knock at my door pulls me out of my head.

Robert's here.

I slide my phone back into my pocket with a quiet groan. "Come in."

The door opens, and Robert steps in. "Mr. Blackwood," he greets. "Apologies for the delay."

I give him a nod in acknowledgment as he sits down in the chair across from my desk. "No problem. What's the situation?"

"We've got a problem," Robert replies, and his tone immediately sets off alarm bells in my head.

I sit up straighter. "What kind of problem?"

"We've received a letter from Alexander." The blood drains from my face. "He's claiming your relationship with Amara is a tactic. A move to secure the deal with the hotel. That it's not real."

My jaw clenches. Are you fucking kidding me?

"I don't talk to my brother," I grit out, fighting the urge to punch something. "He doesn't know a damn thing about my life or Amara. This is none of his business."

Robert nods. "I know that, Nicholas. But the board…" He hesitates, a momentary flicker of concern crossing his face. "They're taking his letter seriously. They want proof. They want to see both of you together, in public. They're going to be at the L.A. opening tomorrow. I think it would be a great opportunity to show them how serious you and your fiancée are."

I exhale slowly, my fingers digging into the edge of the desk, the tension in my shoulders almost unbearable. I wasn't planning on attending the opening, certainly not with the board breathing down my neck. But it's unavoidable. I need to put out any fires that Alexander started.

"Fine," I mutter, grinding my teeth at an attempt to contain my frustration. "We'll be there."

Robert pauses, his gaze flicking to mine as if expecting something more. But when I stay silent, he stands. "I'll let the board know. They'll be expecting you both."

I nod curtly, my mind already racing through the possibilities, a hundred scenarios playing out in my head. I stand up, buttoning my jacket, trying to regain control over the situation.

I open the door for Robert and give him a tight smile. "I'll see you and the board tomorrow."

His nod is stiff, but he doesn't say anything more. I watch him leave, the door clicking shut behind him. The meeting, the board's doubts, it all sinks in like a brick in my stomach. This situation is spiraling faster than I can keep up, and I need to get ahead of it.

I exhale slowly, my fingers flexing at my sides. I pull out my phone, the screen lighting up in my hand as I scroll for Ethan's number.

The phone rings twice before he answers.

"Look who it is. Where the hell have you been? Busy with your fiancée?" he teases.

The muscle in my jaw tightens, but I push the frustration down. I don't have time for this. "Ethan, I need a favor."

"What kind of favor?"

"I need you to take care of a cat for me."

There's a long pause on the other end, and I can practically hear the gears turning in his head before a dry chuckle follows. "A cat? What kind of cat?"

I let out a sigh, closing my eyes as I try to force my thoughts into some kind of order. "An orange one. With a pink bell around her neck. Possessive. Hates men."

Ethan snorts, amusement clear in his voice. "Well, then why the hell did you call me?"

I press my fingers to the bridge of my nose. "Please, man. I never ask for favors, but I need this. I have to fly to L.A. tomorrow, and I can't leave the damn cat on its own."

I hear Ethan's sigh. "Say no more. I'm on my way to buy some cat toys. I'll swing by and grab the little beast."

Relief floods through me. "Thanks, man. I owe you one."

"Yeah, you do," Ethan adds with a laugh before hanging up.

I sit there for a moment, the weight of everything that's still hanging over me pressing down, but at least I've managed to sort out one thing. One small problem is handled. Now, if only the rest of my life could be as simple as getting Ethan to babysit a psychotic cat.

I exhale, running a hand through my hair, trying to calm myself. I've got a lot to deal with, but first things first.

I press the intercom button.

"Mr. Blackwood?" Amara's voice crackles through.

"Can you come in, please," I say, releasing the button a second later.

I let out a heavy breath as I lean back in my chair, rubbing a hand over my face. Fucking Alexander. He took it too far. Jeopardizing this business deal not only fucks me over but fucks him over too. He's playing with fire, and I'll be glad when he gets burned.

The knock at the door pulls me out of my thoughts and Amara steps into my office a second later. My gaze lingers on her a second too long, my mind flashing to last night. Her naked body, the way she felt against me, how every inch of her belonged to me.

"You wanted to see me, sir?" she asks, blood rushing to my cock at how professional she looks in her tight pencil skirt, white blouse and thin pink cardigan around her shoulders when just last night my face was buried between her thighs.

I rub a hand over my mouth, trying to hide the amusement, but the thought of my brother and the L.A. opening flood to my mind, the tension tightening in my chest again.

"Pack a bag," I tell her. "We're going to L.A. tomorrow."

CHAPTER TWENTY-FOUR

Amara

As soon as I step onto the jet, I almost forget how to breathe. The white leather seats stretch out in perfect rows, and there's this plush leather couch in the center that screams *luxury*.

Nicholas walks next to me, his hand lightly resting on my back, guiding me to the back of the jet. I try not to let my awe show too much, but the more I take in, the more it feels like I'm in some kind of dream. It's hard to wrap my head around it all, especially knowing it's only temporary. When this whole contract ends… I'll have to say goodbye to all of this. I'll have to say goodbye to Nicholas.

"Everything okay?" Nicholas asks, slowing his pace, his eyes catching mine like he knows exactly what's going on in my head.

"I'm fine," I say, forcing a smile.

He nods, slipping his jacket off and sinking into the couch with a contented sigh.

I sit next to him, the heat from his body brushing against mine, and my stomach flutters when he turns to look at me.

"Why are you looking at me like that?" I ask, trying to keep my voice even, though his gaze makes me feel nervous.

His grin widens, and he raises an eyebrow, a teasing glint in his eyes. "Do I need a reason?"

I laugh, my cheeks warming. "You're my boss."

His gaze sharpens, and a low groan slips out of him as his hand reaches for my chin. He gently tilts my face up to meet his eyes, the intensity there making it hard to breathe.

"And your fiancé," he murmurs, his lips grazing my jaw.

"Fake fiancé," I add, reminding myself that this is all part of the deal.

Nicholas's eyes flicker, something unreadable flashing across his face. "Not to everyone here."

Before I can say anything, a voice breaks the moment.

"Good morning, sir." The flight attendant stands in the doorway, her gaze immediately locked on Nicholas with an intensity that I can't ignore. Her red-painted lips curve into a smile as she looks down at us—or more specifically, *him*. "I hope you have a great flight. I'm here for *anything* you need."

I blink at her. Was that just my imagination or did that sound suggestive?

I feel something stir in me as she smiles at him, her attention solely on him. I can't help but glance at Nicholas, trying to gauge his reaction.

He glances at her for a second, shooting a quick smile. "Thank you, Savannah."

Savannah's gaze flicks over to me, her eyes traveling down the length of my body before returning to my face with a smile that is just a touch too sweet, almost condescending. I give her a polite smile, but the slight narrowing of her eyes and the curl of her lips tells me she doesn't see me as any kind of threat.

Okay, so I wasn't imagining it.

She wants Nicholas.

Savannah flashes him another pearly white smile before she turns on her heels and walks out. The door clicks shut behind her, leaving just the quiet hum of the jet.

I glance at Nicholas, questions swirling in my mind, but I push them down. Or at least try to.

"Savannah?" I ask, aiming for casual even though curiosity slips through.

His brow furrows, his expression skeptical. "What about her?"

"You know her name?"

He leans back into the couch, one arm draped lazily over the backrest. "She's worked for me for years. She's the main flight attendant when I use the jet."

I nod, trying to keep my voice even. "And how often is that?"

A slow, teasing smile tugs at his lips. "You're my assistant. Shouldn't you know?"

"Right," I shrug. "Except as you've pointed out, I don't know much about your personal life."

He sighs, rubbing his chin thoughtfully. "A few times a month, maybe more. Depends on if I need to be somewhere quickly. I usually prefer the helicopter."

I hum in acknowledgment, pretending his answer satisfies me. But inside, I'm still thinking about Savannah—about how often she's around him... *alone*. It shouldn't bother me. I've been his assistant for two years. I've seen the revolving door of women he's dated. So why does this feel different?

I turn to stare out the window, willing the thoughts to dissolve, but they linger.

Nicholas's hand brushes under my chin, gently tilting my face back toward him. "What's really going on, Amara?"

"Nothing," I lie, my lips pressing together.

"Amara," he says again, firmer this time.

I exhale a shaky breath. "Did you sleep with her?"

Nicholas's brows shoot up, his eyes narrowing in surprise. "Excuse me?"

"I know you've slept with plenty of women," I say, bitterness slipping into my tone before I can stop it. "I'm not clueless. I used to pick out the ones you'd take to bed, remember?"

His expression shifts, his brows knitting together. "And what makes you think Savannah is one of them?"

"The way she looked at me," I explain, fidgeting with my hands on my lap. "Like I was competition."

He lets out a low chuckle, shaking his head as though I've said something absurd.

"It's not funny," I snap, a flush rising to my face.

Nicholas straightens, his smirk deepening. "It is if you think she would have any competition when it comes to you."

My heart stutters. "So... does that mean—"

"No," he says firmly, cutting me off before I can finish. "I haven't slept with Savannah."

Relief floods through me, even though I tell myself it shouldn't matter. I tilt my head skeptically. "Really?"

His expression softens as he leans back into the couch. "I don't mix business and pleasure." His voice lowers. "And for the record, I never slept with those women you picked out either."

I blink, thrown by his confession. "What?"

"That was all PR," he explains. "Just a show to get the gossip sites buzzing. It was never real."

"Kinda like us?" I ask cautiously.

Nicholas shakes his head slowly, his gaze steady as it locks onto mine. "No, baby. Not even close." His hands find my face, his palms warm against my skin, grounding me as every trace of lingering jealousy dissolves. "You're the only exception."

"Yeah?" I whisper.

He leans in, his lips brushing against the sensitive skin of my jaw. Heat spreads through my body, sending a shiver down my spine. "The only one," he murmurs.

Before I can respond, the sound of a soft cough echoes through the cabin.

Savannah stands in the doorway, her gaze flicking between us before settling on Nicholas. Her lips curve into the same flirtatious smile. "Sir, we're ready for takeoff," she announces, her eyes briefly grazing mine before returning to him as though I don't exist.

"Thank you, Savannah," Nicholas replies.

She lingers longer than necessary, her smile widening. "And if there's anything I can do…"

I watch her with narrowed eyes, my fingers curling into fists on my lap.

"Actually," Nicholas cuts in, surprising me. "There is something."

She leans in, her voice filled with sugary sweetness. "Yes, sir?"

Nicholas's hand curls around my waist, tugging me to his side, earning a gasp from me. "My fiancée and I are celebrating an anniversary today," he lies, and I blink at the side of his head, wondering what the hell he's doing. "We'd love a glass of champagne and some strawberries." His eyes finally turn to face me, and he brushes his lips softly against mine, making my eyes flutter. "Anything you want, baby?" he asks, his hand finding its way to my waist, pulling me closer as he presses a soft kiss to the curve of my neck.

I shake my head, glancing up at Savannah, who just blinks, clearly taken aback.

"Of course, sir. I'll be right back with your drinks."

When the door clicks shut again, I let out a breath, shaking my head.

"That was a little unnecessary."

Nicholas arches a brow, looking very pleased with himself as he stretches out on the couch. He taps his leg twice, a silent command.

"Sit, Amara," he orders.

"Nicholas—"

"You're my fiancée. Sit on my lap."

I suck in a breath, my mind racing as I prepare to tell him that, while he might be used to that, I'm different—bigger, heavier. But before I can find the words, his arm slips around my waist, pulling me effortlessly onto his lap. My hips settle over his left leg, my skin tingling at the contact.

"Much fucking better," he murmurs, his voice sending a shiver down my spine. His nose brushes against my neck, lips grazing the soft curve of my skin.

His hands are on my thighs in an instant, gripping firmly as he presses his lips to the sensitive area beneath my ear.

A throat clearing has me gasping when I look up and see Savannah above us, with two glasses of champagne in her hand and a bowl of strawberries in the other.

Nicholas merely smiles, takes a flute from her, before reaching for the other. His gaze flickers to me, a wicked smile curling at the corners of his lips. Savannah's smile falters, and she turns, closing the door behind her with a soft click.

"You think she'll get the picture now?" he asks, taking a slow sip of his champagne, his eyes never leaving mine.

His grin widens slightly as he tips his glass, a drop of champagne falling onto my neck. I gasp as the cool liquid spreads over my skin, and before I can react, he's already trailing his tongue along the path it left, his touch scorching, smooth, and maddening.

"Mmm, you taste sweet," he murmurs, his voice rough against my skin.

"It's the champagne," I reply with a breathless chuckle.

He shakes his head, the sound of a soft growl vibrating in his chest. "No," he says, his voice dark, "it's you."

His hand slides around my waist, fingers firm but slow as they drift down to my thigh. I inhale sharply, the heat of his touch seeping through the fabric, making every nerve in my body buzz. He doesn't rush, as if he's savoring the moment, testing my reaction.

My legs widen of their own accord, wanting his touch, needing it, no matter the consequences. My breaths come faster, uneven, as every inch of his touch stirs something deep inside me. His hands hover dangerously close, teasing the edge of what I've been silently begging for.

I've never felt this desired before. Never felt this wanted by anyone. The sensation sends a dizzying rush through me, making it hard to catch my breath.

I gasp as I hear the unmistakable *rip* and look down to see my tights stretched out around my thighs. I glance over my shoulder to find Nicholas grinning mischievously, and the sight sends a flush to my cheeks, heat pooling between my thighs.

Before I can speak, his fingers graze the hem of my skirt, inching it higher, the fabric bunching at my waist, leaving me exposed. "Spread your legs wider for me, honey," he murmurs, his voice sending a shiver down my spine. "Let me feel how soaked you are."

My breath catches as I spread my legs wider, shifting slightly on his lap, feeling every inch of his hard cock rubbing against the curve of my ass. The realization flickers through me, and suddenly, I'm drunk on the power of knowing *I'm* the one who's making him hard.

A low groan escapes him, rasping with desire, when I grind against him. His hands grip my hips, stopping me. "Do that again, and I'm going to come in my pants," he warns, his hands sliding to my thighs, spreading them wider on his lap. "Is that what you want?" he asks, his teeth grazing the soft skin of my earlobe. "Hmm?"

God, yes.

The thought of someone as powerful as Nicholas losing control just from me grinding on his lap turns me on like nothing else. I do it again, my clit throbbing as I feel his thick, hard cock against me, craving him inside of me again.

A sharp slap lands on my pussy, covered by the thin material of my underwear, and I gasp. His hand covers me a second later, soothing the sting as his middle finger drags along my seam. "Fuck, you're needy," he mutters, grunting as his finger pushes deeper, my underwear a thin barrier between him and the place that's dripping for him. "God, I lose my mind every single time I touch you."

I buck into his hand, moving my hips as his fingers find my clit, rubbing slow, soft circles while his lips brush against my skin. "Look at you. So prim and proper in the office, blushing every time you look at me, and yet you're soaking my fingers, grinding your pussy against me," he grunts with dark amusement, making a flush creep across my skin.

I'm hyper-aware that this jet is small, and Savannah is just on the other side of the door, probably hearing every gasp and moan escaping my lips. The thought should be enough to make me stop, but instead, it only fuels the fire burning inside me. I can feel my pussy leaking as his fingers rub a little harder, increasing the pressure.

"Do you think she'd still be interested in me if she knew where my fingers were right now?" His voice is low, rough and heated, sending shivers down my spine as his hand slides up the bare skin of my thigh, pushing the hem of my skirt higher.

My skin heats as I imagine her walking in, seeing me sprawled out on her boss's lap, while his fingers are covered in my arousal.

Feeling bold, I grab his hand and push my panties aside, guiding one of his fingers inside of me.

He grunts, unashamed and loud, as he thrusts his finger inside, stretching me out, filling me completely.

"Sir?" A knock at the door makes me flinch, quickly trying to cover myself. "Is everything alright? Can I get you anything else?" Savannah asks from the other side.

Nicholas doesn't answer. Instead, his lips brush against my neck, featherlight and teasing, as he whispers, "Should I tell her I'm already taken care of?"

I bite my lip to stifle a laugh, which quickly turns into a moan when he slides another finger inside of me, pleasure curling up my spine.

"You're going to get us caught," I hiss, my body betraying me as I arch into his touch. His other hand slides around my waist, trailing up my shirt.

"Maybe that's what you want," he murmurs, his voice dropping an octave. "Or are you just mad she thought she had a chance?"

My gasp turns into a louder moan as his teeth graze the curve of my collarbone. His hands grow bold, unapologetic, as he cups my breast, pulling down my bra to rub his thumb against my hard nipple.

"You're not being very quiet," he teases, a wicked glint in his eyes, knowing exactly how much I'm struggling to stay composed.

"Then stop making it so hard," I gasp when his fingers pump deeper inside me.

His laugh is dark, vibrating through my chest as he leans in, his lips brushing my ear. "Careful, honey. I don't think you want me to take that as a challenge."

"Yeah?" I ask, grinding against his cock, teasing him, wanting him to go further.

He groans, pulling his fingers out of me. I almost whine, desperate for him to return them. "Lift your ass up for me, baby," he orders, hands tightening around my hips. "I need to get my cock out or I'm going to lose my goddamn mind."

I lift off him, and I hear his belt buckle unfasten. A few seconds later, his hands are back on my hips, pulling me down onto him until I feel all of him. "Your pussy's so slippery already," he grunts, thrusting between my thighs. "It'd be so easy for me to slide my cock inside you."

A low whimper escapes me as I tip my head back, pleasure building inside me. "Please," I beg, needing him inside me again.

His large hands grip my hips, hard enough to leave bruises, as he bucks his hips, sliding his cock against me. "Slide your panties down for me, honey. Let me feel your soaked pussy rubbing against my cock first."

Squirming on his lap, I tug my panties down my legs, along with my ripped tights until I'm completely bare from the waist down.

Nicholas groans, his hands gripping me tighter as he pulls me back down onto his lap. His cock slides between my pussy, brushing my clit with delicious pressure that makes me gasp, my fingers curling around the armrest beside me. "You feel so good, honey, and I'm not even inside you yet," he grunts, every thrust sending a shiver through me. His cock, slick with my arousal, slides against me in slow, teasing motions. "I wish I was on my knees, burying my face in that sweet cunt of yours."

My eyes flutter closed at his filthy words, the tension between us electric as his cock glides against me. "I'm so close," I moan, biting my lip as I realize Savannah can probably hear everything.

A breath catches in my throat as he suddenly lifts me, and with one hard thrust, his cock slides deep inside me, filling me completely. "Fuck, you're so tight," he groans, his hands gripping my hips as he holds me still, his cock pulsing inside me. "I couldn't let you come without feeling you soak me."

The ache inside me intensifies, pleasure building until it's almost unbearable. His hand finds my clit, rubbing slow, gentle circles while his other hand keeps me steady as he lifts and slam me back down onto him.

Normally, I'd be worried about the pressure of my weight on him, about being too heavy or whether I'm moving too fast. But right now, none of that matters. All I care about is the overwhelming pleasure taking over my body.

His cock hits a spot so deep inside me that I gasp, my head falling back. "Oh god," I moan, gripping the armrest tighter.

"Nicholas, baby," he corrects, thrusting into me. "Say my name, Amara."

"Nicholas," I moan when he thrusts into me harder, the sound of his name filling the room as the pressure in my clit builds.

"That's it," he groans, his hands tightening around my hips as he slams into me, each thrust more frantic than the last. "Scream my fucking name, Amara. Let her know who I belong to."

My body jerks as the pressure inside me snaps. The intense wave of pleasure floods me, and for a moment, the world goes hazy. I can't breathe, every muscle seizing as I fall apart.

"Oh, fuck," Nicholas grunts, his thrusts growing frantic, desperate, each one harder and faster as he tunnels his cock into me. "You're gripping me inside of you so fucking tight. I'm gonna—" Nicholas lets out a low, guttural groan as he finally comes, his body shuddering beneath me, as he fills me with his cum.

The sound of his release sends a wave of heat through my own body as he keeps languidly thrusting inside of me.

I melt against him, my body softening as his lips brush against the skin of my back in a trail of heat that makes my heart race. We stay like that for a few moments, until Nicholas grips my waist and gently lifts me off him.

I feel his cum drip out of me the instant I move, and Nicholas groans behind me at the sight. I bite my lip, glancing over my shoulder, my clit throbbing at the sight of his cock resting against his stomach, wet and covered in both of our releases.

His large hands grip my ass, spreading my cheeks as he watches his cum drip from me. His eyes darken with desire as he swipes two fingers, collecting what spilled before pushing them back inside me.

"Don't clean it up," he murmurs, his fingers moving slowly inside me. "I want my cum dripping out of you when we walk out of here."

Our eyes meet as he removes his fingers, lifting me to my feet and spinning me around to face him. The same two fingers that were inside me press softly against my lips, brushing them open before sliding into my mouth without warning. I gasp, my cheeks flushing at how dirty this feels. I can't stop myself from running my tongue over his fingers, tasting both of us together, the sound of his groan making me pulse with need.

He pulls his fingers from my mouth and tilts my chin up with the same hand. "Remember, next time you get jealous," he adds, his voice rough and possessive, "only my fiancée gets to know what I taste like."

CHAPTER TWENTY-FIVE

Amara

I don't belong here.

That's the only thought in my mind the moment I step into the Blackwood hotel lobby. I feel like I've stumbled into an alternate reality.

The marble floors are so shiny I'm convinced if I stare long enough, I might just see my own shocked face staring back at me. It even smells expensive. Like fresh roses, leather, and the kind of money I can only dream about.

Nicholas rests his hand on my back as we make our way toward the check-in counter. He's calm, collected, like he owns the place—which he does. Whereas I'm doing my best not to look like someone who wandered in off the street by mistake.

As Nicholas approaches the counter, the concierge straightens up, a flicker of surprise flashing before it morphs into a practiced smile. "Mr. Blackwood, good evening. We weren't expecting you."

"It was a last-minute trip," Nicholas responds smoothly, pulling his wallet from his jacket pocket, handing them his ID.

"No problem at all." The concierge types away. "We're happy to have you with us. The Presidential Suite is ready and waiting."

My breath catches. The Presidential Suite. Naturally. Because anything less would be unacceptable for Nicholas Blackwood.

Nicholas nods, sliding his wallet back into place. "Thank you."

"If you need anything at all during your stay, just let us know," the concierge adds, handing back his ID with a smile.

Watching the interaction is like observing royalty being served.

Nicholas turns, his hand sliding back to the small of my back as we stroll across the lobby toward the elevator. It's casual, probably no big deal to him, but I can't help but love how he keeps touching me, like he's drawn to it without even realizing.

"So, this is a Blackwood Hotel," I murmur to myself more than anyone, letting my eyes roam over the hotel lobby.

Nicholas halts mid-step, glancing down at me, a brow raised. "You've never been to one?"

The disbelief in his voice makes me bite back a smile. "Not exactly in my price range."

He blinks, his expression blank for a beat. "You're serious?"

"Unfortunately." I shrug, letting out a soft laugh. "Besides, I've never really needed to stay in a hotel. I've always been busy with work. Never had the time for a vacation."

For a split second, his expression softens, a moment of realization crossing his face like he's just realized how different our worlds really are. "You've really never stayed in a hotel like this before?"

"Nope." I shake my head.

He studies me for a long beat before his lips tug into a smile. "Well, that's about to change."

He turns to press the button for the elevator, and we stand there, his hand sliding back to my side just as a guy in a pristine gray suit taps Nicholas on the shoulder.

"Nicholas." He extends a hand. "I wasn't expecting you here this week."

"Michael." Nicholas greets him, his posture somehow even straighter than usual. "Last-minute trip. This is Amara." He looks at me with that easy smile of his. "My fiancée."

Michael's eyes flicker between us, and I'm almost certain I catch a brief flash of surprise before he quickly masks it with a polite grin. He's probably thinking I don't belong with someone like Nicholas.

"Nice to meet you, Amara."

I swallow hard, forcing a smile. "You too."

Michael turns back to Nicholas. "Let me know if you need anything while you're here."

"Will do. Thanks, Michael."

The elevator doors open and Nicholas guides me inside. "Is it always like this for you?" I ask, glancing at him. "People fawning over you everywhere you go?"

He shrugs, adjusting his cufflinks. "You get used to it."

I don't push him further, but I can't imagine ever getting used to *this*.

The elevator dings, and we step into a private hallway. Nicholas swipes his key card, the door opening with a soft click.

The first thing that hits me is the view. Floor-to-ceiling windows stretch across the far wall, framing a breathtaking shot of Los Angeles at sunset, the city sprawling beneath us.

The suite itself is out of this world. Sleek, traditional, and so luxurious I feel like I've stepped into someone else's life. The living room is bathed in muted tones, featuring a velvet couch and a glass coffee table. Off to the side is a small bar stocked with bottles of liquor I can't even name, and a dining table that could host a dinner party for ten.

Nicholas pushes open the door to the bedroom, and my eyes go straight to the king-size bed in the middle, piled high with what looks like a million cushions.

"Wow," I breathe, stepping further into the room, taking it all in.

Nicholas stops by the door and glances at me. "What do you think?"

"It's beautiful," I reply, letting my eyes wander around.

His brow lifts, watching me carefully. "But…"

I turn to face him, catching the knowing look on his face, and hesitate for a moment, chewing on my lip. "The rug," I say slowly. "It doesn't match the vibe. It's too busy. And the lighting in the bathroom… it's too harsh for the marble. It needs something warmer to balance it out. Oh, and that table?" I point toward the dining area. "It's stunning, but it feels too light for the space. A dark wooden table would have made it much more inviting."

I trail off, suddenly aware of how much I've said. "Sorry. I didn't mean to—"

"Don't apologize," Nicholas interrupts. "You're right."

I blink, caught off guard. "What?"

"You're right," he repeats, stepping closer. "The rug, the lighting, the dining table… You nailed it. You have an incredible eye for this, Amara."

Heat rises to my cheeks. "Thank you. It's always been what I wanted to do."

"I know. And you're going to be amazing at it."

His words hang in the air, and for a moment, the raw honesty of them settles something deep in my chest. I've spent so long wondering if I'm good enough for this, if I'm just fooling myself into thinking it's something I can actually do. And the fact that he believes in me—really believes in me—in a way I've never let myself believe, makes my chest flutter with hope.

Before I can process, he steps closer, his hand brushing my cheek. My breath catches as his lips find mine. It's a kiss that feels a little too real, and when he pulls back, I'm dizzy, my head spinning.

I turn toward the window, needing a moment to steady myself. "The view's amazing," I say. "But... I think I prefer the view back home."

Nicholas moves behind me, his arms wrapping around my waist as he places the softest of kisses against my neck. "I prefer the view wherever you are."

My heart stumbles in my chest, and I force out a laugh. "You're laying it on thick, don't you think? No one's around to hear you."

"You are. I don't need anyone but you to hear it."

"Okay," I laugh, spinning to face him. "Are you done?"

"Not quite." He smirks, reaching into his pocket.

Nicholas pulls out a sleek black card and hands it to me. I frown, staring at it in confusion when I see my name printed on the front. "Nicholas... What is this?"

"We have the opening," he explains, leaning in to place a soft kiss on the corner of my mouth. "Go buy something nice to wear. Something expensive."

I shake my head, almost immediately. He's already covered the dress, the flight, the hotel. And now this... I open my mouth, but he stops me.

"Don't argue," he interrupts, as he steps closer. His tall frame towers over me, and that familiar flutter stirs in my stomach. "You need a dress for tonight, and I know you love to shop. Trust me, I want to see you in a new dress. Preferably one you can't wear panties with."

I roll my eyes, but his grin only widens as he gently tips my chin up, locking his gaze with mine. "Spare no expense. You're the fiancée of a billionaire. Start acting like it."

I narrow my eyes. "You're going to regret saying that."

His lips twitch into a smirk. "I doubt it. I'll meet you back here in a few hours."

I hesitate for all of five seconds before plucking the card from his hand. It's surprisingly heavy, and I can't help but grin as I slide it into my purse. "You sure about this?"

"Amara." His tone is dry, a flicker of amusement in his eyes. "If you can max it out, I'll be impressed."

Challenge accepted.

CHAPTER TWENTY-SIX
Nicholas

The opening of the newest Blackwood Hotel location in Los Angeles is nothing short of a spectacle. The lobby drips with luxury. Polished marble floors gleaming like liquid gold, chandeliers so massive they're practically threatening the city's power grid.

There's champagne fizzing in crystal glasses, murmured gossip disguised as polite conversation, and bursts of fake laughter.

And yet, I'm stuck by the entrance, checking my damn watch for the fifth time in three minutes, feeling like the human embodiment of a waiting room. It's been three hours since I told Amara to go out and buy a dress, and she's still not here.

I check my phone again like a lovesick puppy, hoping for a text, a call, *something*. Instead, I'm met with radio silence. For a man used to being in control, this waiting—this not knowing—is maddening. I swear I'm about to lose my mind when the sound of soft heels clicking against marble makes my head snap up and my chest tighten.

Holy. Fucking. Hell.

The conversation, the music, even the obnoxious sparkle of the chandeliers… It all becomes background noise.

My throat goes dry, and my pulse skips as my eyes trace her. Her orange hair is styled in loose waves that cascade over her shoulders, and the dress she's wearing… *Christ*, that dress. It should be illegal. Deep crimson velvet that hugs every curve of her body, clinging to her soft, round belly that has my throat going dry. The neckline dips low enough to tease, the fabric clinging to her full bust before tapering in at her waist and flowing over her wide hips.

She stops a few feet away, her green eyes locking onto mine. She tucks a strand of hair behind her ear. "Hi." Her voice is soft and uncertain as her hands smooth down the sides of her dress. "What do you think?"

What do I think? I think I've forgotten how to speak. I think she's about to single-handedly raise my blood pressure. But all I manage is a rough swipe of my hand over my mouth, my vocabulary wiped clean.

I'm aware that I'm staring, that I probably look like a complete idiot, but I can't stop. My gaze drags down the length of her body and back up again, taking in every detail.

"You hate it, don't you?" she asks, her smile faltering. Her hands hover near her sides, fidgeting slightly. "I can change if—"

"Shut the fuck up," I cut her off, closing the distance between us in two strides. My hand hooks around her waist, and before she can finish her thought, I claim her mouth in a kiss that makes her gasp against me.

Her lips are soft and warm, her body going rigid with surprise before she melts into me, her hands gripping the lapels of my tuxedo. I know I'm smudging her lipstick, but I don't care. Let the whole damn room see. Let them know she's *mine*. The kiss is hungry, desperate, and I pour everything I can't say into it—my frustration, my awe, my goddamn helplessness when it comes to this woman.

When I finally pull back, her lips are kiss-swollen and smudged with a shade of lipstick I now have all over my mouth. Her eyes are wide, her cheeks flushed a deep pink that has nothing to do with her makeup.

"I'll take that as you like it," she teases breathlessly, her lips curving into a small smile.

"Like it?" I shake my head, my hands sliding possessively over her hips. "Baby, I fucking love it."

Her hands press flat against my chest, toying with my bow tie as her lips curve into a smirk. "I'm glad you think so because I did exactly what you said. I bought a very expensive dress."

A laugh rumbles out of me as I lean in and kiss her again, my grip tightening on her hips. "I saw. Two-hundred-thousand?" I shake my head, still chuckling. "What the hell did you spend that on?"

She shrugs, completely unapologetic. "You said 'spare no expense.' So, I didn't. I got a designer dress, and two more, matching shoes, a bag, makeup, jewelry... and of course, Pumpkin needed a new cat tree."

I groan, because of course she couldn't resist spoiling that little attention thief. "She's spoiled enough," I grumble.

Her laugh bubbles up, soft and teasing. "Pumpkin's a sweetheart. You're just jealous she cuddles me first."

I grumble, even though we both know the fluffy demon won this round.

Her head tilts, that smug little grin of hers only getting wider. "I told you you'd regret giving me that card."

Regret it? I groan, my hands sliding down to her waist, gripping tighter than necessary as frustration burns through me. "The only thing I regret is not dragging you back to our room and skipping this whole event altogether. You have no idea how much watching you spend my money makes my cock hard."

She sucks in a breath and her teasing smile only makes the situation in my pants worse.

But before I can haul her off to a more private place, a sharp voice interrupts. "Nicholas."

I turn, my jaw tightening as the board members approach. The moment is ruined, but I slip my hand into Amara's, plastering on a professional smile. "Good evening."

"Where's your brother?" David asks, his brow lifting as he takes a sip of his scotch. "I would've expected him to be here tonight, seeing as he's the head of the L.A. department."

I nod, keeping my expression neutral. My brother's probably at some club or tangled up with his latest fling. Work's never been his thing, which is why it pisses me off that he's suddenly so invested in undermining me for the CEO position.

He thinks he deserves it because he's the eldest. I deserve it because I've worked my ass off for it. And I'll be damned if I let him or anyone else steal this from me.

"You know him, sir. Always somewhere he shouldn't be."

David chuckles, along with Robert and Claire, but my focus shifts as I catch a subtle glance from across the room. James— the youngest board member, mid-thirties, charming in a smug kind of way—is looking at Amara.

And not just looking.

His gaze lingers, too long and too bold, with a flicker of something that churns my stomach. Not admiration. Not respect. *Interest*.

He's not the only one noticing her. Hell, I can't blame them. Amara's absolutely stunning in that dress, her curves commanding attention whether she realizes it or not. But James and his eyes raking over her rubs me the wrong way.

Without thinking, I step closer to her, my hand finding the small of her back. It's a possessive move and judging by the flicker of surprise in her eyes when she glances up at me, she knows it too.

But I don't care.

She's mine. Or at least that's what everyone here is supposed to think.

James notices, of course, his gaze flicks to where my hand rests on Amara's waist, my fingers grazing her curves.

"So, Nicholas," David interrupts, "when's the wedding? I trust it's not too far off now that the engagement is public."

My jaw tightens, but I manage a calm smile, glancing at Amara. She looks up at me, her eyes wide. We hadn't planned for this. Hell, we didn't even want to be here tonight, let alone answer questions about a wedding that won't ever exist.

But this is the game we're playing. The board's watching, and every detail of this relationship has to look as real as the ring on her finger.

"We haven't set an official date yet," I reply, letting my hand slide a little lower on her back, grazing her ass. "Still working out the details, right, honey?" I tilt her chin with my fingers, forcing her to meet my gaze.

Her lips part, and she catches on, nodding with a smile that's so convincing, even I almost believe it. "Right," she says sweetly, her tone dripping with charm. "We want it to be perfect."

"Well, it was wonderful to see the two of you again," Claire adds, smiling at us. "Nicholas, we'll be in touch." She turns, and the other members follow.

But James doesn't move.

His gaze is still locked on Amara, his eyes trailing down her body in a way that makes my blood boil.

"James Sinclair," he greets, his hand extending toward her. His eyes linger on her neckline for just a second too long before he finally meets her gaze. "It's an absolute pleasure, Miss…?"

"Blackwood," I interject sharply, making sure he understands. "Her name will be Amara Blackwood."

The smirk drops from his face. Amara glances between us, her brows furrowing slightly, but she doesn't say a word.

"Of course. My apologies," he says with a smug smile I want to punch right off his face.

I tighten my hold on Amara, knowing I need this asshole's approval to be able to move forward with the deal. I don't respond. I don't need to. The look in my eyes says everything I want him to know.

When he finally turns to leave, Amara pulls back, her brows knitting together. "What was that?"

I smirk, leaning down to whisper, "Just proving a point."

Her brow arches. "By groping me in public?"

"By making sure everyone here knows you're mine," I correct, my voice low. "Especially James."

Her gorgeous eyes blink, frowning. "What are you talking about?"

My jaw ticks. "He couldn't take his eyes off you. I had to let him know you were taken."

Her gaze flickers with recognition, and a small frown creases her lips. "You're delusional. He wasn't checking me out."

I laugh darkly, gripping her waist. "Baby, if you think I'm the only one who notices how fucking stunning you are, you're out of your mind."

I swear her eyes are shining like emeralds as they look at me. "You didn't have to do that. I know you have to play nice with the board to get this deal."

I glance down at her, my brow arching. "The hell I didn't. He disrespected me by thinking he had a chance with my *fiancée*."

She lets out a cute little laugh, shaking her head. "You're impossible."

"And you're mine," I say, my voice firm.

Her cheeks flush deeper, and I can't resist brushing my thumb over her jaw, tucking a strand of her fiery hair behind her ear. "Let's get out of here," she murmurs, her voice a little breathless.

My brows lift. "You're serious? Say the word, and we're gone."

She nods, her teeth catching her bottom lip in a way that shouldn't make my thoughts derail like this, but it does. "We've done what we came here to do, right? We proved to them that we're madly in love, and your little... performance definitely sealed the deal."

Her hands press flat against my chest as her fingers slide upward, sending a trail of heat through the fabric of my shirt. They loop around my neck, her gaze locking onto mine.

"Take me to bed."

It's not a request. It's a challenge.

And the way she says it, her voice low and teasing, makes my restraint snap in half.

Christ. I remember the first time we slept together. How shy she was, how she struggled to say what she wanted, how I had to coax the words out of her.

It turns me on that she's not afraid to speak her mind anymore. She's becoming exactly what I never knew I needed, and it's only making it impossible to hold back.

God help me. I don't think I've ever wanted someone as much as I want her.

As I take her hand in mine and rush toward the elevator I can't help but think that I'm not sure where this thing between us is headed, but one thing is certain.

Amara Blackwood is more than just my fiancée—fake or not.

She's my undoing.

CHAPTER TWENTY-SEVEN
Nicholas

The second I swipe the key card and push the door open, I tug Amara inside, not wasting a second. My lips crash onto hers, and everything else fades away. My head spins, completely drunk off her taste. She's so *sweet*, like champagne and sinful damnation. She's the kind of temptation I can't escape, and every kiss only pulls me deeper.

Her moans—soft, sweet—hit me like a punch to the gut. God, I can't get enough. It's *never* enough. No matter how many times I kiss her, I always want more, my body demanding more of her, wanting her in a way that scares me. This woman is undoing me, piece by piece.

The thought of the inevitable end between us churns in my gut. I don't know what the hell I'm going to do when I have the deal in my hands, and we go our separate ways. I haven't even let her go yet, and I'm already dreading it.

I pull back, just enough to catch my breath, my fingers brushing a strand of hair from her face, tucking it behind her ear. Her eyes flutter closed for a moment, but when they open again, they're full of pure desire, blinking up at me.

God, I'm a sucker for those cute, little, innocent eyes. She doesn't know how badly I want to ruin her, how I'm dying to corrupt her and do things she can't even imagine while her hands are tied behind her back.

I slide my hands down over her back, tugging on the zipper slowly, taking my time, savoring every second as I shift it down her body, easing it off her shoulders until the rich velvet sips off her body and pools at her feet.

Amara shivers, standing before me in nothing but matching red lace underwear that makes my mouth water. She glances up at me, with no urge to hide herself and my lips twitch, loving how much more confident she's becoming.

I move my hand to the back of her head, finding the black, silk ribbon tied in a neat bow. The moment I pull it free, her soft hair falls through my fingers, a waterfall of warmth and silk that catches the light. She's always been beautiful, but right now, she looks impossibly tempting.

Her eyes flicker up to mine, her lips parting slightly, but she doesn't speak. I wonder if she realizes the delicate ribbon I hold will soon bind her completely.

I take her hand in mine, my thumb skimming over the diamond on her finger, the one that reminds everyone she belongs to no one but me. I take a step closer, my lips brushing the curve of her neck as I turn her around, guiding her. Her body tenses, but she doesn't fight me. No, she trusts me. She's always trusted me, even when she's unsure of what's coming.

My lips press against her skin, just below her ear, and I feel her shiver under my touch. "You're going to be a good girl for me," I whisper. Her pulse quickens beneath my mouth, and I can feel the heat radiating from her, responding to me in ways she might not even realize. "And do what I tell you."

With my other hand, I guide her wrists behind her back, slowly wrapping the ribbon around them. She gasps, her chest rising sharply when my fingers tighten around the fabric, pulling it to ensure she can't move them.

"Hold still," I murmur against her skin, kissing her neck again, my lips trailing lower as I finish tying the ribbon. It's tight, secure, and when I step back to admire my work, she's completely in my control, so completely *mine*.

I step in close again, my hand lightly brushing her cheek before moving down to her chin, tilting her head to meet my gaze. "Get on your knees."

She doesn't need to be told again. Her breath hitches, but her body's already responding to the words before she even moves. She sinks to her knees, her eyes never leaving mine. The sight of her kneeling in front of me, wrists bound with nothing more than a simple bow, sends a surge of heat through me.

"You look so beautiful like this," I whisper, my voice almost unrecognizable with the hunger I feel. "So vulnerable. So ready for me."

Her gaze lifts to mine, the heat in her eyes matching my own. My hand gently cups her chin, lifting her face to meet mine. I feel the heat of her skin, the way her lips tremble just slightly under my touch. She's shaking, but not from fear. From desire.

Pulling my belt off, I unbutton my pants slowly, her eyes tracking every one of my movements as I pull my pants off. She scans my body from head to toe, her eyes zoning in on my thick cock springing free when I pull my boxers off.

I grip my cock in my hand, giving it a couple of strokes. Her gorgeous eyes widen as I move, grunting at the sight of her on her knees, waiting for me.

"Suck me into your mouth," I murmur, giving my cock another slow stroke. "Show me how much you want to please me."

Her eyes flicker up to meet mine, her breath quickening before she leans forward, her full lips parting as she takes the head of my cock into her mouth. My hands drop and a low groan leaves my lips the minute her tongue swirls around the sensitive tip, her hot, wet mouth enveloping me as she sucks me down.

"Fuck. That's it. Just like that. Suck me dry."

Her nipples pebble beneath the teasing red lace and she shuffles on the ground closer, her hands tied up behind her back as she looks up at me, her lips stretched around my cock. *Fuck*, she looks so deliciously ruined.

A groan escapes me as I move my hand to her hair, grabbing a fistful and tugging her off my cock, before pushing her back down a second later.

A rough moan leaves my lips, unable to keep quiet from her mouth wrapped around me. My body tenses, fighting the urge to thrust my hips forward, to fill her mouth, to wreck her.

Amara takes it all, her soft tongue swirling around my cock as I thrust her back down on my cock.

"I'm close," I warn her, the pressure so intense my eyes flutter closed. I snap them open, wanting to see her pretty lips sucking me down. Her eyes fill with tears as I continue to push her back down on my cock, moving faster as I feel the pressure building inside of me.

My hips take over, thrusting into her mouth as I tug her head down. My cock hits the back of her throat with each thrust, and I feel every inch of her warm mouth.

I'm so fucking close, my body shudders with the effort to hold back. A groan escapes me when Amara gags once more, her eyes filling with tears and *Jesus*, it tips me over the edge.

My hips jerk, thrusting into her mouth as I grab hold of her head in my hands, fucking her face, every thrust pushing me to the edge.

"Fuck, I'm gonna come." I thrust deeper until she gags, spluttering, moaning around my cock. Her noises, the tears in her eyes, it's all too much. I can't hold back anymore. My hips flex, pushing deeper as my whole body shakes with the intensity, the release ripping through me as I empty into her waiting mouth.

Heavy breaths leave my lips, every muscle in my body tightening as I slowly come down from the orgasm. Once the pleasure rippling through me settles, I pull out of her mouth, my cock glistening with her saliva, and my cum dripping from her mouth.

"Look how fucking perfect you look right now," I tell her, swiping my thumb on her lips, covered in my release. "Swallow it all for me, baby."

Her throat moves as she swallows every drop of my cum down her throat and a shiver runs up my spine. "Open." She opens her mouth, sticking out her tongue to show me. Cupping her face, I caress her cheek, and she melts into me. "What a good girl, baby. You really love to please me, don't you?"

She nods, her eyes fluttering and a heavy breath leaves my lips at her submissiveness. She knows exactly what I need. And I know she needs praise, needs to be treated like a goddamn princess while also begging to be my slut.

Leaning down, I help lift her up until she's on her feet, looking up at me with those gorgeous innocent eyes. Without warning, I spin her around and push her onto the bed, her knees hitting the mattress as I shed the rest of my clothes, gripping her hips and pulling her closer to me as I stand behind her.

"You look like my own personal fuck toy," I tell her, running my hands over her large, plump ass, her pink pussy still glistening with my cum from earlier. "Your hands tied behind your back, with my cum still dripping out of your pussy, your ass in the air, waiting for me."

Kneeling down, I press on her lower back, lowering her until that sweet cunt is right in front of me, waiting for my tongue. My hands grip her ass, spreading her out for me. She's already trembling, her body open and vulnerable. I lean forward, a drop of my spit falling onto her pussy, the wetness pooling on her skin, gleaming under the light.

My mouth hovers over her, the scent of her arousal intoxicating as I dive in with a groan. The first lash of my tongue hits her, and she moans loud, her head hitting the bed. She shudders as I flick my tongue over her, savoring every inch of her.

I want to drown in her, savor the way she reacts to my every touch, memorize her sweet whimpers and the way she melts under me.

Her hips begin to buck, letting me know she's close, and as much as I would gladly die between her legs, I want to feel her pussy tighten around my cock when she comes.

I lift onto my feet and stroke my cock, looking down at her kneeling on the bed, desperate for me.

Gripping my cock in my hand, I bring it to her pussy, swiping it along her slit, covering it in her wetness. "You need my cock inside of you, so bad, don't you?"

She moans, dropping her head when the tip of my cock slips inside of her, just an inch before I pull it out, doing it again.

I reach around, cupping her breasts, my thumbs brushing over her nipples. She moans louder now, a sound that goes straight to my cock. "Say it. Tell me how badly you need me."

"I need you," she gasps when I slide the tip inside again. "Please."

Slowly, I push inside her, the warmth of her tight pussy enveloping me, pulling me in deeper with every inch.

She moans, her back arching slightly as she presses back against me. Her pulse races beneath my fingertips as I run my hands down her spine, over the curve of her hips. The way she reacts to me—her shivers, her soft moans—drives me wild. I press my chest to her back, my hips nudging hers as I drag my mouth along the line of her neck.

"You feel so good." I groan, my hips flexing with each thrust. I begin to move slowly, giving her time to adjust, feeling her body welcome me. My thrusts are slow, wanting to feel every inch of her, every part of her.

Her body shudders beneath me, her breath coming faster.

"Tell me you're mine," I grunt.

She moans, the ribbon pulling at her wrists as she squirms beneath me, her voice breathless and desperate. "I'm yours. I'm yours… please, don't stop."

I lean over her, my chest against her back, my hands gripping her hips tightly. I begin to move faster, harder, my breath ragged as I lose myself in her. Christ, I just came in her mouth, and I can already feel another orgasm cresting. I'm insatiable when it comes to this woman.

Pulling out of her, I grip her waist and flip her over, lifting her knees as I climb on the bed. I guide her hands above her head, position my cock at her sopping wet pussy, and slide back inside her heat.

My girl moans, tilting her head back as her breasts bounce with every hard thrust, driving me wild.

"You're so pretty baby," I grunt, caressing her face as I wreck her pussy, thrusting deep inside of her. "Look at you, taking my cock like a good fucking girl. Completely and utterly wrecked by me."

I wipe her smudged mascara under her eyes, my hands sliding down to her throat, her pulse fluttering beneath my fingers. She gasps, her body stiffening for just a second before she melts against me. The way her body submits to me drives me wild.

I lean in close, my lips brushing her ear, my breath hot against her skin. "You trust me?" I whisper, my thumb gently tracing her jawline.

Her eyes flicker to mine, and she nods. I tighten my grip slightly, just enough for her to feel it. Her breath catches in her throat, a quiet whimper escaping her lips. I can feel the flutter of her pulse, the vulnerability and the want, raw and untamed. She's lost in it, and I'm right there with her.

I draw back, just enough to look at her, and then slowly, I press deeper into her, my hips moving in rhythm with her body. My hand around her neck tightens with every thrust, her breath shallow, coming in quick bursts as I move inside her.

"You're such a pretty little slut, satisfying me. You like being choked, baby?" I murmur.

The pressure of my fingers around her throat makes her gasp, her eyes fluttering for a moment. She's breathless as her head tilts back, offering herself to me. "Yes... sir."

The words hit me like a shock, my body stalling for a second. *Fuck*. I didn't expect her to call me that, but holy fucking hell it makes my blood burn. A low growl escapes me as my grip tightens, my hips snapping deeper into her, every inch of me demanding more.

"God, I love messing you up." A groan crawls out of my throat as I thrust inside of her, the pleasure curling up my spine when her pussy tightens around me. "You look so fucking beautiful right now. My cock deep inside of your pussy, my hand around your pretty little throat."

I feel her pulse quicken with each movement. The way her body shakes under me, the way her voice cracks when she gasps for air consumes me. She's at my mercy, and she wants it. She *needs* it.

My lips crash against hers, desperate, hungry, starving for every single inch of her.

"Say my name," I demand against her lips, my voice rough with desire.

She gasps. "Nicholas."

I shiver, my cock twitching inside her tight cunt. "Again."

"Nicholas..." She breathes my name again, and it sends a shockwave through me, the sound of it driving me even deeper into her.

Her body tightens, and I know she's close. Her moans grow louder, more urgent, and I push harder, deeper, wanting to give her everything.

"Come for me," I grunt. "Let go, baby. I want to feel your pussy tighten around my cock."

I increase the pressure of my grip, which sends her over the edge as she moans loudly as she falls apart beneath me. She floods my cock with her orgasm, her cunt wrapped so tight around me. A couple more thrusts has me following her, coming with a groan as I empty inside of her tight pussy, filling her up.

The only sounds in the room are our ragged breaths as we slowly come down from the orgasm, my heart still pounding in my chest. I pull back slightly, just enough to look at her, my hand still resting lightly around her neck, fingers gently tracing the pulse I can still feel racing beneath her skin.

Her eyes are closed, lips parted, chest rising and falling quickly and I can't help but watch her.

Reaching up, I tug the ribbon from her wrists and run my thumb over her cheek, brushing away the beads of sweat that cling to her skin.

"You okay?" I murmur, my thumb stroking her jaw.

She opens her eyes, a haze of pleasure still clouding her gaze. A shaky breath escapes her lips as she looks up at me. "Yeah. That was…"

"Yeah?" I ask, smoothing the roughness of my touch with my lips on her neck. "You liked it?"

She nods, pulling her bottom lip between her teeth. "I love everything we do."

I chuckle, gripping her waist with a deep need for her. "You're always so eager to please me," I say, pulling back to hold her face in my hands, tucking her hair behind her ear. "But if there's ever a moment you're not comfortable or want to stop, just say the word. I'll listen. Always."

She takes a breath, her voice tentative. "Like a safe word?"

"Kind of," I reply, meeting her eyes. "Are you familiar with the traffic light system?"

She blinks, her eyes searching mine. "Red, yellow, green?"

"Exactly," I say, my fingers tracing her jaw. "If you love what we're doing, use green. You want to slow down or pause, use yellow. And if you want to stop, use red. Although, if you say 'stop,' I'll stop. Your consent means more to me than anything, Amara. More than your submission."

She nods in understanding, and I can't help but dive in and capture her lips, kissing her until I can't breathe.

Two months.

That's all we have left.

It's what I signed up for—what we both signed up for—but I'm already getting withdrawals from her.

And I have no idea how the hell I'm going to survive when she's gone.

CHAPTER TWENTY-EIGHT
Amara

Silence.

Thick, suffocating silence.

As the elevator doors slide open and Nicholas and I step into the office, the room falls into a stunned hush. Heads swivel, conversations die mid-sentence, and even the hum of keyboards fades into nothing.

Nicholas, however, is completely unfazed. He walks through the office, his hand firmly in mine. Meanwhile, my legs are doing their best not to turn into jelly from the attention of every eye in the room.

He insisted we walk in together. To make it clear that we're engaged. Honestly, I'm not sure what I was expecting, but I definitely didn't think it would be this.

We finally make it to my desk, and I'm just about to sit down and pretend none of this is happening when Nicholas grabs my elbow, spins me around, and presses a soft kiss to my lips.

"Have a good morning, honey," he murmurs, his lips turning in a small smirk, and my stomach does a little flip.

Before I can even react, he pulls away and walks off, leaving me standing like a deer in the headlights

I turn toward my desk, only to be met with Jade's wicked grin on her face, her blue eyes practically sparkling with mischief. Sophie eyes me curiously, arms crossed but clearly holding back a million questions.

"Oh. My. God," Jade squeals, dragging each word out. "Tell me everything!"

"There's nothing to tell," I say quickly, dropping into my chair and pulling my laptop open as a makeshift shield.

"Nothing to talk about?" Jade repeats, leaning against my desk with a scoff. "You're telling me there's nothing to say about the fact that Nicholas Blackwood just kissed you in front of the entire office?"

"It was purely for show," I mutter, logging into my computer, trying to focus, though my hands are shaking.

Jade lets out a laugh. "Honey, that was *not* a 'for show' kiss. That was a 'you're mine, and I want everyone to know it' kiss. Now, spill. I want all the sordid details."

"There are no details. Can we just move on? My head's killing me."

Jade scoffs. "Yeah, I'm sure your knees and throat are sore too."

I don't respond, focusing on my typing, but the heat in my face tells me I'm blushing. Sophie's gasp from her desk confirms it.

"Oh my god. You slept with him, didn't you?"

"No," I lie, the words slipping out before I can stop them, and the blush deepens.

Jade's grin widens. "Oh, this is *so* much better than I thought. You're *fucking* your fake fiancé and didn't tell me?"

"Shhh." I glance around quickly. "Can you two keep it down? No one's supposed to know it's not real."

"Relax." Jade waves her hand. "Mum's the word. So, are you two together now?" she asks. "I give you props. I thought this would've happened way sooner."

"No." I shake my head, more to myself than to her. "We're not... This is just..."

Her brows furrow, and she glances at Sophie, who's wearing the same confused expression. "Just... what?"

I let out a sigh. "We're just sleeping together. We're still agreeing to part ways once the contract ends, and I don't need to be his fake fiancée anymore. There's nothing else going on between us."

Sophie raises an eyebrow but doesn't push further. Instead, she asks quietly, "And you're telling me there's no chance, not even a tiny, minuscule chance, that you're catching feelings?"

I hesitate, her question hitting a little too close to home. "Nope," I lie, though my chest aches as I say it.

"Are you sure? First, you two are sleeping together, and then that kiss... You've never really been a casual kind of girl, Amara. We saw how hard you clung to Liam."

"Nicholas is not Liam."

"No," she agrees. "Which is what makes this so much more confusing. Nicholas is successful, rich, handsome, a good guy—"

"Good in bed, I'm guessing?" Jade cuts in with a grin.

Heat creeps up my neck. "I'm not answering that."

Jade scoffs. "No need, babe. Your face says it all. But Sophie's right. There's no way you're keeping your emotions out of this for another two months."

I gulp, realizing they're both right. I hadn't let myself think about it, but now I can't ignore the fact that I'm already starting to blur the lines between what's real and what isn't. And I know these feelings will only grow stronger.

"I'll be fine," I say, though I don't sound very convincing. "Can we please move on? Don't you two have work to do?"

Jade laughs. "Absolutely not. This is way more entertaining."

My phone buzzes on the desk, saving me from their relentless teasing.

"Shit," I say, glancing at the screen.

"What is it?" Sophie asks.

"My sister," I say, scrolling through the flood of texts.

Annie:

> Are you seriously going to pretend like these photos are fake?

Attached is an image of me and Nicholas at the gala, his hand on my waist, and me smiling up at him.

Annie:

> You're engaged? I thought you were dating Liam. What the hell is going on, Amara?

I swallow hard, feeling a lump form in my throat. "She and my grandma found out about Nicholas."

She blinks. "Wait. You hadn't told them you're engaged?"

I shake my head, guilt gnawing at me. "No. I couldn't tell them the truth and I didn't want to lie, so I just told them it wasn't real. But my sister saw the photos from the hotel opening."

Another groan slips from my lips when I see another one of my Annie's texts. "They want to meet him."

Jade lets out a laugh, crossing her legs as she sits on the edge of my desk. "Oh, this is going to be so good."

Before I can spiral any further, the intercom rings.

"Boss wants to see you," Jade singsongs, her smirk widening.

I roll my eyes and stand, slipping my phone into my pocket.

When I reach Nicholas's office. I hesitate for a moment before knocking.

"Come in," his voice calls from inside.

I push the door open and step inside, my heart pounding in my chest. Nicholas is sitting at his desk, his tie slightly loosened, the top button of his shirt undone. He looks up, his dark eyes locking onto mine, and the corners of his mouth tug into a lazy smile.

"Hi," I say, closing the door behind me. "You wanted to see me?"

He leans back in his chair, his gaze sweeping over me, the corners of his mouth twitching into a grin. "Yes, but now I'm wondering if I can actually be professional with you in here."

I roll my eyes, trying to ignore the way my pulse kicks into overdrive. "Be serious."

"I am serious," he replies, a smirk playing on his lips as he rises from his chair. "Come here."

As soon as I'm within arm's reach, his hand shoots out, gripping my wrist and pulling me toward him. Before I can protest, his lips find mine, slow, sweet, unhurried at first... but the kiss deepens quickly as his fingers tangle in my hair, tugging me closer.

"God, I missed you," he murmurs against my lips, his other hand sliding around my waist to lift me, positioning me on the edge of his desk.

"It's been ten minutes since you last saw me," I manage to say, breathless, the words faltering on my lips as his kiss consumes me.

"I know." He chuckles, pulling back just enough to brush his thumb over my cheek, his eyes dark with something that makes it hard to breathe. It's a look that makes it impossible to forget, makes it impossible to push away the thought that I won't see this look again in two months. "You've ruined me."

A laugh escapes me, before his lips find mine again, his hand trailing down my thigh, slowly lifting my skirt.

"What did you want to talk about?" I murmur, trying to catch my breath.

"Hmmm?" he hums, his lips trailing a lazy path down my neck, making it hard to think.

"You... called me in here. Did you need something?"

"Yes," he groans, his mouth hot against my skin, his tongue flicking over the sensitive spot just below my ear. "You."

"Nicholas," I chuckle, pulling back just enough to catch his gaze. "We're at work, remember?"

He sighs, reluctantly pulling away. "I got a call about the new couch, which is coming today." He raises an eyebrow, his lips curling into a teasing smile. "We're getting a new couch?"

We.

I swallow, the word hitting me harder than I'd like to admit, but I keep my expression neutral. "You need a new one."

He scoffs, crossing his arms. "What's wrong with my couch?"

I lift my shoulder in a shrug. "It's too long, too hard. Grey. I thought a light, fluffy fabric one might make the place feel less like a bachelor pad and a little more... homey."

His smile widens, his gaze turning softer. My pulse quickens as his eyes linger on me. "Got any more surprises I should know about?" he asks, teasing.

"A few more," I admit, my lips curling into a smirk. "You told me to redecorate however I'd like. So, that's exactly what I'm doing."

His grin widens, and he steps closer, his hands reaching up to cradle my face, tilting my head back just enough to meet his dark, intense gaze. "Fine by me," he murmurs, before leaning down, brushing our lips together, sending a shock of heat through my body. His lips part slightly, groaning into my mouth as if he can't help himself.

Then, my phone buzzes, immediately pulling me out of the moment. I freeze, remembering the endless texts from my sister.

Then my phone buzzes, loud and intrusive, cutting through the haze of desire. I freeze.

Nicholas pulls back, a frown knitting his brows together as his gaze flickers toward my phone. "Do you need to get that?"

I shake my head quickly, the moment already slipping away. "No. It's just... my family."

His brow arches. "Oh?"

"They found out about us."

Nicholas leans back slightly, crossing his arms as he props himself against the edge of his desk. His eyes narrow, curiosity flickering. "Found out, as in...?"

"As in, I didn't tell her we were engaged," I admit, tugging my lip between my teeth, my words spilling out in a rush. "I didn't want to lie to her or my sister, but now they both found out and they won't stop blowing up my phone with a million questions." I let out a shaky breath, trying to hold it together. "They both want to meet you. And I don't know what to say because I hate lying to them, and now they're asking about Liam, and I don't—"

"Whoa, whoa," he cuts in gently, his voice warm and soothing. "Calm down, honey. It's okay."

"Calm down?" I echo, shaking my head. "That's not exactly an option right now."

His expression softens, the teasing fading. "There's no need to panic. I'd love to meet your family."

I blink at him, stunned. "You would?"

"Of course." His lips curl into that unfairly charming smile of his. "They're important to you."

I stare at him, the tight knot in my stomach slowly starting to loosen. "You'd really do that?"

He tilts his head slightly, the sincerity in his gaze making my heart skip a beat. "It'll be just like a meeting, Amara. I've done hundreds of them. I think I can handle one with your grandma."

A laugh escapes me, but my heart is still racing, too loud in my chest. "We're going to have to pretend in front of her, too."

Nicholas leans forward, brushing his lips over the corner of my mouth. "Fine by me," he murmurs. "I could use another excuse to kiss you."

I laugh again, breathless, my fingers curling instinctively against his chest as I pull him closer. "You don't have enough of those already?"

"Not nearly enough," he replies, his voice dropping lower, as his hand trails down my arm. "It'll never be enough."

Another buzz from my phone brings me back to reality, and I glance down at it reluctantly.

"Answer her," Nicholas tells me, lifting my chin gently so I'm looking at him again. "Tell her we'll be there on Saturday."

I search his face, looking for any hesitation, any sign that he's second-guessing this. "You're sure about this?"

He meets my gaze, unwavering and confident, like he's already planned this out. "I'm sure."

And just like that, the panic that had been clawing at my insides disappears. I breathe out slowly, the tension easing from my shoulders.

"Okay," I whisper, my lips brushing his as I say it.

He smiles against my mouth, his hands sliding around my waist, pulling me closer. "Saturday," he repeats. "We'll be there."

His smile makes my stomach flutter, and for a moment, it's easy to forget where the lines are drawn between what's real and what's part of the act.

But I can't let myself forget.

CHAPTER TWENTY-NINE

Amara

My palms are sweating. My whole body is sweating. The magazine I'm clutching crinkles in protest as I grip it tighter. Modern designs stare back at me from the glossy pages as I flip the page, studying a minimalist living room with a charcoal-gray sectional and a statement coffee table made of dark-stained oak. Too cold. Too impersonal.

I've been slowly transforming Nicholas's apartment, adding little touches to make it feel less like a showroom and more like a real home. A throw blanket here, warmer lighting there, maybe a plant or two to breathe some life into the space. He hasn't said much about it. I'm starting to think he probably doesn't even notice… or care.

My stomach twists with nerves as I flip the page once more. The last time I went home was Christmas. Now, I'm heading back with my fiancé.

My fake fiancé.

Lying to my family has never been easy, and this? This lie might be my worst one yet. They gave up so much so I could chase my dreams, and now…

A flicker of movement pulls me from my spiraling thoughts. I glance up, meeting a pair of dark, intense eyes fixed squarely on me, one hand covering his mouth as he studies me.

"What?" I ask, dropping the magazine to my lap.

His lips twitch, and then a small smile curves them. "You're beautiful."

Heat floods my cheeks, and for one stupid second, my nerves give way to something warmer, softer. He has this way of looking at me like I'm the only person in the world. It's infuriating. It's distracting. *It's also not real*.

He arches a brow. "Are you nervous?"

A dry laugh escapes me as I shake my head and toss the crumpled magazine onto the seat beside me. "Are you kidding? I can already picture my grandma and sister lining up to interrogate me. 'Why did you and Liam break up? Why didn't you tell us you were engaged? And, oh, my personal favorite... Why did the media call you his assistant when you told us you were a designer?'"

His brows lift. "You told them you were a designer?"

I sigh, breathing out a sigh. "I might have. They gave up everything so I could follow my dreams, and I didn't want them to know that the only job I could land was as an assistant," I admit, my voice quiet. "But now, I'll have to tell them the truth."

"Or..."

"Or?" I repeat, my brows knitting.

He shrugs, leaning back against the plush couch. "Or you could tell them you work as a designer under me, and the news just got it wrong. It's not technically a lie. You will be a designer in less than two months. What's the harm?"

I blink at him, surprised. "That's... not a bad idea."

"I know. I'm brilliant," he says, flashing a self-satisfied grin.

I scoff, rolling my eyes. "How are you not nervous? They're going to scrutinize you to death. My grandma and sister will ask a million questions to figure out if you're good enough for me," I warn him. "She hated Liam, didn't think he was good enough for me."

Nicholas raises an eyebrow, looking entirely unbothered. "She was right. Besides, I'm ten times better than your ex."

A laugh bubbles out of me before I can stop it. No argument there.

"What else is worrying you?"

I shrug, trying to brush it off. "I just don't want her to realize I was lying to her."

He pins me with a look. "Amara."

I let out a sigh, closing my eyes briefly. "I didn't have the perfect childhood," I start, glancing at him. "My dad left when I was still a toddler. I don't even remember him. And my mom… died a few weeks after my seventh birthday," I admit, my chest tight at the reminder. I haven't thought about that day for so long, and the reminder is as painful as it was back then. "And after my mom died, it was just me, my sister, and my grandma. She's the one who really raised us."

Nicholas stays silent, waiting for me to go on.

I feel the lump in my throat as my gaze drops to my lap, my chest tightening. "I guess that's why I care so much about what they think. I want them to be proud of me."

Nicholas studies me for a moment, leaning forward to cup my face in his hands. "They will be. They already *are*. You're amazing, Amara, and your family knows it." He shoots me a reassuring smile. "There's nothing to worry about, honey." His smile widens into a grin. "I'll make them love me. So much so that your grandma will be begging me to marry you for real."

My chest tightens at his words, and I force a smile, trying to push down the chaos swirling inside me. Somewhere along the way, I convinced myself I could keep this professional. That I could sleep next to him, kiss him, and not let it get messy.

But it's too late. I've caught feelings—hook, line, and sinker—and they're not going anywhere.

The sound of footsteps in the aisle saves me from spiraling any further. I glance up as a flight attendant approaches. For a split second, I tense, expecting Savannah to appear, but instead, it's a blonde woman with a sleek bob and a warm smile.

"Good morning. I'm Astrid, and I'll be your flight attendant today. Let me know if there's anything you need."

My brows knit together, my gaze flickering to Nicholas. *Where's Savannah?*

Nicholas nods in acknowledgment, entirely unfazed. "Thank you, Astrid. I'll have a scotch."

"Of course." She turns to me with the same practiced smile. "And for you, Mrs. Blackwood?"

Mrs. Blackwood. The title catches me off guard, making my pulse jump. I recover quickly, pasting on a polite smile. "Just a coffee, please."

"Certainly. I'll be back with your drinks shortly." Astrid leaves, leaving a faint trail of floral perfume.

I turn to Nicholas, narrowing my eyes. "What happened to Savannah?"

He leans back in his seat. "She got reassigned."

"Reassigned?" My frown deepens. "I thought she was your personal flight attendant."

"Not anymore."

"Wait…" I lower my voice, the realization dawning. "Did you… *fire* her?"

Nicholas shakes his head, his lips curving into a faint smirk. "I didn't fire her. I had her reassigned. There's a difference."

My jaw drops. "Nicholas…"

The smirk fades as his eyes meet mine. "She disrespected you," he says simply. "I don't tolerate that. I don't want you to feel uncomfortable when we take the jet. She won't be an issue anymore."

Heat creeps up my neck, and I glance down at my hands, suddenly unsure of what to do with them. "But I'm not going to be taking the jet once the contract ends," I murmur.

He doesn't respond immediately, and when I glance up, his jaw is tight, his gaze locked on me. For a moment, neither of us speaks. He just watches me, his eyes searching mine.

Before I can untangle the mess of emotions swirling between us, Astrid returns, setting our drinks down.

"Here you are. A scotch for you, and a coffee for Mrs. Blackwood."

"Thank you," I manage, forcing a small smile as Nicholas nods in acknowledgment.

Astrid disappears again, leaving us in silence.

The rest of the flight blurs by, my nerves simmering as the minutes tick closer to arriving at my nanna's house. Nicholas remains unbothered, meanwhile, I'm doing my best to keep my leg from bouncing.

When the car finally pulls up to the little white bungalow, a wave of nostalgia and unease hits me all at once. The peeling paint and overgrown lawn tug at my chest, a bittersweet reminder of the home I grew up in.

Nicholas steps out first, smoothly rounding the car to open my door. "You ready?" he asks.

Not even a little. But I force a smile, placing my hand in his as I step out. "Yeah. Let's do this."

The door swings open before we even make it up the short path. Annie stands at the door, hands mid-wipe on her jeans, her messy bun frizzing in every possible direction.

"Hey, stranger!" she sighs, enveloping me in a hug that smells like cinnamon and dish soap.

"Missed you," I murmur, my throat tight as I cling to her for just a second longer.

She leans back, her sharp brown eyes zeroing in on Nicholas. Her gaze sweeps over him, taking in every detail from his perfectly tailored jacket to his absurdly symmetrical jawline. Her brows arch, and a grin tugs at her lips.

"And you must be the fiancé."

Nicholas doesn't falter, meeting her gaze with one of his trademark polite smiles. "That's me." He offers his hand.

Annie stares at his hand for a beat too long, then shakes it. "Hmm. Handsome and polite. I'll admit, I was expecting worse."

"Worse?" Nicholas repeats, his brows lifting slightly, amusement flickering in his eyes.

She waves a hand vaguely. "Well, let's just say you've exceeded expectations. For now."

"Annie," I warn, my lips twitching at my sister's interrogation.

She sighs, stepping aside to let us in. "Come on in. Nanna's in the living room."

The moment I step inside, it's like walking into a memory. Nanna is sitting in her wheelchair, her favorite knitted blanket spread across her lap. When spots me, her face lights up, her smile making the corners of her eyes crinkle.

"Amara!" she calls, her voice full of affection despite the pain I know she's hiding.

I feel the lump in my throat instantly, but I push it down, forcing a smile as I lean down to give her a hug. "Hi, Nanna."

"God, it's been too long." She squeezes me tightly before rubbing my back.

"I know," I reply, laughing a little awkwardly when I pull back. "I'm sorry."

She shakes her head, a soft tut escaping her. "Don't be sorry. I'm just glad you're here." Her eyes flick to my ring finger, and I can't help but stiffen as she reaches for my hand. She inspects the ring closely, then glances up at me with a raised brow.

"How the hell do you walk around with that thing?"

I feel a flush creep up my neck, but I try to keep my composure as she turns her gaze toward Nicholas, who's standing behind me.

"I'm assuming this is the fiancé who gave you this ring?" she asks, a touch of suspicion in her voice.

I can't blame her for being skeptical. I've never once mentioned Nicholas, and now here I am, introducing him as my fiancé.

Nicholas steps forward and gently takes her hand, his smile smooth and confident, the kind that probably seals more deals than I'll ever know. "It's a pleasure to meet you, Ma'am."

Her brows lift at the name, and she lets out a small laugh. "Oh, god, please, call me Mary. 'Ma'am' makes me feel like I'm a hundred."

Nicholas chuckles. "Of course, Mary."

I watch as Nanna's initial hesitation fades under his charm, and I can't help but feel a little relieved. I'm so grateful he's here, I could almost cry.

Nicholas sits beside me, his knee brushing mine, grounding me, even though my nerves are still buzzing beneath the surface.

Nanna shifts in her wheelchair, folding her hands neatly in her lap. Her gaze sharpens, locking onto me, like she can sense the hesitance I'm trying to hide. Her smile softens, but there's no missing the curiosity in her voice when she asks, "Well, come on then. Tell me how this happened."

Beside her, Annie raises an eyebrow, leaning forward, her eyes flicking from me to Nicholas, eager for the story.

I glance at Nicholas, my heart racing. "Well…" I begin, the word coming out a little wobbly as I struggle to find the right words. I give a small, nervous laugh, trying to ease the tension. I grip my knee to keep my fingers from fidgeting. "It's a long story."

"That's all right. I've got all afternoon."

My gaze falls to my hands, which I'm twisting nervously on my lap. "Liam and I broke up a couple of months ago," I start, my voice trailing off. "He, uh… He cheated on me."

Nanna's smile falters, her expression freezing. She sits up straighter, her mouth parting slightly. "He cheated on you?"

I nod, keeping my eyes trained on a spot on the coffee table. Saying it out loud again feels like a fresh wound reopening.

Nanna's voice softens, her concern evident. "Oh, sweetheart. I'm so sorry. I warned you about him. I knew he wasn't good enough for you."

"I know. I should've listened," I admit, my voice tight. "He wasn't who I thought he was. But I'm okay now." My eyes flick to Nicholas, grateful for his steady presence. "Nicholas helped me through it."

Nanna's attention sharpens, her gaze moving to him. "You did?"

Nicholas nods. "Of course. Amara's important to me."

Annie leans back in her chair, narrowing her eyes. "Okay," she says slowly. "But how do we go from you comforting her to being engaged? I mean, it all happened pretty fast."

"It wasn't sudden for me," he tells them, sitting up straighter, his gaze flickering from Annie to Nanna, his expression softening as he continues. "I've been drawn to Amara since the day we met."

Nanna raises an eyebrow, and Annie leans forward, both women now fully invested in his words. And so am I, turning my head to glance at him.

Nicholas shifts his gaze to me, the intensity of his stare making my breath catch. "I admired her from the start. But we worked together, and I didn't want to cross any lines. I convinced myself it wasn't the right time, that I'd keep things professional. But..." He hesitates, his jaw tensing before he exhales deeply. "It became impossible to ignore how I felt. The more time we spent together, the harder it was to pretend I wasn't falling for her."

His words hit me like a jolt, knocking the wind from my lungs. I stare at him, momentarily forgetting this is all part of the act. The vulnerability in his eyes is too real, and for a heartbeat, I wonder if any part of his words is real.

Nanna smiles, her gaze warm. "Well, it sounds like you've found yourself a good man, Amara."

Her words linger in the air, weighing heavy on my chest. The guilt swirls within me, mingling with the knot of confusion I've been carrying since this whole thing started. I manage a smile, but it feels strained, as though I'm forcing it past all the unspoken things I'm too afraid to acknowledge.

I glance back at Nicholas. He's still watching me, his face unreadable, but there's something in his eyes that makes my stomach twist.

"Yeah," I say, my voice quieter than I intended. "I guess I have."

The sound of dishes being rinsed and set down fills the kitchen as I pass another plate to the drying rack. Annie stands beside me, sponge in hand, scrubbing at a stubborn casserole dish. It's quiet except for the running tap water. Comfortable. Normal. Or it would be if my chest didn't feel like it was caving in.

"So," Annie begins, glancing at me out of the corner of her eye, "how's work? You must be pretty busy to not tell me you were engaged."

I freeze for a fraction of a second, then force my shoulders to relax, focusing on folding the dish towel in my hands. "Yeah, I'm so sorry, I had a lot on my mind."

Annie rinses the dish, setting it in the drainer. "Yeah, I know how busy *assistants* can get."

My hands pause mid-fold, the towel slipping from my fingers. I glance at her, my stomach twisting. "Annie, I—"

"It's fine," she cuts me off, holding up a soapy hand. "You don't have to explain."

I blink, caught off guard. "I don't?"

Annie shrugs, rinsing another plate. "I get it. You didn't want to disappoint Nanna. I mean, I wish you would have told me, but I get it. You've always been the one chasing big dreams, and you didn't want her to think you'd settled for less. It's not like you're the only one who's ever bent the truth to protect her feelings."

I exhale, a weight lifting off my chest. "You're not mad?"

"No." Annie's smile is small but warm. "But you know you can tell me, right? Whatever it is, you don't have to deal with it on your own."

The lump in my throat is back, but this time for a different reason. I nod, my throat moving as I gulp. "How about you? How are you doing?"

"I'm good." Annie grins, her cheeks tinting slightly pink. "I, uh, started seeing someone."

My eyebrows shoot up, and a genuine smile breaks across my face. "What? Annie, that's amazing! Who is it? How long has this been going on?"

Annie rolls her eyes, laughing. "Calm down. It's new. His name's Derek, and he's… nice. You'd like him."

"I'm so happy for you," I say, nudging my sister lightly with my elbow.

"And," Annie adds, "I got a promotion at work. I'm making a little extra money now, so you can stop sending me cash every month."

I frown, my hands stilling on the damp plate. "Annie, no. Nanna needs that money for her medical bills."

"She's doing okay, Amara. Really. I'm making enough to handle us both. And you need it more than we do. I can only imagine how expensive it is to live in New York City. You've got rent, food, and—"

I shake my head. "I'm dating a millionaire, Annie. I can afford to give you some money."

A deep voice interrupts us from the doorway. "Billionaire, baby. With a *B*."

Both of us turn to see Nicholas leaning casually against the doorframe, a teasing smile tugging at his lips. Annie bursts into laughter, shaking her head as she dries her hands on a dish towel.

She tosses the towel onto the counter and squeezes my shoulder. "I'll let you two handle the rest of the dishes."

Nicholas grins, pushing off the doorframe to step into the kitchen. "Your sister seems great."

"She's the best," I say, unable to help the smile that tugs at my lips.

Nicholas steps closer, picking up a plate from the rack and begins to dry it. "You didn't tell me you send them money to help out your grandma."

I stiffen for a second before lifting my shoulder in a shrug. "Well, there wasn't any reason for me to. It's not your job to worry about your assistant's personal life."

Nicholas sets the plate down and moves closer, his hand slipping around my waist, the intensity in his gaze making my pulse spike. "You're way more than that, and you know it."

I try to pull away, shaking my head. "Nicholas. It's not your problem."

"Make it my problem," Nicholas says, his tone serious. "I don't care about money. I care about *you*. Let me help with your grandma. Let me make sure your sister isn't overworked. You shouldn't have to carry all of this on your own."

I shake my head, a lump in my throat. "Nicholas, that's... It's too much. It's my problem to deal with. They're my family."

He moves closer, the heat of his body and his intense eyes making my chest pound. "They're your family, yes. But they're important to me now, too. You don't have to say yes. But I'm going to help, Amara. Whether you let me or not. You're my fiancée, and I take care of you, that includes your family."

His words hit harder than I expect. It's not just about the help, because Nicholas is a kind, giving man, but it's the way he sees this… my family, as his responsibility too.

I swallow, struggling to keep my composure. "I don't know how to accept this."

"You don't have to know how," he replies, his voice softening. "Just trust me. Let me do this for you."

I exhale, my shoulders dropping in surrender. "Okay."

Nicholas gives me that smile as he leans in again, brushing his lips over mine. It's slow and soft, his hand still resting on my waist, and the tenderness of it almost undoes me.

When he pulls back, I feel the lingering warmth of his kiss on my lips. I touch my fingers to my lips, trying to steady my breath, but it's no use when my heart pounds in my chest as he smiles down at me.

I tried to keep whatever is going on between us casual. Tried to ignore my feelings, but it's impossible to do so anymore.

I'm falling for him.

And all I can think is how much it's going to hurt when this ends.

CHAPTER THIRTY

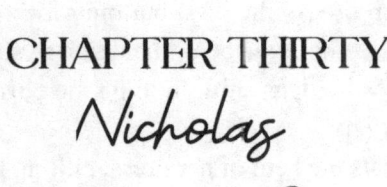

Nicholas

I'm addicted.

It's not something I've dealt with before. I like control—need it. The first time I tried a cigarette, I hated it, put it out before I even got halfway through. I've never been the type to get drunk or let a glass of whiskey become a habit. I've never even touched drugs. I've always thought addiction was for people who didn't have control.

Until I met her.

The woman sitting beside me has me so far gone, I don't even care if I look desperate. I probably do.

Her taste is burned into my memory.

Her scent is all over me, in my head, in the car, *everywhere.*

The shape of her lips.

The deep sage shade of her eyes.

Every part of her has me completely under her spell.

I haven't stopped touching her since the moment we stepped off the jet. I can't. Waiting isn't happening. Not with her. Not tonight.

Amara's hands grip my shirt, pulling me closer as I kiss her like I'm starving for her—because I am—and it's still not enough. I slide my tongue along the seam of her lips, and she opens for me, a soft, breathy sound escaping her that goes straight to my cock.

My hand moves, finding her thigh, bare and warm under my palm. Her gasp breaks the kiss, but only for a second. "We're almost home," she whispers, her voice shaky, her body betraying her as her legs shift, inviting me closer.

"I'm impatient."

My hand fists the hem of her dress, pulling it up. Her skin is soft under my fingertips, and I'm already picturing what's underneath when the car jolts to a stop.

Her whole body goes stiff, her head whipping toward the front where the driver clears his throat. "We're here."

"Perfect fucking timing," I mutter, leaning back, my hands reluctantly falling away.

She pushes at my chest, her cheeks flushed, but I catch the look in her eyes, the same need that's burning me alive.

I lean in, my lips brushing her ear. "This isn't over."

She shivers against me as the driver opens the door, and I step out, adjusting my jacket before turning back to help her out of the car. My hand finds hers, pulling her close the second she's out. Arousal swims in her eyes, and I let out a groan, tearing my eyes off her.

"Don't look at me like that," I warn as I guide her toward the entrance.

"Like what?" she teases, her lips twitching as she walks ahead of me.

The doorman nods as we walk past, but I pay him no mind. All I can focus on is her. The sway of her hips, the teasing glance she throws over her shoulder as if she's daring me to lose control right here.

The lobby is quiet as we head toward the private elevator, and I slide my keycard into the panel, the doors opening a second later.

She steps inside first, her fingers brushing mine, a fleeting touch that sets my nerves on edge. I follow, pressing the button for the top floor, and the moment the doors slide shut, I lose what little restraint I had left.

I have her against the wall in a heartbeat, my mouth crashing against hers. She sighs into the kiss, her arms looping around my neck like she's been waiting for this just as much as I have.

"You drive me insane," I murmur against her lips, my hand sliding down to grip her waist.

"You're insatiable," she teases.

I groan, my forehead dropping to hers. "Baby, I haven't felt your pussy around my cock in days. The bed at your grandma's house squeaked like crazy. I didn't want to give her a heart attack, and you know you wouldn't have been able to keep quiet."

Her laugh is light, but her cheeks flush as her fingers tangle in my hair. "I can be quiet."

"Liar." My lips trail down her neck as the elevator dings, and I reluctantly pull away, grabbing her hand to tug her toward the door.

The penthouse is dark when we step inside, the city lights pouring through the windows as I tower over her, my eyes darkening with everything I don't need to say.

She takes a step back, a grin playing on her lips, but I don't let her get far. I catch her, pressing her against the nearest wall, and crash my lips against hers.

Desperate. Needy. *Starving* for her.

Lifting her up in my arms, I carry her to our bedroom, her arms finding their way around my neck. I kick the door open and flick the lights on, wanting to see every inch of her.

"I've been waiting all night for this. All weekend. My lips graze her neck, my hands already sliding down her sides, gripping her waist. "I *need* you."

She lets out a soft whimper, her body melting into mine, but then she shakes her head, her voice small, almost apologetic. "I need a shower first."

I groan, my forehead dropping to hers as I drop her on her feet. "Please tell me you're kidding."

"I've been in a plane all day," she sighs, her hands resting on my chest. "I just need to get under the hot water for a minute."

I exhale sharply, my jaw clenching as I fight the mental image already forming. "You're trying to kill me," I rasp out. "Picturing you in that shower, naked, wet, alone..."

Her lips twitch, that teasing glint back in her eyes. "Then maybe you should join me."

My head snaps up, my eyes narrowing as her words sink in. "You're playing a dangerous game."

"Am I?" she whispers, stepping away, her fingers trailing down my arm before she disappears into the bathroom.

For a second, I just stand there, breathing hard, trying to collect myself. But then I hear the sound of the water turning on, steam curling out from under the door.

I'm already pulling off my tie as I follow her, the door swinging open to reveal her standing by the glass, the straps of her dress sliding off her shoulders, exposing bare skin that has me cursing under my breath.

"Get in, or stay out there," she challenges over her shoulder.

There's no chance in hell I'm staying out here.

I'm in that bathroom a second later, slamming the door behind me. I don't even give her time to breathe before I'm turning her around, pinning her back against the glass shower door, my mouth claiming hers.

Every inch of her feels like fire under my fingertips, and I can't get enough. Her hands move to the buttons of my shirt, tugging at the fabric with impatience, and I lift her hands away, pinning them above her head.

"You can tease me all you want," I murmur, my voice dark, "but don't forget who's in control here."

I feel her shiver, her body reacting to mine with no hesitation. Her breath hitches, and she meets my gaze, her eyes softening in submission. "Yes, sir," she breathes, the sound sending a rush of heat through me.

I pull her dress over her head, exposing her to me completely, taking in the curve of her body, the way her full breasts sit so perfectly in my hands. I want to devour every inch of her, but first, I want to see her unravel for me.

"You're a little impatient," she gasps out when her dress falls to the ground.

"You have no idea," I murmur, my hands trailing up her sides, grazing over her belly, feeling the heat of her skin under my fingertips. "So beautiful," I whisper, pressing my lips to the hollow of her neck, feeling her pulse beneath my lips.

Her eyes never leave mine as she reaches behind her, unhooking her bra, letting it fall to the floor.

I pull off my shirt, throwing it aside, my eyes locked on her. "Don't stop," I mutter as I unbutton my pants. She's already ahead of me, pushing her panties down her legs, stepping out of them. I can't help but drag my eyes over every inch of her gorgeous naked body.

As I slip out of my pants, she steps into the shower, the water cascading down her body, and I follow her, stepping behind her, and pulling the glass door closed.

I take her mouth in a kiss, deep and slow, and as the water pours down on us, I forget everything else. There's no past, no future. There's only this moment, only her.

She lets out a needy moan when my hands land on her ass with a sharp slap. "That's for making me wait," I murmur against her neck, my grip tightening on her hips.

"Please," she moans, her fingers getting lost in my hair as the water cascades over us.

"Please what? Tell me what you want," I demand against her lips. "I want to hear you say it."

"You," she whispers, our bodies naked and grinding against each other. God, she feels so good against me. Soft, warm, and all fucking mine.

"Where do you want me?" I coax, wanting to hear the dirty words from her lips.

Her head tips back when I part her legs with my knee, and fit it between her legs, positioned so she can grind her sweet little clit against me.

"I want… *Oh god*."

"Not God. *Nicholas*, baby. We've been over this."

Grinding her pussy against my leg, she moans, her eyes fluttering. "I want… your mouth."

"On where?" I ask, feeling her arousal drench my leg as she grips onto me, the orgasm cresting inside of her.

"On my…" Tugging her bottom lip between her teeth, she sucks in a breath when I press my knee harder against her clit.

"Where, Amara?" I say, firmly.

Her eyes open, glancing up at me with those cute innocent eyes as she grinds her cunt on my leg. "On my pussy," she says, making my breath hitch. "I want your mouth on my pussy."

A satisfied groan leaves me. "Such a good girl for me. You know I love when you use your words."

My lips trail down her neck, finding her breasts, my tongue swirling around her tight, pink nipples. A desperate groan grits from my throat when she moans, breathless and quick and utterly delicious. "You're so fucking responsive. Every touch, every kiss, makes you quiver."

My hands clutch her wide hips, exploring her body, feeling every inch beneath my touch. She deserves to be praised, *worshipped*.

When she moans again, her fingers tightening in my hair, I break out into a grin as I kiss down her body, pressing my lips to her soft stomach.

Her legs start to shift as she squirms under my touch, desperate for me. But instead of giving in, I let my lips graze against her pussy so softly, she whines.

I take my time with her. She's not just a woman to me, she's *my* fucking woman, my fiancée, and I want her to feel that with every kiss, every flick of my tongue, every second of the sweet torture I'm giving her.

"Patience, baby," I murmur, my lips brushing the sensitive skin of her inner thigh. "You'll get exactly what you need… but only when I'm ready to give it to you."

Her whimper is soft, her hips bucking, seeking more contact. She's coming undone already, and I haven't even touched her where she wants me most.

My hands slide down her thighs, spreading her open, and the sight of her—glistening, pink and perfect—makes my cock throb painfully. But this isn't about me. It's about her, about showing her exactly how I want to please her.

The first flick of my tongue draws a sharp gasp from her lips. Her fingers tighten in my hair, pulling me closer, and I give in, groaning against her as I take my time tasting her. Her hips grind against my mouth, every moan, every shudder telling me exactly what she needs.

"That's it, Amara," I rasp between strokes, my voice thick and needy. "Let me hear you. Let me feel how much you want this."

She's falling apart under me, her moans turning to broken cries, her body writhing as I lick her sweet pussy. When I slide two fingers inside her, curling them just right, she clenches around me, her fingers clutching the strands of my hair so tight I feel pain.

"Nicholas," she gasps, her nails digging into my scalp. "Don't stop. Please don't stop."

I grin against her, quickening my pace, my tongue working in perfect rhythm with my fingers. Her cries grow louder, and when she finally breaks, it's the most beautiful thing I've ever seen.

Her orgasm crashes over her, her breath catching as she moans my name over and over like a prayer. I don't stop until she's completely spent, until her legs are shaking and her grip on my hair loosens.

When I finally pull away, she looks at me through heavy-lidded eyes, her chest heaving, her lips parted.

"You were so incredible, honey," I say, lifting onto my feet as I brush her hair back from her damp forehead. "And I'm not even close to being done with you."

She smiles, lazy and sated, but the fire in her gaze tells me she's ready for more.

And so am I.

"Open your mouth," I demand, my voice rough.

She obeys without hesitation, her lips parting, and her tongue sticking out for me. Tilting her head back I look down at those wide, innocent eyes and spit on her waiting tongue. My cock aches when she moans, soft and breathy. It's the most beautiful sound I've ever heard.

"See how sweet your cunt tastes, baby?" I rasp, my thumb tracing her jaw before I pull her in for another kiss, my tongue tangling with hers. Her body arches, silently begging for more.

Pulling back, I grip her chin, forcing her gaze to meet mine. "Turn around," I order.

She moves instantly, turning around as she places her hands flat on the shower glass. My hands glide over her wide hips, marveling at how beautifully she fills my palms. I can't stop myself from squeezing, my fingers digging into her softness like she was made to fit my hands.

Dragging the tip of my cock along her slick heat, I tease her, reveling in the way she quivers. "You're dripping for me," I murmur, my voice a mix of awe and hunger. "You want this, don't you?"

"Yes," she breathes, her voice shaking. "I always want you."

Her words drive me wild, and I can't resist her any longer, gripping her hips tighter as I thrust forward, groaning as her body takes me, inch by inch. She's wet and warm and so tight that I almost lose it right here.

"Fuck, Amara," I grit out, my fingers digging into her skin. "You feel like heaven."

Her moan is pure music to my ears, and I start to move, pulling out slowly before driving back in. Each thrust draws another sound from her lips. Soft gasps, breathless cries, desperate whimpers that make my cock twitch inside of her.

Leaning forward, I press my chest against her back, my hands sliding around to her stomach. A groan leaves me as my fingers splay across her, loving the feel of her body beneath my palms.

Beautiful whimpers escape her as my hand drifts lower, finding her clit. My fingers circle it in time with my thrusts, and her body jolts, her cries growing louder, rawer. "You're desperate for my cock to fill this tight cunt, aren't you, honey?" I murmur, quickening my pace. "I can feel every inch of your pussy squeezing me, gripping my cock inside of you." She lets out a sweet little cry at my words, her tits pressing against the glass as I fuck her hard, relentless, wanting to bury myself inside this woman until the end of my days. "Let go, Amara. Let me feel you come on my cock."

The way she tightens around me pushes me over the edge, the orgasm crashing into me hard and fast. "*Fuck*." I bury myself deep inside her, my hips stuttering as I spill into her tight heat.

For a moment, all I can do is hold her, my forehead pressed against her shoulder, my breaths heavy in her ear. I don't pull out, don't let go—I can't.

The thought of impregnating her flashes in my mind as I thrust my cock deeper, filling her with every drop of my cum. Her body full and round with my child, the ultimate proof that she's mine, consumes my mind.

But I force the thought away as I press a kiss to her damp shoulder. That won't ever happen. This thing between Amara and I will be over in less than two months. This is strictly business. Nothing more.

I pull out of her, groaning when my cum drips out of her pussy, and pull her into my arms, turning her so I can look into her eyes. She doesn't see the turmoil flashing through my mind, and I don't let it show.

"You're so beautiful," I murmur, brushing a strand of hair from her face. "You did so well for me, baby."

Her smile is soft, sleepy, and sated, and I press my lips to her forehead, holding her closer as my chest tightens with things I can't afford to want.

CHAPTER THIRTY-ONE

Amara

The apartment is quiet. Too quiet. The only sounds are the faint hum of the fridge and Pumpkin clawing at the cat tree I bought for her... with Nicholas's card, of course.

He left for work a couple of hours ago, and it's ridiculous how much I already miss him. We woke up in bed together—like we do every morning—and he crawled between my legs, making my eyes roll to the back of my head as he ate my pussy for breakfast until my legs were shaking. And then he got in the shower, got dressed and kissed me long enough to make me forget how to think straight before he told me to stay home today while he took care of things at work.

I smirk to myself at the reminder. Dating the boss has its perks. The thought pops into my mind, making my smile drop. We're not dating. This engagement isn't real. It's a contract, a means to an end, nothing more. I keep repeating that in my head, day after day, like a mantra that's supposed to protect me from heartbreak.

But I feel a strange whirling in my chest. It's getting harder to hide my feelings for him, when I wake up in his bed every morning, tangled in his sheets, his arm heavy around my waist, holding me against him.

He doesn't let me sleep in the guest room anymore. Not that I'm complaining. I've stopped trying to argue about it. The way he clutches me to him, burying his face in the crook of my neck until we both drift off, makes it impossible. It's addictive, the way he holds me, like he can't bear to let me go.

My phone buzzes on the coffee table, jolting me out of my thoughts. I reach for it, half expecting a message from Nicholas, even though he's probably neck-deep in meetings by now. Instead, it's from my sister.

Annie:

> Loved seeing you this weekend. Nanna's doing great with the new nurse. Thank Nicholas for me. He seems like a really good guy. I'm really happy for you.

A smile tugs at my lips as our weekend away at home flashes in my mind. I can't remember seeing my grandma so happy for me before, so charmed by a guy. It felt so natural, so easy, like he wasn't just pretending to be my fiancé, like this whole thing wasn't a charade.

But it is.

Once Nicholas gets what he wants, I'll leave this place. I'll leave him. And there's nothing I can do about it.

I'll have to deal with the heartbreak. They'll feel sorry for me, and Grandma will probably shake her head and say she knew it was too good to be true.

And I'll have to nod along, pretending I didn't know that too. Pretending it doesn't hurt as much as it does.

I've known this was coming from the moment I signed that contract. I shouldn't feel sad about it… but the thought of walking away still makes my chest ache.

I shake my head, trying to dislodge the growing lump in my throat. My nose tingles as tears threaten to form, but I force them back. Crying over something that isn't real is pointless. I reach for my phone again, ready to text Annie back, when another buzz makes the screen light up.

But it's not Annie this time.

It's Liam.

My ex.

The air leaves my lungs as I stare at his name, a name I've been trying to forget for months. Against my better judgment, I open the message.

Liam:

> Saw the pictures of you and him.

My heart pounds. I hover over the block button, my thumb twitching, but then another message comes through.

Liam:

> You look so beautiful.

I furrow my brows, my stomach twisting. I can't remember the last time Liam called me beautiful. Certainly not in the last year of our relationship. Not after he started pulling away, finding excuses to stay late at work, his affection dwindling until it was almost nonexistent. And now, suddenly, he decides to say it when I'm with another man?

I see he's typing and my stomach churns.

Liam:

> Can I see you? I really need to talk to you.

My chest tightens, memories of Liam crashing over me. I should ignore him. Block his number and forget he ever existed. But... he was someone I thought I'd marry. Someone I loved. Someone I spent years of my life with.

He also cheated on you.

My phone dings with another text.

Liam:

> Please, Amara. I need to see you.

I suck in a breath. There were so many things left unsaid, so many questions I never got answers to.

My fingers hover over the keyboard, and before I can stop myself, I type:

Me:

> What do you want to talk about?

The reply comes almost instantly.

Liam:

> I think we should talk in person. I'm outside your apartment.

My brows furrow, and my eyes dart to elevator doors as if expecting to see him standing there.

Me:

How do you know where I live?

Liam:

I still have your location on my phone.

Let me come up. Please.

I stare at the message, my thoughts spinning. I don't want to see him. I don't want to talk to him. I don't want to look into his eyes and remember what I used to love about him, knowing someone else saw it too.

Me:

I don't think that's a good idea.
Nicholas will be home soon.

Liam:

All I need is a few minutes. Please.

My jaw clenches, and I pace the living room, glancing at the screen, half-tempted to tell him to go to hell. But then I find myself typing one word.

Me:

Okay.

The seconds stretch into an eternity as I pace the living room, my phone clutched tightly in my hand. I don't know why I agreed. Closure, maybe. Or a reminder of why I left.

The elevator doors open and I stop pacing as I glance toward them, seeing Liam standing there, looking both familiar and foreign. He's thinner than I remember, his jawline sharper, his hair scruffy in a way that used to make me weak in the knees. But now? Now all I see is the man who broke me.

"Thank you for meeting with me." he says, his bright blue eyes scanning my face. "You look really good, Amara."

"What do you want, Liam?" My voice is sharper than I thought it would be considering I was in love with him a few months ago.

He licks his lips, taking a step closer. "I wanted to talk to you."

"About what?" I shake my head, crossing my arms over my chest. "You said everything you needed to say that day. We have nothing else to talk about."

He nods, looking down at his feet for a moment before meeting my eyes again. "I know I fucked up, okay? I know. I... I thought I needed something different—someone different— but I was wrong. I was so wrong, Amara." He steps closer, and I take a step back, his proximity suffocating. "I want you back."

"You can't be serious."

"Of course I'm serious. I told you I made a mistake, but I know what I want now. You can stop playing this game now and come back to me."

My stomach churns. "Playing this game?" I repeat.

"Yeah," he scoffs, his eyes narrowing. "Playing hard to get. Trying to make me jealous by fucking your boss." His eyes scan the penthouse. "We both know Nicholas Blackwood will never end up with someone like you. This is just a phase. He'll get bored and leave you. Come back to me, Amara. We can spend the rest of our lives together. Just like you wanted."

I can feel my heart race, my pulse hammering in my ears. I take another step back as he reaches out for me. "Wanted," I say. "Past tense. I don't want that anymore. Especially not with you. I'm engaged to Nicholas, and whatever happens between us isn't any of your business, Liam. You need to leave."

Liam's face hardens, his eyes narrowing. "I need to leave?" He steps closer, his jaw clenching. "You act like you're some kind of saint, giving me shit for cheating, when you did the exact same thing."

"Excuse me?" I say, my eyes widening at the audacity.

"You were working for Nicholas while we were together," he points out, a sneer curling his lips. "And a week after we break up, you two are engaged? Don't stand there and pretend like you didn't open your legs for him when we were still together."

My whole body stiffens, but I don't back down. "Get out," I say firmly, every inch of me resisting the urge to break down. I won't cry over him anymore. He isn't worth it.

Liam's face tightens with disgust as he steps into my space. "Don't play innocent, Amara. You want to know why I fucked someone else?" His eyes scan me coldly. "You were boring." I suck in a breath at the cruelty in his voice. "You were so fucking vanilla and predictable. You think you're some kind of catch?" he sneers. "I couldn't fucking stand the thought of touching you anymore. Fucking you was a chore. You didn't even *come*."

My chest tightens, but before I can speak, a deep voice cuts through the room. "She's never had that issue with me."

CHAPTER THIRTY-TWO
Nicholas

My blood is burning in my veins.

Every inch of me is coiled tight, my muscles tense, my eyes locked on them. The way he's standing way too fucking close to Amara, the way he speaks to her, like he still has some kind of claim. I don't know what pisses me off more. The fact that he's even here or that Amara is letting him get this close.

He turns around, his eyes widening when he sees me standing in the doorway and Amara's eyes widen. What the fuck is she doing here alone with him? Does she still want something with him? Does she miss him? The thought hits me like a punch to the gut, and I have to fight to hold it together.

"I was just—" he starts to mumble, but I'm done with his excuses.

"Trying to insult my *fiancée* by insinuating she cheated on you?" I cut him off, anger boiling inside me. I won't give him a chance to speak. I won't let him act like he has any right to be here. No one gets to talk to her like that. Especially not this asshole.

His eyes narrow as he breathes through his nose. "I know she—"

"You know *nothing*," I interrupt. My fists itch to pound into his face, wanting him out of my sight, away from my penthouse, away from my fiancée. "Amara and I only happened because you made the mistake of even looking at another woman," I tell him, the sound of my shoes against the hardwood floor the only noise as I approach the bastard, seeing his chest rise and fall as he breathes hard, anger building inside of him.

"*You* walked away from her. Don't blame anyone else for your actions. You decided you didn't want her anymore, and I took my chance with her. I didn't waste any time, because I knew someone like her deserved the world, and unlike you, I wanted to give it to her."

The words feel like they're coming from somewhere deep inside me, as if I've been holding them back for too long. But now that I've started, I can't stop. My hands are shaking from the overwhelming need to stake my claim on her, to remind him—and myself—that Amara is mine. I look at him, daring him to say something, to contradict me.

"While you were busy looking at other women," I continue, pressing a finger to his chest. "I was looking at yours, wishing she was mine."

He shakes his head, breathing out a scoff. "Amara and I have history. We dated for years."

The audacity of this asshole. God, I want to punch him. "And yet you threw all of that away for some easy pussy. You might have history but *I'm* her future. So, remember that when you think you have some kind of claim on her, because you don't. Not anymore. She has *my* ring on her finger, she sleeps in *my* bed, and it'll be *my* last name on her documents."

I feel her eyes on me, wide with surprise. She never realized how much I thought about her. Even when I shouldn't have. How often her face came to mind when I was alone. How I would do anything to make her feel safe, to make her feel like she's the only woman in the world.

I move forward, approaching Amara who's still glancing up at me with her lips parted and I stake my claim, clutching her waist in my hands as I look down at her, not bothering to give him any more of my attention.

"You gave up your shot," I say, brushing a strand of her orange hair behind her ear. "You had your chance, and you blew it." I lift my head, glancing at Liam. "Now you regret it and want her back. But you thought she would be here, begging to have you back." I tut, shaking my head. "You were fucking wrong. She traded up, so thanks for letting her go. I'll make sure she forgets you ever existed."

Liam laughs bitterly, his gaze shifting to Amara. "Forget me? She'd have to stop stuffing her face long enough to even look at someone new."

The blood in my veins boils. Every muscle in my body tightens as fury takes over, and before I can stop myself, my fist flies through the air, slamming into his jaw with a sickening thud. He stumbles back, eyes wide with shock as he blood trickles out of his mouth.

I close the distance, my fist aching with the force of the hit, and I grab him by the collar, lifting him off the ground. "Don't you *ever* talk to my fiancée like that again. If you do, I swear to God, I'll fucking kill you. You don't fucking know me. I can make a body go away."

Liam spits out blood, sneering as he tries to regain his composure. "Enjoy my sloppy seconds."

Fuck, I want to pummel him into the ground. "The only sloppy thing here is your inability to actually make a woman come."

His nostri_s flare, blood staining his busted lip, and I can see the fury building in him. I release my grip on his collar, my chest pounding with anger. "Get the fuck out of our apartment, and don't ever contact her again."

Liam wipes his lip, a scoff escaping his lips as he tries to compose himself. "Fuck this." He turns on his heel, storming out of the apartment.

I glance at Amara, her eyes wide with shock, her breathing uneven. "Nicholas, what—"

I don't give her a chance to finish. My lips crash into hers with a deep urgency, my hands gripping her face as if it's the only thing holding me together. I pour every ounce of the rage and the relief I feel into that kiss, reminding myself that she's mine.

She always has been.

CHAPTER THIRTY-THREE
Amara

His lips crash into mine before I can say another word. It's intense, heated, pouring all of his frustration into the kiss. His hands find my face, cradling it like he's afraid I might disappear if he lets go. Every inch of me melts into him, and for a moment, I forget everything else. Liam. The insults he threw at me. Everything.

"Nicholas…" I murmur against his lips.

"Let me kiss you," he mutters, his voice rough… pained, even. "Just… *fuck*. I need this."

He closes the distance again, and I gasp into his mouth as he kisses me deeper, rougher, desperate. I feel the tension rolling off him, the clench of his jaw, the faint tremor in his fingers as he grips my waist.

"Nicholas," I whisper.

He groans, pulling away with a ragged breath. There's a flicker of something dark in his eyes as he steps back, running a hand through his hair in frustration before he turns around. "Fuck."

"Nicholas?" I breathe, a frown tugging at my lips.

He turns toward me, his face suddenly hard. "What the hell was he doing here, Amara?" His eyes lock onto mine, dark and intense. "Why were you alone with him?" he presses. "In our apartment?"

The word snags in my chest. *Our*. Not his. Ours. Even now, with the flicker of hurt in his eyes and the tension radiating off him, he still calls it ours.

"How did he even know where you were?" His nostrils flare, his jaw tight.

"He still had my location on his phone," I tell him, my throat feeling tight at the way his expression shifts. "I didn't tell him, Nicholas. I swear."

He takes a step closer, his gaze boring into mine. "Do you still have feelings for him?" His thumb brushes against my bottom lip.

I shake my head, firm and certain, not an ounce of doubt in me. "No, Nicholas. I don't."

The relief on his face is instant but fleeting. His shoulders relax, but his grip on me tightens, his hands sliding firmly to my waist. "Then tell me." His voice drops lower, sending a shiver down my spine. "What the fuck was that asshole doing here? Why did he think he still had a chance with you?" His eyes burn into mine. "When it's *my* ring on your finger?"

I suck in a breath, his words sinking deep into my chest. There's something about the way he says it that makes me dizzy. *This isn't real*, I remind myself. *It's all fake*. But the way he's looking at me, the way his voice wavers as he waits for my answer... feels anything but fake.

"He texted me," I admit. "He said he wanted to talk, and I—" I falter, shaking my head. "I don't know. I thought maybe I needed closure."

His jaw tightens, his brows knitting together. "Closure," he mutters, almost to himself. "You wanted to see if you'd made a mistake. In choosing me."

"No. Of course not. I just… We dated for a long time, and I thought I owed him a conversation."

"You don't owe him *anything*, Amara." Nicholas's voice is firm, his hands tightening around my waist as though he's afraid I'll slip away. "He insulted you, broke your trust, and turned his back on you. That's on him, not you. Never you, baby."

I blink up at him, trying to hold back the sting in my eyes, but he tips my chin up so I can't look away. "What you said before," I ask. "Did you mean it?"

For a moment, his expression softens, and I know he knows exactly what I'm talking about. The words he said to Liam, the ones that had left my stomach twisting and my heart racing. When he'd said I'd been in his head long before this fake engagement started.

At first, I'd assumed it was a lie, a tactic to throw Liam off, to make it clear that I wasn't an option anymore. But now, looking at him, I can't shake the feeling that there was truth in it.

He holds my gaze for a long moment. And then, finally, he nods.

"I meant every word I said to him," he tells me. "It might've been wrong. You were my assistant, you had a boyfriend, and I had no right to think about you that way." The confession sends my heart racing. His gaze never wavers, holding me captive in a way that leaves me breathless. "But I thought about you anyway," he admits. "I pictured you. Wondered what it'd feel like to touch you." His fingers graze down my arm, my skin breaking out in chills. "I wondered what it'd be like to kiss you," he continues, leaning in until his lips are a breath away from mine.

The softest brush of his lips against mine steals my thoughts, my breath—everything. My knees threaten to give out, and I grip his arms to ground myself.

I let out a shaky breath, my chest rising and falling too quickly. "Nicholas…"

"I didn't lie to him, Amara." His eyes darken, his grip tightening as if he's afraid I might disappear. "Not once." His hands slide to my waist. "You've been living in my head for months—no, years. And I wanted him to know you weren't an option. You're mine, Amara," he says, the words rough and soft all at once as his lips capture mine.

When he pulls back, his forehead rests against mine, his breath mingling with my own. "My assistant," he murmurs, his lips grazing mine again before they drift to my jaw. He trails a path of kisses there, each one slower, softer, as though he's memorizing every inch of my skin.

"My fiancée." He pauses, breathing me in like I'm the only thing keeping him alive. The warmth of his breath sends shivers down my spine, and when his tongue flicks against my skin, followed by the scrape of his teeth, I gasp.

He groans against me, the sound deep and raw, as if simply kissing me is driving him wild. His lips, his teeth, his tongue… All of it works in perfect rhythm to mark me, claim me, and I feel myself surrendering completely.

"My fucking woman," he says, his voice filled with possessiveness, one arm wrapping around my waist, the other slipping beneath the hem of my sweater.

"You're all. Fucking. Mine." His hands tug at the hem of my sweater, inching it up over my hips, until the fabric is slipping over my head and pooling on the floor.

"Nicholas," I whisper, half naked as he devours me with his eyes. His hands slide to the waistband of my pants, and before I can catch my breath, they're off. Those dark brown eyes roam over every inch of my skin.

"You're so insanely gorgeous," he says, and I don't know what to do with the raw honesty in his voice.

Before I can respond, his arms are under me, lifting me off my feet like I weigh nothing. I squeak, my hands clutching at his shoulders. "What are you doing?"

He just laughs, the sound low and smug. "Carrying my woman to bed."

He nudges the door open with his foot, the hinges creaking, and he lets me down gently, turning me around swiftly until we're both facing his huge floor-length mirror. My reflection stares back at me, flushed and disheveled, and I hate the way my gaze immediately falls to the ground at the sight of him, tall, handsome, full of muscles… and then me beside him—the complete opposite.

I try to look away, but his fingers are under my chin, gently lifting my face until I meet his gaze in the mirror. "You think I don't see you looking away every time you look in the mirror?"

I don't answer, my eyes glued to my reflection as I swallow hard. All I can see are the parts of myself I've spent years trying to hide. The curve of my stomach, the softness of my thighs, the roundness of my arms.

His hands slide down to rest on my shoulders, his touch warm. "Don't you see how fucking beautiful you are to me?" he asks, his thumb brushing across my jaw, making my skin tingle.

I shake my head, but he doesn't let me look away. His fingers trail down my arms, then back up to cup my face, tilting it toward the mirror, his lips brushing against my temple. "Look at yourself, Amara."

My gaze flickers, unsure, but his hands move again, skimming down my sides, tracing every curve like he owns them. He cups my breasts over my bra. "I love these," he murmurs, his thumbs brushing against the fabric. "The way they feel under my hands, how perfectly they fit in my palms."

Heat rushes to my face, but he doesn't stop, his hands trailing down to my stomach. "And this," he adds, pressing his palm flat against my belly, making me suck in a breath. "This is sexy as hell. I love kissing it. Love how it tugs at the fabric when you wear a tight dress."

I shake my head, the words catching in my throat, but he grips my chin, turning my face to meet his gaze in the mirror. "Don't do that. Don't act like you're anything but fucking perfect."

He leans down, pressing a kiss to my shoulder. "I wish you could see yourself the way I see you." His hands roam lower, over my hips, my thighs, pausing to squeeze gently. "These," he continues, his hands gripping my thighs, "are my favorite sight in the world. Thick and gorgeous, fills my hands perfectly." His eyes lock on mine in the mirror. "I especially love when my head is buried between them."

I breathe out a laugh, and he spins me around, his hands flying to my hips as he looks down at me with those dark, gorgeous eyes of his that make me melt.

Slowly, he tips my head back, tracing my jaw with his lips. "You are my everything."

My breath catches at his words, the intensity of them making my heart race. I feel his lips move lower, trailing down my neck, pausing at my collarbone. "You're so incredibly beautiful, Amara. Every time I look at you, touch you, I can't believe I get to have this. Have *you*."

A shaky breath escapes me as his hands trace my curves, leaving no part of me untouched. "It kills me that you don't see what I see. Because when I look at you, all I see is perfection."

His words, combined with the way his hands and lips trail over my skin, undo me completely.

"You might not see it yet, but you will," he promises. "I'll make you see that you're everything I want."

Pulling back, he turns me back around to face the mirror and this time I don't look away. I stare at our reflection. His hands, large and confident, framing my body like I'm his masterpiece. My hair is messy, my skin flushed, but the way his eyes devour me makes me feel like the sexiest thing he's ever seen.

"I want to show you something," he murmurs, his lips grazing the shell of my ear as he kisses my cheek, my jaw, every part of me that he can.

I feel so drunk on his kisses, my eyes close as I let myself be consumed by his touch. His hands come to rest on my hips, fingers spreading wide, and he pulls me back against him. I can feel him—hard and thick—pressing against my ass, and the pulse between my legs throbs in response.

"Show me," I breathe out, because I don't give a damn what it is. I love everything this man does to me.

"Not here," he replies, his fingers sliding down my stomach, dipping into my panties as he begins to play with my clit, soft, slow, and torturous. "It's a place."

My brows knit together, but when he circles my clit again, I let out a moan, leaning back against him. "What kind of place?"

"The fun is in the mystery, baby." Amusement coats his tone as one hand slides down my back, cupping my ass. A gasp escapes me as his fingers knead my flesh, slow and teasing. His hands are everywhere—gripping, claiming, lighting my skin on fire.

"God, I can't wait." His voice drops to a low rumble, his fingers tugging down the hem of my panties.

I feel my pussy dripping onto his hand as he plays with my clit, his other hand spreading my ass wider, his fingers dipping lower to tease my untouched hole, which makes a gasp leave my lips.

"Relax, honey," he murmurs, spreading my legs wider with his knee. "I won't touch you here if you don't want me to." His finger brushes it again and I swallow hard. "What color, Amara?" he asks.

The sensation is strange and foreign and everything I shouldn't want, but I find my body arching into him, my thighs pressing together in anticipation. "Green," I whisper.

"That's my fucking girl," he murmurs, the praise hitting me like a jolt of electricity straight to my clit. He pulls his hands away and I almost let out a whimper as Nicholas heads toward his nightstand.

I turn around, watching him open the drawer, and when I see the small metallic plug in his hand, my eyes widen.

His lips twitch. "I need to stretch that tight little hole out before you even *think* about having me inside of you."

His words send a shiver through me as Nicholas approaches me. "Hands against the mirror, honey. Bend down and spread those pretty legs for me."

I swallow, my clit throbbing with anticipation as I turn around and press my hands against the cold metal, glancing at the reflection as I see Nicholas walk toward me, his eyes fixed on my ass in the air for him.

He lets out a groan, as he grabs my ass in his big hands before he kneels behind me, spreading me wider, completely exposing me to him. I know without a doubt my face has never been this red or hot before.

"That's it. Fuck you're so beautiful everywhere."

A moan rips from my throat when I feel his finger graze my hole, slowly pushing inside.

"Goddamn, you're tight," he grunts, pressing into me deeper, filling me in a way I've never been filled before.

"Please," I find myself saying, a cry ripping from my throat.

"Please?" Nicholas repeats. "You want more, honey?"

I nod, my face pressed against the mirror as he continues to work his finger slowly inside of me.

"Christ, you're going to kill me," he murmurs, pulling his finger out of me. I hear the sound of a cap opening and then the feel of cool metal pressed against me.

The sensation is sharp at first, and I gasp, but Nicholas moves slowly, carefully, working the plug inside of my ass until it slides in. I let out a mix between a moan and a cry as my body stretches around the intrusion, unfamiliar but so fucking exciting.

"Breathe," he urges, his hands steadying me. His lips brush the curve of my back as I adjust, the fullness making me hyper aware of every shift, every twitch of my body. "That's it, baby. Let it stretch that pretty hole out."

I exhale slowly, letting my body adjust, but then I feel Nicholas pull back. His hands trail back up my sides, pulling me into him.

He presses a soft kiss to my back, before stepping away. Without a word, he heads toward his closet. "Get dressed," he says, like he didn't just shove a plug in my ass.

I blink, turning my head to look at him over my shoulder. "What?"

"You heard me." He shoots me a grin as he shrugs on his suit jacket.

I blink again, wondering if I heard him wrong. "With this inside of me?" I shake my head, flustered. "I can't—" I groan as I stand up straight, the pressure inside me intense, every small movement sending a ripple of pleasure through me.

"You'll get used to it." His hands cup my face as his lips find mine. "I promise."

My body twitches involuntarily, and he chuckles, the sound dark and full of amusement.

"Or maybe not," he corrects, a smirk curling his lips. "But I think you'll enjoy it either way."

CHAPTER THIRTY-FOUR
Nicholas

What the fuck is wrong with me?

Since the moment we stepped into this limo, I've looked at no one and nothing but the girl sitting beside me. I can't seem to tear my eyes away from her, memorizing the shape of her lips, the color of her eyes, every single part of her.

My heart thuds against my chest again. *Fuck.* I need to call my doctor because this can't be normal. It shouldn't beat out of my chest every time I look at her. Has the stress of this merger finally caught up with me and is now taking a toll on my body?

I push the thought aside, focusing on Amara. She has no idea where we're going and what she's in for, and the thought makes me that much more excited.

My eyes drop to her figure, lingering on her dress, which is a big problem. A slinky, black number that hugs her in ways that make my mouth dry. The neckline dips just enough to cause the perfect torture.

Amara doesn't realize the kind of power she holds, and I don't know whether to be frustrated or grateful. She's looking out the window, distracted, while I'm fighting every instinct to pull her into my lap.

I've never had an issue with control. It's the cornerstone of everything I am—my business, my reputation. But Amara wrecks it all.

The car slows, and I reach for a small black mask, realizing we're almost there.

Her eyes land on the black mask in my hand, her full lips parting. "What's that?"

A smirk tugs at my lips. "Do you trust me?"

Her brows furrow slightly before she nods. "Of course."

Of course. She says it so easily, so earnestly. I adore how effortlessly she hands her trust over to me.

Leaning closer, I slip the mask over her head, tying it up in the back. My fingers brush against her neck, and she shivers as I pull away to look at her.

"You look so beautiful, honey," I murmur, taking in her full cheeks, plump red lips and green eyes visible underneath the lace mask, just enough to hide her identity without covering her features.

She lifts a hand absentmindedly, and feels the mask under her fingers, her eyes widening when I pull out a simpler black mask for myself.

The car comes to a stop as I slide on my mask, climb out of the car, and adjust my jacket before circling to her side. I open the car door and offer my hand, which she takes immediately.

And when she steps out, I stop breathing.

Christ, that dress was torture when she was in the car, but now that she's here, right in front of her, the fabric clinging to her curves and her heels making her legs look endless, my self-restraint is hanging on a very thin thread.

"Are you ready to go in?"

Her cheeks flush as she nods, and I slide my hand over hers, leading her to the door.

When Ethan first told me he wanted to open a sex club, I thought it would be a loud and flashy strip club, but this is nothing of the sort.

Shadows and Silk is unassuming, sleek with no sign to mark it. Just a glossy black door with a keypad and a waiting list longer than the population of California.

Everyone wants to be a member of S&S but only some get invited. And being the best friend of the owner has some advantages.

I tap the keycard against it, and it beeps before swinging open.

The sounds hit us first. The air is humming with noises of pleasure—gasps, moans, the rhythmic slap of skin against skin.

Amara's grip on my hand tightens as we walk in deeper, the smell of sex, sweat and something faintly floral filling the room. It's dark inside, lit with soft red and gold lighting, but I know Amara can see the scene in front of us very clearly by the way she sucks in a breath.

A crowd gathers to watch a woman, tied up and spread open while two men share her, one thrusting into her mouth, while the other fucks her pussy.

"What... What is this?"

I glance down at her, a smirk curling my lips. "This is Shadows and Silk," I inform her. "An exclusive sex club."

"You've... been here before?" she asks, her voice hushed as her eyes widen.

"A few times," I admit with a nod. "I used to come here occasionally when I needed to blow off some steam."

Her head snaps toward me. "You did?" She glances at the other side of the room when the woman moans loudly and I smirk, watching her take in the sight around us. Bodies intertwined, couples bent over furniture, women tied and gagged, men groaning as they sink deep into willing partners.

"I liked to watch," I tell her, leaning down to whisper in her ear. Her breath catches, her body going stiff as I curl my hand around her waist, pulling her into me. "Just like you're doing now. I like to see a woman consumed by pleasure. To hear her. To watch her partner take her apart, piece by piece."

Her lips part, a soft breath escaping when I circle my hand around her neck, tightening ever so slightly.

"Or punish her," I add, testing the waters.

Her eyes flick to mine, and there's a flicker of something—curiosity, maybe even desire—before she looks away, her fingers curling tighter around mine.

I guide her further in, weaving through the crowd. Amara's gaze snags on a woman pleasuring herself in the center of a group, her cries echoing as she sinks two fingers into her slick pussy. The people around her watch her climax with undeniable hunger.

Her eyes slide to the two women on the ground, one with her back on the floor, while the other is on top, her hand wrapped around her neck as they grind their pussies together.

Amara's hand grows slick in mine as I guide her deeper into the club. She pauses to watch a group of men lining up to empty their loads into a willing bottom, her lips parting at the sight.

She was so innocent when I first got my hands on her, didn't even know how she liked to have her pussy eaten and yet here she is now, curious, hungry, *intrigued*.

My lips twitch as I open the door and pull her into a playroom, guiding her inside before closing the door behind us. The room is dim, lit only by a few sconces on the walls, casting soft, shadowy light. It's enough to obscure everyone's identities while still allowing people to watch.

"Where are we?" she whispers.

"We're in a group playroom," I tell her, leading her toward the back. "This is where couples can fuck while other people watch."

Her eyes widen as she watches a man grip a petite woman by the waist, driving into her with slow, deep thrusts. Amara freezes, utterly hypnotized.

I stop too, but my attention isn't on the couple. It's on her. Her breathing, her chest rising and falling faster with each second that passes. Through the thin fabric of her dress, I see her nipples harden, and I clench my jaw, fighting the groan that wants to slip out.

"Are you turned on?" I whisper, my hands skimming over the curves of her hips, feeling the heat of her skin beneath the dress.

She stiffens at my touch, but then, almost imperceptibly, she nods.

"You like watching him wreck her pussy?" I ask, my lips skimming her jaw. "You like watching his big cock push inside her tight pussy? Hmm, baby?" My hands slowly run down her body, feeling every inch of her as I slide them down to grip her thighs, feeling her soft skin warm and supple beneath my fingertips. She nods, sucking in a breath.

"Good." My lips brush her ear as my fingers slide down, bunching the hem of her dress. "Because I'm going to make sure everyone in this room knows how gorgeous you look when you come."

My fingers tease the edge of her dress, lifting it higher as her breath hitches, sharp and audible over the low hum of music and murmured conversations. Her hands clutch at my arm, nails digging into the fabric of my jacket as I trail my touch along the smooth skin of her thigh. "Open your legs for me, Amara," I rasp, my free hand gripping her thigh firmly, urging her to part for me.

Her gaze darts around the room, wide and filled with the delicious mix of nervousness and arousal that drives me wild. "Nicholas," she breathes. "What if someone sees?"

"Let them. Let them wish it was them instead of me."

A shiver races through her, and her lips part, her breathing erratic as I press my mouth to the corner of her jaw, just below her ear. Her scent—sweet, vanilla, soft, and utterly hers—wraps around me, making it impossible to focus on anything but the need to ruin her in the best possible way.

Sliding my hand higher, I find the edge of her lace panties. My thumb brushes against the damp fabric, and I groan into her ear. "*Soaked*. You're soaked for me."

Her hips jerk instinctively, seeking more, and I grant it, pressing the pad of my thumb against her swollen clit through the lace. Her head falls back against my chest, and she exhales a moan that has my cock straining painfully against my pants.

She lifts her hips, a silent plea for more, and I slide one finger inside her tight, welcoming heat.

Her gasp is loud enough to draw a few glances, and I tilt my head to watch. Across the room, a group of men have shifted their attention from the stage to us, their gazes hungry and fixed on Amara.

"You see them?" I murmur, curling my finger inside her, finding the spot that has her breath catching. "They can't take their eyes off you. They love the way your body reacts to me."

Her eyes flutter open, and she follows my gaze, her cheeks flushing as she realizes they're watching. But instead of shrinking away, her body tightens around my finger, her hips moving to meet my touch.

A groan rips from my throat. "You like it, don't you?" I whisper, sliding a second finger inside her, stretching her, teasing her. "Knowing they're watching your cunt tighten around my fingers."

Her only response is a strangled moan, her head tilting back, her body arching against my hand as I pick up the pace, fucking her with my fingers in deep strokes. Every sound she makes, every quiver of her body fuels the fire burning through me.

"Be a good girl, Amara. Come for me. Let them see how beautiful you are when you coat my fingers with your cum."

She grips my arm, her breath quickening, as I curl my fingers inside her, hitting that spot I know makes her lose control.

"Nicholas," she moans as she comes on my fingers, a shudder running through her.

Fuck. The sound of my name leaving her lips has me unraveling. I yank my hand away, spinning her around without a second thought. Her eyes widen in shock, but before she can say another word, I push her onto the empty bed beside us, her body sinking into the soft mattress with a gasp.

Her gaze locks onto mine, wide and questioning, as I strip off my suit jacket with one fluid motion. She lifts herself onto her elbows, anticipation written all over her face.

I want her to feel this, to know how beautiful she is, how badly I need her. And I want every goddamn person in this room to witness it.

"I love to watch," I murmur as I slowly unbutton my shirt, throwing it carelessly to the floor. "But right now, I need your mouth."

Her chest rises and falls, each breath sharp and shaky as I strip off my belt and pants, my cock aching and already leaking for her.

I've never done this. Never been the one on display. Never been exposed in front of so many eyes. But with Amara here, not touching her is pure fucking torture. I don't care about anyone else in this room. Not a single person. Just her.

I step closer, letting my hand glide along her jaw, my thumb brushing her bottom lip. Amara's tongue darts out, tasting me, and it's the sweetest invitation I've ever received.

Her eyes flicker, a mix of hunger and hesitation. "Nicholas…"

"Color?" I ask.

"Green," she murmurs, her gaze locking onto mine.

I nod, loving how open she is to this. "Then be a good girl for me and get on your knees."

Amara shifts, positioning herself on her knees as her hands slide up my thighs. The heat of her touch has me clenching my fists to keep control. She looks up at me through her lashes, the flush in her cheeks making her look even more irresistible.

She presses her lips to the tip of my cock, her mouth warm and soft as she takes me between her lips. My head falls back, a groan rumbling deep in my chest as she moves, her tongue swirling, teasing.

The low hum of the gasps and moans fades into the background. The only thing I can focus on is her. Her lips sliding over me, her nails digging into my thighs as she takes me deeper, her soft little moans vibrating against my cock.

I glance down at her eyes on me, and her red lips stretched wide around me.

"Taking me so well," I murmur, brushing a strand of hair from her face. "You love my cock deep in your throat, don't you?"

She doesn't respond, but the way her eyes darken tells me she does.

Around us, I feel their eyes on her—or us—and I know they're hungry, envious... but they'll never have her.

Amara pulls back, gasping for air, her lips swollen and glossy. Her hand wraps around the base of my cock, stroking as she licks her lips.

"Don't fucking stop. I want you to suck me dry."

Leaning forward again, she takes me back into her mouth, this time slower, sucking me deeper. A groan leaves my lips as my hand grips the back of her head, guiding her.

"Fuck," I mutter, my voice strained. "You're going to make me lose my goddamn mind."

Her pace quickens, her moans vibrating against me as she works me closer and closer to the edge. My knees threaten to give out, but I hold, watching her, soaking in every second of this.

Amara's eyes flick up to meet mine as she takes me even deeper. The sight of her—on her knees, her lips stretched around me, her cheeks hollowing with every pull—sends a surge of heat through my body.

"Just like that," I rasp, my breath hitching. "Fuck. Your mouth feels like heaven."

Her free hand slides up my thigh, her nails dragging lightly over my skin. The slick sound of her movements, the way her tongue swirls and presses in all the right ways, has me teetering on the edge of control. I feel her moan reverberate through me, her confidence growing with every twitch and groan she pulls from me.

"Fuck. I'm close." I grit out, my voice low and broken.

She doesn't let up. If anything, she doubles down, her hand working in tandem with her mouth, her tongue flicking over the sensitive head before she takes me back in, deep. My head tips back, a curse tumbling from my lips as the pleasure coils tight.

"Fuck—" My words cut off, my body locking up as the release hits me hard. She doesn't flinch, taking everything I give her.

When she finally pulls back, her lips are swollen and glistening, her tongue darting out to catch the last traces of me. She looks up at me, her expression a mix of satisfaction and mischief, and I know I'm done for.

"You're going to be the death of me," I murmur, crashing my lips against hers, tasting myself on her mouth. I pull back, holding her face in my hands, staring at those eyes through the lace mask. "You want more?"

She nods, licking her lips as she waits for my next command.

I reach for the cuffs attached to the bed, holding them up so she can see. Her lips part, her breathing quickens, and I can see the faintest tremor in her hands.

"Color?" I ask, tilting her chin up so her gaze locks with mine.

"Green," she whispers without hesitation.

"That's my girl." I press a kiss to her forehead, before stepping back. "Lie down."

She obeys, her body sinking into the soft mattress, her hair fanning out like a halo. I secure her wrists to the headboard above her head, the soft click of the cuffs locking into place. I take a moment to admire her—completely at my mercy, laid bare before me.

"I wish you could see how you look right now," I murmur, running my fingers down the length of her arm, across her collarbone, and down to the curve of her waist. Her skin shivers under my touch.

Her legs shift restlessly, and I catch the smallest whimper escaping her lips. "Patience. You'll take what I give you, when I give it to you. Understand?"

"Yes, sir," she breathes.

I smile, dark and slow. "Always such a good girl for me."

My hands find the hem of her panties, and drag them down her legs, taking my time, letting the cool air kiss her skin. I toss them aside, knowing every pair of eyes is on her now, on the curve of her thighs, the glisten of her arousal.

I drop to my knees between her legs, spreading her wide with my hands. The sight of her makes my mouth water. I lean in, pressing a soft kiss to her inner thigh before dragging my tongue along her slick cunt. She gasps, her body jerking against the cuffs, but I pin her hips down, holding her in place.

"Stay still," I command. "You don't move unless I tell you to."

"Yes, sir," she whimpers.

I take my time, licking and sucking, alternating between gentle strokes and firm pressure. Her moans grow louder when I circle her clit with my tongue, teasing her just enough to make her squirm.

"You sound so fucking pretty when you moan for me. Let them hear you. Let them know how good I make you feel."

My tongue slides over her, savoring every taste of her, and her body jolts at the contact, her hips twitching despite my earlier command to stay still.

"Please," she cries, her voice desperate. "Please, sir, I—"

I slide two fingers inside her, curling them just right, and her words dissolve into a broken sob.

I pull back, my fingers teasing and denying her. "Not yet," I say, my grip tightening on her hips. "I want to make you beg."

I keep her on edge, my fingers stroking deep, slow, the pace just enough to tease but never let her tip over.

"Please," she whispers, her voice shaky, the word catching on a soft sob. Her body trembles under my touch, flushed skin and shallow breaths, and I can feel how badly she wants this.

But I want to play with her first.

"Come on, you can beg better than that."

"Nicholas," she pleads, tugging at the cuffs. "I need—"

"I know what you need." My thumb brushes over her clit, featherlight, and the sound she makes is desperate, hungry. "But you need to ask me properly."

Her head falls back against the pillow, her lips parting on a sharp inhale.

"You're so close, aren't you?" I ask, my voice tinged with just enough command to make her toes curl. "I can feel it."

"Yes," she gasps, her voice breaking on the word.

Her whole body tightens as I curl my fingers inside her, stroking the spot that makes her fall apart every single time. I suck her clit into my mouth, teasing her further. And just as she's about to tip over the edge, I stop, her broken whimper filling the room.

"You can take this, baby. I know you can." I lean in, pressing a kiss to her clit as my fingers slide back inside her.

She shudders, her body clinging to the edge of control, and I can't help but smile against her. "That's my girl," I murmur.

Her moan is quiet, pleading, as I circle her clit with my tongue, teasing her. When I suck her into my mouth once again, her thighs tremble around me, her cries growing louder.

"Please," she begs again, her voice cracking. "I can't—I need—"

"I haven't heard you beg properly yet," I cut her off, wishing I could stay between her legs for the rest of eternity.

"Please, sir," she sobs. "Please let me come. I'll be good. I'll do anything."

This time, I don't hold back. My fingers work her faster, my tongue circling her clit, and her cries reach a pitch that tells me she's right on the edge.

My free hand trails up her body, wrapping gently around her throat. I apply just enough pressure to make her gasp, her eyes fluttering shut as her body arches into my touch.

"Look at me," I demand, my grip tightening slightly. Her eyes snap open. "You keep those beautiful eyes on me when you come. Understand?"

"Yes, sir," she chokes out.

I thrust my fingers deeper, my tongue relentless against her clit. Her body arches, her sweet moans echoing in the room as she shatters under me. She's breathtaking, every part of her quivering as she clings to the moment, her sobs turning into soft, gasping breaths.

But I'm not done with her. Not even close.

I keep my tongue on her clit, licking and sucking and tasting her as she coats my fingers. Her legs shake as she tugs at the handcuffs the more I play with her sensitive clit, her voice breaking as she sobs my name.

"You wanted to come, didn't you?" I ask, curling my fingers into her deep enough to make her hips buck.

"Yes," she gasps.

"Then we're not stopping until I suck every single drop of cum from you," I murmur, pressing a kiss to her thigh before diving back in.

"Oh god," she moans, her hips bucking against my mouth.

I don't let up. My tongue works her clit, flicking and circling, while my fingers slide back inside her, curling to hit that spot that makes her gasp. Her moans are louder, her body straining against the cuffs as she climbs higher and higher.

She cries out as another orgasm slams into her. Her body tightens around my fingers, her moans breaking into sobs as she comes hard once again. But I don't stop. I don't even give her a chance to recover.

My tongue stays on her clit, relentless, while my fingers keep thrusting, pushing her straight into another climax. She moans loudly, her head thrashing against the cushion, her wrists pulling against the cuffs.

"Too much," she whimpers, her voice high and shaky. "Fuck, it's—"

I lift my head just enough to meet her gaze, my fingers never stopping. "Color?"

Her eyes flutter open, glazed and desperate. "Green," she gasps. "It's green."

"Then you'll take it," I murmur, flicking her clit with the tip of my tongue, smirking when she shivers from the contact. "Because I know you can. You're going to be a good girl for me and give me another one. Understand?"

"Yes, sir," she sobs.

I add a third finger, stretching her further, and her back arches off the bed as another wave of pleasure crashes over her. She's shaking, her thighs quivering uncontrollably as I push her into overstimulation.

Her cries turn into broken, breathless sounds, her body writhing as she tries to escape the intensity. But I hold her steady, one hand gripping her neck while the other works inside her.

"Look at you. Falling apart for me again and again," I rasp, my voice rough as I look down at the bed, the sheets drenched from her orgasms. "You can do it, baby. Give me one more."

She shakes her head weakly. "I can't—"

"Yes, you can," I cut her off. "Let me make you feel good. Let go for me. Just one more."

I lean down and tongue her clit again, feeling her thighs squeeze my head as another orgasm builds inside of her.

My lips wrap around her swollen, overused clit, and I suck it harder. Her body locks up, her cries echoing through the room as another orgasm tears through her. Her entire body trembles as the pleasure overwhelms her.

When I finally pull back, her body is limp, her skin flushed, her chest heaving. I lift onto my feet, my face covered in her arousal.

I let my hand run along her pussy. Down, down, down until I find the butt plug lodged in her ass. She glances up at me, and I lift a brow, asking a silent question.

She nods and I remove the butt plug slowly, watching her reaction as she gasps, her body arching off the bed.

"You're so perfect," I whisper, my eyes locked on her stretched hole. I quickly grab the lube and pump some out onto my hand, wrapping my fist around my cock, covering it. I press the head of my cock against her tight cunt, my hands gripping her hips. "You want this, honey?"

"Yes," she begs, a whimper escaping her. "I want you to own every part of me."

I groan and press forward, my cock inching into her tight heat, and she gasps, her hands tugging at the cuffs. I pause, letting her adjust, my hands smoothing over her hips.

"Breathe, baby," I murmur, my voice low and soothing. "You're doing so good for me. Just relax and let me in."

She nods, her breathing shaky as I sink deeper. The sensation is almost too much. Her ass is so fucking tight, gripping me inside of her and... *Christ*. It takes everything in me not to lose control. I grit my teeth, forcing myself to move slowly, savoring every inch as I fill her completely.

"Fuck, Amara," I groan, my voice rough. "Your ass was made for me."

Her moan is loud and needy, her head turning to the side as she pulls against the cuffs. "You're so deep inside me," she whispers.

I smirk, my teeth grazing her shoulder as I pull back just enough to thrust into her again, this time deeper, harder. She cries out, her body tightening around me, and I can feel the tremor in her legs.

"You're taking it so well. Breathe, baby."

The moan she lets out is delicious and desperate, her body writhing beneath me. A heavy breath leaves her lips, each thrust dragging her closer and closer to the brink.

"Look at them," I murmur, my lips brushing her ear. "They're all watching you, wishing they could have you like this. But they can't. You're mine. Only mine."

"Only yours," she moans.

"That's right," I growl, my hand sliding up her back to grip her hair, pulling her head back gently. "You're mine to use, mine to worship, mine to fucking *ruin*."

She cries out, her body shaking as I thrust deeper, hitting the spot that makes her moan my name like a prayer.

"You're going to come for me again," I command, feeling my own orgasm crest. "I'm not stopping until you do. I want to feel you come on my cock."

Her body tenses as the pleasure builds up, and my god, she looks so fucking beautiful like this. Tied up, naked and desperate for another orgasm. My thumb finds her clit, rubbing it gently in time with my thrusts and in no time, she moans out, her body convulsing as another orgasm rips through her, her ass squeezing me so fucking tight it nearly drags me along with her.

"Fuck yes," I grunt, pushing her through the aftershocks, her cries turning into broken whimpers as I drive her into overstimulation again. Her body shakes, her voice hoarse as she pleads for more, for mercy, for everything I'm willing to give her.

"I thought seeing people look at you like this would make me want to kill someone," I murmur, my voice barely audible over her soft, broken cries. My hand tightens on her hip, holding her in place as I thrust into her again, savoring every second. "But seeing how beautiful you are, how gorgeous you look when you come…" I pause, my words catching as I push deeper. "I couldn't keep such a masterpiece to myself."

Her moans are raw, her body arching against the restraints, her wrists pulling at the cuffs as I push her higher, harder. She's gone—lost in the pleasure, lost in me—and the sight of her like this, completely undone, is maddening.

"Amara," I groan, her name breaking from my lips. My control slips as I thrust harder, my pace quickening, chasing the edge that's been taunting me since the moment I touched her.

She sobs my name, her voice cracking, her body clenching around me as another orgasm rips through her. Her head falls forward, her hair sticking to her damp skin, and her legs shake as she collapses beneath me, spent but still taking everything I give her.

"Fuck," I rasp, my grip tightening on her hips, as I bury my cock inside her.

A deep groan rumbles from my chest as I spill into her. My forehead drops to hers, my breaths ragged and uneven. She's still shaking, her body so soft, so pliant beneath me, and I can't help the way my hands roam over her, grounding her as much as myself.

When I finally still, I press a kiss to the curve of her neck, my hands moving to the cuffs, unlocking them carefully. She leans into me, her breathing still uneven, her body exhausted but sated.

"You did so good for me," I whisper, my hands smoothing over her skin, brushing her hair back from her face.

She doesn't reply, her head resting against my chest as she tries to catch her breath, but I feel the way her fingers curl into my shirt, holding onto me like I'm her lifeline.

And maybe I am.

Because I know one thing with absolute certainty.

I'm not letting her go.

CHAPTER THIRTY-FIVE

Amara

I wake up with Nicholas's lips on mine. It's a soft kiss, slow and lazy, like he has all the time in the world, and I break out into a smile, my stomach fluttering.

His lips leave mine, trailing down my neck. I feel his lips curve into a smile before he pulls away. "Morning," he murmurs, his voice still rough from sleep.

My eyes flutter open, seeing Nicholas above me, already dressed, in a crisp suit.

"Where are you going?"

A sigh leaves his lips. "I need to head into work."

"Today?" I ask, my brows dipping.

He nods, a groan leaving his lips. "All I want to do is get back into this bed and bury my head between your thighs until you scream my name. But I have a meeting with the board this morning to discuss the details of the merger." He breathes out a sigh, shaking his head. "There's still so much we need to figure out and the deadline is coming up soon."

I blink, pushing myself up onto my elbows. "Yeah... I know." I press my lips together, trying to act like the thought of us ending soon doesn't affect me. I want Nicholas to get what he's always wanted. I want him to succeed. But once this deal goes through and Blackwood Hotels go international, everything between us will end.

His gaze flickers to mine, sensing the sudden shift in my mood. He gives me a small, almost apologetic smile. "Stay. Don't go anywhere. I'll be back later."

I try to smile, but it doesn't quite reach my eyes. "Okay."

He leans down, pressing another kiss to my lips, but this one is firmer, more desperate, before he turns and shuts the door behind him.

I lie in bed for a while after he leaves, the thought of everything between us ending making my chest ache. Goddamn it. How did I let myself get so attached to him? This deal was supposed to be easy, beneficial even, but all it's bringing me is pain. I let out a sigh and reach for my phone from the nightstand, scrolling through the missed texts from Sophie and Jade.

Jade:

> We're going out tonight. I don't want any excuses.

> Hello?

Sophie:

> She's probably still sleeping. Not everyone wakes up at the crack of dawn like you.

Jade:

> Lucky. Insomnia's a bitch

Sophie:

> Texting me this early should be illegal. It's a Saturday.

Jade:

So, where did we land on the whole going out thing?

Hello?

???

Sophie:

I give up.

I chuckle at their texts, my fingers hovering over the keyboard.

Me:

I'm in.

Jade:

WOOOO.

The door creaks open, and I glance up, hoping Nicholas came back, but my assumptions are crushed when I see Pumpkin jumping on my bed, meowing at me like she hasn't been fed in days.

I let out a laugh, rolling out of bed before walking to the kitchen to feed her.

Her paws claw at my ankles as she follows me, meowing along the way.

"Calm down. You'll get your food soon," I mutter, filling her bowl and her water dish.

Once she's taken care of, I wander back into the bedroom, shedding my clothes as I go, until I'm standing in just my underwear.

My eyes drift toward the mirror, and this time, I don't look away. I let my eyes settle on my reflection, taking in the curves of my body, soft and round, with old white stretch marks that cover my skin.

My thighs brush together as I shift and run my hands over my stomach, the knot in my throat thick as I attempt to swallow it down. My fingers brush against each groove, and roll, my eyes tracking every movement. I've spent so long trying to avoid the mirror, but for the first time in... forever, I'm starting to love myself more, feeling comfortable in my own skin.

I let my fingers wander, my hand brushing along my sides, imagining Nicholas's hands on me, picturing what he sees when he looks at me, thinking of the way he looks at me like he's never seen another woman before.

Sometimes, I still catch myself avoiding my reflection, wishing certain things were different, but I'm getting there. Slowly but surely.

Then, an idea hits me. A sudden rush of confidence runs through me, and I step back, drop my panties, and reach for my phone. I quickly flip the camera on, angling it just right, and snap a couple of pictures. My teeth tug at my bottom lip as I sit on the bed, lying back and angle the camera to catch my naked body as I cup my breast.

I take a couple more pictures, my confidence growing with each one. When I'm done, I glance down at the images, scrolling through them as my heart hammers in my chest. It's me. My body—every curve, every inch—no filters, no shame.

Just… me. And for the first time, I can't help but smile, because I look good.

I attach the pictures with a quick message.

Me:

Miss you.

I press send, and immediately, my neck flushes with warmth, wondering if he'll reply. He's busy, tied up with the merger, and I'm sure the last thing on his mind is me. But I still feel a little thrill coursing through me.

I shrug it off when there's no reply a couple of minutes later, and grab a towel, heading for the shower. The water engulfs me immediately and I let out a groan, closing my eyes. I'm going to miss this shower when I have to leave.

When I'm finally done, I step out, drying off my hair as I spot one of his t-shirts lying on the bed. I used to be so curious about what he would wear when he wasn't in the office. But, of course, Nicholas looks as amazing in a t-shirt and sweatpants as he does in a fitted luxury suit. I throw the towel on the ground and pick up his light grey t-shirt, tugging it on. I bring the soft fabric to my nose, a smile tugging at my lips as his scent fills my senses.

My eyes squeeze closed. God, I miss him. It's irrational to miss someone this much only an hour after they left… but I do. I miss his smile, miss his kisses, miss the way he cups my face in his large hands as if I'm the most precious thing to him.

My stomach growls, snapping me out of my thoughts, and I head to the kitchen, opening the fridge as I scowl for some ingredients to make a sandwich.

The bread only just hits the counter when I hear the familiar ding of the elevator.

My eyes snap toward the doors, seeing them open, my eyes widening when Nicholas steps into the room. His eyes lock onto mine, and before I can get a word out, he's walking towards me, closing the space between us in seconds.

"Wha—" I don't even get the chance to speak before his lips crash into mine. His hands grip my waist, and before I know it, he lifts me effortlessly, placing me on the kitchen counter like I weigh nothing.

"What are you doing?" I ask, breathless, pulling away from his mouth. "I thought you had a meeting."

Nicholas's lips curl into a grin as he leans in close, his breath hot on my neck. He slides his hand onto my thigh, making me shiver under his touch. "I needed to fuck my *fiancée* instead."

His words hit me like a jolt of electricity, his grip on my waist, possessive, claiming, and I can't stop the smile that tugs at my lips. I love the way he says that word.

Nicholas groans. "You think it's funny making me rock fucking hard at a business meeting, sending me pictures like that?" he asks. "You think I could handle another second without leaving that room and rushing back here?" I shiver again. "You underestimate the hold you have on me, Amara," he continues. "God, the sight of you—wet and warm, smelling like candy, dressed in my clothes. Fuck, you've ruined me."

Before I can process it all, his lips are on mine, his tongue brushing against the seam of my mouth, making me gasp. But my stomach growls loudly, interrupting the moment.

He chuckles against my lips before pulling back. "Hungry?"

A smirk curves my lips. "Kind of. I was about to make a sandwich."

He gives me one last kiss, before straightening his tie. "Eat, baby. I can wait."

I arch an eyebrow. "You're not going to ravage me?" I tease.

His lips curl into a smirk as he shakes his head. "Not right now. I can wait."

He takes over, grabbing the bread and the fillings as he finishes making my sandwich. I give him a smile as I take it from him, feeling his gaze lingering on me as I take a bite. I swallow down the sandwich, my lips tipping up into a smile of their own accord. "Stop looking at me like that," I murmur.

His smirk widens, breathing out a laugh. "How are you so damn beautiful?"

Before I can reply, his lips find mine again, his hands sliding up my thigh, gripping my skin, and—

"Fuck," Nicholas groans, pulling back suddenly and looking down at his leg. "What the..." I follow his gaze, my brows knitting together as I see Pumpkin, clawing at his legs, letting out a meow.

Nicholas groans, rolling his eyes. "What a cockblock."

Pumpkin leaps up onto the counter, climbing into my arms, her purrs vibrating against my chest as I pet her. "Poor baby is jealous," I tease, lifting Pumpkin closer to my face and pressing my nose against hers. "You want Nicholas to give you kisses, too?"

He scrunches his nose, the corner of his mouth tugging into a small smile. "I'll end up with a scratched face, and then your mommy wouldn't want to kiss me anymore."

I roll my eyes, a playful grin tugging at my lips. "That's not true. I'll want to kiss you even more."

Nicholas glances at me for a moment, then turns his attention back to Pumpkin, who's now trying to nuzzle against his chest. "Well, in that case..." He leans closer to the counter, his hand moving to Pumpkin's back. "Scratch away, Pumpkin."

She stretches out, curling her little paws against Nicholas's chest, her tiny nose nuzzling him.

Nicholas chuckles as she climbs into his arms. "I guess she is pretty cute." His gaze shifts back to me, his fingers lightly brushing my leg. "I think I've fallen in love with your cat," he says, with a smirk.

I let out a laugh, shaking my head, feeling my heart soften at the look on his face. "It was inevitable."

Nicholas chuckles, but his smile falters, just slightly. The playful gleam in his eyes dims, and he swallows, his Adam's apple bobbing as he looks at me. "Yeah."

My heart stutters, the beat picking up pace, each thump like a drum in my chest. The way Nicholas looks at me, the way we fit together, the way he makes me feel...

This might all be fake, for the sake of the deal, but there's something else, something I can't pretend isn't there anymore. My feelings for him have been growing, building, until the realization slaps me right in the face.

I've fallen in love with my boss.

CHAPTER THIRTY-SIX

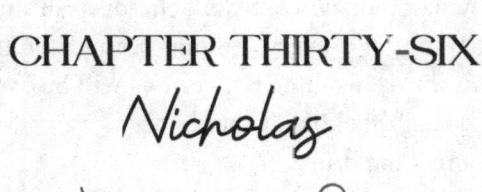

Nicholas

Inevitable.

That's the only word that keeps running through my head as I stare blankly at my screen. It was inevitable that Amara would end up working for me. Inevitable that I'd kiss her. Fucking inevitable that in just one month, everything will be over between us, and I'll never see her pink cheeks or those deep green eyes ever again.

My pen taps against the desk. I should be finalizing the details for the international expansion. Should be reviewing the quarterly reports. Should be doing *anything* that doesn't involve thinking about her.

But I can't stop it.

The deadline for our fake engagement is fast approaching. Only a matter of time before we both walk away from each other and leave everything that happened behind.

And that sinking feeling in my gut grows heavier with every second that ticks by.

The thought of her no longer being a part of my life—the thought of her not living in my penthouse, not working beside me, not filling the space with her warmth and her goddamn laugh—hits harder than I ever expected.

I didn't plan for this. I didn't want this.

But it was fucking inevitable.

I run a hand over my face, gripping the pen tighter, as if doing so will somehow ease the ache deep in my chest. The clock is ticking, and every passing second reminds me that soon—*too soon*—this thing between us will be over.

And it doesn't feel like it should be.

I need a fucking drink.

"Jesus Christ, Nicholas. You look like you're about to explode."

I barely look up. "Ever heard of knocking?"

"Nah." Ethan flops down in the chair across from me. "Keeps you on edge," he says with a smirk. "So… guess what I found out today."

My eyes flick to him, but I'm not in the mood for his bullshit. "What?"

"Your membership at the club was reinstated," he says, tilting his head with that teasing glint in his eyes. "Sneaky dog."

I let out a groan. "How the hell do you know that?"

Ethan raises an eyebrow. "I own the damn club, remember?" He kicks his feet up on my desk.

I exhale sharply, running a hand over my face. "Get your feet off my desk."

I try to focus on him, but my mind's miles away. I don't have the energy to deal with him right now.

Ethan studies me for a few seconds, shaking his head. "Alright, what's going on with you? You look like you just walked face-first into an existential crisis."

I rub my temples. "I don't fucking know." Everything. Nothing. *Her*.

Ethan sighs. "I thought you were getting some action. Should've loosened you up by now."

I shoot him a glare. "I'm not the fucking mood, alright?" I shake my head, frustrated. "It's… My chest feels tight, and… my head's all over the place… Fuck."

Ethan lets out a low whistle, holding his hands up. "Almost sounds like you're in love or some shit."

My whole body locks, the thudding of my heart ringing in my ears as if to confirm his suspicions.

I stiffen, fingers twitching on the desk.

My jaw clenches.

The truth smacks me in the face like a slap.

And suddenly, it's so damn obvious that it's almost suffocating.

I'm in *love* with her.

I'm in *love* with Amara.

"Of course, that would *never* happen," Ethan continues, his tone dripping with sarcasm. "Not with your assistant-slash-fake-fiancée who you took to my club, just last week, right?"

I ignore the nosy fucker and picture her. Her laugh, her smile, and the thought of not seeing that ever again is like a knife twisting in my chest.

Fucking hell.

This is the worst complication possible.

Before I can even process the feelings coursing through my body, the door swings open.

And there she is.

Amara steps in, eyes glued to her tablet. "So, I think I found the perfect color for the bedroom—" She stops mid-sentence when she sees Ethan. "Oh, I'm sorry, I didn't know you were here. Am I interrupting?"

She tucks the tablet under her arm, and all I can do is stare at her. She has no fucking idea. No clue that she's the reason my whole world just flipped upside down.

Ethan arches a brow at me. "You're painting the walls again?"

My teeth grind. "We're redecorating."

Ethan squints, confused. "Didn't you just hire a decorator like… five months ago?"

That fucking big mouth of his.

Amara freezes, her eyes widening. "What?"

I don't look at her. Can't. I can feel her eyes on me, though. Sharp, searching.

"But…" She shakes her head. "You told me you needed a decorator."

Ethan whistles, his eyes twinkling as he meets my gaze.

I'm struggling to think of reasons why I shouldn't punch my best friend of twenty years.

I ignore him and meet Amara's confused gaze. "I did."

She narrows her eyes, trying to make sense of it. "Ethan just said you hired one only a few months ago."

I lift my shoulder in a shrug. "That was before you."

Her frown deepens. "Nicholas…" She whispers my name like a question, and everything inside me breaks.

I swivel out of my chair, all the words I've been holding back rushing to the surface. I can't fucking hold them in any longer. "I wanted you to do something you loved," I admit. "My penthouse was just a place for sleeping before you stepped through the door, but now it's a home. Our home, and I wanted you to decorate it any way you wanted to."

Truthfully, I wanted her to turn it into somewhere she would have hated to leave.

I wanted her to want to stay.

I wanted those things months ago, before I realized I was in love with her, before I had even tasted her.

And I still want those things.

Want them more than anything.

"I wanted *you* to do it. No one else. You." I cup her face, glancing down at those gorgeous eyes I love so much. "You're amazing, Amara, and you shouldn't have to wait another month to finally do what you love."

Her eyes fill with tears. "Nicholas..."

Ethan's sigh drags me out of the moment, suddenly remembering he was still in the room. "Welp. That's my cue to leave." He stands up, reaches into his jacket pocket, and pulls out a condom, tossing it onto my desk with a smirk. "Stay safe, kids."

The door closes behind him, leaving just the two of us.

M thumbs brush over her soft skin as she breathes in sharply, her eyes wide, searching mine.

"Nicholas. Why would you—"

And then I kiss her.

I don't think, don't question it. I kiss her to stop the words, to stop the thoughts of how this is all going to end in a month.

It's not gentle. It's not careful. It's raw, needy, a desperate attempt to keep her, to not face the fact that in just thirty days, everything will be over. I need more. More of her. More of this. It's everything I've been holding back pouring out all at once.

Her gasp vibrates against my lips, and I feel her hands clutching at my shirt, pulling me closer, like she can't get enough, like she doesn't want to let go either.

"Do you have any idea what you do to me?" I ask her, frustration and desire laced in my voice.

Her lips part, her breath hitching as she looks up at me. "I—
"

I don't let her finish. My hands grip her hips, pulling her flush against me as my mouth crashes back down on hers.

I guide her backward until her ass hits my desk. She gasps as I slide my hands down her thighs, lifting her skirt just enough to expose the tops of her tights. With a sharp tug, I rip them open right in the crotch, the sound tearing through the room.

"*Nick*," she breathes, her voice a mix of shock and arousal.

"*Fuck*. Call me that again," I groan, lifting her leg to hook around my waist.

Her moan is soft, but needy as her nails dig into my shoulders when I thrust against her, my body heating up.

"Nick. What are you doing?" she asks, hooking her arms around my neck, her lips parting on a soft moan when I grind against her pussy. "Someone could come in."

"You have no idea what you do to me," I murmur against her ear. "Every time you walk into a room, I can't fucking breathe. You've *ruined* me, Amara."

Her response is a broken moan, her head tipping back as I grind harder, my cock throbbing with the need to be inside of her.

I tug her blouse free, pulling it over her head in one swift motion. Her bra follows, the lace slipping from her shoulders and falling to the floor. She doesn't stop me, doesn't question me. She just keeps her eyes on me, her chest rising and falling.

God, this woman is the most beautiful thing I have ever seen in my life. I don't know how I ever thought I wouldn't fall for her. It was *inevitable*. Just like I fell for her damn cat.

I stare at her, my gaze dragging over the curves of her chest. My mind floods with the thought of those soft, perfect tits in my hands, feeling the weight of them, the way they'd look when I make her squirm. I want to twist, tease, and take, show her just how much control I can have over her body. My cock stirs at the thought, and I reach for a pair of binder clips on my desk.

Her lips part on a sharp gasp as her eyes dart between the clips and my face, and I can see that mix of excitement and fear that drives me fucking wild. She knows what's coming—doesn't know *exactly* what—but that's what makes this so much better.

Slowly, I trace the cold metal along her tight, pink nipples, groaning as they harden under my touch. She sucks in a breath, her body arching toward me, gripping my arms for balance.

"What color?" I ask, my eyes locked on hers.

Her tongue darts out to run over her lips. "Green," she answers without hesitation.

I cradle her face in my hands, my gaze locking with hers. "Remember, I will always listen to you. If you don't like something, you tell me. Understand?"

She nods, eyes wide, her trust in me unwavering.

I place the binder clips on her nipples carefully, watching her face for any sign of discomfort. She gasps, her lips parting, but she doesn't pull away. Doesn't tell me to stop.

"God," I whisper, pressing a kiss to her temple. "You have no fucking idea how beautifully wrecked you look right now."

A needy whimper escapes her, and I tug on the nipple clamps a little, her lips parting on a cry.

My lips twitch, my cock straining against my pants. "You take pain so well for me, baby. I promise I'll make them feel good after."

My hands fly to her hips, and I turn her around, bending her over the desk. My hands slide up her thighs to the hem of her panties, and with a quick tug, the delicate fabric is shredded and discarded. The sound tears through the air, and my cock throbs at the sight of her exposed skin.

"Fuck, you're a sight," I say, my voice rough as I spread her legs wider, pulling down my pants to free my cock. "Bent over my desk, ready for me. Do you have any idea how badly I want you?"

She moans, her hands gripping the edge of the desk as I slide a finger along the seam of her pussy.

"You're so wet for me," I grunt, teasing her with the tip of my cock, already so fucking hard and leaking for her. "You like being like this, don't you? Completely at my mercy."

"Yes."

I slide inside her in one smooth thrust, groaning as her body clenches around me. She cries out, her back arching as I fill her, stretching her, owning her.

"Fuck, Amara," I groan, my hands gripping her hips as I start to move. "You feel so fucking good."

I thrust harder, the sound of our bodies colliding filling the room. Her moans grow louder, turning desperate as I slide in deeper.

"Tell me how it feels," I demand.

"So good," she sobs. "So fucking good."

When I can't hold back any longer, I pull out of her, guiding her toward the large windows. The city sprawls out behind us, but all I see is her. Her flushed cheeks, her parted lips.

"Keep your hands on the glass," I command, my tone firm. "Don't move unless I tell you to."

"Yes, sir," she breathes.

I step back, taking her in. Her hands pressed flat against the glass, her legs slightly parted.

Opening my desk, I pull out a ruler and head toward her, dragging the cool, flat edge up the inside of her thigh, her body shivering under the touch. "You drive me fucking crazy," I grit out. "Tell me why I can't stop thinking about you."

Her breath hitches, her fingers curling against the glass. "I don't—"

"What the fuck did you do to me?" I cut her off, bringing the ruler down lightly against her ass.

She gasps, her body jerking at the sting. "I don't know."

"You don't know?" I ask, tilting my head as I examine her ass, plump and red. Marked by *me*.

I press the ruler between her legs, the edge teasing her as I slide it against her slick heat, letting it get coated with her arousal. Her moan is soft but desperate, her hips pressing back instinctively.

"Fuck, look at you grinding against my ruler," I muse, watching her hips buck against the wooden material. "You're so fucking needy."

Her body arches, her breath hitching as I tease her, never giving her exactly what she wants.

"You're so beautiful like this," I murmur, setting the ruler aside and sliding my fingers between her legs, circling her swollen clit, pinching it between my fingers. "So perfect."

Pulling my hand away, I position myself behind her, sliding inside her again. The angle makes her cry out, her body arching as I thrust into her.

"Look out the window," I murmur, my lips brushing her ear. "Look at everyone out there who doesn't get to have you like this. You're mine, Amara. *Only mine*."

Her moans grow louder as my cock tunnels into her, deeper, harder, needing to feel every inch of her tight pussy. "Come for me," I demand, my voice raw as I tug on one of her nipple clamps. She cries out, drowning in both pain and pleasure when I smooth my thumb over her sensitive nipples. "I want to feel you drench my cock."

Her head tips back, a delicious moan leaving her lips as her pussy clenches around my cock and I bury myself deep inside her, feeling her pulse around me. The tension in my body snaps, and the pleasure is so intense it's almost painful.

My hips jerk uncontrollably, driving into her as the pleasure coils low in my spine as I empty myself inside her.

The world fades away. There's no city, no office, no one but her and the way she feels, the way she moans my name.

"Amara," I rasp, her name a prayer on my lips as the last shudder wracks through me. I lean forward, pressing my forehead against her shoulder, trying to catch my breath.

I don't let go. I can't. Not yet. My arms wrap around her middle, holding her upright as her head falls back against my shoulder.

"Easy, baby," I murmur, brushing my lips against her temple. "Just breathe. I've got you."

Her fingers curl against the glass, her body melting into mine as I press a kiss to her damp skin. She smells like us, and I can't stop myself from inhaling deeply, committing this moment to memory.

I pull my spent cock out of her slowly, and she gasps at the loss, her body tightening instinctively. My hands stay on her hips, grounding her, as she shivers against me.

I scoop her into my arms, her body soft and pliant against mine, and carry her to my desk. She doesn't protest, just lets her head rest against my shoulder as her breathing starts to even out.

When I set her down, she leans back on her hands, her hair messy, her lips swollen, her eyes half-lidded and hazy, and I can't help but smile.

This woman has me completely and utterly under her spell.

"Stay still," I tell her, crouching in front of her as I carefully remove the binder clips from her nipples. She flinches slightly, and I lean in, pressing gentle kisses to the reddened marks, my lips soothing the tender skin.

"Are you okay?"

Her eyes soften, and she nods, her lips widening into a smirk. "That was fun."

Relief washes over me, and I let out a chuckle, leaning in to kiss her, my lips moving against hers like I'm trying to tell her everything I can't say out loud. She sighs into the kiss, her hands sliding up to tangle in my hair, pulling me closer.

When I finally pull back, her lips are swollen, and she looks at me like I've just changed her world. I don't know how to tell her she's done the same to me.

"I'm going home this weekend," I tell her, my thumb brushing over her plump cheeks, reddened to a perfect pink.

"You are?" she asks, her brows knitting together.

With one hand, I hold her face, glancing down at those bright green eyes that make my heart jump in my chest. "I want you to come with me. I want you to meet my mom."

Her lips part. She doesn't pull away. She doesn't laugh it off or tell me it's a bad idea. Instead, she nods. "Okay."

My shoulders drop in relief, and I release a breath. "Good," I murmur, leaning in to press a soft kiss to her forehead, my lips lingering as I close my eyes.

I've never brought a girl home. Never wanted to. But I want to bring Amara. I want her to meet my mom, see my childhood bedroom, have her around my family.

Because I know now, with a certainty that shakes me to my core.

I'm not letting go of her.

Not now. Not ever.

CHAPTER THIRTY-SEVEN

Amara

I'm about to hurl. My stomach churns, and my head's spinning like crazy, like we're still in the air. But we're not. We landed thirty minutes ago, and now we're on our way to his mom's house.

I glance over at Nicholas, seeing him focused on his phone, completely unfazed. I envy how calm he is, how he's always collected, always in control.

"I can feel you stressing."

"I'm fine," I mutter, though my white-knuckled grip on the seat says otherwise.

His dark eyes flick to mine, brow arched as he tilts his head.

I exhale, the tension in my shoulders releasing a bit. "Okay, maybe I'm not fine. But can you blame me? You're not the one about to walk into a room full of strangers who think this—" I gesture between us "—is real."

He sets his phone down, turning toward me, his gaze sharp. "It is real. At least for the next month. Remember that."

The reminder that this thing between us is coming to an end in less than thirty days has my heart pumping in my chest.

"What if she doesn't like me?" I blurt out before I can stop myself.

His brow furrows, and for a moment, he looks almost confused. "She will."

I shake my head, exhaling. "I know it's stupid to think about because it's not like we're really together, but…" His jaw ticks as I tuck my hair behind my ear. "I really want her to like me," I admit, quietly.

He drops his phone, his hand cupping my face, as he gazes into my eyes. My stomach flips. *I love his eyes.* "It's not stupid. I thought the same when I met your family. I was worried they'd think I wasn't good enough for you. I wanted them to love me."

I suck in a breath. He never told me that. He always seems so confident, so sure of himself. I thought he didn't care about their approval.

"My mom will love you, Amara." His lips twitch. "Especially since you're the first girl I've ever brought over."

My brows shoot up. "Seriously?"

He shrugs. "I've never dated much," he admits. "I had a few girlfriends, but nothing too serious." His thumb moves gently back and forth against my cheek. "You're my *fiancée*. It's different."

The way he says fiancée makes it sound like it's fact, not fiction, and it breaks my heart a little. Because in less than one month, I won't be his fiancée anymore, I won't even be his assistant. I'll be nothing to Nicholas, and he'll forget all about me.

I nod, my throat tight, and close my eyes, begging myself to keep it together. I've known the terms of this deal from the start. I've been bracing for this, preparing myself. I need to accept that this won't be my reality much longer. I won't wake up next to him. I won't kiss him. I won't make love to him.

Leaning back in the seat, I stare out the window, doing my best to keep the tears in check.

When the SUV finally slows to a stop, my breath catches in my throat. *Holy shit*.

The Blackwood estate is massive. The kind of place that only exists in my unrealistic vision boards. The driveway stretches for what feels like forever, decorated with perfectly manicured hedges, with a fancy fountain sitting in the middle.

And the house itself is just as beautiful. White stone with tall windows, and a front door so big, I'm pretty sure it could fit a car through it.

I turn to Nicholas, my brows shooting up to my hairline. "*This* is where you grew up?"

He looks over, a smirk on his face. "You seem surprised."

"A little. I definitely didn't expect *this*." I motion vaguely toward the entire estate, feeling a little out of place in my jacket, barely thick enough for a cold breeze, and my worn-out boots. "It's stunning."

He gives me a half-smile. "You want one like this?"

My eyes widen. "What? That's crazy."

"It's just a house. Say the word and it's yours."

Just a house. I shake my head, not knowing how to respond. My home was cramped, the walls were too thin, and we were lucky if the kitchen sink didn't leak. "I'm good. You've given me more than enough."

Nicholas opens the car door and steps out, offering me his hand. It's become second nature, and I can't help but wonder what I'll do when it's no longer there. The cold hits me as soon as I step out of the car, and I instinctively pull my jacket tighter, the chill nipping at my skin as we make our way toward the front door.

We're halfway down the driveway when the door swings open, and out steps a woman.

Eleanor Blackwood is everything I expected Nicholas's mom to be. Tall, effortlessly elegant, with blonde hair pulled into a perfect bun that looks like it could never have a single hair out of place.

"Nicholas," she greets her son, her smile widening as she spots him. "You're here."

He smirks at her, leaning in to give her a hug. "Good to see you, mom."

"And you must be Amara," she says, her smile growing as her eyes move over me. She shakes her head. "You're even more beautiful than the pictures I've seen."

I offer her a warm smile, my hand tightening in Nicholas's. "Thank you."

"I've heard so much about you," Eleanor continues, smiling at me with a warmth that almost makes me forget how out of place I feel here. "It's wonderful to finally meet the woman who's captured my son's heart."

"I, uh—It's great to meet you too," I stumble over the words, letting out a nervous laugh.

Eleanor's smile widens, but before she can say anything else, a voice cuts through the air.

"Well, well, well. The infamous fiancée."

I freeze, and Nicholas stiffens beside me, his body going rigid as he slips his hand to the small of my back.

I follow his gaze to the man now standing in the doorway. Alexander Blackwood.

He's everything Nicholas isn't. Sharp angles where Nicholas is smooth, relaxed where Nicholas is controlled, and a cockiness radiating from him that sets me on edge.

"What are you doing here?" Nicholas asks him, his voice sharp.

Alexander grins, and lifts his glass to his lips, taking a slow sip as if he's enjoying the moment a little too much. "When I heard you were bringing your fiancée, I thought I should see for myself."

He takes a step forward, his gaze flicking over me like he's sizing me up. There's nothing overtly rude about it, but the way his eyes linger makes me want to squirm.

Before I can even react, he takes my hand, pressing a kiss to my knuckles.

"Alexander Blackwood. A pleasure to meet you, Amara."

I pull my hand back a second later. "Nice to meet you, too," I reply, pressing my lips together in a smile.

"That's enough," Nicholas snaps.

The shift in his tone catches me off guard, and I glance up at him, my eyes widening.

Alexander's smirk doesn't even falter. If anything, it widens. "Don't be so territorial, little brother. I'm just being polite."

I shift on my feet, unsure of what to do, as the tension from whatever history they share hangs in the air, thick and ready to snap at any moment.

"Okay, boys. Shall we go inside?" Eleanor suggests, trying to defuse the tension between them.

Alexander smirks, his hand outstretched. "Come on in, little brother." I glance back at Nicholas, catching the tightness in his jaw.

The inside of the house is just as beautiful as the outside, with high ceilings, marble floors, and a sweeping staircase that leads to the second floor, the railings sleek and dark against the light colors of the foyer, with a long crystal chandelier hanging in the middle. The walls are filled with abstract art, paintings and sculptures I can't even begin to name, and a grand piano tucked in the corner.

Eleanor leads us through the house, showing off room after room as we make our way toward the living room, where the fire crackles in a huge brick fireplace.

"So, tell me about the wedding." Eleanor grins, her eyes sparkling with excitement as we finally sit down on her plush white couch. "Have you guys decided on a date yet? What's the guest list look like?" She gasps. "Have you picked out a dress?"

I glance at Nicholas, anxiety twisting in my stomach. We haven't planned a single thing because… this isn't real. There won't be a wedding. I won't stand at the aisle, gazing into Nicholas' eyes as I say *I do*.

But before I can answer, Nicholas speaks up, his arm wrapping around my waist and pulling me a little closer to him.

"We're still in the early stages of planning. But we want something small," he begins, his arm curling around my waist. "Just close family and a few friends. In the fall, with the leaves falling and the warm breeze, crisp air. And of course there will be ducks."

Ducks?

Oh my god. He's describing the exact wedding I've always dreamed of; the intimate gathering I told him about months ago.

My brows furrow in confusion as I glance up at him, my heart thudding as I wait for an explanation, but Nicholas glances down at me with a smile. *Right*. Of course. He's simply pretending we'll have a future together. I manage a tight smile as I swallow back the rising ache.

Eleanor's expression softens, her eyes glistening. "Your father would have loved to see that," she adds. "He would have been so proud of you, Nicholas."

Nicholas's hand flexes around my waist as his shoulders drop. I can only imagine how much that must have meant to him.

But then, Alexander's voice cuts through the moment as he lets out a scoff. "Dad coddled you too much," he says, shaking his head as he leans back in his chair.

I glance at Nicholas, watching the tension tighten in his jaw. "He gave me what he thought I deserved," Nicholas replies, his tone colder than I've ever heard it. "I worked beside him day by day. You, however, did whatever you wanted, whenever you wanted."

"Boys," Eleanor interjects, trying to diffuse the brewing tension. "Let's not do this now. We have company."

Alexander rolls his eyes. "You always think you're the one who worked the hardest. Always the golden boy, huh?" Alexander slaps his hand down on the table, the force making me jump. "I deserve that position."

Nicholas stands up suddenly. "You deserve nothing," he snaps. "You're lucky I even gave you the position in L.A. Without me, you would have been on your own. I gave you a lifeline, and you've done nothing but disrespect me."

There's a beat of silence where neither of them says anything, but I can see the fury in their eyes.

Finally, Nicholas glances at his mother, his expression softening a little. "Excuse me, Mom. I'd like to show Amara upstairs."

Eleanor gives a small nod, her smile apologetic. "Of course, darling."

Nicholas takes my hand as we make our way to the stairs, his grip tightening. Once we reach the top, he pushes open a door and steps into what I assume is his childhood bedroom.

I follow him inside, my eyes widening when I glance around. His room is different than I expected. Expensive, sure, but there's something oddly comforting about it. A few soccer jerseys hang on the walls, trophies are lined up neatly on a shelf, and posters cover every inch of space above his bed.

I wander over to the shelf, running my fingers lightly over a framed photo of a younger Nicholas, grinning with a group of boys, all wearing the same soccer jersey.

"I didn't know you played soccer," I say, trying to fill the silence.

Nicholas lets out a sigh, rubbing the back of his neck as he steps closer, his eyes following mine. "I told you," he says quietly. "You don't really know me."

I turn to face him, raising an eyebrow. "I know you a little," I tease, though curiosity bubbles inside me. There's still so much I don't know about him, about his past, the person he used to be.

He groans, and then, before I even have a chance to react, his forehead presses against mine. His eyes are dark and unreadable as his pulse thumps against mine.

"If I wasn't so messed up over my brother…" A rumble erupts in his throat. "I'd bend you over my bed and fuck you."

My breath catches in my throat as I wrap my arms around his neck, leaning into him. "What's going on between you two?"

Nicholas pulls back slightly, his jaw tightening as he glances away. He's silent for a beat, and I brace myself for him to shut me out.

But then he lets out a sigh. "Alexander thinks he deserves the CEO position just because he's the oldest," he says, frustration lacing his words. "He's trying to sabotage everything, trying to make the board think I'm not fit to run Blackwood Hotels. He wants it all, and he's willing to tear me down to get it."

My stomach sinks at the thought. "That won't happen," I tell him with certainty. "Everyone knows how hard you work."

Nicholas looks at me, the hardness in his expression softening just a little. Without saying anything, he steps closer, removes one of my hands from around his neck, and kisses the back of it. It's so soft, so unexpectedly gentle, it catches me off guard. Slowly, his lips move up my arm, inch by inch, kissing my skin before they finally find mine.

My heart beats in double time as I melt into his kiss, a soft moan leaving my lips. He pulls back just enough to speak. "God, I'm so happy you're here with me."

His words hit me in the chest. "Me too," I whisper as he kisses me again.

He pulls away a few seconds later, his hands lingering on my waist. "I'll be right back."

I nod, and he turns to leave the room. My gaze returns to his jerseys, and I can't help but smile at the young, carefree version of him frozen in time in the pictures.

"My brother left you alone?"

I gasp, turning to find Alexander leaning against the door, shaking his head with a smirk. His eyes skim me from head to toe, his gaze lingering in a way that makes my stomach churn. "He should know better than that."

I've heard of Alexander, talked to him plenty since he always calls the office, but being in the same room with him is a different story. My stomach churns as he lazily swirls his drink, his eyes locked on me with a look I can't quite decipher.

"Nicholas will be right back. He just went to get something."

He hums, nodding as he pushes off the doorframe, walking toward me. "So, what's it like being engaged to my brother?"

"It's... nice," I reply, the uncertainty creeping into my voice. I don't even know how to answer him, especially with the way he's looking at me.

"Nice," he repeats, his tone dripping with amusement. "That's quite the endorsement."

I stiffen, but before I can respond, he leans forward. "You seem too sweet for him, you know."

"I—"

"He can be..." Alexander pauses, his gaze searching mine as if he's trying to gauge my reaction. "Intense. Boring. A workaholic. Way too fucking controlling. Are you sure you're up for that?"

I suck in a breath as he takes a step closer, my hands pressing against Nicholas's dresser. "I can handle it," I tell him, narrowing my eyes. "What I can't handle is you invading my personal space."

His smirk returns, darker, dangerous. "Feisty. You've got my brother wrapped around your little finger, huh? What's he promised you to go along with this? A raise? A promotion? Or is it just his cock you're after?" He tilts his head. "Tell me, and I'll sweeten the deal."

"I'd rather die than go anywhere near you."

He laughs, leaning in closer, his fingers grazing my cheek lightly. I turn my head, shuddering at his touch. "You know, if you ever get bored of Nicholas, and change your mind—"

"Alexander." Nicholas's voice cuts through the room, and Alexander steps back, slowly... unbothered. Nicholas enters the room, setting a bottle of white wine and two glasses on the dresser. "Get the fuck away from her."

"Relax." Alexander raises his hands, a smirk on his face. "I was just getting to know her."

Nicholas doesn't respond, his eyes sliding to mine. The muscles in his jaw ticks as he stares at me. "Amara, come with me."

He doesn't give me a chance to respond before he's guiding me out of the room, his touch on my back heavy.

Once we're in the hallway, I finally gather enough courage to speak. "How much did you see?"

"Enough," he says, his voice cold and clipped.

A breath catches in my chest. "Why didn't you say something?"

Nicholas stops in his tracks and turns to me, his gaze locking with mine. "I wanted to see how you'd handle it."

My eyebrows lift in disbelief. "You think I would take him up on his offer?" Is he out of his mind? Does he really think I'd want his brother when I'm madly in love with him?

He doesn't respond immediately, but his eyes soften just a little. "It wouldn't be the first time."

I shake my head. "I would never. You know that, right?"

He finally relaxes, his hands slipping around my neck, pulling me closer. "I know." He leans in, his breath warm against my lips. "Why don't you go downstairs? My mom keeps grilling me about you."

I let out a small laugh. "Really?"

He nods. "I fear she might like you more than me."

I nudge his chest, shaking my head. "That's not true."

Nicholas chuckles, leaning in to press a soft kiss to my forehead, his thumb gently tracing my jaw. "I'll be down soon. I promise. I've just got to take care of something first."

CHAPTER THIRTY-EIGHT

Nicholas

I step into my bedroom, shutting the door behind me with a quiet click. My chest tightens at the sight of Alexander standing by my desk, holding one of the framed photos. It's a picture of me from years ago, fresh off the soccer field, dirt smudged on my face, my arm thrown over my teammates. I remember the week after that picture was taken, Alexander signed up for my team, out of pure jealousy that I had our parents' attention.

"Always after what I have," I mutter, shaking my head as a dry scoff escapes me.

Alexander doesn't react at first. He sets the frame down, his back still to me. His shoulders are relaxed, as if he belongs here, as if my room is just another one of his playgrounds. When he finally turns, his lips curl into a familiar smirk I want to punch.

"I don't know what you're talking about," he says with a shrug. "I was just admiring her."

Admiring her. He made a mistake by just *looking* at her.

"Bullshit. We both know what the fuck you were trying to do."

He gives up pretenses, letting out a sigh. "I've always had a thing for your girlfriends, little brother," he says with a tut. "Candace was so sweet."

I stalk toward him, my lip curling. "Go near her, and you'll regret it. I don't care who you think you are."

His laugh is instant, cutting through the air, and he tilts his head back with a smirk. "Jealousy doesn't suit you. It's been years, Nicholas. Time to let it go."

"This isn't about Candace, and you know it. You think I give a fuck about her? She was just a distraction. Doesn't mean shit to me. None of it was ever real. Just a dumb fucking arrangement I had to make the best of."

Alexander's smirk falters just slightly, his gaze sharpening. He's not used to me brushing off his attempts to dig into old wounds. Candace was never what he wanted her to be. She wasn't a trophy he could dangle in front of me. She wasn't a loss. She was simply a pawn. Nothing more than a name on a checklist my father handed me.

His lips press into a thin line, his eyes narrowing. "And what about Amara?" he asks, leaning forward slightly, his voice laced with something that sounds almost too eager. "Do you care about her?"

I freeze for a second, my body rigid, my fists curling. "Don't talk about Amara," I warn him.

His grin widens. "So, you *do* care," he says slowly, letting out a dark laugh as he leans in slightly, just enough to make my blood boil. "That's fun. I bet she'll taste sweeter knowing you want her, and I got her instead."

The anger hits me, and my hand shoots out before I can stop it, grabbing the front of his shirt and yanking him toward me. His smirk doesn't falter, but I catch the flicker of something in his eyes, a sliver of hesitation.

"Keep your eyes and hands off her. You hear me? She's not yours to play with." My grip tightens on his shirt, pulling him closer. "Not now. Not ever. You'll never get her." I shove him back, hard enough to make him stumble. "And you won't get the company either. Forget about it."

He smooths his shirt. "You always did have a flair for dramatics."

My jaw clenches, and I take a step closer. "You've crossed the line, Alexander. You seem to forget who's in charge here. Your current position is thanks to *me*. So go ahead. Keep pushing me, and you might just find yourself out of a job."

He stills, but I see the subtle twitch in his jaw, the flicker in his eyes, calculating, weighing his next move.

But there's no move for him. Not this time.

He's gone too far, and we both know it.

I take another step forward, letting my words settle between us. "You think you can taunt me, push me, and I'll just let it slide?" I shake my head, scoffing. "You're sorely mistaken."

The silence stretches between us, but he says nothing. Doesn't blink. His mind is racing, but there's nothing left for him to do.

And this game between us?

It's over.

CHAPTER THIRTY-NINE
Amara

"T his is the one." Jade spins around, holding up a red, lacy, crotchless bodysuit. "Classic. Sexy." She smirks, waving it in Sophie's face. "He won't know what hit him."

Sophie's eyes widen like the lingerie might leap off the hanger and attack her. "I was thinking something... less intense. Like this," she replies, holding up a pale blue babydoll.

"Less intense?" Jade scoffs, her voice dripping with disbelief. "Babe, the whole point of lingerie is to *be* intense. If you're not leaving him speechless, you're doing it wrong."

Sophie's cheeks turn bright pink, but she lifts her chin in defiance. "I'll have you know, Sebastian is very satisfied."

"I'm sure he is," Jade quips. "But this couldn't hurt." She thrusts the lace bodysuit toward Sophie. "Humor me. Try it on and see how you feel."

With a long, exaggerated sigh, Sophie disappears into the dressing room, the curtain swishing closed behind her. Jade immediately turns to me, eyebrows practically jumping off her face.

"No." I shake my head, stepping back as she snatches another hanger off the rack.

"Come on," she whines.

"You told me we were going to lunch," I say, narrowing my eyes. "Not lingerie shopping."

"We are." Jade shrugs, unconcerned. "I just wanted to make a quick stop here first. Here," she says, holding a black lacy number in front of my face. "Try this on."

A laugh escapes me. "No way."

"What? Why not? It's hot."

A flush of heat creeps up my neck at the thought of wearing something so revealing. "I'm not the type of girl who wears that."

She scoffs. "Bullshit. Lingerie is for everyone. You walk into a room wearing this, and trust me, Nicholas will be on his knees."

I laugh, shaking my head. "You're relentless."

"And yet, you keep me around," she quips, grinning as she shoves the bodysuit into my hands.

Before I can talk myself out of it, I step into the dressing room, the mirror greeting me with brutal honesty, the harsh lighting doing me no favors. My first instinct is to look away, but I force myself to stay. My reflection stares back, every curve and dip exposed under the unforgiving fluorescent light.

I inhale deeply, strip down, and slide into the lace. It's delicate against my skin, the intricate pattern hugging my curves in all the right ways. The plunging neckline is daring, and for the first time in a long time, I feel sexy. *Really* sexy.

A small smile tugs at my lips as I grab my phone. I snap a picture in the mirror and send it to Nicholas before I can second-guess myself.

His response is almost immediate.

Nicholas:

> Holy fuck.

> You're killing me.

> Please buy that.

> Buy ten more.

Warmth spreads through me as I read his words, my heart racing. I bite back a grin, change back into my clothes, and step out of the fitting room.

"Well?" Jade asks, her eyes sparkling with anticipation. "Is it a winner?"

"It's a winner," I say, holding up the black lace.

"Hell yeah. I knew it would be." Jade nudges Sophie. "And you?"

Sophie exhales, defeated. "Fine. You were right. It's hot."

Jade beams as we head to the register. "I'm a genius. You both owe me for the best sex of your lives tonight."

I let out a laugh, swiping the card Nicholas gave me, to pay for the lingerie.

"God, I'm starving," Jade groans as we leave the store. "Do you guys want sushi or tacos?"

"Tacos," Sophie counters. "I'm not in the mood for raw fish."

"I'm cool with tacos," I agree, but my attention shifts as my phone buzzes in my bag. Expecting another message from Nicholas, I pull it out, only to see an unknown number on the screen.

"Who is it?" Sophie asks, noticing my pause.

"Uh… no one," I reply, unlocking the phone.

Jade smirks. "Let me guess. It's Nicholas. The lingerie killed him, didn't it?"

I let out a laugh, but my stomach twists as I open the message. It's an audio file. No name, no explanation—just the file. My gut tightens as I press play and hold the phone to my ear.

"And what about Amara?" I furrow my brows, recognizing Alexander's voice.

"You think I give a fuck about her?" Nicholas spits, venom dripping from each word. My brows raise as I hear the fury in his voice. "She was just a distraction. Doesn't mean shit to me. None of it was ever real. Just a dumb fucking arrangement I had to make the best of."

The recording ends, but the words echo in my mind. My hand trembles as I lower the phone, staring at the screen like it might somehow explain what I just heard.

"Amara?" Sophie's voice pulls me back to reality. "What was it?"

I shove the phone into my bag, forcing a smile that feels too stiff. "Wrong number," I lie.

She seems to buy it, her attention shifting as we head to lunch, but my mind stays stuck on the recording. Nicholas's voice, so cold and detached, echoes in my head, replaying endlessly.

By the time I'm home, I'm drained—physically and emotionally—and teetering on the edge of tears. I sit on the edge of the bed—*his bed*—staring blankly at the lingerie bag in my hand.

I thought Nicholas was different. I thought I could trust him. But his words keep running through my mind, over and over, until they're all I can hear.

I mean nothing to him. None of it was ever real.

And I realize, too late, that I was naïve enough to believe otherwise.

Hours pass before Nicholas finally arrives. The elevator doors open, and he steps into the apartment, sending a chill down my spine.

It feels like I'm a stranger in this place, like it's my first time stepping into this penthouse all over again. It doesn't feel like home anymore.

"Fucking finally," Nicholas mutters with a grin, already tugging at his tie. His eyes find mine, and that familiar spark flares to life. My heart stumbles, traitor that it is, his gaze glimmering as he walks toward me.

"Goddamn, I missed you," he grunts as he closes the distance between us. His hands slide to my waist, his cologne enveloping me as he leans down to kiss me.

At the last second, I turn my face, and his lips land on my cheek instead.

He pauses, his breath warm against my skin, and pulls back slightly. "Everything okay?"

I force a smile. "Yeah. Just tired."

He chuckles. "I bet." His eyes flick to the boutique bag on the couch. "How was shopping?"

"Good."

His grin widens. "I've been thinking about it all day. What'd you pick out?"

I step back, trying to shove down the ache in my chest. "I should get Pumpkin some food."

"I can do that," he offers, crouching down to scratch Pumpkin behind the ears. She arches into his touch, purring contentedly. I watch him for a moment, the tenderness of his movements stirring something deep within me.

She used to hate men, but like me, she fell for him. And it was all a lie.

For months, I lived in a bubble, thinking this life was somehow... real. A life where he treated me like I was everything, where he took care of me, kissed me like he meant it, told me I was beautiful.

I let myself believe it.

The ache in my chest sharpens, and I turn away, grabbing Pumpkin's food. "I'll do it," I murmur, knowing it's better she doesn't get any more attached. In two weeks, we'll be gone, and it'll hurt her more then.

"Okay." He stands straight, his eyes locking on mine. "Are you hungry? I can make us something."

"No, I'm fine," I say, busying myself with the food.

He doesn't press, but I can tell he knows something's off. He presses his lips to the top of my head, and the intimacy of the gesture freezes me in place. How could he do that when it means nothing to him?

"I'm gonna go take a shower," he tells me, stepping away.

Once the bedroom door shuts, I close my eyes, and tears fall freely. How can he lie to me like this? How can he pretend to care when his words are so cold, so detached, when he thinks I'm not listening?

I thought I could handle it. I thought I could make it through until the contract ended. But I can't. I can't stay here, sleep in the same bed as him, knowing it's all just a game to him, a way to pass the time until we're out of each other's lives.

After feeding Pumpkin, I crawl into bed, pulling the covers up tightly around me.

Nicholas joins me a few minutes later, the bathroom door swinging open, steam billowing out as he walks in, a towel wrapped around his waist, droplets of water clinging to his body.

Against my will, my eyes drop to take him in. Hot and wet and *ugh*... I roll over quickly, my back to him, squeezing my eyes shut. I'm still so attracted to him. My heart still beats for him. And he doesn't care about me at all.

A minute later, I feel the bed dip as he slides in beside me. I hold my breath, hoping he'll just go to sleep. But I feel him inch closer.

"You never did show me what you bought," he murmurs, his hand grazing my hip. His lips find my neck, and I freeze.

"*Red*," I whisper, the word slipping out before I can stop it.

He pulls away immediately, his hand falling back. "Okay," he says, his voice soft but tinged with a hint of concern.

"I'm sorry," I whisper. I've never turned him down, never wanted to. But the thought of him touching me when I know he doesn't feel the same hurts too much. I can't do it. Not tonight.

There's a pause. Then he shifts closer, his lips brushing my temple. "You don't need to apologize, honey. I'm more than happy to just lie here with you."

My heart twists painfully. The sincerity in his voice almost breaks me. But I can't. Not after what I heard.

"Everything okay?" he asks, quietly.

"Yeah," I lie, trying to keep my voice even. "Just tired."

He hesitates, then pulls back, pressing another kiss to my temple before settling against the pillows. He doesn't push further. Doesn't touch me again. Soon, his breathing evens out, and I know he's asleep.

But sleep doesn't come for me. Instead, my mind races, already planning what I'll do once he leaves tomorrow.

CHAPTER FORTY
Nicholas

I glance at the clock again, the relentless ticking echoing in the silence of my office.

It's been over an hour now, and Amara still hasn't shown up to work.

Where the hell is she?

She told me this morning to go in alone because she'd be a little late, but this? This is different. She's never been this late before, and every minute that passes feels like a weight on my chest. If she needed a break, if she wanted to stay home, she could've just told me. She could ask me for anything, and I'd give it to her.

Another glance at the clock.

Still nothing.

The frustration inside me tightens, curling in my stomach.

I grab my phone, my fingers itching to send her a message, but before I can hit send, a knock at the door breaks through the chaos in my head.

Fucking finally.

"Come in," I say, my lips twitching into a grin, anticipation swelling in my chest. Is it normal to be this obsessed with your fiancée? I don't think so, but right now, I don't care.

The door creaks open, but my grin quickly fades when I realize it's not Amara.

It's Sophie.

For a moment, I don't know whether to feel relieved or frustrated that it's not Amara standing there. Maybe Sophie has answers. Maybe she knows something I don't. I feel like I'm teetering on the verge of losing my mind.

"Sophie. What can I do for you?"

Sophie doesn't seem to notice the shift in my mood. She steps into the room, holding a stack of papers in her hands.

"These came in for you," she says, her tone sharper than usual, a bite to it I'm not used to hearing from her.

I nod, momentarily confused. Sophie's never sounded like this before. But I don't have time to think about it. Amara's still not here. And I have no idea why.

"Thanks," I mutter, grabbing the papers, already half-turning to reach for my phone.

She turns around and leaves, the door clicking shut behind her.

I glance down at the papers in my hands, expecting nothing more than routine contracts, maybe a report or two to sign. But then my eyes catch the words on the first page. My stomach drops, and for a moment, the room feels like it's closing in around me.

Amara's name.

And under it, in bold letters: *Resignation*.

What the fuck?

She still has two weeks left on her contract. Two weeks before I can finalize the deal that'll get her everything she wants. That'll give her the promotion, the stability, everything she's worked for.

I scan the letter again, my confusion growing with every word. There's nothing in here about a transfer, a raise, or a move to another department. Just... resignation.

I drop the paper like it's burning my hands, my thoughts spiraling, but I immediately grab my phone, dialing her number.

The phone rings.

And rings.

And rings.

No answer.

I try again. Four. Five times.

Still nothing.

Frustration and panic claw at me. I stand up, the office chair swiveling as I push away from the desk, my mind racing.

My hands shake as I walk toward the door, determined to find out where she is. Sophie and Jade look up when they see me coming, their eyes widening before they quickly turn back to their work, pretending to be busy.

I stop in front of their desks, my voice low and tight. "Where is she?

Sophie avoids my gaze, shifting uncomfortably in her seat. "Um… we don't—"

I cut her off. "Don't lie to me. Where the hell is my fiancée?"

"She's packing," Jade says, crossing her arms over her chest.

Packing.

I blink, the word not quite registering in my mind. "Packing?" I repeat, my confusion clouding my thoughts. "Packing for what?"

Jade scoffs, sharp and loud. "She's moving in with me," she tells me, her words slicing through me, turning my world upside down. "Are you seriously going to act like you don't know why she wouldn't want to live with you anymore?"

I don't answer, turning away, my mind racing to connect the dots. Why would she be packing? Why would she be leaving?

I check the security feed on my phone. My heart clenches when I see her standing in the living room, suitcase in hand, struggling to close it.

The air in my chest tightens as a mixture of dread and anger rises inside me.

I swipe the screen away and call for my driver. "Lionel, get the car ready. I need to go home. Now."

"Right away, sir."

It feels like the longest ten minutes of my life. My leg jitters nervously, thoughts spiraling out of control. Everything was fine between us, right? We were good. We were perfect. How did it all fall apart so fast?

The car pulls up in front of my building, and I barely wait for it to come to a full stop before I'm jumping out, heading inside. The elevator ride feels like an eternity, each second stretching longer than the last. My hands tug at my hair, frustration clawing at me.

Please, let this be a mistake. Let her still be here. Let this all be some kind of misunderstanding.

Because I can't lose her.

I reach my apartment door, heart pounding in my chest. I step inside and freeze when I spot her, standing by the doors, suitcase in hand, looking like she's ready to walk away for good.

She blinks, her expression unreadable. "What... What are you doing here?"

I swallow hard, fighting to keep my voice steady. "What am I doing here? The real question is, where the hell are you going, Amara?"

Her gaze drifts away, her eyes avoiding mine. "I thought you'd be at work." Her voice is small, distant, and it fucking tears at me.

"Why would you want me to be at work? Why are you trying to run away from me?" I take a step closer, my chest aching.

She shakes her head, her eyes glued to the floor like she can't bring herself to meet my gaze. I reach for her, my hand hovering near her cheek, but she flinches, stepping back. The rejection hits me like a physical punch to the gut.

"Amara, what the hell did I do?" I ask, my voice strained, cracking. "Please, tell me. Whatever it is, I'll fix it."

She lifts her head, finally meeting my eyes, and the green I love—wet and blurry, full of tears—rips through me.

"I know," she whispers.

"Know what?" My brows knit together, frustration and confusion crashing through me. I don't understand. What the hell is she talking about?

She takes a deep breath, her hands trembling at her sides. "*I know*, Nicholas. I know none of this was real to you." Her voice wobbles. "I know I was just a means to an end to you. You never cared about me. Not really." She shakes her head, the sound of her voice breaking something inside me. "I just don't understand why you had to lie and pretend to care about me this whole time."

My frown deepens, the confusion settling deeper into my chest. What the hell is she talking about?

"I would've gone along with it if you asked. You didn't have to—" Her words cut off as I take a step toward her.

Her lips press together, her gaze falling to the floor. The pain in her eyes twists my insides. "I would have done *anything* for you."

Her words hit hard, landing like a punch to the gut. I take a step back, struggling to understand.

"Amara, what the fuck are you talking about?"

She lets out a bitter laugh, hollow and broken. Tears streak down her face, leaving wet trails. "You don't have to keep pretending. I heard what you told your brother."

I freeze. The air seems to leave the room, suffocating me as the blood drains from my face. "My brother?"

CHAPTER FORTY-ONE

Amara

"**M**y brother?" Nicholas repeats, his face eerily still. The muscle in his jaw tenses, and I can feel the anger rising inside him.

I turn away, my heart pounding in my chest. I can't do this. I can't listen to his lies anymore.

"Amara…" His voice breaks through the silence.

"Please… leave me alone, Nicholas." I can't look at him. Not now. Not after everything.

"Fuck," he mutters under his breath, his voice breaking. "What did—*Goddamnit*. Tell me, Amara. What the fuck did my brother tell you?"

I scoff, shaking my head as I walk away from him, dragging the suitcase along with me. "Don't worry, he didn't tell me anything. I heard it straight from your mouth."

His steps falter, and I hear him curse under his breath. "What are you… Amara can you please just *stop* for one second?"

I freeze, the wheels of the suitcase halting as my body shakes. My eyes squeeze shut at the sound of his voice, so raw, so desperate.

I just want to forget it all. Forget how he looked at me, how I let myself believe in the lies he told me. Forget how my heart raced every time I thought there was something real between us.

"Please, Amara," he pleads, his voice low and soft, a desperation in it I can't ignore. "Please, just turn around and look at me. *Please*."

The silence stretches between us, and I fight to swallow the lump in my throat.

I turn around anyway, not strong enough to ignore him. As soon as our eyes meet, he lets out a breath, shaking his head slightly as if he's trying to process everything I've just said. His gaze shifts over my face, his brows knitting together in confusion.

"What did you hear?" he asks, his voice hoarse like the words are stuck in his throat. His eyes lock on mine, pleading. "Tell me."

I shake my head, my throat tightening, feeling the familiar sting of tears building behind my eyes. "I don't want to repeat it," I whisper.

He steps closer, just a few inches, his hand reaching out to touch me. But I take a step back, and his hand drops to his side, clenched into a fist. "Fuck," he mutters under his breath, running a hand through his hair in frustration. "I don't know how to fix this if you won't tell me what you heard."

"There's nothing to fix. Not anymore." I take a deep breath, forcing the words out even though they hurt like hell. "I know how you really feel about me."

His brow furrows, confusion flickering in his eyes. "Tell me. How do I really feel about you?"

"I don't—"

"Tell me, Amara," he cuts me off. "Fucking *tell me* what you think you know. Tell me what he—"

"*And what about Amara?*"

Nicholas stops dead in his tracks, his face draining of color as he hears his brother's voice on the recording.

"*You think I give a fuck about her?*"

I hold my phone in my shaking hand, my stomach dropping when I hear Nicholas's cold, unattached voice talking about me.

"*She was just a distraction. Doesn't mean shit to me. None of it was ever real. Just a dumb fucking arrangement I had to make the best of.*"

I squeeze my eyes shut, my heart breaking. I loved him—love him still—but it was all just a game to him. A means to an end until he got what he wanted. He didn't need to pretend to care about me, because I would've followed through with everything, no questions asked. I had already signed the damn contract.

He didn't have to lie.

The tears fall freely, streaking down my face as I try to catch my breath.

Nicholas takes a step forward, his face contorting in disbelief. "Amara, I did *not* say that."

"Are you telling me this isn't your voice?" I ask, my voice cracking with frustration. "I know what I heard, Nicholas,"

"I did *not* fucking say that," he insists, closing the gap between us. He runs a hand through his hair in frustration, his eyes darting away as if he's searching for the right words. "Alexander, he…" He stops, visibly struggling to find the right explanation. "He edited the clip to make it sound like—"

"You don't need to lie, Nicholas," I cut him off. "I don't want any favors from you. I've already put in my resignation. I'll find a job somewhere else, whether it's as a designer or a waitress. I don't want anything from you." My voice cracks but

I shake my head, trying to keep it under control. "Don't worry. I'll keep my end of your stupid deal. I'll pretend to be your fiancée until you can get what you really want."

"Amara." His voice tightens. "I do not give a fuck about that right now. I need you to believe me when I tell you I did not say those things."

He holds my face in his hands, but I pull away, his touch feeling like a lie. "It's better this way," I murmur.

"Amara." His voice breaks as he reaches for me again, but I take another step back.

"The contract was going to end in two weeks anyway," I continue, sniffing as my nose tingles. "It's best if I leave now so I don't get even more attached." I bend down to pick up my suitcase, but before I can move, Nicholas's hand lands on mine, forcing the suitcase back onto the floor.

"You're not going anywhere." His eyes narrow, fire burning in them.

"Nicholas—"

"You are not leaving."

"The contract ends in two weeks," I remind him.

"I told you, I don't give a fuck about the contract. How many fucking times do I need to tell you, you're all I fucking care about!"

I shake my head, unable to believe anything he says.

He sees the look in my eyes, the confusion, the hurt, and it makes him pause. He straightens up, his jaw tight, and then he turns, walking away from me. The sharp click of his footsteps echoes in the silence.

"Nicholas?"

He doesn't turn back, his silhouette fading into the hallway as he walks into his office. Less than a minute later, Nicholas walks out of his office, a piece of paper in his hand.

"Is that…?"

"The contract?" He holds it up, and without another word, he rips it to shreds, the paper falling to the floor like confetti.

"What are you—"

"Is that enough proof for you that I don't give a fuck about the deal or the contract or *anything* else except for you?"

I shake my head, confusion flooding my thoughts.

He takes a step forward, throwing the shredded paper onto the ground, his hands reaching for me. His thumb rubs along my jaw. "I don't want to end this," he breathes, shaking his head. "Not now, not in two weeks. Not *ever*."

I suck in a breath, my chest tightening at his words.

"I want you, Amara," he continues, his eyes softening as he looks into mine. "I want you and Pumpkin and everything that comes with the two of you. How could you ever question that for a single second?"

My breath hitches in my throat, my mind reeling at the sincerity in his eyes. But my mind floods with the reminder of the recording. "But what about—"

"I did not say that," he interrupts, shaking his head. "I swear to you, Amara. At least not about you."

My brows furrow in disbelief. "What are you talking about?"

He exhales sharply, stepping back just enough to rake a hand through his hair. "When I was eighteen, my dad was trying to land some investors. His business partner had a daughter. Candace. He wanted her to be set for life, taken care of. So, he made a deal with my father. Alexander wasn't interested in anything that wasn't getting drunk and high out of his mind, so my dad came to me. Told me what was at stake, how much it meant to him… and I agreed. I made her think we had a future together to keep her father happy." He shakes his head, his expression tightening. "But it was never real for me. Not even for a second. It was all for my dad's business. And I'm pretty sure Candace knew that, too…" His jaw clenches. "Which is why she slept with my brother."

My eyebrows shoot up. "Alexander?"

He scoffs, the muscle in his jaw ticking with tension. "He thought I'd be pissed. Thought he'd be hurting me by sleeping with her. But I didn't care. She could've married him for all I cared. Once the deal was done, I ended it with her. And since I didn't want her, neither did Alexander." He shakes his head, frustration coursing through him. "The whole thing was his way of getting back at me. And he tried doing the same to you. That recording you heard…" He pauses, his jaw tensing. "He twisted it. Took bits and pieces and made it sound like I was talking about you. But I *never* once said we weren't real."

He reaches up, brushing my hair behind my ear, and my eyes flutter shut at the touch. He lifts my chin gently, his gaze piercing mine. "Of course it's fucking real. This thing between us has never once been fake to me, Amara."

I search his face, my heart hammering in my chest. "Really?"

He nods, his eyes softening as he moves even closer. "You could tell the world I was lying about you being my fiancée, I could lose the deal, and I wouldn't care as long as I had you." He cups my face, his touch warm and tender. "I love you, Amara."

363

My eyes snap wide open, my stomach dropping. *Did he just say*—?

"I. Love. You," he repeats, making my chest pound. "I don't know when it started, but you're all I think about. You're all I want."

The ground beneath me shifts as he kisses me again, his hands cupping my face like he can't bear to let me go. "I know it with every sense in me. *I love you.*" His lips find mine once more. "I adore you," he murmurs against my jaw, his breath warm on my skin. His hands slide down to my hips, and before I can even process what's happening, he lifts me off the ground, wrapping my legs around his waist. "I want you to stay. Forever. Please don't leave me."

His kisses trail down my neck, his hands gripping me tighter, pulling me closer. "Please don't ever leave me." The urgency in his tone makes it impossible for me to breathe, let alone think.

And as he walks us... somewhere, I feel everything shift, the walls I've built crumbling under his admission.

"I can't imagine my life without you." He lowers me to my feet, his hand brushing against my stomach as he lifts my shirt over my head. "I can't imagine sleeping in this bed without you. I don't want to."

My shirt flies off, leaving me completely braless, and Nicholas groans when he cups my breast. "*Mine,*" he groans, leaning down to flick his tongue over my nipple. "*My* fucking woman."

"Nicholas. Oh god."

"Need these off," he groans, pulling down my pants and panties all in one go. "Need you bare." He keeps his lips on my body as he pulls his own pants down, freeing his cock. I whimper when he pulls away, tugging his shirt off. His hand curls around his length as he pumps it slowly, his eyes roaming every inch of me. "Need to be inside you."

Spreading my legs with one hand, he kneels between them and positions his cock against me. His eyes lock on mine as he thrusts inside me to the hilt in one smooth motion.

I let out a moan, throwing my head back, his thick cock stretching me open.

"Tell me you're mine, Amara," he grunts, his hand wrapping around my throat, squeezing gently, making my eyes flutter. "Tell me I won't lose you. Tell me you feel the same." He begs with each kiss, breathy noises leaving his throat every time he pumps inside me.

"I'm yours," I tell him, every part of my body aching for him. "I'm not going anywhere," I promise him, running my hand over his hair. He closes his eyes, melting into my hand. "I love you."

He pauses, opens his eyes, staring at me for a while as if making sense of my words, and then groans, kissing me as he thrusts inside of me even deeper.

"Goddamn, I love you," he murmurs, breathy and so fucking sexy. "I." *Thrust*. "Love." *Thrust*. "You."

Pressure builds inside me until it's so intense and... *Oh god*.

"Nicholas. I'm gonna—"

"I know. I can feel you." He kisses me, his tongue brushing against mine as his thrusts become deeper, harder, faster, my nails digging into his skin. "Fuck. That's it. Squeeze your pussy around me, baby. Come all over my cock."

My head lolls back as the orgasm floods me, my legs shaking as he continues to thrust inside me, his cock hitting the spot that makes me see stars.

Nicholas groans, gripping my breast in his hands and a few seconds later, I feel him spill inside me with a groan.

He drops onto the bed beside me, his cock slipping out and grips my waist, pulling me into him, his lips brushing mine. "No more contract," he whispers against my lips. "No fake engagement and no more pretending." When he pulls back, his eyes bore into mine and he brushes my hair out of my face. "It's just you and me."

"For real this time?" I ask.

He smirks. "Forever, baby. Until we're old and gray and have a bunch of grandchildren." My heart soars as he kisses me again, soft and pure and *real*. "Does that sound good to you?"

I smile, feeling my heart flutter and my stomach settle. "It sounds perfect."

CHAPTER FORTY-TWO

Nicholas

I storm into Alexander's office, slamming the door so hard the walls rattle. The sound echoes through the room, cutting through the heavy silence.

Alexander doesn't flinch. He doesn't even look up. He's slouched in his chair, feet propped on the desk, scrolling through his phone. His tie is gone, his top buttons undone, his hair slightly disheveled, as if showing up was effort enough.

When he finally glances up, he smirks lazily, tossing his phone onto the desk. "Nicholas," he drawls. "To what do I owe the displeasure?"

"I know about the recording you sent Amara."

His lips curl into a mocking grin, and a dark chuckle escapes him. "Ah, I see." He leans back, crossing his arms. "So, the fake engagement's over, then? My condolences."

My hands ball tighter, my nails biting into my palms. "You're wrong," I bite out. "What I feel for Amara isn't fake. Your pathetic attempt to break us apart didn't work. And whatever you're scheming with the board won't work either. You can keep trying to undermine me, Alexander, but you'll never succeed. I'm the CEO. Not you. And there's nothing you can do about it."

The smirk vanishes. His feet hit the ground with a thud as he stands abruptly, slamming his hands on the desk. "I'm the eldest. It should've been mine."

"You think you deserve it because of your age?" I snap, stepping closer. "While you were jetting off to islands, getting wasted out of your mind, I was here. Every weekend. Every late night. I worked for this, Alexander. I earned it. You treated this company like a backup plan."

Alexander's jaw tightens, his hands gripping the desk until his knuckles turn white. "You think that makes you better than me?"

"This isn't about being better," I fire back. "This is about doing the work. About respecting Dad's legacy. You tried to sabotage my career, ruin my relationship, destroy everything I've built. And I'm done letting you get away with it." I lean forward, my hands flat on his desk. "You're fired. Effective immediately."

The silence that follows is deafening. Alexander doesn't move, doesn't even blink. I can almost see the gears turning in his head, his mind scrambling to process what I've just said. I expect him to shout, to argue, but he's quiet, quieter than I've ever heard him before.

The color drains from his face. "You can't do that," he stammers. "I'm your brother."

I feel a pang of guilt—just a flicker of it—but it's quickly drowned out by the anger bubbling under the surface. He's my brother, yes, but that doesn't mean anything when he's tried to destroy everything I've worked for.

"Being my brother doesn't give you immunity," I shoot back. "You've crossed every line, and now you're out of chances. I own this company. Which means I own you. I told you if you kept pushing me, you'd find yourself without a job. Well, congratulations, Alexander. Welcome to unemployment."

His face flushes with rage. He steps around the desk, pointing a finger at me. "You're going to fire your own brother? You don't have the guts."

I step closer, unflinching. "You didn't think about family when you went behind my back, when you tried to humiliate me in front of the board, when you tried to ruin my engagement. You don't care about family, about this company, or about Dad's legacy. You only care about winning. Well, guess what? You've lost."

His mouth twists into a snarl. "I still have the recording. I can convince the board you were talking about Amara. They won't trust you after that."

I take a deep breath, forcing calm into my voice. "Go ahead. Play it for them. Hell, I'll tell them myself. Because unlike you, I don't hide behind threats and manipulation. I don't need to."

His expression falters, the smugness draining as he realizes I'm serious. "You won't do it."

"Watch me," I reply, turning on my heel, already pulling my phone from my pocket. I step into the hallway, dialing Robert's number. The first ring buzzes in my ear as the door clicks shut behind me.

For the first time in years, I feel like I've taken back control. Alexander's games are over. He won't win. Not this time. Not ever again.

CHAPTER FORTY-THREE
Nicholas

"Thank you all for coming on such short notice." I close the door behind me, my eyes sliding to where the board members are seated.

Robert breaks the silence first. "Care to tell us what this is about? I thought everything was settled last week. Were there any changes to the contract you wanted to make?"

I shake my head, my mouth dry. "No, the contract is exactly what I wanted." I pause. "But I couldn't sign it without being honest with you first."

The board's expressions shift. Curiosity, confusion, a few exchanged glances.

"My father built this company from nothing," I begin. "He made Blackwood Hotels what it is today. A legacy. One that I've worked every day to honor. When he passed…" I swallow the lump in my throat. "When he passed, I promised myself I'd do whatever it took to protect it. To protect his dream."

A heavy silence fills the room. Robert watches me intently. Claire leans forward, her brow furrowing. But I keep going, the words pushing their way out.

"And in trying to do that, I made some decisions I'm not proud of." I hesitate, locking eyes with each of them in turn. "Choices like faking an engagement."

Robert's eyes widen, Simon's jaw tightens, and even David looks up from his notes.

"Amara isn't really my fiancée," I admit. The words taste bitter, like betrayal on my tongue.

Richard clears his throat. "Nicholas, are you saying—"

"I asked her to lie," I confirm, cutting him off. "After my father's death, the media focused on him. His funeral, his life, his death. No one was talking about the company. Our revenue was dropping, we were losing customers, and I didn't know how to stop it." I glance out the window, the city sprawling beneath me, too vast to seem real. "A friend suggested a PR move. A harmless dating scandal to shift the public's attention back on me, away from the company's struggles to my dating life, instead. And it worked. For a while, anyway. But then this deal came along. And I realized the image I'd created, the dating scandals and gossip, was getting in the way of everything I wanted. So, I did the only thing I could."

"You faked a relationship," Richard finishes.

I glance at each of them, and nod curtly. "Yes. I asked my assistant to pretend to be my fiancée. It was a desperate move. Not one I'm proud of. But this company was my father's dream, and I couldn't let it slip away."

"This seems like an elaborate scheme for a simple business deal," Claire adds.

"It was," I admit. "But it was also the only thing I could think of to protect his legacy."

Richard's brow furrows. "And Amara? Was she just… part of the act?"

I hesitate, the answer catching in my throat. "At first, yes," I say finally. "But somewhere along the way, it stopped being fake. My feelings for her stopped being fake. And now…" I blow out a breath, running a hand through my hair. "Now, I'm in love with her. And this whole charade—as ridiculous as it sounds—turned out to be the best thing that's ever happened to me."

The room is silent, their expressions unreadable.

"I'm telling you this because I want to be honest," I continue. "If you decide not to move forward with the deal, I'll understand. But I couldn't go through with it without telling you the truth."

The room falls silent. My pulse kicks into overdrive, the ticking of my clock making the sweat build on the back of my neck.

Finally, he stands, adjusting his jacket as he faces me. My stomach clenches, preparing for the rejection I'm sure is coming. This is it. He's going to thank me for my honesty, shake my hand, and walk out.

"I appreciate your honesty, Nicholas," he says, extending his hand.

I nod, forcing a smile as I shake his hand, my stomach dropping.

"And we'd love to move forward with this merger."

My head snaps up. "Excuse me?"

Richard smiles. "Your father was a good man. And after hearing this, I know you're committed to carrying on his legacy. We'd be honored to partner with Blackwood Hotels."

Relief floods my chest, and I let out a shaky laugh. *Holy shit*. "Thank you. Thank you so much."

Claire steps forward, shaking my hand with a smile. "We're looking forward to the future together."

David pats me on the back, a genuine grin on his face. "We all have our moments, Nicholas. Don't worry about it."

But it's Simon who catches my eye last. The same Simon who spent the entire gala checking out Amara. He smirks as he extends his hand. "Hell of an act, Nicholas."

I force a tight smile. "Not sure how much of it was an act." I don't know how much of it was for the company or how much it was my sheer possessiveness over Amara.

Robert slaps me on the back. "Let's expand your father's legacy. Together."

I let out a deep breath. For the first time in weeks, the weight on my chest lifts. I might have lied to get here, but I'm going to prove that I'm the right person for this job.

And when I get home to Amara, I'll make sure she knows that she's not just part of my success. She's the reason for it.

CHAPTER FORTY-FOUR

Amara

My phone buzzes on the desk, and I glance down, seeing Nicholas's name lighting up the screen.

Nicholas:

> Come to my office.

It's my first day back at the office since I tried to quit—which Nicholas flat-out denied—and I haven't even made it through ten minutes of catching up on emails.

A smile tugs at my lips as I quickly type a response.

Me:

> We're not having sex in your office again. People will talk.

Nicholas:

> Couldn't care less what people say, baby. But it's not that. I promise.

I laugh under my breath, shaking my head as I stand up, smoothing my skirt down my thighs before heading toward his office.

When I reach his door, I don't bother knocking. I push it open, not expecting to find anything different. But instead of sitting behind his desk, buried in paperwork like usual, he's standing by the window, his arms crossed in front of him, watching the city below.

I stop just inside the doorway, feeling a small flutter in my chest at the sight of him, and clear my throat. "You wanted to see me?"

He turns to face me, and his lips quirk in a smile, his eyes softening the moment they land on mine. "I always want to see you." He steps forward, his hands flying to my hips as our lips meet. I part my lips, gasping when his soft tongue brushes against mine.

"Nicholas," I murmur, pulling back with a chuckle. "You're not even pretending to be professional anymore."

His forehead drops to mine, a soft groan slipping from his lips. "I've become an addict when it comes to your lips. I need them, Amara. Always."

"Later," I murmur, fingers toying with the smooth fabric of his tie. "What did you need from me?"

His hand lingers at my waist for a beat too long before he turns toward his desk. He grabs a stack of papers, his fingers grazing mine as he hands them over. "I need you to sign these."

I flip through the pages, my stomach twisting the moment I register the bolded words at the top. Resignation papers.

My head snaps up. "Wait... You're firing me?"

He shrugs, a small, amused smile pulling at the corner of his mouth. "Not exactly," he replies. "I'm promoting you."

The words don't quite make sense at first. My brain races, struggling to catch up. "What? But... there's still a week left."

"I told you, Amara. No more contracts. No more pretending. No more lies. It's just you and me now. And this—" He gestures to the papers. "This is me making good on my promise to you."

I blink, my heart thudding in my chest, unsure of how to respond.

"You'll have a new position in the New York designer facility," he continues, "and a raise, of course."

A breath escapes my lungs, disbelief flooding my mind. This is everything I've ever wanted. I've worked for this moment, fought for it. But my heart clenches at the thought of leaving this role behind. I've grown so used to being here with him, sharing this space every day. I glance up at him, a little hesitant.

"So…" I pause, taking a deep breath. "I won't be your assistant anymore?"

"No," he confirms. "You won't. I'm in the process of hiring someone new. He's organized. Smart. Graduated from Harvard."

"Wow." I feel a small jolt of jealousy, though I don't want to admit it. "He sounds great."

He meets my gaze, his expression sharpening. "Remind me never to introduce you two."

I can't help the laugh that bubbles up. "You're such a caveman."

His gaze softens, and he steps closer, a playful glint in his eyes. "I'm in love," he corrects, his thumb brushing against my bottom lip. "And love makes men do strange things."

My heart skips a beat at his words. "Like what?"

He doesn't answer right away. Instead, he pulls me into his arms, eliciting a gasp out of me when he picks me up and places me on his desk, his breath warm against my ear.

"Spread your legs, sweetheart."

I let out a laugh. "You promised we wouldn't have sex in here."

He hums, smoothing his hand up my thigh. "I also promised myself I wouldn't fall for you, and yet here we are." His brow lifts. "You want me to eat your pussy on this desk, honey?"

I should say no. I should hop off and go back to work. Try to keep some semblance of professionalism. But the way his eyes burn into mine, and his hands warm every inch of my skin, has my resolve melting into a puddle in my underwear.

I spread my legs wider, and he breaks out into a grin as he kneels to the ground and grips my thighs in his hands.

"I'm going to miss these office visits," he grunts against my skin.

I breathe out a laugh. "Is that all you're going to miss?"

He arches his brow, lifting his gaze to meet mine. "You forget, I've been gone for you for *years* before I even tasted your lips." His fingers slip under the hem of my sweater, gently tugging it over my head. "I loved looking into your eyes. Loved seeing you smile. Loved picturing what color sweater you'd wear to work that day."

My heart thuds harder in my chest. I had no idea he thought that much about me.

His hands cradle my face, his lips brushing mine so softly that I melt into him. "I'm going to miss *you*, Amara. Not just the sex or the kissing. I'll miss your damn presence. I hate the thought of not having you right here, a few steps away from me… Of not having to make up reasons to call you in here so I could see you."

I blink, surprised by the admission. "You really did that?"

He smirks, his thumb tracing my bottom lip. "I even debated changing the walls to glass so I could look at you all day… but then again," he leans in, his voice dropping, "if I had, we couldn't do this." He punctuates his sentence by gripping my thighs, spreading them wider on his desk.

I can't help but laugh, feeling both flustered and turned on by the thought. "You're insane."

"Call it whatever you want, baby," he murmurs, his lips brushing against mine. "Insane. Obsessed. Out of my mind in love. Doesn't fucking matter as long as you're with me."

My heart swells at his words, but then he steps back, his expression turning serious. "I'm going to miss having you here. You're irreplaceable, Amara. But I can't hold you back because of my feelings. I want to see you do what you love. I want to see you succeed."

My chest tightens, and I find myself smiling, my breath hitching in my throat. My heart feels like it's about to leap out of my chest… or maybe it already has. Because my heart no longer belongs to me. It belongs to him. And it's his to keep.

"I love you," he whispers against my lips, his words so raw they make my chest ache. "So much, I don't even know how I functioned before you."

I suck in a deep breath. "I love you too," I reply, my arms curling around his neck, fingers tangling in his hair. He groans, leaning in, brushing his lips against mine, pouring everything he feels into this kiss.

EPILOGUE
Amara

"Where are we going?" I ask for the tenth time tonight, though I know I won't get an answer. Nicholas has been annoyingly secretive, only telling me to get dressed and that we'd be taking his helicopter. I'm not great with surprises. I need to know or at least have a hint.

He just grins at me, his hand gently cupping my face as he looks down with that twinkle in his eyes. "You look so fucking beautiful," he murmurs, his lips brushing mine in a kiss that sends my heart racing.

I narrow my eyes. "You think sweet-talking me will distract me from the fact that you're still not telling me anything?"

A slow grin spreads across his face. "No."

Before I can press him again, he reaches into his pocket and pulls out a strip of black silk. Nicholas twirls the fabric between his fingers, tilts his head. "Do you trust me?"

I swallow hard, heat creeping up my neck. "Always." *With my life.*

A slow, satisfied smirk tugs at his lips. "Good."

He steps behind me, and I stand perfectly still as he ties the silk in place, his fingers brushing the sensitive skin at my nape. The moment my world fades to black, every other sense sharpens. The warmth of his breath at my ear, the featherlight touch of his hands adjusting the knot, the steady press of his palm against my lower back as he guides me forward.

I hear the helicopter door open, feel the shift as he helps me inside and buckles me in, sliding into his seat a minute later.

"The last time you didn't tell me where we were going, you ended up fucking me in front of an audience," I remind him, my face flushing at the reminder. We've been back to the club a few times since, and the anticipation of returning has my heart knocking against my chest.

Nicholas chuckles as the sounds of flips and switches fill the cabin. "And you loved every second of it, didn't you?"

Heat floods my cheeks, and I'm grateful for the blindfold hiding my expression. "So... is that the plan tonight?"

His fingers find mine, lacing through them. "Not tonight," he murmurs. "Tonight, I want you all to myself."

His words send a flutter through me, and as the helicopter lifts off, my heart starts to pound. The first time I was up here, I was nervous. My hands were sweaty, my breath shallow... but ever since then, whenever we've taken Nicholas's helicopter, there's no fear, only anticipation.

The flight feels endless. Without the ability to see, every sensation feels heightened, the sounds and subtle tilts of the helicopter invading my senses as I feel Nicholas start to descend.

When we finally land, Nicholas moves first, unbuckling my seatbelt. I hear the door open, a rush of cool air hitting my skin, and then his hands are on me again as he guides me onto the ground.

As soon as my feet hit the ground, the scent hits me.

Peonies.

The air is thick with them, filling the air with the sweet, floral scent.

Where is he taking me?

Nicholas leans in close, his lips brushing my ear with a whisper. "Ready?"

I nod, my heart thudding in my chest.

He unties the blindfold, gently, the silk slipping off my skin, and my eyes blink rapidly, adjusting to the light as I glance around.

The first thing I notice are the skyscrapers, towering over New York City, a view I've become way too familiar with during the last six months I've been working as a decorator for Blackwood Hotels.

I feel a subtle warmth at my back, and I turn, a gasp catching in my throat when I see hundreds of candles spread out on the rooftop, and peonies scattered on the ground.

I look up, finding Nicholas standing behind me, hands in his pockets, his smile warm as he watches me.

"Nicholas…" I breathe, shaking my head.

His smile widens as he nods toward the skyscrapers. I turn around, brow furrowed, not sure what I'm supposed to be seeing. But then a light flickers on one of the buildings, grabbing my attention.

A giant W lights up, and my heart stops. I glance to the building beside it as the lights flash again—an I.

L.

L.

No. This isn't… Is he… He can't be… right?

The lights keep coming, forming the message, letter by letter, until it's complete.

Will you marry me?

I freeze, hands flying to my mouth, tears welling up as I spin around to face him. He's smiling, watching me, and I'm shaking my head, unable to believe this is real. Unable to do anything but look at him.

The man I love… lighting up the sky for me.

"I could've taken you anywhere," he says, his voice rough as he swallows harshly. "Paris, Rome, a private island—hell, I own one." His lips twitch into that infuriatingly gorgeous smirk before his expression softens again. "But this city is where I met you. It's where you stormed into my office and turned my world upside down."

His hand curls around my waist as the other cups my face. "I've spent so much of my life chasing things that didn't matter. Money, business deals, headlines. But you've made me realize that none of that means anything without you. Without *us*. You're the one thing I know I can't live without."

Tears fill my eyes. "Nicholas."

"We may have entered an engagement under false pretenses, as a business deal," he continues, "but what I feel for you is real." His hand shifts from my waist to my hands, his thumb brushing over my engagement ring. "The moment you put this ring on your finger, I knew there would be no one else for me. No one else could've been my fiancée. It was you. Only you. And tonight, I want to make it official."

I gasp, my tears drying as I shake my head up at him. My heart feels like it might burst, and I'm still not sure this isn't all a dream. But being with Nicholas feels like a dream every single day.

Nicholas drops to one knee, and my breath catches in my throat as he opens a small velvet box, revealing two gold wedding bands.

"You already wear my ring, and we're as good as engaged, but this is me asking you, not out of obligation or a deal, but because I want you. I need you, and I want to spend every day with you, loving you, cherishing you. I want to be the man who makes you smile, who makes you feel safe, who makes you feel like the most important person in the world. I want to love you for the rest of my days. I want to make you mine, completely and forever."

More tears well up, and my heart swells with emotion. I don't try to stop them. This is everything I've ever wanted. I've spent so long wondering if I'd ever get engaged for real, if I'd ever find someone who would love me the way I've always wanted to be loved. And now, I've found it.

The words swirl in my chest for what feels like forever, before they tumble out in a rush. "Yes. Yes, Nicholas. Of course I'll marry you."

In an instant, Nicholas stands, pulls me into his arms, and lifts me off my feet, spinning me around as I let out a laugh, tears still falling down my face. His smile is wide, his eyes locking on mine as our lips meet in a kiss.

"I love you, Amara Winslow," he whispers against my lips, his forehead resting against mine. "I love you more than I ever thought possible."

"I love you too," I breathe, my heart full to bursting.

I used to wonder if heartbreak could somehow kill you. But now, feeling his warmth, his touch, I realize that the pain is worth it, because it brings you exactly where you're meant to be. I don't regret a single thing. Not the heartbreak. Not the loneliness. Because it all led me here… to him.

And this is exactly where I'm supposed to be.

The End

Acknowledgements

Writing a book always feels impossible until it's done. Somehow, through the late nights, the rewrites, and the moments of doubting everything, it comes together.

Strictly Business was one of those ideas that hit me right as I was falling asleep—because apparently, that's when my brain decides to be the most creative.

I told myself I'd think about it in the morning, but instead, I grabbed my phone and started typing in my notes app. And once Amara and Nicholas took shape, I couldn't stop thinking about them. Their tension, their chemistry, the way they challenged each other—I was obsessed. So much so that I pushed back my other book releases just to write this one first.

Now, after months of living in their world, this book is finally in your hands.

Whether this is your first book of mine or you've been here for a while, thank you. Your support, your excitement, and your love for these characters mean everything. I'm beyond grateful that I get to do what I love, and that's entirely because of you.

A special thank you to my incredible Patreon members. You helped shape this book from the very beginning, from choosing Amara and Nicholas's names to enduring my unhinged, messy first draft snippets and all the name changes. Your excitement and support mean more than I can put into words. Knowing you were just as invested in this story as I was made the entire process even more special. I appreciate you all so much.

To my family, thank you for letting me disappear into my office for hours at a time without (too many) interruptions.

And finally, to my editor, thank you for taking my manuscript and helping shape it into the best version of itself.

I hope you guys loved Amara and Nicholas's story and here's to more stories, more spice, and plenty of fun ahead.